Advance prai~
Firewo~

"The Independence Day celeb.   .ollier, Georgia, is
disrupted by the crash landing of .   .ntic UFO. A quarter
of the townspeople are killed or maimed, and worse follows,
as the forces of the secret agency ONYX descend, appropriately enough in black helicopters, not to mention black combat gear, weapons, Hummers, and everything else an elite
special-operations unit uses. The ONYX troopers' security-
oriented paranoia elicits a similar response from the remaining townsfolk, who aren't fond of the government to begin
with and grows less fond with each passing hour, day, and
incident. Chief of Police Frank Osborn and ONYX CO Colonel Anderson try to cool the hotheads and remember that
Americans constitute both sides. But incomprehension and
violence (willful on the part of come white supremacists)
escalate to a gruesome climax that erases Collier from the
map, just in time to see the UFO go back to wherever it
came from. Irony, tragedy, regional color, memorable character sketches, horror, and literate paranoia mix together in
Moore's disturbing, absorbing novel."—*Booklist*

"James A. Moore's *Fireworks* is a masterful, cruelly ironic novel
that somehow melds the folksy, small-town atmosphere of the
best King and McCammon novels with an examination of the
disturbing dichotomy that is 'the American way.' Moore grows
increasingly assured with each new book, and *Fireworks* exhib-
its a confidence and skill that represents his own declaration
of independence. Great things are to be expected of Jim
Moore, ladies and gentlemen. Get your tickets early; you don't
want to miss the *Fireworks*."—Christopher Golden, author of
Strangewood and *Of Saints and Shadows*

"James A. Moore has crafted a terrifyingly real scenario, a "What If" that could happen . . . and heaven help the common man if it does."—P.D. Cacek, author of *Canyons*

"With Fireworks, James Moore mixes a powerful blend of science fiction and horror that asks the question...what would you do when —overnight — freedom was replaced by terror? Jim puts the people of Collier into that strange, frightening situation, and readers will hang on every step of the way for the exciting twists and turns of their fight against a faceless enemy."—Matt Costello, author of *The 7th Guest* and the upcoming (2002) *Unidentified* (Penguin Putnam).

"This is the latest from Moore who wrote the well-received *Under the Overtree* and now presents us with a picture of another small town that will end up fighting for its life against forces from too close to home."

"It looks like it's going to be another typical 4th of July. Everyone is preparing for the fireworks show that draws visitors from all around. Collier, Georgia is a small southern town that takes care of its own. Neighbors care for each other in sickness. The town mill makes sure everyone who wants to work has a job, and all that is about to change."

"The fireworks are almost over when a gigantic craft crashes into the lake turning it into steam, green lightning danced around the park and the wail of a banshee turned out to be the last thing around 200 people every saw. The next thing the survivors remember are helicopters filled with masked armored soldiers that have cut the town off from the rest of civilization. Project Onyx has now taken over the town with the intent to recover the mysterious disc shaped object at any costs."
"Moore has written a tale where the government suspends the Constitution and tells the townspeople to co-operate or be

wiped off the face of the Earth. Moore knows his background and shows how a small Southern town would react to being forced into aiding an occupation force until pushed to the limits. This is a marvelous novel of suspense as we watch the characters fight for their freedoms against a superior force. Moore has done it again; pick this one up for sure."
—*Baryon Magazine*

"Collier, Georgia is a quiet little town, typical of rural America in composition and attitudes. Although it is populated mostly by plain, simple folk, it still has its share of colorful characters and bad apples. There is, however, very little about the town to distinguish it from its neighbors. At least that is the case until the Fourth of July, when an enormous alien spacecraft crashes in a local lake, vaporizing its contents and killing dozens of locals. That's the day the lives of the citizens of Collier change forever, in ways you might not expect. This is not a novel of alien conquest, or even of alien contact. Eschewing predictable plot lines, Moore instead poses two simple questions, namely, 'How would the federal government react in such a situation?' and, 'Given that reaction, how would it affect the lives of the local populace?'"

"Moore provides a suitably chilling answer to these queries, positing a special branch of the armed forces created to handle just such a task, a grim cadre of soldiers dressed in high-tech body armor, their faces concealed by black visors. Immediately after the crash landing, these soldiers descend on Collier, cutting it off from the rest of the world under the pretext of battling terrorist activity. Their main objective: to secure the apparently inert craft. Their secondary objective: to maintain secrecy, even if it means killing everyone in the town.

This then is the focus of Moore's narrative, as he chronicles the reactions of everyday people to the invasion of their town by their own country. Although at first they are cooperative, the townspeople come to realize that they are in fact prisoners. Their resentment and anger grow by the day, building to a surprising crescendo. Moore populates his book with living, breathing characters, human beings on both sides of the conflict who, despite their fears, are only doing their best to cope with a stressful situation."

"Moore is more in control of this narrative than he was of his prior effort, the flawed but highly readable *Under the Overtree*. The writing here is crisp and clear, the pacing is almost flawless, and, with the exception of the appearance of the spacecraft which triggers these events (its origins and purpose remain a mystery throughout), the subject matter is utterly believable and involving. Moore effectively milks the situation for all it's worth, filling the novel with telling incidents and detail, forcing readers to confront the brutal reality that true horror may lie in something as simple as losing the simple freedoms that Americans take for granted. A twisted combination of Sinclair Lewis' *It Can't Happen Here* and Thornton Wilder's *Our Town*, *Fireworks* is a great read, a book that merits your attention."—*Hellnotes*

"If a person were asked to describe the works of James A. Moore, one could easily respond that the author combines the best of Koontz and Little in a unique style of his own.

Fireworks is another one of Mr. Moore's usual cross genre appeal tale that will more than enthrall horror and conspiracy buffs with its out of this world story line."—Harriet Klausner

Fireworks

by

James A. Moore

Meisha Merlin Publishing, Inc
Atlanta, GA

FIREWORKS

An MM Publishing Book
Published by Meisha Merlin Publishing, Inc.
PO Box 7
Decatur, GA 30031

Editing & interior layout by Stephen Pagel
Additional editing, copyediting & proofreading by Josh Mitchell
Cover art by Kevin Murphy
Cover design by Neil Seltzer

ISBN: 1-892065-40-1

http://www.MeishaMerlin.com

First MM Publishing edition: May 2001

Printed in the United States of America
0 9 8 7 6 5 4 3 2 1

Fireworks

Prelude

1

Collier, Georgia

July third was a very busy day for Bobby Carlson. Bobby had to set the fireworks displays in place and he had to triple-check every fuse, every electronic detonator, and every stand before lunch. Bobby'd been setting up the fireworks for the Collier, Georgia Fourth of July bash every year for the last seventeen years straight. It would have been twenty-five straight, but the year he had his appendix out, the city'd had to hire professionals instead of Bobby. Everyone still claimed that Bobby's were better than the pros', and that was a big source of pride for him.

Bobby hopped in his rowboat with the practiced ease of a long-time fisherman, and rowed slowly out to the buoys he set in the center of Oldman's Lake every year. No speedboats were allowed in the lake, nor had they been since Jeffey Wilkes got his head smashed into jelly by old man Carnes, back in '73. Carnes was pickled so badly that he never even realized he'd pulped Jeffey's skull; wouldn't believe he had either, until they pointed to the patch of bloodied scalp painted to the front of his Waterhawk.

Bobby liked the lake just fine without the roar of engines and the stench of burnt diesel fuel in the air; the land was plenty polluted on its own without adding the filth to the waters, thanks just the same.

Robert Jonathan Carlson grew up in Collier, and he planned to die there, certain that no other place was quite as fine. Oh, the place had its ups and downs, and these days there seemed to be more downs than ups, but at least there was still a sense of *community* in Collier, a sense of family and belonging. Collier took care of its own, like when Mable Cradsworth had broken her hip falling from her stepladder while trying to pick apples. Did she have to worry about the state or federal government paying for her mistakes, like they all seemed to in the big city? No sir. Her whole block chipped in, taking turns caring for her, making sure her eight cats were fed. It'd only been eight cats then, but these days it was closer to thirty; the damn cats were going at it like bunnies and every time you turned around there seemed to be another litter ready for passing out to friends and family. Collier took care of her own, and that was really the way everyone preferred it, especially Bobby.

Bobby double-checked the fireworks packages, the ones his drunken fool nephew Artie would be handling, satisfied himself that everything was fine, and headed on his way back to the other buoy of fireworks. The gentle rocking of the waves was a lovely feeling; like being cradled in the arms of some magnificent mother who cared for her own. Like being held by Collier.

The sun was too damn hot, and the humidity was nearing the level where it made his chest work like a bellows to gulp air, but that was still fine; as long as Collier was the place, the weather mattered little. He wiped his brow with a withered forearm that had seen the summers come and go in Collier for over fifty of the last sixty years. He noticed the speckled brown spots on his arms were coming in closer together this year. With all the gloom and doom talk on the radio, he wondered how much longer before the doctor told him he had to stay out of the sun or worry about skin cancer. He shunted the thought aside, forcing himself to think of cheerier things, like tomorrow's fireworks display which was, he was certain, going to be the best ever.

He thought of Marion, his wife of forty years, and was saddened as always that she couldn't be with him on this occasion. Marion had died of bone cancer five years past, writhing in pain at the end and begging the Lord above for the mercy of death. She suffered more than any person was meant to suffer, and she died without even her dignity left intact. Her thick hair became pale wisps towards the end, her heavyset body metamorphosed into a skeletal frame with little but withered flesh to hold all that he loved together. The doctors' tubes and pills had kept her going for a while, allowed him extra time to make absolutely certain that she knew the depths of his love; not that she ever really doubted, but he needed to know that she understood. In the end, he was glad to see her go because her suffering was done, and she could once again know peace. Still, he missed her deeply everyday and more so when the night came to his king-sized bed and he rested alone on the right-hand side, leaving the left for his Marion.

He forced the thoughts away, knowing that he and Marion would be together within a few more years. He checked the connections one last time and slowly rowed back towards the pier, a smile on his face that was part pride and part bittersweet memories. While it's true that Fourth of July was the last time Bobby Carlson ever did the fireworks, everyone had to agree it was also the most memorable.

2

Milo Fitzwater checked and rechecked the figures from the last three Fourth of July picnics and groaned. He chewed anxiously at the plastic bottom of his pen and wiggled his foot impatiently under the desk. Every year there were more people from outside of Collier coming to see the fireworks displays, and every year they left a bigger mess than the year before. Herb Cambridge and Billy Lanier were already grumbling about there being too much work for just the two of them to handle and, much as it pained Milo to admit it, the time had come to hire another person for town maintenance. Two full-timers just weren't able to tow the line by themselves and even with the summer help from a couple of the local boys, there was no denying the need for at least one more city employee in the Maintenance Department. One more drain on the town's coffers, which hadn't been doing all that well lately.

Milo jotted himself a note and prepared to face the town council again on the need to start charging a parking fee for anyone spending time over at Oldman's Lake. He set the note on top of the already towering stack of other notes about how to handle the next town meeting and went back to chewing on his Bic Pen.

Milo found himself looking forward to the time when he could step down from office and just go back to running the family store, or maybe even move all the way into full retirement. Judd was doing a fine job of handling the Fitzwater Ace Hardware without his father's interference, and maybe the time had finally come to just step down and let the boy handle the show. As far as Milo was concerned, he'd more than earned the right—not even fifty-five and he already felt like he was in his eighties. It was the pressure. He'd never handled pressure well and he knew it.

He pushed away from the desk and pulled his pants back up to their proper location, all the while wondering what had made him run for mayor in the first place. Arnetta Wilcox looked up briefly from her phone conversation as he walked past her desk, and he gestured to let her know he was leaving for lunch. She nodded without much expression and went back to talking with whichever of her gaggle of friends she was exchanging gossip with this time around. Milo was the first to say that Arnetta was sharp and efficient, but he surely did hate to hear her flapping her gums constantly. Her waspish voice started driving spikes into his temples if he had to hear her for too long.

He left the mayor's office and walked past the double doors leading into the local police offices without even looking. With any luck he could avoid another argument with Captain Frank Osborn, his least favorite civil servant.

He hadn't made three feet past the frosted windowpanes in the double doors before he heard Frank's throaty voice calling to him. "Milo, we need to talk. Now."

Milo mentally set his armor in place and turned to face the man who had recently become his number-one enemy. "Hi, Frank. And how can I help you today?"

"Milo, you know what I want to talk about. It's the same thing I always want to talk about. I need more men, at least for the Fourth of July and the month of August. I've already got three of the boys working double shifts. You know and I know that there's gonna be nothing but more people coming into town from here on. It's the same thing every year."

Milo could have recited the words from memory, but knew better than to press his luck. It wasn't that Frank Osborn was a bad man—the Good Lord knew that wasn't the case; it was just that he was a little shortsighted when it came to the expenses of running a town the size of Collier. "Frank, I can't give you what I don't have. What I don't have is any more money in the town's accounts. We're gonna be scrapin' the bottom of the barrel to survive through the rest of the year as it is."

Frank's bushy eyebrows grew together, and for a second Milo expected to see steam whistling from the police chief's ears. Those eyebrows looked almost comical resting under Frank's crewcut hair, but only almost. He was far too big a man to look cartoonish up close and personal like he was right now. "Milo, where does this town get most of its revenue come the summer?"

"From the tourists. You know that and so do I."

"So how can we give the tourists proper police protection if all of my men are sound asleep behind the wheel? They can't work all the time. Now and then we gotta let them rest. It says so in the labor laws."

Milo felt his own blood pressure rising. He'd heard the same argument too many times, and he just didn't want to deal with it any more. "Frank, you know I'd give you the money if I could, and I know I said the same thing last year, but that was before the damned floods washed away any chance we had of staying in the black. I'm already planning on trying to squeeze in a parking fee for tomorrow, but I'm running on short time here, and I just can't talk to you right now. If I get the fee, I'll give you one more man. That's the best I can do."

Frank swelled his chest like a male pigeon preparing to face off against another male for the attention of a possible mate, and then slowly exhaled, letting himself relax. Milo managed to stare the man down, but it was not an easy task, and certainly not one he enjoyed. "All right, Milo. I'll let it go for now, but I'm not happy about it, and I want you to know that. Just for the record."

"Duly noted, Frank. Just try to be patient with me; we'll get it all worked out." Frank turned briskly away, and stormed back into his office. Milo gave thought to just quitting again, a thought that came to him regularly these days. In the end he just shuffled off towards the diner, prepared to face another chef's salad in the ongoing battle to beat his waistline into submission.

Collier had thirty-five hours to go before the town would be changed forever.

3

Marty Wander stared at the distant lake and increased his speed, eagerly looking forward to hitting the cold water and washing away the sweat from his chores. Summertime was great, but Marty hated mowing the lawn, and he sure hated having to help out with repairs around the house. At thirteen years of age, Marty had long ago decided that he had better things to do with his life than work; that could wait until he was older as far as he was concerned. The hot tarmac under his tires was cracked and lumpy, but Marty had spent his entire life in Collier, and he knew the dangerous parts of the roads almost as well as he knew the freckles on his hands. Millwater Street was no exception to that rule. He could name every single shop on Millwater Street, from the Fitzwater Ace Hardware to Dewett Hamill's Sunshine Bakery.

Marty pedaled furiously to the crest of a small hill, gaining momentum for the downhill race to the edge of the lake, where Mike Summers, Andy Newsome and Tom Thornton would be

waiting for him. They always managed to get to the lake before Marty did. All three of them had parents who could afford gardening services from Wander Lawn Maintenance;
Marty's family could too, but his dad believed in Teaching
Children Responsibility from a young age. Besides, why should
his dad pay his own company to do the lawn when he had
perfectly good slave labor waiting at home?

At the crest, the old Huffy launched through the air, sailing gracefully over the top of the hill. With a precision born of
too many years spent ignoring any possible threat of bodily
injury, Marty landed perfectly on his back tire. The bike's front
end hung suspended in the air for a few seconds longer, before
it came crashing down onto the road again. Had any cars been
coming, Marty would have been perfectly positioned to get
himself crushed under the front tires. But no car was coming.
There were never any cars in Marty's way; he was lucky along
those lines.

At the bottom of the long hill was the artificial beach built
along the shore of the lake that seemed to go on forever from
where Marty was. To the left of the road, the docks ran for a
good quarter mile, holding boats of all sorts in place and sup-
porting a few small shops for visiting summer people, even a
small restaurant that sold seafood, despite the lack of ocean
for a hundred miles in any direction. To the right the beach
ran on its course around the lake's perimeter. Directly ahead
the lake glistened like a small ocean. In front of that body of
fresh clear water was the entrance to the parking area for
Oldman's Lake and just past the entrance, Marty's friends stood
leaning against their bikes and smoking more of Tom's stolen
Marlboros. Tom pilfered cigarettes from his old man all the
time and his old man never noticed or, if he did realize they
were missing, he never complained.

Marty pushed his legs to their limit, forcing every last ounce
of speed from his bike, and aimed directly towards the trio
waiting at the base of the hill. At the last possible moment, he
reversed direction on the pedals, activating the Huffy's brakes,

and turned the low-slung bicycle sideways, leaning forward, into the skid and forcing a good portion of the tires' outer skin to kiss the asphalt. The bike trembled and the rough-terrain tires screamed in protest, a high-pitched shriek of pain, but the bike stopped less than three inches away from the front tire of Mike's Schwinn and left a very impressive skid-mark running for several feet behind it. Tom, Mike and Andy all looked at Marty as if he'd lost his mind. Andy actually looked ready to run but apparently forced himself to stand still. Marty smiled broadly, revealing even white teeth.

"Hi guys." Now and then it was fun to leave a really righteous skid-mark, but it was always even more fun when you could scare a few people along the way. "How's things?"

Mike just shook his head and grinned. Nothing ever fazed Mike. The two of them had a long rivalry to see who could be the most outrageous in their escapades. Much to Marty's chagrin, Mike still had him beat in their unofficial competition.

Tom just stared at him, slack-jawed, as he always did when either of them pulled one of their stunts. Tom was pretty much in awe of both of the daredevils, but at least he was willing to play along from time to time. Andy, on the other hand, looked a little green around the gills and would surely complain about the whole scene when his blood pressure lowered itself down to the normal range. Andy wanted a world that was calm and serene. Marty often thought Andy was never really meant to be a youngster, but rather should have come out of the womb as a middle-aged man.

Mike nodded his hello and ground out the cigarette butt under his Reebok. Tom was far more enthusiastic in his greeting. "Man! That was bitchin'! Geez, I wish I could do that, you musta slid a good fifteen feet! Hey, how are ya, Marty?"

Andy just gasped like a fish out of water, reaching for his asthma inhaler and waving with his free hand. Andy didn't really have asthma, but he was allergic to damn near everything under the sun, and the only way he could do anything strenuous was to have his medication. Marty guessed that was a lot of the reason that he was always so pissy about everything; it was hard to be happy when you were allergic to every pollen and mold on the planet, especially when you lived in the south, and probably suffered from the allergies at least nine months out of the year. Marty watched Andy inhale the chemical mist that aided his breathing with the same fascination he always had. Even after being friends for the last seven years, Marty couldn't get over the sound of those chemicals going into Andy's chest. Andy sounded just like Darth Vader when he did that, and Marty tended to think of the wet, hissing noise as somehow sinister. It was like watching his friend inhale demons.

The sun beat down on their heads, as the four young men turned and walked their bikes over to the bike racks not far from the picnic areas. The racks were placed out of sight, in the shade between two oak trees draped with Spanish moss, reinforcing the illusion that very little had changed in the area over the last hundred years. They had the bikes chained in place—it was summertime, and too many tourists came into the area for anyone to really trust that their possessions would remain unharmed like they did in the winter—and their street clothes shed before they reached the shore on the other side of the grassy knoll.

The water was just cool enough to be refreshing instead of downright cold, the benefit of a few days of nothing but sunshine. Marty always loved the little undercurrents in the lake, though; the ones that carried waves of deeper water, water that was much colder than at the surface, upwards, shooting goose-pimple chills across his body when they touched him. The rest of the day was his, at least the remaining hours until dinner. His family ate later than most, normally around 7:30, so he still had plenty of time to enjoy the lake and the company of his friends.

That would change soon enough, sooner than Marty knew. It was 4:02 P.M., and Collier was only thirty hours away from changing forever.

4

Durango Military Installation, Sector 17, Arizona: July Fourth

Colonel Mark Anderson was not a happy man. The last four days had been spent either in his apartment, when he could escape from the pressures in the command center, or in his office. The majority of that time was spent in communication with various people he only knew by codenames. In less than three hours all of the years spent preparing for Project: Onyx would either bear fruit, or prove to a large number of critics that the money could have been better spent elsewhere. Thirty-seven years worth of funding and training, well over one billion dollars in funding siphoned away from every possible section of the United States government and the last twelve years of his life would either be a minor investment with much more to come, or would prove once and for all that the U.S. was pursuing a pipe dream. Anderson had a headache the size of Texas, and no amount of aspirin seemed capable of mending the problem.

Anderson ran a hand through his silvering crew-cut hair and tried to will his headache away. The pounding in his skull had grown harsher over the last few hours, and he was beginning to wonder if he would ever get rid of the vise-grip that had forced itself over his temples and mercilessly constricted. The tension was understandable enough. He was at the threshold of greatness, and the next few days would make all the difference in the world. There was no doubt in his mind that failure in his task would lead to his being buried alive by the people who knew what Project: Onyx was all about, and there would be absolutely nothing that he could do about the situation. Even thinking about the circumstances on a conscious level was enough to start his stomach acid rebelling, start his

body breaking into a cold sweat, the sort that positively stinks
of fear. Everyone in Sector 17 was suffering from the same
symptoms. Everyone knew what was on the line.

But, in all honesty, they didn't know the possible reper-
cussions as well as he did.

When his phone rang the noise made him jump in his seat,
a luxury he only allowed when he was alone, much like the
thick sweat that built on his brow. No sign of weakness was
ever allowed in front of the troops, but here, in his office and
alone, he could permit the reaction. He let the shrill buzzer
drive spikes into his skull for another three rings before he
finally answered the phone.

"Anderson."

"Mark, it's Steve. We have a problem."

"Talk to me." Major Steve Hawthorne was not a man to
mince words. While they were often together in easier times,
when it came to business Steve had no time for anything but
the task at hand. That was the primary reason he'd managed
to remain Mark Anderson's second in command for the last
ten years.

"The Target is already here, three days ahead of schedule."

"What? You've got to be kidding me! We've been tracking
the damned thing for two weeks! It can't be here already!"
Colonel Anderson felt his stomach turn to ice for a moment,
and then melt into a burning pool of lead. No one was fully
prepared. The stations were all manned, but the orders had
not yet been sent out to the numerous bases that they should
ignore any bogeys coming their way. "This is bullshit, Steve.
Absolute bullshit!"

"Yes, sir, it is. But there's nothing to be done about it.
The target is here and it's moving fast. If we want to net this
bitch it's going to have to be now." For the first time in their
long association, Anderson heard a note of panic in Steve
Hawthorne's voice. The cold, efficient baritone he'd grown
to depend on was shaking, ever so faintly, but shaking just
the same.

"Get it done. Screw the countdown and get it started. Send the message to all concerned bases and list it Priority Black One. If any news of this leaks I want the heads of whoever is responsible. Is that clear, Major?" Now that the worst was starting to happen, Anderson felt a flood of calm moving through his body. His headache faded instantly, followed by the burning in his stomach. He felt alive, invigorated and ready for action.

"Sir, yes sir." With the harsh tones from Anderson, Hawthorne's voice grew calmer, steadier. Anderson understood why: the burden was no longer his alone.

"'I'll be in Ops in three minutes, Brief me when I get there." Anderson slammed the phone into its cradle, grabbing his jacket at the same time. The corridors were empty of any other soul, and the only sounds were the muted buzz of the station's alarm and the sharp, measured slaps of his shoes striking the concrete floor beneath his feet. But in his mind, the sounds were much louder. They were the sounds of gunfire and fiery explosions. Deep inside, below the calm that surrounded him, Anderson was already running through every possible scenario for how this day would finish.

It was the Fourth of July. Colonel Anderson, commander of one of the best-hidden government agencies in the United States of America, had no doubt that the fireworks were about to start.

5

Collier, Georgia: July Fourth

Bobby Carlson was once again floating on Oldman's Lake, his rowboat bobbing gently in time with the waves. The sky above Collier was clear and beautiful, a perfect night for a fireworks display. Bobby rechecked the connections leading from his fuses to the fireworks, fearful the water might have somehow ruined the water proof thermite strings. His fears were unfounded, just as they were every year.

Artie waved with his flashlight to indicate that all was well on the far side of the lake, and Bobby flashed his own light three times to indicate the same. Artie was a good boy, better than most, but the spirits got to him now and then and he found himself in trouble with the law whenever he sucked down a little too much Jack Daniel's. Artie's fondness for the bottle would be the end of him yet, at least as far as Bobby was concerned. The good news was that Artie had managed to stay sober this year. That was almost a first for the man; he always drank himself into a stupor at any given chance. Obviously, he'd taken Bobby's threat to find a new assistant seriously.

Bobby looked towards the shore, saw the numerous families situated on the sand of the artificial beach and planted in the picnic area on the grassy hill and smiled. "Best turnout ever, no doubt about it." The Coca-Cola stand had a long line of people waiting to get drinks and overpriced hotdogs. That was always a good sign. Several kids who should have known better at their age were sneaking around and throwing firecrackers of their own. He couldn't blame them. That was what the Fourth of July was all about. Emily O'Rourke was standing on the shore, resplendent in a long dress that showed off her figure. Too fine for a woman in the last year of her fifth decade, but she still managed to carry herself like a much younger woman. Her husband, the pastor of the Lutheran Church on Maple Avenue, was standing with his arm around her waist and looking like the cat who swallowed the canary. Had every right to feel that way, too. Emily was a fine catch, faithful, hardworking and still beautiful. She'd even managed to turn Bobby's head a few times, and that was no easy feat. He looked briefly over at Artie, keeping his face calm and knowing that his nephew was thinking dirty thoughts about Emily, just as he had since the first time he'd seen her. Twenty years separated his nephew and the pastor's wife, but the young fool still pined away for her. Bobby knew, because he'd heard his sister's son calling Emily's name in a drunken stupor on several occasions.

As far as he could see, there were people gathered and waiting with fading patience for his time to shine, his little moment of glory for the year. His show; the fireworks display. Bobby made them wait a little longer, knowing full well that the anticipation always made the end results even sweeter.

He flashed his light five times, the signal to Artie that it was time to start lighting fuses, and lit a Camel cigarette with his sterling silver lighter. The lighter bore the faint reminders of his time in the Second World War: a scarred, faded insignia of the battalion he'd been with when Normandy's beaches were stormed. The lighter was an old and familiar friend, and really the only one left around that remembered the war as well as he did.

The Camel was in turn used to light the fuses. A brilliant spark danced and spit at the end of the long fuse that started the show for the people on the shore; Bobby Carlson smiled, proud, as always, to be an American.

6

Durango Military Installation, Sector 17, Arizona: July Fourth

The Operations Center was filled with nervous people, all of them watching the same screen. A satellite set in orbit twelve years earlier beamed a direct, tight signal to the base, and everyone there watched the information that the Onyx V offered up. The grid squared laid out over the computer image of the United States were small, covering only one hundred square miles each. In one section, directly over a substantial stretch of desert inhabited only by animals and plants, the squares were enlarged, literally dwarfing the rest of the map. A tight V formation of jets moved slowly across the digital map in close pursuit of a single object that dwarfed them all.

Colonel Mark Anderson watched the symbols move, and felt in his bones that something was wrong. The fucking bogey was toying with them.

Onyx V had spotted the craft four weeks ago, literally remaining stationary in the shadow of the moon. For four weeks, Anderson and his crew watched the disc-shaped object, trying to make out details on something that simply should not have existed. Four days ago, the damned thing had moved. One second it was where it had been all along, and the next it was slipping out of the range of Onyx's sensors. Four days ago, Onyx had once again spotted the shape, this time on the other side of the moon, moving very slowly and all but drifting in space. Computers that would have shamed any mainframe on the market carefully calculated its every move, calibrating and readjusting estimates faster than even the creators of the Onyx V and its base computer could have imagined.

Anderson knew where the little circle was going before whatever might be piloting the thing knew where it was going. As a test once, Anderson had ordered the satellite's human operators to aim at New York City with the array of sensitive equipment. He'd decided to see what Onyx could really do. Onyx transmitted pictures back to the station that were beyond belief. From a distance twice again as far away as the moon, the satellite successfully transmitted photos of a cafe during lunch hour. The images were clear enough to allow identification of virtually every item on the diners' plates, and precise enough to allow an accurate count of the number of hairs on each of their heads. Anderson was surprised by the clarity, but he shouldn't have been. He'd seen the craft the sensor designs had come from, and he had no doubt that the originals had done an even better job.

Anderson focused his thoughts back on the task at hand, scolding himself for letting his mind wander. Not much had changed on the giant screen, the ship was still moving smoothly across the screen, with a series of arrows following close behind. The only difference was that the enlarged squares had changed, indicating a different section of the continent, east of where it had been seconds before. Again he suffered that flash of dread, that burning, falling sensation in the pit of his stomach. He didn't know yet what would go wrong, but he knew with a dreadful, sick certainty that all hell was about to break loose.

Transcript of Radio Transmission— Sector 17 and Onyx V flight wing— 07-04-95 21: 43 Hours Eastern Standard Time—Extremely confidential

Onyx: Black Leader, this is Onyx One. Is Target Black in sight?

Black Leader: That's affirmative, Onyx. Jesus, what a sight. I never imagined it would be so big.

Onyx: Orders are as follows: Pursue Target Black for observation purposes. Do not, I repeat, do not attack unless there is no other course of action available, do you copy?

Black Leader: Affirmative, Onyx.

Onyx: Additional orders are as follows: Black Wing is to maintain radio silence with all bases, military and otherwise, with the exception of Onyx One. Do you copy?

Black Leader: Affirmative, Onyx. Wait a minute, something... Sweet Jesus! Did you see that? Sonuvabitch! Uh, Onyx. Target Black has just accelerated, moving away from us like we were standing still. Orders?

Onyx: Pursue to the best of your ability. Do not let Target Black out of your sight.

Black Leader: Affirmative.

Onyx: Black Leader, this is Colonel Mark Anderson. If Black Target proves impossible to follow, you are to bring the target down, do you copy? Repeat, you are authorized to splash the target, weapons free if you are unable to pursue.

Black Leader: Affirmative, Colonel. Uh, sir?

Onyx: What is it, Captain?

Black Leader: Sir, I don't know if that's possible, sir. This thing is huge.

7

Anderson watched the map, knowing without a doubt that there was just no way for the Black Wing Squadron to match pace with the target. The damned thing was moving away from the jets at speeds that just shouldn't have been possible. Whatever was propelling the bogey was far beyond anything that the U.S. had, even with the projects they didn't want to mention. He'd never seen anything cross the map at speeds anywhere near what Target Black was reaching, nothing except a few missiles, at any rate.

Without warning, even as he was preparing to issue the command to fire missiles, Anderson saw the disc symbol on the large screen connected to Onyx V veer sharply to the south. He felt his stomach do a few fast spins on an imaginary axis as the shape literally flickered across the Southern states, moving at speeds that were damned impossible. As far as he knew any craft moving anywhere near that speed would leave a friction trail of epic proportions. He cringed inwardly as the disk suddenly veered again, moving with amazing precision. The enlarged squares of the map grid were now separated by most of the southeastern states; Louisiana, Mississippi and Alabama all blurred past, a kaleidoscopic flash of grid squares blasting to increased magnification and then dropping to their original size at a pace that the naked eye could not hope to match.

Over Georgia, the disk ripped across the sky and then disappeared, dropping from sight and leaving a confused computer system unsure what to do about the enlarged map section. After a second the grid square vanished and took with it all of Mark Anderson's hopes for a quick retrieval. Twenty-five years of military training had become instinct somewhere along the way; he barked orders to scramble the retrieval team in Florida and the one north of Atlanta while his mind still refused to consciously acknowledge what had happened seconds before.

Already, Onyx V was making calculations, pinpointing the exact spot where the ship must have gone down. Anderson watched the targeting lines move from various spots, narrowing down on a square before finally magnifying the grid for better detail. The crosshairs converged and pointed to a spot on the map, a tiny town that was hardly worth noticing. Mark Anderson shivered inside, even as he gave commands and moved towards the airfield to oversee the deployment of jets. His would not leave for almost six hours: a preposterous amount of wasted time, in his eyes. Still, there were details to handle, last minute arrangements to take care of. Colonel Mark Anderson prayed with all of his heart that the town of Collier, Georgia had somehow missed the spectacle, but knew where it counts that they must have seen at least something of the crash or landing, whichever was the case.

He had his orders, and he would follow them, even if everyone in Collier ended up in prisons or coffins before he was done with the task ahead. But he would not like it, no sir, not one damned bit. He had no idea, none whatsoever, of just what the good people of Collier had just seen. He tried to prepare for any eventuality, but what he saw when he arrived was worse than he could have ever dreamed.

8

Collier, Georgia: July Fourth

The night was only beginning; the fireworks were flashing above the lake and everyone was enjoying them as best they could. Mosquitoes swarmed through the humid night air, finding new targets and generally annoying everyone that they fed on. Beer and cola were being consumed from picnic baskets laden down with food that no one would eat: every year people brought too much food and most of what they brought became fodder for the ants and other scavenging insects. In the long set of docks, where thirty or so boats ranging from rowboats to monsters just shy of yachts rested, more people sat in their leisure craft and enjoyed the gentle lulling motions of the waves.

Out on Oldman's Lake, Bobby Carlson was having the time of his life, lighting fuses and listening to the cheers from the shore. He could just see Frank Osborn staring up at the sky, a cigarette burning in the corner of his mouth. Frank always pissed and moaned about the Fourth of July, but Bobby knew well enough that the man was having fun. Frank had grown up on Bobby's street, and had always been one to pretend that he was less impressed or pleased than everyone else.

The time for the grand finale was finally approaching and that was a good thing, because Bobby didn't quite feel his best. He suspected he'd maybe pushed himself a little too hard, maybe even started the old ticker arguing about going to sleep without his consent again. Just as soon as the last fuse was lit he'd have to take a nitroglycerin tablet and hope for the best.

A barrage of pyrotechnic blasts rocketed through the night sky and, for a few seconds, the night was as bright as the noonday sun, but far more colorful. Popping, hissing, shrieking explosions rocked the heavens and, in the lake below, Bobby Carlson reached for his bottle of heart pills. Under the tongue with practiced ease and he could already feel the pressure in his chest easing slightly. He often wondered if the pill really worked that quickly or if he just imagined the change taking place. Damn, but it was a fine feeling either way, give or take the taste in his mouth and the burning under his tongue.

Bobby let his eyes wander towards the distant, fading constellations of his own creation, and reached for the final fuse. The night had been perfect as far as the fireworks were concerned. Artie had managed to stay sober all the way through the evening, and Bobby was almost ready to believe the boy had finally wised up enough to stay away from the hootch. Time would tell. He signaled Artie and his nephew nodded back, reaching for the final fuse on his end.

The waves were gentle on the lake, and that was good too. Bobby lit his fuse, and Artie lit the last in his selection as well. Both of them waited, breathing a sigh of relief that all had gone smoothly, and watched the skies above as the fuses counted down their last seconds.

Artie noticed it first, the faint burning luminescence coming towards them at unnatural speed. It looked almost like lightning running across the sky instead of falling towards the ground, but the color was all wrong, and it wasn't quite fast enough to be electricity in motion. Then it shifted directions even as Artie was calling to his uncle. It started coming straight towards the lake.

Artie opened his mouth to call his Uncle Bobby's name at the same time that the fireworks escaped from their perches and screamed an arc into the heavens. Everywhere around the two men, missiles flared into colorful trails of light, smoke and thunder as they did what they were created to do. If Bobby Carlson heard his nephew's words, he never gave a sign. He too looked towards the sky, and he too saw the object coming down. Eyes watched from all around them, staring towards the stars and waiting with growing anticipation to be dazzled. Bobby looked away from the darkness above for only a few seconds, long enough to finally see that his nephew was trying to be heard over the sound of the grand finale. Bobby saw the fear written on his face and nodded back; he had seen the falling thing too.

As the final volley of explosions ignited the air above the lake, people on the shore stood cheering, amazed by the spectacle. A few, and only a few, noticed that something was amiss, realized that at least one of the streaks of light in the air was moving not upwards, but towards the lake with deliberate fury. Worse still, it was growing bigger.

Then the sound hit: a screaming banshee wail that seemed to switch frequencies as quickly as it reached one. The electrically enhanced sounds of the Collier High School Marching Band on the P.A. system were replaced by white noise caused by whatever energies danced around the falling object. High, keening screams and low mournful howls filled the air. Everyone stopped cheering as the vibrations falling towards the ground started teeth rattling in their sockets. Artie dove from his raft as the light grew closer, making for the shore on limbs powered by adrenaline. On the beach, the people were either running away from the water or covering their ears and falling to the ground. Collier's canine population tried to match the pitch of the howls from above, with minimal success.

Old Bobby Carlson knew long before the light hit the lake that he was a dead man. He felt the vibrations in his bones, saw the light plummeting towards him with all the intimacy of a new lover. "I'll be home to you soon, Marion. You wait there for me." The light filled the sky and before the impact occurred, Bobby Carlson felt his heart stop beating, felt his brain start to boil in his skull, along with his eyes... eyes that had seen and loved Collier for most of his life.

The sounds reached their highest level, and even those who tried to run were forced to fall and cover their ears. The noise became everything for them, a primal scream threatening to break their bodies and their minds. Amilee Foster, only eight months old, and momentarily out of reach of her parents, cried futilely, calling for help against the sound. The doctors would later say it was a miracle her eardrums hadn't ruptured.

Marty Wander and Mike Summers were actually looking up towards the sky to see what was making the sound. What they saw, even though it only lasted a second, was enough to make them believe in God as all of the teachings in Sunday school could never hope to. Green lightning lashed from some dark object, danced in a corona around the edges and roared across the dark thing's surface in random, furious arcs. The sight alone was impressive, but the scope of the thing was too much to fully comprehend. It seemed to fill the entire sky already, but even as they watched it expanded, growing larger as it fell towards the waters of Lake Oldman.

Retinal burns made new homes in their eyes, and both screamed out in pain as the object hit the surface of the lake. Beside them, Billy and Andy Newsome screamed as well. Tom Thornton simply curled into a ball and prayed to God Almighty with the passion of a condemned man.

The reaction was instantaneous and the impact rocked all of Collier. On the beach and in the grass-covered picnic grounds, people were lifted into the air and dropped back to the lawn. The earth moved in a wave of protest, pushing the Independence Day celebrants as easily as a hurricane moves leaves. Arthur McMurphy managed to break his right arm and dislocate his left knee when he fell. The burger and Coca-Cola he carried were hopelessly crushed into his Braves' T-shirt.

Several cars were thrown into the air as well. The entire Habersham family, down for the weekend and visiting Mrs. Habersham's mother, were crushed along with their Mercedes Benz station wagon when Doug Martin's Ford Ranger landed atop it. The windows in Milo Fitzwater's Ace Hardware exploded from their frames and shivered across the ground. Several other storefronts followed the new trend.

But the worst of the damage happened at the water. The surface of Oldman's Lake swallowed the fiery object and immediately gagged. The water went to the boiling point and beyond, converted into steam in seconds. Artie Carlson lived through the collision only though the dumbest of luck. The first scalding wave threw him from the water and onto the shore with second- and third-degree burns across most of his legs and back. Had he worn shorts as he originally intended, his legs would have cooked like stewing beef. As it was they were protected by denim and only burned severely. Bobby Carlson was crushed under the thing that struck the water, forced deep into the silt and baked by the heat of the craft. The fish in the lake disappeared in the roiling foam, reappearing seconds later as steamed meat and flash-fried scales. The long docks exploded into flames. The old, weathered wood of the boat landings took only a few seconds to reach the burning point. The boats themselves were thrown high on the first of the massive waves, and those who were unfortunate enough to be standing on the vessels were hurled into the scalding waters or launched ashore. The heat from the falling star set many of the boats ablaze. Only two people lived through the experience; Mark Walton and Mary Chambers. Both were burned over most of their bodies. Neither would ever be the same. The Lobster Hut, the only seafood restaurant in the entire town, had the misfortune of being too close to the water. The propane tanks stored outside of the actual building went up with a roar that most people could not hear over the sound of the ringing in their skulls, and took most of the restaurant along for the ride. Thirty-five people inside the building, or standing too near, were erased from the history books in a massive, blinding flash that still failed to compete with the actual landing site.

Fully four feet of the sand at the shoreline fused together and took with it fifteen people, four picnic baskets, seven coolers and three dogs. Pieces of all would be found melted into the glass over the next few days. Most of the people were spared the worst of the impact, only being bruised and battered. The sound that had driven people to their knees and then to the ground; saved them from the worst of the heat blast. Amilee Foster, uncovered save by a blanket, suffered blistering burns on one half of her face, and her mother, finally able to think again after the sensory overload, suffered second and third degree burns on her arms, chest and the top of her head. Altogether, one hundred and fifty-seven people died in the accident, and one hundred and seventy-two were injured.

The flames which managed to maintain their hold on the boats along the docks soon added a new measure of noise to the cacophony of screaming people and boiling water. Propane tanks within the vessels—initially shielded from the worst of the initial wave of incinerating energies—soon felt a heat they could not withstand and exploded in brilliant fireballs of shrapnel that rained down over the woods and the picnic area.

Those few boats left unscathed by the initial wave of heat soon began to burn despite their luck. Along the shore a fire built that defied the boiling waters of Lake Oldman.

Frank Osborn placed a call to the Parrish County Hospital and demanded they send as many ambulances as they could. His hair was singed and a few minor burns kissed his face and hands, but otherwise Frank was fine, if severely rattled. Uncertain as to just what had occurred, Frank explained that the fireworks had gone bad and "lots of people are screaming like it's the end of the world." It may as well have been the end of the world that day; Collier would never be the same.

The aliens had landed, and landed poorly at best.

Book One:
Frank's Story

Chapter 1

1

Frank Osborn spent three years of his youth wallowing in the worst sorts of filth the Vietnam War could produce. He'd seen friends and enemies alike torn into shredded meat and viscera by bullets, bombs and napalm. He'd watched the shattered remains of young soldiers try to pull themselves across the ground, too hurt to understand that they should just lie still and die. He had killed other people simply to stay alive. Sometimes, when the world was too quiet, he still struggled with the images of children doing a wild dance caused by the bullets he fired into their bodies. He had, God help him, murdered those children because they were too friendly and they *might* have been booby-trapped. Not all of them were, but he could live with that. He'd long since adjusted to the violence he had committed in Asia so long ago. Or at least he liked to tell himself that he had.

For the first time in his life, he understood what some soldiers meant when they spoke of flashbacks. Right now Collier sure as hell seemed like it had been transported through time and space to end up right in the middle of that nasty war.

After the noise and violence of a few moments ago, everything seemed almost quiet. But the activity taking place removed that illusion quickly, and the ringing in Frank's ears was certainly in part responsible for the lack of noise. He wondered idly if he might have been deafened, but with everything else going on around him, that was a minor concern for the moment.

People walked around with dazed expressions on bloodied, burnt faces, trying to understand what was going on. Those who *could* walk, at least. Seemed like a lot of people couldn't even manage that. The trees closest to the lake were scorched and charred, their leaves blackened and the Spanish moss hanging from their branches incinerated. There wasn't a single weeping willow he could see that hadn't had most of the thin, vine-like branches burnt completely away, and even the stronger oak and maple trees were burned so badly that he knew they wouldn't survive the damage. Even from a dozen yards away he could see that the heat had ruined the outer layers of the wood. Even if it hadn't, most of the trees were now leaning crazily away from the water, pushed by the impact of the thing that even now sent columns of steam into the air. Most of the plants in the area had been fully incinerated, at least those closest to the lake. The grass of the lawn was seared brown, and even from a distance he could see that something was *wrong* with the sand near the lake, though he couldn't quite decide what that something was. *Looks like a nuclear burn,* he thought. *Heat that intense should have killed everything moving, but it happened so damned fast that it only caught bits and pieces of most of us. Hell, if it'd gone on any longer, we'd all be dead now.* He moved forward, setting aside the unsettling thoughts going through his head and concentrating on helping those not beyond his meager abilities to assist.

His first stop was at the massive permanent concession stand halfway between the water's edge and the parking lot, which had managed to lose most of the paint on its upper third before the—whatever the hell it was—landed in the water. He pulled Albert Waller from inside. Albert was alive, but his face and neck looked like they'd met up with a bucket of boiling oil and lost the fight. His hair was damn near gone along the front, and what was left in back was smoking. Hell, even his shirt and apron had scorch marks, though they ended right around where the window the man had been looking out to see the fireworks would have blocked them. Frank frowned at that, worrying about whether or not the heat had been maybe something a little more like radiation and not just flame. It wasn't a comforting idea, but it explained the way the burn marks worked on Albert's chest. That the propane tanks for the grill had not ignited was something of a miracle in Frank's eyes. If they had, Albert have been blown into flinders and would have never even known what hit him. Albert was unconscious, and the lump on the side of his head matched up just about right with the dent in the Sprite canister. Frank rolled the man on his back and tore the apron he was wearing clean off his body. Then he grabbed some of the ice from the concession's bins and used the mustard-stained cotton fabric as a crude ice pack on Albert's face.

He moved on to Emily O'Rourke, lying only a few feet from the concession stand, a fine lady who'd never failed to make the people around her smile and made about the best baked beans he'd ever found at a church social, and did what he could for her. The poor woman was just about one big blister. Her plastic glasses were partially melted to her skin, and her eyes were sealed shut by the swelling in her flesh. William O'Rourke, her husband for almost forty years, was doing his best to comfort her. Her voice was harsh and ragged, her breathing frantic. Frank hated to imagine the sort of pain she was in. The heat rising from her skin was enough to make him wonder if she was burning on the inside.

He worked to cover the worst of her burns with the crushed ice he had salvaged from the concession, taking his own shirt this time for fear that any contact with the scorched polyester fused into Emily's neckline would cause her more harm. He clutched the ice-laden shirt in one hand and used his other to guide the package into William's big, blistered palms. "William, you're gonna have to hold this to her face. She'll scream, like as not, but you hold it there anyway. We need to get that swelling down and we need to do it right now. You understand me?"

"Yes, Frank. I do. You go take care of the others now. I'll take care of Emma." The man sounded winded, almost on the verge of tears, but he managed to do as Frank instructed.

Frank moved on, almost completely on autopilot. Faces blurred and his ears rang anew from the sound of constant screams. He barely even noticed when the ambulances arrived. There were too many wounded for the small company of paramedics to handle alone, so he just kept on doing his thing.

Bethany Harper died in his arms. She was a sweet little girl, only seven as he recalled. Such things should not happen.

He didn't dare let himself dwell on her death. Instead he simply rushed on to the next in line, Beth's father, Wade. Wade was barely hurt at all, but you'd have thought his arms were gone by the way he carried on. Wade Harper only found out later that his only child was dead. Suzanne Harper was worse off than her husband but had the decency to keep her pain to herself. No, on second glance she was in shock. He lifted the woman and carried her towards the waiting ambulances.

And as he walked the magnitude of the disaster hit him again, damn near making him drop Suzanne and just give up. Ten paramedics and a handful of others were doing their best to work on over a hundred people. Despite their efforts, three others screamed for attention as a loved one or family member writhed in pain for every one they treated.

He set Suzy down near the closest ambulance and wandered towards his squad car. More people needed to come in for this one. The clinic and the five ambulances just couldn't handle a disaster on this scale. But when he tried to hail anyone on the radio, all he got was static.

He was starting towards the bank of pay phones at the park's entrance when he saw Milo Fitzwater directing a small fleet of emergency vehicles into the area. The pudgy little fart looked like a general, hollering at the top of his lungs and pointing to this spot and that, directing traffic flow with the efficiency of an air traffic controller. Miracle of miracles, they even followed his orders. More medical technicians started moving about, grabbing those people who stumbled around and moving them aside to reach the seriously injured.

Frank felt suddenly at a loss. He was no longer needed. His knees started shaking as the excess adrenaline caught up with him, and he slumped back on the hood of his patrol car. He looked at the now controlled chaos around him and sighed. Damn, but he needed a cigarette. Before he could so much as reach for the pack of Marlboros in his pants pocket, Milo was at his side, urging him to lie down and just stay calm.

"Milo, what the hell's wrong with you? I'm just fine. Tired, but fine."

"Frank, you need to just rest yourself. You look like you're about to have a stroke." The mayor's voice was filled with concern, and his little piggy eyes had that fretful look he got when he was thinking about the budget. But his stance demanded that Frank follow his orders, and Frank was just too tired to put up a fight. Milo, with surprising strength, helped him lie back and Frank was grateful for the assistance. He felt about as weak as a kitten right then. Confused by the sudden exhaustion, Frank lay back and tried to catch his breath. Despite his best efforts, nothing seemed to help much. He couldn't think straight. He had enough energy going through him to make his whole body twitch, but he couldn't get his body to respond to his mind's orders.

Then Sam Morrisey from over at the Parrish County Hospital was at his side, putting an oxygen mask over his mouth and shoving a rubber cuff over his arm. Sam looked too much like a thirty-year-old Santa Claus for Frank's comfort. He could see the man building toys and wearing granny glasses easier than he could imagine him performing any sort of medical procedure. If Sam wasn't so damned good at what he did, Frank would have shoved him away. The oxygen helped. The blood pressure cuff just annoyed the hell out of him. Morrisey was looking as worried as Milo, but, considering the situation, that wasn't too surprising.

Frank turned his head to look back at the lake and got his first real glimpse at the cause of all his problems. Huge. That was a good word for describing the thing. Through the smoke

of burning yachts and boats, Frank studied the newest addition to Collier's landscape. Though he could not see the whole
of the object, if the curve peering from the boiling waters was
any indication, he'd have to guess the structure was wide enough
to cover half a dozen football fields. The thing looked metallic, but between the steam rising from Oldman's Lake and the
milling people he could not be certain.

"Frank? Are you listening to me?" Sam Morrisey stared at
him worriedly, a slight scowl on his face. "Have you checked
your blood-sugar lately?"

"No." His voice sounded funny to his own ears, and because he couldn't stand not being heard clearly, he tried to pull
the oxygen mask off his face. Sam shoved it back into place,
and Frank let him. The motion had left him feeling strangely
disconnected from his own body. He was annoyed by Sam's
attitude. Damn it, he wasn't the one bleeding or burning or
screaming. He wanted to help! "I've been a bit busy, Sam."
Every time anyone asked him about diabetes he felt like a six-
year-old caught with his hand in the cookie jar. Guilt was one
enemy he never managed to escape.

Sam didn't speak, he simply shook his head and reached
for the glucometer in its brown vinyl bag. Milo made annoying
little 'tsk' noises and wandered off to see if anyone else needed
help. Frank winced when the lancet poked his finger, but more
because of the surprise than the pain. After thirty seconds of
waiting, Sam shook his head and reached back into his medical bag. "Here. Eat these." He held out a set of plastic pack-
ets with foil backings. Each of the two-inch squares held a
small white wafer-shaped lump.

"Are those what I think they are?"

"Yes. They're glucose tablets. Now eat the damn things
so I can get on my way."

"I don't want 'em. They taste like shit."

Sam hauled on his pants, forcing them partially over his
large belly and did his best to look stern. "They're not made to
taste good, Frank. If they tasted good you and every other

diabetic would want to eat them like candy. I'm not going anywhere until you eat the damn things. So eat, I've got people to tend to." He paused and looked around for a few seconds, his face stunned. *Santa Claus on a war front.* The idea was almost enough to make Frank chuckle, but he was afraid if he started laughing he wouldn't be able to stop.

Frank smiled, "Yes, Mom." He opened the packs and chewed on the sickening sweetness of the wafers. "Damn. These things are nasty."

"Well, eat food next time and you won't have to eat them. I've told you before about skipping meals, and I know my dad's told you at least a hundred times." Sam frowned. "Your blood pressure's too high, your sugar's too low. Your heart's a little irregular, too. Have you been for a real physical lately?"

"Yeah. Your father said I was just fine." He shrugged. "You and your dad are both pains in my ass."

"Yeah, and I'm sure he loves it just as much as I do. Stay sitting for a while and then get some rest. We'll take care of things here."

"Rest? Yeah, that'll happen soon."

"I mean it, Frank. You get some rest. You aren't doing anyone any favors by being macho."

Frank waved Sam away and the paramedic left. Frank pulled the oxygen mask off again, and this time no one stopped him. The air was too hot and smelled far too much like places he didn't want to remember, but it beat all hell out of trying to talk through the cold blast of air and annoying plastic muzzle. Sam and his father, John Morrisey, were both fine men. But they harped like old women when it came to Frank's diet. John had an excuse at least; he was Frank's doctor. Four years since he'd been diagnosed as a diabetic, and Frank still never managed to keep his food intake and insulin injections balanced well enough to keep the old fart happy.

Still, he took Sam's advice and stayed where he was for a few minutes, waiting for his blood-sugar to increase back into the normal range. He wanted to get back to work, but the world kept trying to tilt on him and he just didn't dare try standing. Getting older sucked.

While he sat near his patrol car, he looked around the area and watched with something akin to awe as the people finally got around to helping each other with the worst of the mess. Damn near everyone had something wrong with them, from scrapes all the way up to broken bones.

Two medics walked past with a stretcher between them. Emily O'Rourke lay on the stretcher, bundled into a sheet and looking twice as thin as a snake. She was normally so active, so full of energy that she seemed larger than she really was. Now, injured and motionless, she seemed like a different person altogether. *Too frail to be Emily,* he thought as he watched them carry her past. *Not feisty enough by half.* Her face was a mess and Frank had to admit he doubted if she'd live through the rest of the night. Bill was still with her, walking beside her and gingerly holding her hand. He completely ignored the blisters on his own body, too worried about his wife to give them consideration. Frank admired William, but at the present time he did not envy the man.

Finally, unable to stand still a second longer, Frank grabbed one of the ambulance attendants from over in Stockton—how Milo had convinced them to make the trip from so far away was something he'd never understand—and told the woman to put an extra person in the back of his car. She looked at his badge, now pinned to belt, looked at the mounting number of people who desperately needed medical attention and then looked at the dwindling number of ambulances. As another one started moving towards Roswell Avenue, the only road out of Collier, she nodded and called for assistance.

A beanpole of a man came over and helped move not one but two of the victims into the back of the patrol car. Andy Newsome and his little brother Billy. The two looked relatively unscathed, except for the burn marks. Nothing as bad as Emily's, thank God, but fairly substantial just the same. But when Andy settled into the seat, Frank saw the heavy bandages wrapped around one part of the boy's scalp and saw the blood leaking through the thick cotton padding. Billy sat next to his brother, looking hideously pale except where he was scorched. He held a small package in his trembling hands. When he noticed Frank looking, he opened the bundle briefly and closed it again without a word. Going on the location of the bandages and the shape of the meaty lump in the ice-laden cloth, Frank was pretty sure Billy had a grip on his brother's ear.

He made both boys buckle into their seats and turned on the siren. A few seconds later they were on their way to Route 65. Next stop: Parrish County Hospital.

He drove as quickly as he dared, firing up the flashers and the siren both, and pressing on the accelerator hard enough to get them up to 50 miles per hour. Any faster on the winding little two-lane road and he'd have more than a few burns and a severed ear to worry about...

Just as well he kept the pace light, because as he rounded the final bend in the road before everything straightened out and became more than an over-glorified biking trail, he damn near slammed into the back of one of the ambulances. He barely noticed the flashing red and white lights reflected off the trees in time to bring the cruiser to a shuddering, sideways halt. One of the two munchkins in the back squealed in perfect time with the tires. *Jesus please-us! What the hell's wrong with those boys.*

"I dropped Andy's ear, Officer Frank." He could barely hear Billy in the back of the cruiser through the pounding of his own heart.

"What?" He was annoyed by the kid's voice, and did his best to control his temper. Everyone was on edge enough as it was. "Speak up, Billy." Frank moved the car to the side of the road, just in case there should be anyone coming up from behind him who was in as much of a hurry.

The boy's voice was at the edge of panic, and Frank made himself remember that he wasn't alone in is confusion. "I dropped Andy's ear. I can't find it back here."

Frank sighed, pulling his eighteen-inch flashlight from the massive belt he always wore on duty. "Here. Use this and stay put. I'm gonna see what the delay is up ahead."

"Thank you, sir." The kid sounded like he was about to cry and Frank softened up.

"That's okay, Billy. You just stay calm and we'll see about getting Andy all fixed up." He reached out and tousled the kid's slightly greasy hair, for lack of any other way to express his sympathy. Then he got out of the car fast. He hated kids. Not because they were mean or anything, more because they were confusing. They just didn't act like real people. He wasn't fond of that little flaw in his make up, but there it was and he had to live with it.

Up ahead, he saw a continuing line of ambulances. Seven in all, and every one of them with the lights painting the world in stark white and red relief. He thought about running to the end of the line to see what the holdup was, but decided to satisfy himself with walking at a brisk pace.

Frank swatted a few bugs away from his face as he walked, remembering why he hated summertime in Georgia so damned much. Bugs and sweat, sweat and bugs. Always too hot and too humid this time of the year, and the worst was yet to come. August would turn the sultry evenings into an endless sauna. The heat had never bothered him much as a kid, but these days it made him restless and angry.

Just up ahead, he could see the backs of all the ambulance attendees, lined up like a group of well-groomed prisoners. His built-in trouble-sensors—better known to most people as instincts—started screaming up a storm as he took them in. One after another, lined up with their hands on the tops of their heads. None of them even fidgeted. They were standing as still as the oak trees lining the road. The only motion came from a mild breeze ruffling their hair and their shirts.

Frank carefully slid the .38 revolver from its holster and thumbed the safety off. He was not liking this at all. No sir, not one damn bit. The light from the ambulances and even from his police car were going to make sneaking forward a task if he stayed on the road, so he slipped behind the next tree and waited a few seconds. Then he made a dash to the next tree in line and tried to see what he could of the situation. All he could see were the backs and partial profiles of the paramedics. They did not look happy. They looked very, very scared. Sam Morrisey was the only exception. He looked pissed off in a big way. Thinking the situation over, Frank decided he'd rather not get Sam angry. Sure, he looked like Santa most of the time, but just then he looked like an angry grizzly bear.

Whatever was out there in front of them did not seem at all impressed. Frank moved forward again. When he looked around the new tree, he had a perfect view of Sam and another technician in profile. The second paramedic was familiar enough, another local gone off to work in another area. Sam's sister, Denise. Denise did not look like Santa, she looked like a heavier Annette Funicello. Cute, but only pretty if she'd drop about thirty pounds. Beyond her chest and Sam's belly, the others were lost from sight.

Frank cranked his head to the right, trying to see what was in front of the group. All he saw was darkness. Right up until the time the rifle butt filled his vision. The blow was deliberately gentle; he knew that from the second it connected with his forehead. Still, even a light tap from a rifle butt is enough to make a person rethink his position. Frank staggered back a few steps and landed on his ass.

Before he could stand back up, or even really give much consideration to the idea, the revolver was yanked from his loose hand and he was forced face first into the wet mulch on the ground.

His arms were yanked back with enough force to make him cry out, and then cold metal snapped into place over both of his wrists. Whoever cuffed him worked him like a pro. A moment later he was hoisted to his feet and half carried past the paramedics. He wanted to protest, but his head was still buzzing and refusing to lift from its downward-facing position. The smack on the skull had been harder than he had first realized. So solid in fact, that his knees kept wanting to fall away in all the wrong directions.

Finally, after what seemed like too long for the short distance they traveled, the people carrying Frank brought him to a halt in front of a pair of black boots. He took his time and did it right. This time when he decided to raise his head, he was successful.

He almost wished it hadn't worked. The thing in front of him did not look human. The black boots lead up to pants just as dark and just as glossy. The pants were part of a full body suit, divided by a large belt holding half a dozen devices from a radio to what looked like a cattle prod. Over the shins, the thighs and the groin, heavy metallic-looking pieces of armor had been set into the fabric. Above the belt, a flak jacket covered over most of the figure's torso, which seemed like overkill when you considered that more of the armored segments covered the stomach, back, arms and neck of the outfit. And from the neck up, the entire face of whatever was under all that clothing was concealed by a helmet and what looked like a modified gas mask. Where a mouth should have been, a long metallic trunk slid down and then over a heavy-set shoulder. Directly behind the imposing figure, Frank could see the silhouette of a very large and heavily armed helicopter. At least his assailants were human. They only looked like they belonged on Mars.

One of the thing's hands, also covered in black, reached out and grabbed the badge hanging at his belt. The badge was yanked away and held before a heavily tinted visor. He wondered how the hell the guy in the monkey suit could see anything at all.

"Captain Franklin Osborn?" The voice sounded all wrong through the filters over the face. It sounded like something that would come out of an insect. Which, when he considered the face, almost made sense. Frank shivered, despite the heat.

"That'd be me. Who the hell are you?" He wanted to sound stern, but the bonk on his noggin stopped his desires from being fulfilled.

"None of your business, sir. This road and all of Collier are now under quarantine. Nobody leaves."

"What?" He refused to believe he was hearing the words, even though his ears seemed like they were working again. "You've got to be out of your cotton-pickin' mind, mister! We've got over a hundred people in need of medical attention!"

The glass bug-eyes of the mask stared back without expression. "Medical help is on the way. As it stands now, no one leaves this area. Anyone attempting to leave will be shot. We have orders to shoot to kill. Do I make myself clear?"

Frank tried to break away from the two holding his arms, but managed only to make them tighten their grips. "Who do you think you are? You can't do this to me! You can't do this to the people of this town!" He felt his blood pressure jump a few notches. "God damn it, this is still America! And every last one of us is an American citizen!" He gestured at the line of ambulances with his head. "These people are injured, and they'll die if they don't get help. Let us pass!"

The man in black reached out his hand again. This time it held what his buddies in 'Nam had termed a 'BFG,' a Big Fucking Gun, and the business end of the gun pointed directly under his chin. "I know. I know you are all citizens of the United States. Count your blessings on that point. It's the only thing keeping you alive right now. Now get in your patrol car and go back the way you came." The figure moved closer, until Frank could see his distorted face reflected back at him in the black bug-eyes of the man's faceplate. "The injured will be attended to. There're a lot of people coming here within the hour. A lot of doctors are among them." The condescending tone in the man's buzzing voice filled Frank with the simple need to lash out. Sadly, there was the problem of his hands being cuffed to consider.

He spat instead, sending a wad of spittle raining across the left side of the bug-faced mask. Before he could even grin in satisfaction, the man in black slammed a big, gloved fist into his breadbasket. "Whoof!" The sound escaped his lips with a rush of air and everything inside of Frank Osborn seemed to try leaving his body. Certainly his wind was gone, and so were all of his motor functions. His knees gave up completely this time, and he felt his legs just sort of dangling beneath his body. The hands holding him still were all that kept him from crashing into the ground. What little was in his stomach attempted to rebel, but he managed to avoid vomiting all over himself. He tried to curse the man in front of him, but only managed a weak mewling sound instead.

"Let's try this again, Captain Osborn." The same hand that had gut-punched him now yanked at his crewcut. It hurt like hell, but he refused to let it show. Just the same, he moved his head up to ease the pain. The other hand held forth the machine gun, damn near managing to fit the barrel inside his right nostril. "I have my orders. No one leaves here, period. I have orders to kill anyone who tries. That includes you. Now, you can go back to your car and tend to your wounded, or you can stay right here and keep giving me lip. One of those options means you end up in a body bag. The other one means you get to stay alive and help us keep the people of this town from getting stupid and ending up in a morgue." The tip of the short rifle—not one he could recognize, which bothered him in a vague way, as he kept up on all the rifleman's magazines—stopped worrying about his nose and started tapping impatiently at his forehead instead. "Which will it be?"

"I suspect I can manage to find my way back to town."

"I'm glad to hear that, Captain Osborn. Because I really don't want to see anybody die who does not have to." The helmeted face looked away from him, the whole head turning to find one of the figures holding him up. "Escort the captain back to his squad car. Make sure he gets back to town."

"Yes, sir."

The two walking armrests turned him around and started moving towards the car in the distance. Right past the row of paramedics and the line of ambulances waiting to move on. Sam Morrisey looked at him with eyes both angry and afraid. Frank tried his best to look like he was in control, a situation which proved impossible when one considered his current position. As they reached the car, he could see more of the uniformed figures gesturing for the long line of ambulances now behind his cruiser to turn around. One by one, they did just that.

The escorts eased him against the car and removed his handcuffs. Frank took a minute to stand and make sure everything inside his body was where it was supposed to be. Luckily, everything was. Frank looked at the two figures dressed the same as the one in charge of them and shook his head. He was about to say something when he heard the sounds coming from out of the car.

He turned towards the back seat and walked the short distance to where Billy Newsome held a bloodied, soiled pile of gauze in his hands. The ear sat atop the mess like a trophy. The little boy was crying, tears ran from his eyes and mucus ran from his nose to cover the lower half of his blistered face. The ear was held before his brother like an offering to a pagan god. Andy paid it no attention.

Billy whispered hoarsely between jagged breaths. "Come on, Andy. I found it, see? You can talk to me now. Please talk to me, Andy. Pretty please..." He said the words over and over again, like a prayer. Andy continued to ignore him.

"Billy..."

Billy damn near jumped out of his skin when he heard Frank. He looked around with wide, terrified eyes and finally managed to focus on the police chief after several frantic seconds. Billy scrambled around on his knees, holding the torn lump of flesh out towards Frank with desperate glee. "I found it, Officer Frank. I found his ear!" A fresh collection of tears erupted from Billy's eyes and his seven-year-old face squinched up into a pathetic pout. "I found his ear but now Andy's mad at me. He won't talk at all and he won't even look at me!"

"I—Billy—"

"Please make him understand I'm sorry. Puh-leas-hease!" The boy hitched in another breath and collapsed into jagged sobs of grief.

Frank reached forward and took the child in his arms. He held him tight and turned him away from the sight of his dead brother. He'd known both of the boys since the day they were born. He'd never expected to outlive one of them. "Shhh, Billy. It'll be okay. You did good, son. You did just fine." Hot tears ran down his shoulder and he felt the cold, dead flesh of Andy's ear pressed against his neck. "Everything's gonna be just fine, you wait and see."

Frank spared one last glare at the two people in black armor and fatigues, then he started walking back to town. Behind him, the blue and white lights from his cruiser cut wounds through the darkness.

2

Collier looked like shit. He was able at last to see the town as he walked back up the Route 65 extension and into the town proper. He ignored the ambulances that passed him on the way, needing the time to walk and reflect. His arms were threatening to cramp up on him, but he refused to put Billy down until he could find Mark and Sue Newsome.

The thought of telling them that Andy was dead made him want to weep. Andy was Sue's pride and joy. After the rough time she'd had delivering him, it was no wonder that he was a bit on the spoiled side. True, he tended to wince at the thought of pain, but Frank knew that came from too much mothering, not from anything else. Now he was dead, and it was Frank's duty to tell his parents. He'd sooner have castrated himself. The only consolation was that Billy was still alive. Injured, asleep and drooling all over Frank's shoulder, but alive. Surely that had to count for something. If not, what the hell in the world did?

The area was less crowded than when he had left. Those people who remained were either wounded, attending the injured, milling about in a daze or dead. Far too many filled the latter category. From where he stood surveying the scene, he could count over fifty bodies. The only person he saw moving with any real energy was Milo. The little bastard was dashing from place to place and pausing only long enough to assess the situation. The wild look in the mayor's eyes made him wonder if the man had slipped into shock, simply going through comfortable motions until his mind re-engaged.

Finding Mark and Sue proved easier than he could have dreamed. They were lying near the shore of Oldman's Lake, frozen in the molted glass. The glass itself was smoky, thick with veil gray tints, like wispy clouds. The parts of the people in the glass that were above the ground were charred into little more than blackened bone and ash. Enough of Sue's head remained in the melted sand to make identification easy, despite the burns. One eye, suspended and preserved in the glass, stared in frozen shock at the massive structure still sending columns of steam into the air above the lake.

He backed away from the spot slowly, not wanting Billy to see his parents should he awaken. His foot slipped in what was left of someone else—not enough to recognize, little more than congealing body fat—and he had to fight to keep his balance. He managed to make it all the way back to the concession stand without dropping the boy and simply losing his mind, but he would never understand just how the feat was accomplished.

He sat down carefully, leaving the boy against his shoulder despite the cramps complaining in his shoulders. He chose the side of the concession that faced away from the lake—and the mortal remains of people he'd known and cared for—as a backrest. The thought of looking at the shore and the ruins of so many lives was just too much to face.

Every muscle in his body felt loose. Tiny tremors rippled through his back, chest and arms, and finally he was forced to set Billy Newsome down. Billy whimpered once in his sleep and curled himself into a ball. Frank sat watching him for a time, staring away once in a while as Milo passed through his field of vision. His eyes seemed to have a mind of their own, refusing to ignore the sights laid out before him. There were fewer bodies on this side of the stand, but the injured people could still be seen lying in the grass of leaning against each other like crude, human sculptures. The stores on either side of the road leading to the lake looked like derelict buildings in some big city slum. Broken glass dotted the sidewalks and where windows once reflected light there were only pools of darkness as far as he could see. Cars rested on their tops and sides along the road and in the sprawling parking lot off to his left. How they'd managed not to have a massive explosion was beside him; the smell of spilled gasoline was still strong in the air, and the earlier crash of the

Starship! It's a goddamn flying saucer if ever there was such a thing.

meteor or whatever it was seemed like a thing from the distant past. At least two hours had passed between the fireworks and now. It seemed more like a couple of days.

When sleep hit Frank Osborn he was still staring at the cars on their sides and backs. Still wondering just what in God's name had happened. He slept deeply and dreamt of bloody ears, glass-coated eyes and terrifying figures dressed in black. Figures with no faces save for large black orbs where their eyes should have been.

Chapter 2

1

Waking up was sort of like getting hit with a splash of cold water. He was up and ready to scream for a second, ready to swing his fists at the remnants of his tortured dreams. Then reality came back around and made him want to cry instead. Billy Newsome was gone. He'd slipped away while Frank was asleep. It only took a few seconds to spot him standing with his tiny hand in Milo Fitzwater's hairy paw. Milo was wearing the same clothes he'd been dressed in the night before, and Frank wondered if the man had managed any sleep at all.

A loud crashing sound made Frank turn his head sharply , sending a hot wire of pain though his neck. Nothing like sleeping in a sitting position to remind a man that he's getting on in his years. He scanned past Milo and Billy until his eyes focused on the source of the loud noise. Ten of the armored men from the night before had just thrown over Doug Martin's Ford Ranger, revealing the mortal remains of the Habersham family and what was left of their Mercedes. A cursory examination ensued, and four of the men were dispatched, coming back a moment later with two power saws, the Jaws of Life and four body bags. Frank watched them in action as they tore the top off the Mercedes and got to the business of bagging a slightly pudgy male corpse, a female whose head looked like a squashed berry and two young children. Milo pulled Billy away from the sight and ushered the boy over to where Linda Arminter was watching over a handful of other children. Linda was good with kids, that was likely why she worked as one of the teachers over at Fowler Elementary. Then he headed towards one of the soldiers—they had to be soldiers:

everything from their posture to the precise creases in their uniforms screamed military—standing by himself and studying a long list on a clipboard.

Frank stood and stretched stiffly. He lit a Marlboro, going into his usual early morning coughing fit as he sucked in the first lungful, and started walking in the same direction. He met up with Milo just as the mayor was pointing angrily over his shoulder and looking hard at the man in front of him.

"Is that entirely necessary? Those ruffians of yours are treating those people like they were only so much meat."

"With all due respect, Mayor Fitzwater, they are. Those folks are dead and they can't feel a thing. My men have their orders, and those orders include clearing the parking lot to make way for our equipment." The man never even looked up from his paperwork.

Milo looked fit to be tied. "I don't rightly care what they're supposed to be doing. Around here, it's considered proper to give the dead a little respect!"

"Mayor, I don't have time for this. If it'll make you feel better, I'll personally apologize to the corpses later. But for right now, I'm pressed for time."

Milo made a gasping sound, and his mouth opened and closed like a large mouth bass trying to breathe on the land. "I want your name and your identification number, young man. Then I want the name of your commanding officer!"

The man slapped a pen into its slot on the clipboard with sharp angry gestures. He then slipped the bundle between his left elbow and his side. "Captain Osborn, would you like to discuss the facts of life with Mayor Fitzwater? Or would you like me to do it? Your way will be less painful."

Frank stepped forward. "Come on, Milo. This old boy don't like to deal with us mere civilians. Like as not he'll pistol-whip you before he'll give you a straight answer on anything."

"My duty is to secure this area. When my commanding officer lands," the man pointed to where the soldiers were throwing over a Toyota Camry—"which will only happen when my men have removed the vehicles from that lot, you can talk with him about what's going on here. In the meantime, get the hell out of my face and let me take care of business."

"Fuck you, too, asshole." Frank's words were out of his mouth before he could give them any thought. He was lucky. The soldier had already gone back to his clipboard.

Milo sucked in a massive breath and lowered his head until he had an extra chin where his neck usually was. From hardware salesman to charging bull in only a matter of seconds. Before he could speak, Frank hauled on the mayor's pudgy arm and started dragging him away. "Don't even start on me, Milo. I'm doing you a favor. That bastard slammed me in the gut last night. I don't think he's likely to be any nicer today." He looked around and then started down Millwater Street. After two blocks, he cut across over to Oglethorpe Road.

"Who do these people think they are, Frank? No sooner did things start to calm down this morning than they were all over the place and acting like they'd been appointed by God Himself."

"I don't know who they are or who they think they are, but I intend to find out." Frank moved along at a steady pace and was surprised that Milo managed to keep up with him. Now and then he forgot that Milo was used to hauling lumber and moving heavy stock in a hardware store. There was little about the man that did not look soft, from his too small feet to the bald spot on top of his head. Normally the look on the mayor's face was a constant battle between confusion, a frown and a stuck sneeze. Right now he looked ready to head back the way they'd come and go a few rounds with Darth Vader Junior.

"Where are you going, Chief?"

"Back to my office to make a few calls. I want to see what Paul Moody with the Highway Patrol can tell me about these assholes. If Paul doesn't know who they are, he can find out in a short time."

"Well, I certainly hope he does know something. Because I don't think these people have any idea at all what they're doing. I truly do not."

"We'll know soon enough, Milo." Frank started across Seventh Street, past the Hav-A-Feast diner and towards the one-story town hall. "We'll know soon enough." The two of them walked a little faster, Frank supposed that was only natural under the current circumstances. Desperation almost always made people move faster. Right now he was starting to feel a little desperate and a lot paranoid. He hadn't said a word to Milo, who was still rambling on about the lack of proper etiquette on the part of the black-clad forces in the town, but he was starting to get scared.

Last night he'd almost convinced himself that the incident at the exit ramp to I-65 was just an isolated case. Today, he'd started to realize just how many of the dark soldiers were around the town. They'd only walked a total of eight blocks. In that time he'd counted over twenty of the armored figures. Assuming they still had the road cut off as well, there could be one hell of a lot of the goons hanging around.

He walked into the police office and headed straight for his desk and his Rolodex. The blast of cold air that greeted him from the central air conditioning vents was a welcome friend. Buck Landers, his second in command, looked up with a relieved smile spreading out under his oversized mustache. "I've been trying you all morning and half the night, Frank. You had me worrying you were one of the dead."

"I'm still among the living, Buck. Now shut up a minute while I try to get Moody on the line."

"I'll shut up, but it won't do you any good."

"Why not?"

"Cause them bastards in the black suits have control of the phone lines, and they ain't letting anyone make outgoing calls."

"My ass! Are you serious?"

"As a heart attack. I've done everything from begging to screaming at them bastards and not a thing's come of it."

Frank lifted the receiver and listened carefully. There was no dial tone, but a hard-edged voice spoke up. "This is a secured line. State the nature of your problem or hang up immediately."

"This is Frank Osborn, I'm the police captain here in Collier. I need to make a call to the Highway Patrol."

"For what reason, Captain Osborn?"

"Because it's a part of my job, mister. Now will you please give me an open line?"

"I cannot do that, Captain."

"Why the hell not?"

"Until further notice, no outgoing calls are permitted without the direct order of the commander."

"Well, fine then. Put me in contact with your commander."

"I cannot do that, either, Captain."

"Why not? How am I supposed to handle my job if I can't even make a phone call?"

"You may speak with the watch commander if you desire. I'll pass on the message and he should return your call at his earliest convenience."

"You just do that, mister. I'll be right here waiting." Frank slammed down the phone.

Buck stirred uncomfortably, clearing his throat. His voice, which had a moment before been almost cheerful, was now somber. "Doug Calvert and Rick Simms are among the injured, Frank."

"Shit. How bad are they?"

"They're pretty bad off. Massive burns on the both of 'em. Frank..."

"What is it?" He knew the news was bad, and braced himself against the sinking ice pit in his stomach.

"Willie and Lennie are dead. Neither of 'em felt a thing as far as I could tell, but they didn't make it."

Frank sat down hard, and for a few seconds the only noise he could hear was the sound of his own blood rushing in his ears. William Slater and Leonard Slater Junior were two of his officers. They were good men and they were dead. Two more were in a bad way. That left four officers, including himself, to run the town. His mind refused to grasp the idea firmly. Two dead and two injured. One half of his force decimated along with all of the other wounded and dead. The thought slipped through his mental fingers even as he felt his body going numb.

Frank pulled an old stunt from his time in the military and clamped his teeth down on the inside of his mouth, drawing blood from the soft flesh. The numbness left him instantly. He shoved all thoughts of the accident victims aside and forced his muddy thoughts into focus. There were things he had to do. The rusty taste of the blood in his mouth helped more than he'd honestly expected.

"Buck, get on the radio and connect me with the Highway Patrol."

"Can't do it, Frank. Been trying every ten minutes, but I can't pick up anything but static. Whatever fell into the lake seems to make a lot of white noise."

"You gotta be kidding me."

"'Fraid not. Messed up all the walkie-talkies too. Unless you want to try smoke signals, we're cut off from the outside world."

Frank sat down hard in his chair, a scowl on his face and dark thought racing through his mind. "How about the CB in your car?"

"Same problem."

"Well, shit. I guess we'll have to wait for Highway to figure out there's something wrong." Frank wanted to hit Buck, not for giving him the bad news, but for doing it so calmly, when he felt like going into a panic attack himself.

"Oh, they already know something's up."

"They do?"

"Sure. Had it on the news at eight o'clock sharp. We made the number one story today." There it was again, the urge to hit the man. He quelled it.

"Yeah? What'd they have to say about us?"

"I ain't even gonna try to explain. But I recorded it on the VCR at home and brought the tape in for you to see." He reached down and pulled an unmarked video cassette from a bag next to his desk. He wheeled the TV/VCR and its stand out of a small closet where they kept everything they didn't have room for. There was a lot of crap in that closet, but it was all important crap. In a matter of only a few seconds, he'd set the VCR to play and inserted the tape. "It's all set to run. Keep your eyes peeled."

Frank watched the screen as the picture slowly glowed into existence. Channel 2 from Atlanta flickered into life. The anchor woman flashed a smile as artificial as the color of her hair and greeted anyone who cared to pay attention. Then she grew somber and stared intently out from the tube. *This just in: A tractor-trailer, reportedly carrying dangerous stolen materials, has jackknifed near the south Georgia town of Collier. It is unknown at this time exactly what materials were being transported, but inside sources have stated that the stolen substances are toxic and potentially deadly. One source in the state capitol told Channel 2 reporters that the truck was actually carrying several vials of plague-viruses taken from the Center for Disease Control here in Atlanta. However, another source in the Governor's office has told Channel 2 that the stolen material is actually plutonium and/or uranium taken from a government storage facility near Birmingham, Alabama. All that is known for certain at this time is that the entire town of Collier and the immediate surrounding areas are officially under quarantine until such time as the federal agencies called in to investigate the theft have finished a thorough examination of both the truck and the cargo carried inside.*

"While we have no official word at this time, sources close to the Governor have also told Channel 2 that the driver of the hijacked tractor-trailer is none other than Amir Hal Densalid, a Palestinian

radical linked to several terrorist attacks in Jerusalem and allegedly one of five men sought in connection to the attempted bombing of Maine's Bangor International Airport last February. Channel 2's own Ben Johnson is en route now to Collier and should be ready to give us an up-to-the-minute report from the site of the accident within the hour.

"The GBI, in cooperation with federal authorities, has issued a quarantine of Collier. No incoming or outgoing traffic is permitted in the area, and all commercial flights moving in the general vicinity of Collier have been rerouted. Hartsfield International Airport spokes-person, Angela Walker assured Channel 2 earlier this morning that the change in scheduled flight paths should cause no major delays.

"On the lighter side of the news, the Braves have done it again, defeating the New York Yankees eleven to three-" The anchor woman's face disappeared in a nimbus of contracting colors as Buck hit the 'off' switch on the remote in his hand.

"Seems we had a toxic spill in the area. One caused by terrorists, no less."

"Looks like these boys thought of everything."

"Yeah. 'Cept where they're gonna put the bodies."

"What do you mean?"

"With what's sitting in the lake and all the precautions they're taking, I don't think they plan on letting us go alive, Frank." Buck lit a cigarette and kicked back in his chair, propping his feet on the desk in front of him. "I figure we're pretty well screwed at this point. Might as well relax for a while. Oh, and make out your will, too."

He wanted to reprimand Buck, but in the end decided against it. He half-suspected the man was right. The future looked bleak.

2

Two hours later, Frank finally managed to get home and take a shower. The heat outside was enough to make him sweaty and rank. He didn't care what the deodorant company claimed; the stuff was good for twelve hours tops in this sort of weather.

When he'd finished with the shower, Frank made himself a lunch of tuna fish sandwiches and sugar-free Jell-O. It wasn't the same as a good meal at the diner, but he supposed he should go light on the sugar intake for a little while. Last night's drop in blood-glucose levels left him a little skittish. Besides, if he didn't eat the tuna, it would go bad. He hated wasting food.

He turned on the television and flicked past a dozen cable channels before deciding to go back to work. The place was always too empty since Kathy took off a year before. He wanted to stay bitter with her for leaving him, but just couldn't do it. These days he was simply depressed about it. Even after all she'd said towards the end, he still loved her. His eyes wandered over to the picture of his ex-wife in her little one-piece suit, standing on the deck of their houseboat and smiling. Her black hair was pulled back and her nose was spattered with freckles. He wanted her here, now, so he could just hold her and lose himself in her presence. Some things aren't meant to be. Kathy was gone and, while the divorce wasn't finalized, her living in California sort of put a damper on their ever getting back together. Hell, even the houseboat was gone now, burned into so much ash and flotsam the night before. All in all, his life was a shambles and only getting worse.

He slipped on his clean pair of uniform pants and a fresh khaki shirt, then added all the necessities. Time to get back to work and check on how the clinic was holding up with all of the newly injured. Just before he left the house, he remembered to take his insulin and a few syringes. Then he added a few glucose tablets to the normal junk in his pockets and moved outside. With the cruiser like as not in the hands of Collier's visitors, he had to take his old Mustang instead. It was stupid of him to leave it behind the night before, but he hadn't really been thinking too clearly. At least he'd have fun driving around today. He hated the cruiser. It made too much noise and handled about as well as a grocery cart from the Piggly Wiggly.

It only took Frank five minutes to reach the Collier Medical Clinic and Emergency Services Building. It took him two

more minutes to find a parking spot. The entire lot around the
clinic was filled to capacity with the ambulances from the night
before. Ambulances, and their occupants. A small army of
paramedics sat in the growing heat of the day, sipping coffee
or, in some cases, catching a few minutes' sleep inside the
backs of the vehicles they'd driven into town. Every last one
of them was sweating through the blood-stained clothes they'd
worn the night before.

Sam Morrisey nodded a greeting as Frank approached.
"Morning, Frank."

"Morning, Sam. How's everyone holding up?"

"Do you want an honest answer?" The exhaustion in Sam's
voice was evident, and emphasized by the heavy bags under his
eyes. Frank nodded and Sam sighed. "We lost seventeen more
last night. Seventeen more." Frank put one hand on the
paramedic's shoulder, feeling the tension in Sam's muscles even
through the scrub shirt and the layer of cellulite beneath it. "Carl
Timbury died on the way back into town." His voice choked on
that last bit and he blinked his eyes angrily as they tried to tear up.

"I'm sorry, Sam. I know you two were close."

"Close, hell. He was my best friend, Frank. Me and him
grew up right next door to each other. I did my best, but he
just wouldn't respond, not even to the defibrillator."

Frank squeezed affectionately on Sam's shoulder, word-
lessly expressing his own feelings of loss. But there was no
time for pleasantries. "Is you dad in there?"

"Yeah. He might be trying to sleep. Hell, Frank. Him and
Doc Johnson are the only two people in town qualified to handle
some of the cases in there. Ain't neither of 'em had any rest
since the whole mess started."

"I'll give him a few hours. You get a chance, let your dad
know I'll be back to speak with him around two-thirty."

"That I will. Frank?"

"Yeah, Sam?"

"What's going on here? Who are those people in the black
suits?"

Sam wanted answers, and much as he wished he could give them, Frank was at a loss to help. "Look at the lake and ask that again, Sam. Whatever crashed here last night is the reason those bastards have locked up the town."

Frank moved back to his car. He waited a moment after climbing in, his keys just an inch from the ignition. He could think of nothing to do, save wait for the commander of the men in black to arrive. After lighting another cigarette, he turned the Mustang around and aimed himself back in the direction of Oldman's Lake. The commander would land there, and they would have words, whether the man wanted to speak with him or not.

3

Frank stopped his car just outside of an area the soldiers had cordoned off. The entire parking lot for the lake was separated from everything else by a long line of sawhorses, complete with yellow flashing hazard lights. He was partially amazed by the speed with which the black-clad figures worked and partially amused by the CAUTION: BIOHAZARD banners running just above the tops of the wooden barriers. *Biohazard my ass. The only biohazard around here is them.* But he thought of the intense heat just before the thing crashed the night before, the scorch patterns in the park that looked too much like footage he'd seen of Hiroshima after it was nuked, and shivered a little. The mass of wrecked cars was gone, vanished as if they had never been there. They'd even swept up the broken glass and other debris.

He looked away, his eyes drawn back to the lake and the massive vessel gleaming dully in the sunlight and mostly surrounded by a thick cloud of rising steam. Over a dozen hours later, the damned thing was still boiling the water.

It simply should not be there. He'd spent most of his life in Collier, and a portion of that time was wasted hanging around the lake or cruising on the sailboat. The monolithic metallic object looked like a tombstone half-submerged in the waters of the lake, and looking at it made him feel dirtied somehow. Like he'd stepped in dog shit.

Looking around some more, he located the ruin of his boat about fifty feet out in the waters. She'd caught fire when the thing crashed. He knew she was beyond repair; she was half sunk already, and probably going lower even as he watched. Even from this distance he could see the scorch marks and peeling paint on what had been his pride and joy. Finally, he forced himself to look at the stretch of lawn leading to the beach. Despite his fears, there were no bodies there anymore. Apparently the soldiers wanted everything just so for when their commander showed himself. *Can't have any corpses littering the yard,* he thought. *That just wouldn't be proper. What the hell is next, they want the band to get out their spare uniforms and play Hail to the Chief?*

Disgusted with the situation, and with his inability to make anything better, Frank leaned against his Mustang's hood and lit himself another cigarette. He'd just exhaled the first cloud of smoke when he heard the sound of Dewett Hammil screaming up a blue streak somewhere behind him.

Frank turned to his left until he was facing in the opposite direction of a moment before. When he stopped turning, his eyes focused on Dewett pointing a massive finger at one of the soldiers. Hammil was on the wrong side of the barrier, standing next to the door of his bakery. Just like that, Frank had his headache back again.

Dewett was a very large man, downright intimidating in his way. His skin was as dark as a well-polished piece of ebony, and he stood an easy six feet, eight inches tall. That was with his shoulders slumped and his head lowered. In his prime, Dewett had earned the respect of damn near every white man in the entire town. Not a one of them could take him in a fair fight, and his marksmanship had prevented too many from thinking about bothering him in groups. The one time a group of the local farmers in white sheets and hoods decided to "drive the nigger back to Africa where he belongs," Dewett left two of them dead and three more badly wounded. That had been in the Forties, when he'd come back from the Second World War and decided to settle himself in Collier. He might have gotten himself lynched after that, but Lucas Brightman, the man who ran the textile mill in Collier, had decided he liked Dewett's feistiness almost as much as his bread. There was no proof that Brightman had been the one to decide what happened to the baker, but Frank would have put money on that being the deciding factor. Brightman owned most of Collier, and that meant people listened when he talked.

Fifty years had taken their toll on old Dewett. What was left of his hair was white, and he was forced to wear thick glasses over his eyes in order to see anything at all beyond about ten feet. These days, Dewett was a far milder man most of the time. But he was still big enough to scare anyone who didn't know him.

Right then, the soldier was looking through his bug-faced mask and doing his damnedest to look like he was in control of the situation. The way he had to crane his helmeted head back to look at the baker and the death grip he had on his weapon took away from the image he wanted to portray. Frank gave the man marks for bravery just the same; he'd seen plenty of folks run from Dewett when he was in a tirade.

Frank moved as fast as he could, hoping to avoid a confrontation that would leave someone dead or injured. Dewett was already building a full head of steam, and even from a dozen yards away Frank could hear the man's deep voice roaring. "I don't take well to bein' told I can't go into my own shop, sonny-boy! I don't take well to that at all! That's my property, and I intend to keep it!" Dewett's heavy brows had joined above his wide nose, and his lower lip was thrust out in defiance. His arms and neck were corded, and every loaf of bread the man had ever kneaded with his bare hands showed clearly in his muscular frame.

Frank opened his mouth, prepared to interrupt, but stopped when Dewett looked his way, jabbing a finger the size of a Kielbasa in his direction. "You keep out of this, Frank. Me and your daddy went back a long ways, and I know that you want to do what's best. But I pay my taxes and I know what my rights are. This young fool can't keep me from what's mine!"

"Don't be stupid, Dewett. The man's got a gun and he's just following orders."

"Don't you sass me, Franklin Alexander Osborn. I ain't lived to be seventy-five to have a guppy like you come around and sass me."

"Yessir. But—"

"Ain't no buts to it. You tell this young man to leave me be, or I'm gonna get my own rifle and show him two can play that game."

Frank walked over to the soldier, moving easily and speaking in a soothing voice. "Just relax, mister. Dewett's a big man, but his bark is worse than his bite."

The unnatural voice coming from behind the mask still sounded like a swarm of bees trying to mimic human speech, but there was a definite note of panic mixed in with the anger Frank heard. "My job is to secure this area. I will shoot this man if I have to."

"There's no need for guns." Frank turned to Dewett and tried his best to look official. The task was made harder by the fact that Dewett's wife had to change his diapers when he was a baby. "Dewett here's gonna leave peacefully. Aren't you, Dewett?"

The old giant crossed his arms and shook his head, obstinate to a fault. "I ain't going anywhere until I check on my store. I got money in there, and I don't aim to leave it sitting where any of these damn fools can take it!"

Frank looked long and hard into the old man's eyes. Finally he turned away, imploring the soldier with his facial expression. "Can't you just let him check out his store? The bakery's all he has, and I can promise you there's nothing in there he could use as a weapon."

The soldier looked from Frank to Dewett, turning his whole head several times as he moved from one face to the other. After a few moments of continuing this exercise, he finally sighed deep in his chest. "All right. But make it damned quick, old man. I don't like the idea of getting my ass in a sling so you can count your money."

Just like that, the fearsome expression faded from Dewett's face and was replaced by a friendly grin. Dewett had a smile that could light up half a city block, and even his eyes seemed suddenly warmer. "Thank you, sir. I won't be but a minute." The baker turned and stepped through the remainder of his glass door, careful not to cut himself on the jagged teeth stuck in the frame as he entered.

The soldier spoke again. "Jesus Christ. That is a big man."

"That he is." Frank smiled tightly, his eyes still looking at Dewett with affection. "Old Dewett's about as big as any man I've ever seen. He's also one of gentlest souls you'll ever meet. He's just a mite dangerous when you get him riled."

"Thank you for your help, officer. I didn't want to hurt him."

Frank looked at the glass orbs of the man's mask. "You would have, wouldn't you?"

"I have to follow orders, officer. It's my duty."

"You'd have shot an old man? Just to stop him from crossing into his own property?"

"Like I said. I have my orders. If you hadn't shown up, I'd have done my best to stop him by any means available. Even if I had to shoot him."

They stood in silence for a while, neither of them willing to initiate another conversation. Not but a minute later, Dewett came out of the store with a zipper bag from the local bank held in one hand. He seemed smaller than before, but much happier. He nodded and then waved a silent thanks. Seeing the old man happy made that nasty headache fade down to a mild roar.

After Dewett had gone on his way, Frank lit another cigarette and leaned against the sawhorse. After a second he realized he was still on the wrong side of the barrier and stepped
back. The soldier nodded his thanks.

"What's with the get-ups?" Frank asked when the silence
stretched too long.

"What's that?"

"The mask and the hose where your mouth should be.
What's up with them?"

"Oh. Safety precaution. We don't know where that thing
has been." The man pointed to the steaming mass buried in
the lake. "It might have bacteria unknown to human life. For
all we know the thing's carrying a plague that could kill us all."
The man's voice suddenly stopped. He had apparently said
more than he was supposed to say.

Frank nodded, looking at the craft. "Figured it was something like that. You protected from any radiation too?"

"Uh. Yeah. We are."

"That the reason for the quarantine? To make sure we don't
contaminate everything else?"

"Pretty much." Frank could tell the man wanted to say
more, but he didn't push the subject.

"Frank Osborn. I'm the police chief around here."

"I—I'm not allowed to volunteer my name, Captain Osborn."

"That's okay. I kinda figured it was something like that."
After the silence stretched for a few more minutes, Frank
looked at his watch. Ten after twelve. "You have any idea
when your commander is supposed to be here?"

"Yessir. He's expected in any time now."

As if on cue, the sound of helicopters became audible.
Frank looked over the lake, where the sound was coming from.
Twenty-five small specks on the horizon began to grow larger,
even as the sound increased. He counted again to make sure
he wasn't seeing things. He wasn't. To add to his fun, it looked
like another squadron was coming in behind the first.

"Soldier?"

"Yes?"

"Just how many people is you commander bringing with him?"

"I'm not at liberty to say, sir."

"Uh huh. That sounds about right."

Frank watched on as the copters came closer and grew louder still. Looking at the numbers of ships in the sky, he wondered is the parking lot would be enough.

It wasn't.

Not by a long shot.

4

Frank was very impressed by the sheer number of helicopters in the air. He was almost speechless when he realized how little noise they made. Dozens of aircraft hovered over the area, low enough that they were barely noticeable above the trees, but their collective sound was only a little louder than an idling motorcycle. Far more ominous than their lack of noise, however, was the array of attachments he saw on the wings of each and every one of them. He was hardly an expert, but he was also willing to bet most of them held missiles or heavy caliber firepower. He saw the racks for the artillery, loaded with long, bullet-shaped missiles, under at least two of the damned things. Frank had no doubts that they were meant for more than merely transportation.

He watched as several of the craft came down, immediately disgorging more armored men. It took a minute for him to realize what worried him the most about the helicopters, more even than their silence or the blatantly obvious artillery each carried: they had no serial numbers. No identifying marks of any kind. They were anonymous.

He was hardly the only person in Collier to notice the helicopters. Even as he watched the sleek black craft descending, a good number of Collier's citizens and a sizable group of the unexpected visitors stuck in the town came forward in their cars or on foot. They gathered around the area to watch as the hovering craft landed briefly, disgorged a number of people and then lifted into the air again.

Frank tried to count the number of tourists stuck for the duration of what was now the government's show, and couldn't keep up with the numbers. Somewhere along the way he'd forgotten all about the people who'd just shown up for the fireworks and wound up trapped in the town. Where they would stay and how they would be taken care of was a new concern. Most of them came forward with locals, and he even recognized a large percentage of them, but only now was he realizing just how many *guests* were imprisoned along with everyone else.

"Damn. I don't need this shit."

A voice came from his right, in response to his comment. He hadn't even realized he was speaking aloud. "Yeah. I know what you mean, Frank. I don't think any of us need this nonsense." The twangy voice of Lucas Brightman was recognizable immediately. Lucas was as much a foundation in Collier as Lake Oldman. He'd been on the town council for as long as Frank could remember, and he was almost always on the side that cried out against anything resembling growth in the area.

Frank looked at the lean, angular man standing beside him and forced a smile. It wasn't easy. Hatred was just barely too strong a word for how Frank felt about the old bastard. Lucas was an oily old dog, and that was being kind. In addition to owning the textile mill at the edge of town, Brightman also owned half of the buildings rented out to the stores in Collier. That wasn't what made Frank antsy around the man. Oh, no. What made the captain of the Collier City Police want to reach out and strike the man down was his constant need to find a scapegoat for all of the ills inflicted upon mankind. The number one target of his accusations was normally anyone whose skin wasn't quite white enough. When failing to find a racial target for his animosities, Luke often chose anyone from another country as a good mark. While he had no proof, Frank figured Lucas was the main source of racial tensions in town. Brightman would never speak directly against anyone, but his cronies always seemed ready to do the speaking for him.

That wasn't to say that Brightman was all bad, by any stretch of the imagination. Lucas Brightman was not only the wealthiest man in town, he was also one of the most generous with his time and his money. The library near the town hall was one of his donations, and the medical center had been bought and paid for by the man. Hell, when he wasn't being a sly old weasel, Brightman was generous almost to a fault. He was the first to offer financial aid when it was needed by the town or by a person—and oddly enough, that included those who weren't the right color to satisfy his own personal preferences—and he normally either waived the loss of money completely or merely asked that the person he was giving the loan to pay it back in a fair amount of time. He didn't loan money to people who wanted to buy houses or new cars. The bank took care of that sort of thing and, as a major investor in the bank, Brightman didn't want to cause himself damage. He loaned the money to people who actually needed it to survive. Frank just didn't trust that there wasn't an ulterior motive to any good the man did.

Frank thought the man was trouble, pure and simple. "How are you, Lucas?" The smile and handshake he offered were strained, but the best he could manage under the current conditions.

Brightman shook his hand in return, surprising Frank with how warm his flesh felt. Considering the pale color of the man's face and the dry, flaking skin on his old hands, Frank always expected the man's touch to be as cold as a snake's hide. "Why, I'm just fine, Frank. Mighty interested to see where all of this will go." He nodded his head towards the landing pads marked on the parking lot near the lake. Another 'copter lifted from the ground even as a dozen men in black clothes and gear ducked away from the whirling blades. Like the people already holding the town at bay, they wore goggles and respirators under their helmets. None of them bore any marks to indicate their rank or names.

"Just do me a favor, okay, Luke?"

"You name the one you want and you can call it a done deal, Frank."

"Just leave the talking to me and to Milo. I don't think this is gonna be an easy situation. I think it might just get messy, if you know what I mean. I think it's best if they think the two of us are the only real officials around here."

Lucas Brightman considered him with eyes that glittered in the sunlight. His mouth worked silently for a few seconds, and Frank could tell he wanted to say something nasty. But Lucas never said anything foul in public, only when he and his cronies were able to take control without fear of reprisal. "That I will, Captain. But I expect to be kept informed of what occurs here."

"You and everyone else." Frank watched as the old man moved away. The expensive suit covering Brightman's body did not hide the anger in his stride. It did nothing to lessen the stoop in his shoulders, either. Frank always thought of vultures when he saw the richest man in Collier walking away: the man's posture and his long, dour face made the image of a carrion eater seem frightfully appropriate.

He turned back to watch as one of the armored figures walked over to speak with the soldier Dewett had almost turned into a corpse. By the stiffening of the guard's posture, he suspected he might have found his man. Without waiting to see if the guard would point to him, he walked straight towards the two men.

As he approached, Dewett's little friend did exactly what he'd been expecting and pointed in his direction. He decided the time was right for taking the initiative. Looking at the newcomer, he nodded briefly and spoke. "You the commander of this operation?"

The figure regarded him silently for a moment. Frank knew his measure was being taken, and regretted that he could not stare the man in the eye and do the same in return. "Yes, Captain Osborn, I am."

"That's sort of what I figured." He gestured once with his right hand, sweeping the entire area. "This here's my town. I understand that you're only following your orders, mister. But I expect you to come to me as soon as you can. We need to talk about what your plans are for Collier." He hoped that sounded professional enough.

The bug-eyes of the man's mask moved slightly, following Frank's hand and then going back to a silent study of his face. Finally, the static-hiss of the man's voice started up again. "I'll be with you in about fifteen minutes, Captain. In the meantime, please keep your people away from the barrier. Trespassers will be shot."

Frank nodded, pulling his cigarettes from his breast pocket as he moved to park his butt against the Mustang. Despite the occasions when he'd spoken to others of the armored men, this one's voice seemed worse. It went beyond the buzzing of insects; it was cold and alien. He was afraid to consider what might actually be inside the special equipment.

He watched as another of the men came forward. This one was armed with a clipboard and a ramrod-stiff back. Frank knew right away it was the asshole from the night before and from that morning as well. Watching how quickly the two soldiers responded to the newcomer, he was once again struck by the fact that none of them wore any identification. Only the single man with his pen and paper stood out from the others. Frank couldn't for the life of him figure how they recognized each other.

A few seconds later, a very tired looking Milo Fitzwater, along with his secretary, Arnetta Wilcox, marched up to confront the trio of armed men. His conversation lasted about twice as long as Frank's little chat. During their very short conversation, Milo's face grew redder and redder. Then the leader of the dark men gestured for Frank to come join them.

Frank sighed, moved away from his car and back over to the small gathering. Out of the corner of his eye, he saw Lucas Brightman wearing a satisfied grin two sizes too big for his face. He resisted the urge to give the old buzzard a one-finger salute.

Milo was standing in a combat-ready stance. His pudgy hands were pressed into his fat hips, and the color of his ears was almost as red as the minor burns on his cheek and neck. Frank hadn't noticed before, but Milo had a few injuries of his own to contend with.

"Howdy. What's up?"

The commander spoke again, and Frank's skin tried to crawl. "Captain Osborn, would you be kind enough to escort Mayor Fitzwater over to your vehicle, and would you also explain that I will answer his questions in a few minutes?"

"Sure thing." Frank nodded to the man and then grabbed hold of Milo's bicep. "Come on, Milo. Let's get over to my car while these nice men with the big guns and heavy artillery discuss their business."

Milo turned even redder, but did not struggle until they'd reached the Mustang. "What the hell's gotten into you, Frank?" The mayor's face was sweaty, and the dark circles under his eyes seemed even more pronounced than they had that morning. "When, exactly, did you lose your mind?"

"Funny, Milo. I was just about to ask you the very same thing."

"What are you talking about?"

"I'm talking about not pissing off the bad men in black," he hissed as he grabbed both of Milo's arms and spun him around. Behind the mayor, Arnetta gasped and then sucked in a huge lungful of air. "I'm not sure if you've really noticed, Milo, but these boys are holding all the cards."

"I will not stand idly by and let these people run over the citizens of this town!" Despite the almost whispered quality of Milo's response, Frank could tell the man was close to blowing his top. "I'll be damned before I'll let these bastards take control around here. That's not the way the United States of America is supposed to be run."

"Milo. Who the hell said anything about them being with the US?"

Milo's face lost all of its color, and he turned his head slowly, looking back at the group with a sudden, dawning comprehension. "Do you mean they might be with someone else?"

"That's exactly what I mean. I suspect they *are* with the US, but I don't really feel up to pushing the issue just yet." He pointed to the thing boiling away their lake and then pointed back to the armored figures in the distance. "All I know for certain is that they ain't here 'cause of you and me. They're here because of that thing. If that thing's important enough that they got here so quickly, I'm betting they think it's a helluva lot more important than whether or not you and me are breathing by this time tomorrow. Do you get my picture?"

Arnetta made a few wheezing sounds behind Milo, and Frank turned to face her. "Arnetta? Why don't you go get some rest? You look a mite tuckered out."

"I'm just fine here, thank you, Captain Osborn." The stuffy old bat sniffed disdainfully as she glared in his direction.

Milo looked at Frank for a second and then looked at his secretary. "Arnetta? Go home. That's an order. You take the rest of the day off and you come in bright and early tomorrow."

She nodded, her already thin lips fading into an angry white line.

"Arnetta?" Milo's voice sounded almost too sweet.

"Yes, Milo?"

"If you say a word to anyone at all, darlin', I'm gonna fire you. Go straight home and keep your mouth to yourself." Arnetta stormed away, never looking back at either of them.

"You figure that's gonna do any good?"

"What? Threatening her?" Frank nodded. Milo shrugged. "Not likely. But at least it'll make her think about what she wants to say for a while before she actually starts flappin' her gums."

The two of them leaned against the Mustang, staring out over the lake and watching as the helicopters came and went. Most of the machines seemed to settle down in other parts of town, but a few actually lifted away into the air and vanished in the distance instead of dropping from sight.

"Be straight with me, Frank?"

"Sure."

"You think these here soldiers are gonna let us go?"

Frank nodded to where another helicopter was being un-loaded. All of the packages bore the symbol of the Red Cross. "I have my hopes, Milo. I figure if they just wanted us dead, they wouldn't be wasting their time with medical supplies."

"They might."

"How you figure?"

"They might be expecting us to fight back before we all go down."

He had no answer for that one. Instead, he shrugged his shoulders and went back to staring at the curved edge of the thing in the lake. Looking at it for too long was something of a task. The steam kept getting in the way. Also, it hurt his eyes for no reason he could easily discern.

It wasn't long before Frank had to handle the head goon's requests. Frank had to stop seven different people from break-ing through the flimsy barrier to either speak with one of the soldiers or try to find out what was going on by just standing close enough to hear everything. A couple of them were just kids, and they listened well enough. But the adults seemed intent on getting closer, and damn the consequences.

Frank had no real difficulties explaining why bothering the soldiers would be bad, until he encountered Alan Stoner. Stoner was not one of the locals. He was a trucker who'd stopped for the Fourth of July festivities and wound up as stuck as everyone else. Frank had met the beefy man once earlier, and had arrested him for drunken and disorderly. Back then he'd just been a patrolman. The man was older, but looked even sleazier than he had ten years ago, when he'd cracked two of Frank's ribs before Frank and another man had taken him down. One look at Stoner and Frank knew he'd be trouble. Stoner looked like the sort of man who kicked puppies for fun. He had a wide, crooked face with narrow piggish eyes set too close together. His mouth looked slightly sunken in from a lack of teeth, but Frank knew full well the age added to his face by the effect was a visual lie. He'd looked just as toothless ten years ago. He was also built like a gorilla. He wasn't all muscle, but there was enough there to make sure he could carry out any threats he felt like offering. From the heavy hiking boots on his feet to the *Jack Daniel's* baseball cap set on top of his graying hair, he was a wide load of trouble.

Stoner took one look at the badge on Frank's uniform and immediately spat a wad of tobacco juice across the sidewalk. This, while he had one leg and half of his belly hoisted over the sawhorse barrier. Frank had no doubt the man would have merely shoved one of the wooden barriers aside, if not for the length of chain marrying one to the next.

"Y'all want to step aside, Mister Stoner. The government boys don't want anyone in their territory." Frank did his best to sound stern and friendly at the same time.

He shouldn't have bothered. As soon as he opened his mouth, Stoner was back over the barrier and hauling his pants back into their proper place, just beneath his beer gut. Stoner opened a mouth with less than half the normal number of teeth and made a face. Frank couldn't tell if he was wincing, smiling or preparing to burp. Any which way, it was an unpleasant sight. "I remember you. Are you the sheriff these days?" The man's sounded like an old steam engine just starting to get up to pace. His words grumbled from deep inside of his gut and whistled past his remaining teeth. The thick stubble on his jaw glistened in the sunlight. Even from a distance, Frank could smell the stench of beer on the man's breath and in the sweat coming from his pores.

"I'm the chief of police. Frank Osborn."

"Can you tell me when I can take my truck and get the hell out of this shithole?"

"No sir, I can't. That'd be up to those fellas over there."

Stoner nodded his head once, and his brows pulled closer together. "Then I don't want or need to talk to you. I need to talk to them." Without another word, the man started back over the sawhorses.

"Get your flabby ass over here, mister! Now!" Frank's voice fairly boomed across the distance between them, and Stoner hesitated. All around them the people who'd been looking at the men in black turned to the noise and focussed their attention on Frank and his new dance partner. Frank sighed mentally. This wasn't what he wanted. This was more like what Stoner probably thought of as a good thing. His sort always worked best with an audience. It gave them an extra dose of courage for those rough times, like when somebody dared defy them. Times like this very moment.

After a few seconds, Stoner came back over. He did not looked cowed by Frank's Tough Cop voice. He looked amused. "What can I do for you, officer?"

"I just told you, you aren't allowed over that barrier. If you try it again, I'm gonna have to place you under arrest."

"That so? Under what charges?" The man crossed his beefy arms over his chest, putting an incredible strain on the faded, blue cotton of his shirt. He pursed his lips and lowered his head. Frank didn't know if he wanted an answer or a kiss. There was only one of the two the man would get willingly.

"I'll think of something. Hell, I could always bust you for indecent behavior if not for anything more serious. Fact of the matter is, you're making my life harder. That's all I need."

"I ain't even *begun* makin' your life hard, Sheriff. But I will if you don't get out of my face." The trucker moved closer, actually pushing Frank back with his gut, as if they were engaged in a belly-bucking contest. Every third brewery-breathed syllable was another reason for the man to push against Frank, knocking him a little farther back. "I ain't broken any laws, I just want to get on with my load. That there's a refrigerated trailer I'm pulling, and I don't want my stock going sour."

Frank stepped forward slightly, using his knee to shove Stoner's own knee out of the way. When the trucker lost his balance, Frank gave a light shove and sent the man down to the ground in a blubbery avalanche. Stoner hit the asphalt with a squeal of surprise. The look on his face said he wasn't used to being defied. Frank knew just how he felt. He placed one hand on the holster for his .38, looking at the man with through a red haze. "You don't ever want to push me again, Stoner. If you do, I'll bust your ass from here to Alabama."

Despite his ponderous size, the trucker came back up in a blur, one hand already swinging in a wild arc. Frank ducked under the flabby swipe, and realized too late that he'd been set up. Stoner's knee slammed into his groin with enough force to take all of the air out of his lungs. Frank knew, just knew, dammit, that he was going to feel that a second later, and he was right. For a few seconds he forgot what he was doing, and to whom he was speaking. The world blurred into a distant memory, replaced by the burning ache where his privates used to be. It took an effort to focus his eyes, to breathe and to think. He was vaguely aware that he'd fallen to the ground, but beyond that he really couldn't have cared much about anything.

Many people speak of a time when it was considered improper to hit a man when he was already down. Many people talk of chivalry and how the world used to be. Fair to say that Alan Stoner was not fond of the old ways. He did his best to smash Frank's head into jelly under his shitkicker boot heels. Frank was down, but he was not out. He managed to roll away from the point of impact. Doing so hurt more than he'd have ever thought possible.

Frank pistoned his left heel into the trucker's knee, provoking a loud yell in return. Stoner wobbled for a moment then shifted his weight to his other leg. While he was making himself more comfortable, Frank rose back to his feet.

Adrenaline and anger were working wonders numbing the pain in his groin, but he didn't trust them to keep him mobile. Frank reached for the gun in his holster again, ready to shoot the man if necessary.

Stoner reached into the back pocket of his pants and, even as Frank was pulling his revolver, drew a long-bladed hunting knife.

"Put the knife down, you idiot." Frank's thumb depressed the safety on his pistol, as he spoke.

"Fuck you."

"I'm only gonna warn you once, mister. Put the knife down or I'll shoot."

"I got a bunch a witnesses here, Sheriff. I don't think the law would go easy on you. All's I got is a knife." Frank was used to a certain level of difficulty when confronting some of the bullyboys in Collier, but Stoner was going far beyond the level of trouble he normally ran across.

Frank cranked back the hammer on his pistol, leveling the barrel at a spot between the fat trucker's eyes. "Put. The. Knife. Down. Or. I. Will. Kill. You."

For the first time, Alan Stoner looked nervous. "You wouldn't dare."

"Man kicks me in the nuts, he don't exactly get on my good side. Put it down."

Stoner looked into the police chief's eyes and Frank could tell he was gauging his chances of making a lunge to him before he could react. Finally, the man lowered his blade, slowly starting to squat. Then Alan Stoner flexed his legs, and lifted forward and off the ground.

Frank shifted his target and squeezed the trigger. The gun kicked in his hands, but his bullet hit its mark, opening a wet red wound in the trucker's right bicep. Frank could actually see the stream of meat and blood that exploded outward behind the man's arm. Stoner's right hand jerked spasmodically, dropping the blade even as the force of bullet's impact spun the man to the right. Frank was dimly aware of Stoner screaming, but the sound was secondary to the echoing report of the revolver going off in his grip. In all his years in law enforcement, he'd never once had to fire on anyone.

He leveled the pistol at Alan Stoner again, not allowing himself to think about what he'd just done. A voice in the back of his head reminded him that Cambodia had been far worse. He'd killed people over there. Here he'd only wounded a drunken asshole. Working on automatic, he raised his arms until the pistol aimed only at the sky above.

Stoner turned to look at him, his left hand clamped over the hole bored through his right arm. Red trickles were already moving through his clenched fingers, running across his hairy hand. The trucker's heavily jowled face was set in an expression of sheer surprise.

"You sumbitch," the man said in a voice an octave higher than was normal. "You shot me!"

"Just like I said I would. You should have listened."

"You shot me!"

Frank looked at the rising color in the man's face and was grateful he'd kept the pistol drawn. He'd seen enough drunks in his life to know that Stoner was about to do something stupid.

Frank Osborn managed to keep his voice level and authoritative, but it wasn't easy. Right then he wanted little more than to be sick on the ground. It had been a long, long time since he'd been forced to fire on anyone. "Don't move, Stoner. Don't give me a reason."

Alan Stoner let out an incoherent scream, and charged like a bull. His face was dark red, and his nostrils flared out over his remaining bared teeth.

Stoner made one step, then another as Frank moved his weapon towards him. Then the trucker did a funky jittering dance as the sound of a dozen firecrackers exploded behind him. Bright red fans of blood erupted from his torso and legs. The lower left side of his face disappeared in a crimson haze and something wet slapped against Frank's shoulder. Stoner took two more steps and then fell to the ground, a bloody red sack of meat.

Frank stared down at his fallen enemy, stunned for a moment. He looked at his pistol. It had not moved from its upward position. *What in the name of God?*

His eyes slowly moved away from his hands and back to the body twitching on the ground. After a brief pause, they traveled farther, looking beyond where Stoner stood only a few seconds before. One of the armored men stood in a combat-ready stance, a few feet away and to the right of where Stoner's corpse lay, his snub-nosed machine-gun still smoking in his hands. The blank glass eyes seemed to look into Frank's soul, mocking him. The thought that the man's bullets could have killed him was heavy in Frank's mind. *A few feet to the right and I'd be just as dead as Stoner.*

He lowered his pistol, taking careful aim at those insectoid lens pieces. God, how he wanted to pull the trigger. For several seconds—during which time the people in the area let out several belated screams and Milo Fitzwater called his name repeatedly—he aimed at that alien face. Finally, he lowered the pistol and slipped it back into its holster as he thumbed the safety back on.

The buzzing voice of the soldier called out. "I thought you might need some help, Captain Osborn."

Frank made no reply. He merely moved over to the trucker's body and checked for a pulse. There was none to be found, and even the wounds entering into the man's lungs and heart offered blood. A large crimson stain was growing under Stoner's body.

Frank closed the man's eyes, and moved to his car to get a blanket. His steps were jerky, and he had trouble maintaining a straight course. The adrenaline in his body made him feel like he'd slurped down about five too many pots of coffee. Milo helped him cover the body.

Frank sat against the car and waited for the commander of the armed men to come to him. He tried to call into the office, but received only static in response. He looked back at the soldier, who had once again resumed a position near the barrier. Damn, but shooting the bastard would have been a lot of fun. Dying for his efforts, however, would not.

Milo spoke next to him. "Damn, Frank. They just did us in."

It took him a moment to realize the mayor was talking to him. "What do you mean, Milo?"

Milo wiped his brow with a yellowing handkerchief. "I mean they just took a volatile situation and turned the thing over. They came out of this looking cool and collected, you came out looking like you couldn't handle that man on your own."

It took all of half a second for Frank to realize Milo was right. "Shit. There goes any chance of maintaining authority. God *damn* it!" He looked at Stoner's body, then looked at the eyes of the people in the crowd. Faces he'd known all his life were suddenly looking less familiar. The expressions on many people's faces seemed colder. "One damn minute, and they screwed us up, right and proper."

"I don't like this one little bit, Frank. Not one little bit."

Frank looked at his own hands, which were still doing the adrenaline tango, and thought about what was going on around him. "Milo?"

"Yeah, Frank?"

"I think maybe things are gonna get a lot worse around here, unless we can sweet-talk the leader of this group."

"You want to 'sweet talk' that bastard?" Milo's ire was up, and despite what the man might think normally, he was sorely pissed at the present.

"No, Milo. I most definitely do not. But I think we're gonna have to, just the same."

"They just killed a man, Frank."

"That's just my point, Milo. They killed him and never even flinched. I don't think they were so much worried about taking authority from us as they were about making a point. They'll kill anyone who disobeys their orders."

"Damn, Frank. I wish you'd let me have my delusions." Milo's voice was testy and a little shaky.

"What do you mean?"

"I mean that, until a second ago, I had a hope that we could all live through this."

Frank was about to reply when he saw the leader of the armored men walking in their direction, with Clipboard in tow. He guessed any more comments would have to wait. The meeting he'd requested was about to begin.

5

The armored men stared at them through their dark lenses, waiting patiently for Frank or Milo to speak. Frank spoke first. "Do you have a name? Or am I just supposed to call out and wave at every space suit I see until I get the right one?"

The sound that escaped the man's helmet sounded like a laugh mixed with a swarm of angry bees. He reached out one gauntleted hand and waited patiently until Frank reached out to shake it. "You can call me by my name. I'm Colonel Mark Anderson." The man had a grip like steel, and Frank almost wished he'd avoided the contact. The firm handshake was too alien for him. Everything from Anderson's voice to his grip seemed wrong when studied through the environmental gear.

Milo shoved his own hand forward, not to shake, but to point a pudgy finger at the man's armored torso. "Colonel Anderson. I'd like to ask you a few questions about what's going on here. There are injured people in this town, and they need medical help. Not tomorrow, not the day after and not in a couple of hours. They need it now."

"I'm well aware of the situation, Mayor Fitzwater. As you may have noticed, we had a rather large medical shipment brought in with us. Two of those 'copters were loaded down with doctors as well. Your people will be taken care of."

Frank took that moment to interrupt, before Milo could come up with a counter-argument. "Colonel? I need to know what's going on here. What is that thing?" he asked, pointing to the monolith still bathed in steam. He didn't look at it. He didn't want to; it hurt him to look at the damned thing, but he knew just where to point. "Who are you people, and what are you people doing here?"

"Captain Osborn, I'm afraid we don't quite know what that thing is. That's what we're here to find out. As to who we are, we're a part of the United States Government. This area has been sealed off, because that vessel over there presents a potential threat to national security. We cannot let anyone know what is here and, unfortunately, that means we can't let anyone in Collier leave at the present time."

Damn, but didn't that sound well rehearsed. Frank squinted around the area, looking at the number of black-clad soldiers moving around and carrying any number of items, some familiar and some as alien as the saucer cooking away the rest of Oldman's Lake.

Frank nodded. "Okay, I can accept that as a starter. What's with the costumes?"

"The environmental suits are for our protection and for yours. The suits provide us with armor and with protection from possible radiation."

"Radiation?" Milo's voice was little more than a squeak.

"Yes sir. That craft landed several hours ago, but your lake is still heated to beyond the boiling point. That tells us that something's going on out there, but we don't know if that something is just heat or if there's a possibility of hard radiation mixed in just for fun."

"I don't suppose you brought extras?" Frank looked at the craft with a slightly higher level of apprehension than he had before. He looked away again quickly, not wanting to let himself focus on it. For now he could almost make himself believe it wasn't real and he rather liked that little escape.

"No, captain, I'm afraid not."

"Somehow, I didn't think you had."

"For what it's worth, we haven't seen any signs of dangerous radiation leakage so far."

"So why are you still wearing the costumes?"

"Because there are other concerns as well." The colonel's voice grew slightly deeper from behind his mask. "There's always the possibility of a firefight breaking out between us and the people of your fine town."

"Yeah? What makes you think the people of my 'fine town' would shoot at you?"

"Nobody likes being a prisoner, Captain Osborn. Frankly, that's what the citizens of Collier are at present. There is no escape from here at the moment. Every possible access point to and from Collier is blocked off, and that's going to make the civilians in this area antsy."

"Maybe you should have a meeting and let people know what's going on from your side. Might be just the thing needed to calm down the situation.

"Actually, I was going to ask you gentlemen if you could assist me in arranging something along those lines."

Milo snorted loudly, shaking his head. "Well, we can't exactly call 'em all on the phone, now can we?"

"No, but it might be easier all the way around if you could arrange a time and a place for the meeting."

Frank shrugged. "How's eight o'clock at the high school sound to you?"

"That sounds just fine, but make it the elementary school instead, okay?" The Colonel's patronizing tones were starting to grate the nerves in Frank's body, but better to agree with the man than to have him starting off with a bad attitude in town.

"What's wrong with the high school?"

"We've already commandeered the high school."

"What the hell for?" Milo's temper did a fine job of starting up, and Frank wanted to clamp a hand over the man's mouth.

Anderson turned and looked directly at the mayor's angry face. "To better facilitate the recovery of your injured. The clinic is never going to hold them all. We need a place with enough space to allow for surgery if necessary, and with enough additional rooms to hold all of the supplies we brought with us." The man's voice lost all semblance of a friendly tone. "I trust that is sufficient, Mayor Fitzwater. Now if you'll excuse me, I have business to attend to."

"What about using the hotels? We got the Dew Drop Inn and the Collier House. Both of 'em have rooms aplenty. It's gotta be better'n having them folks in classrooms." Milo was trying to keep his calm, but he was having to work at it. Frank could see the veins in the mayor's temples pounding.

"No can do, Mayor Fitzwater. Those buildings have been commandeered for use in holding my men. With everything else we had to carry, we haven't gotten around to sorting through tents and, frankly, there isn't enough room in this town to accommodate the number of tents we'd need."

Milo sputtered again and then turned away, mumbling under his breath.

"One more thing, Colonel?"

"Yes, Captain Osborn?"

Frank pointed to the body of Alan Stoner. "You think you could get a few of your boys to move him out of the street and into a private place? You won't win any popularity contests leaving corpses wherever you go."

The man stared for a moment, and Clipboard's free hand clenched into a fist for a second before relaxing. The colonel nodded and left without another word.

Milo and Frank watched as the two men moved away.

"Pompous asshole," Milo muttered under his breath.

"No, Milo. He's a pompous asshole with a lot of guns. There's a difference."

Milo slapped him on the shoulder, nodding wearily. "You think you can handle the arrangements for the meeting?" He yawned, shaking his head. "I'm too damn tired, Frank. I need to sleep."

"Go on. I'll take care of it."

"You're a good man, Frank. I don't care what everyone else says about you."

"Yeah. Your wife seems to think I'm pretty damn fine, too."

Milo looked at him for a second, a stunned expression on his round face. Then he grinned, realizing that Frank wasn't serious. "Guess she didn't talk to your ex about it, huh?"

"Ouch. Low blow. Get to sleep, Milo. You're starting to act like a real person."

Milo nodded as he left, all but staggering towards his car. Frank watched as two of the men in black grabbed Stoner's corpse from the ground and placed it on a stretcher. They never said a word. He returned the favor.

Frank climbed into his Mustang, thinking about the black ink they called coffee that was waiting at the office. He hoped it had been sitting for a while. He needed all the caffeine he could get.

Chapter 3

1

Frank returned to his office to find Buck Landers stretched out on the long wooden bench in the lobby. The man was snoring loud enough to drown out the sounds of a dozen heavy trucks moving around outside. The soldiers continued to pour into town, but now they were moving in with trucks and jeeps. None of the vehicles had license tags or any identifying numbers. They were all black.

Frank woke Buck and told him to get his sorry ass home and into bed where it belonged. His assistant did not argue, he simply left. Two other officers showed up—Ricky Boggs and Jay Freisner and, after he'd finished chewing them apart verbally for taking their own sweet time to report, Frank sent them out to do what they could to keep order. He also warned them that the armored men in control of the town were not to be toyed with, ordering them to shoo away any nosy civilians, and to lock up any who decided to get pissy about the situation.

Arranging the meeting that Anderson had requested did not prove exceedingly difficult. With the help of the new, government-issue operator and a few angry words about Colonel Anderson's request that he handle this situation, Frank was allowed to use the phones in order to call several of the town's people and gather assistance in handling the details. Sadly, the soldier did his job too well. As soon as Frank dialed the number for the Highway Patrol, the disembodied voice came back over the line and told him that the call could not be made without the direct orders of his commander. Frank hadn't expected to get through, but he'd have hated himself if he hadn't at least tried.

After the calls were made and the details of the meeting were cemented, Frank climbed back into his Mustang, completely ignoring the squad car the soldiers had returned in his absence, and drove back over to the clinic. The situation there was much changed from earlier in the day. John and Sam Morrisey were sitting on the small rise of steps leading to the front door of the building. Where Sam looked like Santa Claus, his father looked more the part he played in life. He was just a little on the heavy side and clean-shaven. With the glasses perched on his small nose, he looked about right for kicking back on a porch and reading stories to a gaggle of grandkids. Right now, they both looked tired, over-heated and ready to collapse. Both were drinking coffee. An elderly doctor and his paramedic son, just stopping to enjoy the day. Not likely, at least if the angered expressions on their faces were any indication.

The doctor noticed him first, a frown of concern showed on his face. "Howdy, Frank. You had those burns examined yet?"

"No, Doc. I've been a bit too busy."

"You should at least put some aloe on them, keep the peeling from getting too nasty." The man sounded too damn tired and Frank could guess that neither father nor son had slept in the last twenty-four hours.

"Did the medical supplies and extra doctors help any?"

Sam snorted, turned his head and spat. "Oh yeah, they helped one hell of a lot, Frank. They helped so much that we ain't even allowed to see the patients anymore."

"'Scuse me?"

John Morrisey answered before his son could speak again. "The medical team came in and took over all medical operations. My files have been cleaned out, Frank. They took every bit of information on every patient I have. Then, just to make sure we understood our place properly, they took the patients that went with the files."

"Well, what the hell made them do a fool thing like that?"

"'This is a matter of national security.' That's the only answer they gave us." Sam that time, once again punctuating his comment with a spit wad.

"Look, I'll do what I can, talk to Colonel Anderson and see what's what. In the meantime, why don't you two take advantage of the break and get some sleep?"

"It isn't that easy, Frank," John explained. "If we head out of here, there're gonna be an awful lot of people wanting to know what happened to their family and not getting any answers."

"Well, they can wait until tonight to get their answers. You two are damned fast to jump on my case when I forget to eat, so I'm returning the favor now. Get your butts into bed and get some sleep, or I'll lock the both of you in holding cells until I'm certain you've had a nice, long rest."

Sam looked ready to argue, but Frank stared him down. Finally the two men agreed and went off to John's house, just down the road. Frank stared at their retreating figures, puzzled by what they'd said. Why would the Feds want all of the serious victims under lock and key? He didn't know for certain, but he knew he probably wouldn't like the answer.

After mulling over the implications of the latest development for several minutes, Frank left to head over to the Hav-A-Feast Diner. Laurie Johnson's cooking sounded far better than another dry tuna sandwich, and he needed a treat.

The diner was not exactly overflowing with business. Laurie herself sat at the counter, reading a copy of People Magazine. She was a skinny little thing, with hardly any meat on her bones. Frank suspected that was because the closest she ever came to eating was taking a few sample bites from whatever specials she prepared on any given day. She looked up at Frank as he entered the restaurant, beaming a smile his way. "Hi, Frank! Don't you look like a mess." Laurie hopped off her stool, shaking her head and sending her short, bleached blond hair snapping around her ears. She wrapped her hands around his left bicep and led him over to one of the booths along the bank of windows. Ten years younger than he was, and she was already adept at mothering him.

"Aw, I don't look so bad," he complained. "And I feel fine, Laurie, there's no reason to fret." He tried brushing her hands away from his arm, but she held on and all but forced him into a seat. Before he could do more than adjust his position on the bench, she had a glass of ice water and a menu in front of him.

"I'm sure you feel fine, sweetie. But you need a little tee-el-cee right now, just like everyone else around here does." Laurie was possibly the only woman in town he'd let call him 'sweetie,' and that was only because she called everybody by that title. When she called you by your name and your name alone, you were on her bad side. Only about five people in town were stuck with only the use of their proper names. She moved out of sight again, then reappeared a few seconds later with a set of flatware wrapped in a checkered linen napkin. She moved discreetly around the area, waiting for him to finish reading his menu. As soon as he did, she was back and asking for his order.

Then she disappeared for around ten minutes, during which time he smoked another cigarette and watched the people moving around outside the Hav-A-Feast. Strangers filled the streets. Or at least it seemed that way. Most of the town's surviving population were in their homes, but the tourists were either at the motel or wandering the streets for the most part. No one walking out there looked happy. It was too hot, too humid and the wrong place for most of them. They probably all had families outside of Collier. Families who'd be worried about their safety.

Spaced out at regular intervals, faceless armored men in environmental protection gear stood with small, deadly weapons held at the ready. He'd looked at the firearms again, tried to study them and still couldn't figure out the make or model. That made him uncomfortable as all get-out. Already the people walking the streets were doing their best to give the figures a wide berth. The glances they cast towards the men in black were almost always furtive.

Frank crushed out his cigarette and was about to light another when Laurie deftly slid a platter topped with a chili burger and fries under his nose. "Lord above, Laurie, that smells wonderful."

"It should, I cooked it myself." She smiled quickly, and Frank saw the worry lines around her eyes. "Why don't I turn on the TV?" She suggested. "We'll see what the news has to say about what's going on here?"

He looked at his watch, frowning. "It's two-thirty, Laurie. There's no news on, just the soaps and a few of those damn talk shows."

"You better believe there's news. After they said there might be a terrorist stuck here in Collier, that's all they've been talking about."

"Sure, let's hear about the nasty ol' terrorist. I could use a laugh or two."

Laurie reached into her apron and pulled out a battered remote control. With a flick of a button, the television mounted above the condiments, behind the counter, squealed into life. The picture was fuzzy and too bright behind the layer of grease and dust, but the volume was okay. Several mediocre actors were on the screen, going over the lines for their daily soap opera. An attractive woman, dressed in clothes that should have gotten her arrested for indecent exposure, was just finishing a particularly acid remark when the screen changed to the station logo and call letters.

The deep, serious tones of an announcer explained, for the terminally stupid, that this was a Channel Two Special Announcement. One of the regular anchors on the news stared somberly at the screen before proceeding. On the announcement board beside her, an illustrated building was in the process of exploding. Written in bold letters beneath the illustration was the legend: TERRORISM IN GEORGIA. *"Good afternoon. Channel Two News has been following the terrorist crisis in Collier, Georgia. Inside sources at the state capitol have recently passed on information that the situation is far more severe than originally believed. The Palestinian radical, Amir Hal Densalid, believed to be responsible for the hijacking and subsequent destruction of a government owned tractor-trailer has also caused the derailment of a train carrying toxic waste from New Jersey to a special holding facility near Savannah. Still more troops have been brought into Collier, where the city remains under quarantine.*

"We now go to the town limits of Collier, where Channel Two's own Ben Johnson is currently waiting for the latest news..."

The scene changed abruptly. On the screen a moderately handsome man with too many dimples and a ridiculously warm-looking suit appeared, replacing the stern looking black woman with coifed red hair. The man stared intently at the camera, seemingly oblivious to the heat, save for the moisture on his brow. Behind him, the Spanish moss-decorated oaks and weeping willows loomed over the familiar highway off ramp leading into Collier. A massive tractor-trailer lay on its side, blocking the road. In front of the trailer, three men in standard Army fatigues stared out into infinity, guarding a line of sawhorses. On each of the wooden structures, a bright orange sign bore the words Caution: Biohazard and the universal emblem for the same.

"Good afternoon, Monica." The man spoke in a deep, non-accented voice, carefully pronouncing every word he spoke. Frank pegged him as the sort of man who'd argue over a penny. *"As you can see, the military is taking no chances with any of the potentially disastrous events surrounding the normally sleepy town of Collier. Behind me, the capsized tractor trailer believed to have been carrying potentially dangerous virus samples stolen from the Centers for Disease Control in Atlanta still blocks the only road into Collier. Since last night, when the government forces moved into the sleepy southern town, all access to the town has been denied. Several of the citizens of Collier who were away at the time of the incident have expressed concern over loved ones and family members now trapped within the confines of Collier."*

Frank leaned forward as Ben Johnson moved to his left, where several people stood waiting near the sawhorses. Among them were Robert Summers and his wife, Jennifer, the parents of Mike Summers. It was jarring seeing them on the television. It wasn't right. They were supposed to be here, where he could see Bob's easy smile and too-thick eyebrows, and where he could think bad thoughts about how shapely Jenny was, despite having borne a child and spending far too many years working as a housewife. Even as Frank was trying to hear what Johnson was saying to the couple, Laurie was sticking her head out the door and calling out in a voice almost loud enough to shatter the windows of her diner. A second later, Frank noticed why she was so noisy. Mike Summers and his friend Marty Wander fairly flew through the entrance to the building.

"What are they saying?" Mike's voice was filled with worry, but Frank waved his hand frantically and told him to shut up so they could all hear.

When silence reigned again, Laurie increased the volume just as Bob Summers started talking, his heavy southern accent almost jarring after the nondescript speech of Ben Johnson. *"We just want to know that our son is okay. Jenny's Mom is in the hospital over in Parrish County, and we wanted to wish her a happy Fourth of July in person. Next thing we know, there's a whole bunch of men in special suits pointing guns our way and saying that we can't go home. The town's been cut off. What kind of nonsense is this? My little boy is stuck behind those barriers, and for all I know, he's being held captive by an Palestinian terrorist."*

Ben Johnson nodded his understanding, all the while looking dreadfully concerned. Then he turned back to the camera and spoke again. *"Even outside of Collier, the tension here in southern Georgia is high. We stepped away from the main road earlier, to take some footage of the defenses already set in place by the military forces in Collier."*

The scene changed again, and Frank stared slack-jawed at the screen as images appeared and held for a few seconds before moving to other camera shots that were just as surprising. More military personnel stood behind massive structures of wood and razor-wire. Each of the figures shown wore traditional gas masks under their helmets. In comparison to the dark figures walking inside the town, far away from the camera's prying eye, they looked like boy scouts. Their uniforms were merely fatigues and their weapons were standard issue. They did not wear armor, or carry fully automatic assault rifles. They looked more human, despite their completely hidden features.

Ben Johnson continued speaking. *"Nuclear threat? A potential plague waiting to sweep through the town of Collier? A dangerous spill of toxic waste waiting to ravage this peaceful community? Whatever the case, the military forces that have seized control of Collier are not giving any answers. This is Ben Johnson, reporting for Channel Two News."*

Frank looked over at Laurie and shook his head. "When, exactly, did we become a 'sleepy southern town?' Sounds like we don't even get out of bed in the mornings..."

Laurie punched a button and the volume faded to a whisper as the anchorwoman came back into view, another practiced look of concern marring her features. Laurie reached over and wrapped one of her bony arms around Mike Summer's shoulders, giving him a tight, one-armed hug and smiling down into his somber face. "See, sweetie? I told you your parents were okay. They just can't get into town anymore than we can get out."

Mike forced a smile for her, and she ushered the two boys over to a table, promising them ice cold Coca-Colas and sundaes if they could just wait a minute or two. Both boys did their best to be patient as she came back over to speak with Frank.

"You're bein' awfully sweet to them two, Laurie."

"Oh, they're good kids. They just like to have a little fun now and then."

"A little fun? I don't call letting the air out of all the school buses fun, Laurie. I call it vandalism."

"That was half a year ago, and neither of 'em was dumb enough to actually cut the tires; they just let the air out." She frowned, placing her hands on her narrow hips. "It's not like they was doing crack cocaine or any of that stuff, Frank. They were just having fun." Her mischievous smile grew lopsided on her face, and she nudged him as she leaned in close. "Besides, I don't think either of 'em's gonna do too much wrong anymore, not since you put 'em both in a jail cell the last time.

"Yeah, well you can mark my words. Those two better be on their best behavior if they want to get through this mess. I don't think the assholes outside are too picky about who they shoot, if you catch my meaning."

"Yeah." Laurie's face grew stormy as she looked out the window at one of the armored men. "I heard about you and that trucker. I'm really sorry, Frank. I know you didn't want that to happen."

"Hell, Laurie. I don't think anyone ever wants that sort of thing to happen." He shrugged, then grabbed the sweaty diet cola glass near his meal and sucked half the liquid from the container into his mouth. He didn't want to talk about dead drunks and the idea of speaking about the current state of Collier was getting tiresome. "Any chance you can get me a refill, sweetheart?"

Laurie smiled, turned and walked away. She knew him well enough to understand that he didn't want company. A few minutes later, she dropped a new glass of soda on his table, deftly sweeping the other glass up and onto a tray in the same motion. She then delivered the promised sundaes and refreshments to the Summers' boy and his little friend.

Frank ate in silence for a few minutes, watching Laurie with the two kids and wondering what having children was like. Laurie had never had any, but she almost treated every customer like a child. Maybe that was her way of dealing with the void in her heart where true love was supposed to be. Frank had known what he thought was true love; then Kathy told him she wasn't happy, and that she had to move on. Maybe

Laurie's way was the best: treat them nice and be their friend, but drop 'em when they start acting up.

When Frank was finished with his meal, he went over to where Marty Wander and Mike Summers sat eating enough ice cream for five. He gestured Marty over and sat down next to the boy. Both of them smelled of summer heat and mown grass. Frank loved the smell of summer, surely the best cologne nature ever made. The two were nervous around Frank, but that was what he expected. He was friendly enough with them when he saw them on the street, but he always made it clear that he was watching them. A little fear went a long way to making sure the two of them kept their noses clean.

After a few strained seconds of silence, Frank spoke up, doing his best to sound friendly. "How you two boys doin'?"

The two mumbled something along the lines of "Fine, thank you," and stared at their deserts.

"Mike? You have a place to stay while your folks are out of town?"

"Yessir. I'm staying over at the Wanders' place, least until my folks come back."

"Well, that's mighty nice of your folks, Marty. Mighty nice indeed."

"Heck, Officer Frank. I think Dad just did it so he could have two of us to keep the lawn neat." Marty's smile was infectious, and Frank couldn't help returning a grin. Even Mike managed one.

"Well, I want you two to keep yourselves outta trouble." Frank raised his hand before either of them could protest. "Don't go gettin' defensive on me. I know you two don't mean any harm with your pranks, but I don't like the way them fellas out there are treating the people of Collier. I'm afraid they might get a little trigger happy if they heard a cherry bomb going off behind them, and I know they don't like anyone who's breaking their concentration. Just stay clear of 'em, okay?"

It took the two boys about fifteen seconds to agree. Neither could quite look him in the eye when they did. Frank hoped they'd keep to their word, but doubted it just the same. He thanked Laurie for a wonderful meal, paying her for the eats despite her protests that it was on the house, and leaving her a nice tip besides. The food was worth the cost, and her cheeriness was absolutely priceless.

After a few minutes of contemplation, he decided to find Colonel Anderson and give him the details on the meeting himself. Despite the lack of distinctive clothing, Frank found locating the man relatively easy. All he had to do was ask any of the guards where Anderson was, and they told him. Most seemed a little taken aback that he knew their commander's name, but after the initial surprise they were actually very efficient about getting him the information he needed. He learned quite a bit by just watching the guards in action. When one of them touched a small button on the underbelly of his mask's artificial elephant's trunk, Frank learned that they had radio communications, despite the fact that all of the radios in town were on the fritz. He learned that the guards were ready to roast alive in their uniforms—not surprising, since the temperature was in the high nineties and the humidity around the same level—and he learned that their deodorants were not living up to the advertised promises. Both of the soldiers stank to high hell.

That knowledge made Frank feel better. They were human under all of that gear, and they had to deal with the heat just like he did. The difference was, they had to deal with the heat while wearing enough rubber and armor to make a battalion's worth of firefighter's helmets.

He asked every guard he passed if they knew that a heat wave was coming, just to see if they'd groan out loud. None of them did, but a few of them weren't standing quite as tall when he saw them again. It was a petty, childish gesture but it made him feel good.

The search for Anderson was short and sweet once he found the right area of town to look in. He was the one everyone else bowed and scraped to. He stood up when Frank entered the area near the lake where he had set up his command post. No one stopped him from entering the giant green tent, though a dozen armed men stood around the perimeter of the place. "How can I help you, Captain Osborn?"

"Well, you could all pack up and get the hell out of town, but I don't expect that's an option from where you are."

"No, I'm afraid it isn't."

"I just thought I'd let you know that everything is set up for the meeting tonight."

"That's much appreciated, Captain."

"So why don't you prove that, and tell me why the town doctors can't get in to see their patients."

"Because they don't have the experience and training necessary to deal with the sorts of burns that we're dealing with."

"Well, they did go to medical school." There was more than a little edge in his voice and he almost wished he could have toned it down. Fortunately, the Colonel seemed to take it in stride.

"Did they specialize in radiation burns and high risk trauma cases?"

"Nope. They just did that general practitioner thing. Oh, 'cept that John Morrisey went back to school in his spare time to study forensics. He's hell on wheels with a scalpel and a body bag."

"That's always good to know. Listen, Captain, I don't want us getting off on the wrong foot. Despite the need to...well, to take control of your town, I am not a power monger. I just need to ensure that there are no leaks on this one. This is a very dangerous situation. We don't know what that thing is, or what it is capable of doing. Just as importantly, we don't know for certain just how deep the burns go on the victims, or even if any of them will survive. If the damage they've suffered was caused by heavy radiation, we want to give them the best possible chance for survival."

Frank hated that the man sounded so damn reasonable. Logic and a good dose of placation was taking the wind out of his sails. "Well, Colonel, I still don't see the harm in letting the local doctors look in on their patients. A lot of those folks have never been far away from here, and they've never seen doctors aside from John Morrisey and Walt Johnson." Frank shrugged, looking around for a moment and gathering his thoughts. "We're talkin' about doctors who still make house calls, here. We're not talkin' about doctors who leave every detail about a patient in a paper file, either. How are you gonna tell if one of them burn victims has a seizure caused by an allergy to a medicine or by epilepsy? I know for a fact that Doc Morrisey never bothers putting things like that on files, 'cause he already knows the information. He don't need to sweat it, none of the locals do. This is a very small town and a very tight community."

Judging by the man's posture—which was really all Frank had to go by—the Colonel was still capable of listening to reason. He seemed more attentive behind the mask and breathing apparatus.

Frank moved in for the proverbial kill, adding a last bit of ammo to his argument. "Besides, Colonel, you aren't gonna win a lot of support from the locals once they hear that you've quarantined their family and friends. Having Morrisey and Johnson on your side to answer questions is a far better idea than having them blab that they aren't even allowed to see who's doing well and who's fading away."

"All right, Captain Osborn. I'll do what I can to get the good doctors reinvited to the party, as it were. But I can't make any promises."

Frank was about to respond when he heard a massive electrical hum, followed almost immediately by the sound of running water. "What the hell is that?"

"That's the pumps we've placed into the lake, Captain."

Frank looked through the mosquito netting, out towards Lake Oldman. Several large hoses ran into the water, and were apparently draining the lake. The massive rubber tubes shuddered and twitched, despite the ropes anchoring them in place. Somehow, he'd managed to overlook them before they started moving. He liked his recently discovered ability to ignore even the blatantly obvious less every second.

"Why in the name of God would you want to drain the lake?"

"Because we can't examine the—the target if we can't reach it. We can't reach the target with all of that water in the way. Beside, the water needs to be purified and examined to ensure that there are no health risks to the people of Collier."

"You can say it, you know."

"Say what, Captain?"

"Spaceship, UFO, alien vessel, satellite from beyond the stars..." He shrugged. "Ain't anyone in this town dumb enough to think that ship is manmade. If the Russians had anything that big and that powerful, we'd have lost the cold war a long time before the Communist Bloc fell apart. Hell, Colonel, just the size alone would have lost it for us. That's one hell of an intimidation factor."

The Colonel was silent for a long moment, and even through the dark glass lenses that hid them, Frank could feel the man's eyes on him.

Frank spoke again, just to break the silence. "You do understand that the lake is the primary source of water for the entire county, not just the town of Collier, don't you?"

"Yes. We've already made arrangements to draw water from the neighboring counties for the next few days, possibly longer." There was something different in the man's voice, some missing quality that had been there before. Frank could not place exactly what that property was, but he wished it would come back. The man sounded even more alien than before.

"Colonel? What are the chances of this whole thing just blowing over and all of us going back to life like we had it before that thing crashed?"

After a pause that stretched longer than Frank liked, the man responded. "That depends on the cooperation of the citizens in Collier."

"Give me a ballpark estimate."

"I can't do that just yet, Captain. I wish I could."

"Call me Frank."

The Colonel was silent for a few heartbeats before answering. "Frank it is. Call me Mark."

"That I will, Mark. Mind if I take a look-see at the lake?"

"Go right ahead. Just be careful; the water is well past the boiling point."

"You know it."

Frank left the tent, doing his best to ignore the weak feeling in his knees. He walked to the edge of the lake, noticing with a sense of disorientation that the fused glass and human remains were all gone. A long strip of soil and red clay rested where the sand had been this time yesterday.

Lake Oldman was a very deep drink, well over sixty feet deep under normal circumstances. So Frank was taken aback when he saw the level had dropped by easily ten feet already. The surface of the lake was buried under debris ranging from parts of a dozen shattered boats to the bloated corpses of countless fish. The smell of the cooked fish was enough to make him nauseous, and the frothing waters with their heavy cloud of steam did nothing to make him feel better.

Somewhere down there, old Bobby Carlson was boiling away, cooking in the intense heat. He didn't want to be around when they found his remains. Gathering up his nerve, Frank looked out to the ship in the lake. It shouldn't have existed. It should never have come down in Collier. But just to prove him wrong, the damned thing sat gleaming in the water, releasing waves of heat. *How could something so big ever get into the air in the first place? It's twice the size of any plane I've ever seen, and I've seen a lot of planes.* The surface of the thing looked almost oily from this distance. It carried reflected colors as surely as a puddle of water at a gas station does, like little swirling rainbows on a stagnant pool. He couldn't understand how something so hot could look wet.

Frank continued to look at the lake that had always brought him peace. All the while he grew more and more unnerved. The 'copters had no serial numbers. The same was true of all the vehicles the group had brought with them. The uniforms on the soldiers' bodies bore no markings of any sort. Even the firepower they carried had no serial numbers that he could see. So why in the name of God

My name is Colonel Mark Anderson

had the man given his name? Either it was a fake name or *Call me Mark.*

they—or maybe just Frank—were in one hell of a lot of trouble. The only possible reason that a group as seriously paranoid about being recognized as the armored men in black would even consider giving out names had to be the certainty that no one would report those names to anyone else.

Ain't no way he actually thinks a town this size can keep a secret. No way in hell. I don't think I like this. I think this is a damn big mess waiting to happen.

Frank stood after a while. He looked at the tent behind him and took one last look at the lake below. The pumps and the boiling water continued to take their toll. At a guess, the water level had dropped another few inches while he watched. Feeling less like a man relaxing then when he had started, Frank walked away. Behind him, he could feel the presence of the ship as surely as he could feel the sun on his burns from the night before.

The meeting was only hours away. It was time to get some rest in before he had to play mediator.

2

Frank talked calmly with his men about just what was going to happen and exactly how he expected everything to go down. They listened intently, acknowledging that he was in his "No time for nonsense" mode. When he was like that, even Ricky Boggs knew better than to give him any sass. There were going to be some very angry people at the meeting, and whether or not any of them agreed with the anger of their friends and families, they had no choice but to remain calm. Each officer took a position at an exit point for the Fowler Elementary School gymnasium, where the meeting was to take place. All save for Frank, who would be on the stage itself. Frank had no intention of speaking, and certainly did not intend to add his endorsement to whatever the Feds had to say about the situation. But he had every reason to believe that his being there would help diffuse at least some of the tension brewing in the town.

Frank cautioned all of them to avoid having any sort of violent conflict unless there were simply no other options. He also made clear that under no circumstances were they to leave the doors manned only by the men in black. He opted not to answer when Buck Landers asked him why.

Frank really didn't want to think about it himself. He would much rather have avoided the idea creeping into his mind, the idea that—*God above, we're all gonna be in an enclosed place. What's to stop them from just opening up with those guns of theirs and mowing us down like wheat?*—the armored soldiers would consider declaring open season on Collier's citizens. Speaking from a strictly mercenary perspective, the meeting was a perfect chance to remove most of the threats to their little matter of "National Security."

In the same situation, he'd seriously consider doing the exact same thing. Hell, for all he knew the military boys were wearing those suits because they'd already dropped a powerful virus in the air, or added it to the water supply they were re-routing from somewhere else. While he was on the subject of betrayals, what guarantee did he have that Colonel Anderson was telling the truth when he claimed the radiation from the thing in the lake was at a harmless level? All he had was the man's word, and he just didn't feel safe taking what the leader of a secret military force in the United States had to say as gospel. Nossiree, he didn't like the idea at all. All he knew for certain was that he'd be checking his toilet before he flushed. First sign of blood in his urine or stool, and he was going to blow Anderson's head right off his damn shoulders and consider the consequences later. That sentiment went double for sudden massive hair loss, or severely bleeding gums.

Just to be safe, he made a mental note to search out his father's old mail-order Geiger counter and see if the stupid thing had a hope in hell of ever working. The more his mind worked at the chances of the people in Collier living through the next few days, the more paranoid he grew. He'd started chewing his nails again, for the first time in over seven years. Every time he looked at one of the soldiers—which was basically every time he left an enclosed space—all he could think about was whether or not the person inside the armored uniform had ever killed before. He was willing to bet that most of them had.

Not much after 7:00, the first of the townspeople began coming into the auditorium. Almost immediately, they reached for their brows, wiping the sweat away. Despite having the air conditioners running since just after five, the air was still sweltering. Twenty days of sealed doors and closed windows had done nothing to keep the school safe from the blistering heat. Frank had pretty much acclimated to the temperature, but he still had to pull his kerchief every few minutes to mop away another layer of perspiration. Thinking about the soldiers who would soon enter the room, he was almost tempted to turn off the air altogether. Maybe they'd all get lucky and the bastards would roast alive in the heavy garments.

"Whattaya think them boys are gonna want to discuss, Frank?" The voice was from the past, and not one he honestly expected to hear. He turned his head sharply and was rewarded by a sudden burning pain, caused by his over-tense muscles protesting, and by the smug face of Peter Donovan. Peter was six feet, one hundred and eighty-four pounds of lean, hard redneck. His short red hair was clean, and framed a hard face with an easy smile. The smile never reached his eyes. Peter's black T-shirt was adorned with a rebel flag carried by an elderly Confederate soldier with a savage scowl on his face. In a word balloon, the soldier cried out 'Hell no! I'll never forget!' Between that and the swastika tattooed on Donovan's arm, it was easy to tell the man still preferred the company of whites to that of anyone else.

"Pete, nice to see you." He managed to keep his voice calm, but with what he'd already been through in the last two days, he had to work at it. "Now, what the hell are you doing in Collier?"

"Oh, that's a real nice greeting, Frank. I was here to see the fireworks. Funny, but I never quite got around to leaving." The man's eyes were dark enough to counter the almost-pleasant tone of his voice. "Figured since them fellas with the guns wanted me to stay so bad, I'd just hang around for a while."

"I'm gonna say this once. I will not repeat myself. If you go anywhere near Karen, I'll have your ass in the slammer before you can think about going near her again."

"I ain't even seen Karen." Peter Donovan lifted his fingers in Boy Scouts salute, a big grin splitting his face. "The thought never even crossed my mind."

"Bullshit. You might not have seen her, but I'd bet money you've thought about it. Hell, I should probably bust you here and now, just to avoid another situation."

"Won't be any situations, and you can't bust me. I ain't done nothin' wrong."

There it was again, that belief that the law always protected the innocent, and spewing forth from the mouth of someone who hadn't been anywhere near innocent in over a dozen years. Frank managed to avoid actually laughing out loud, but it was a close thing. *Why do the assholes always know their rights better than the nice people do?* "Law says you ain't allowed within a hundred yards of Karen, Pete. I'm betting they'd believe me if I said you'd been closer. Hell, she shows up at the meeting here and you will be breaking your probation. You think about that, and remember that I'm being nicer than you deserve."

"Oh come on, Frank. You don't really think I'd hurt her, do you?" Frank looked at the overly sincere expression on Peter Donovan's face and gave serious thought to caving the man's handsome features in on themselves with the butt end of his revolver.

"Lessee here," Frank lifted a hand and started ticking off fingers with each point he made. "Breaking and entering, attempted kidnapping, assault and battery, attempted rape. Do you want me to go on, Pete?"

"I told you before, it was a misunderstanding. I'd had too much to drink and I was missing her something awful."

"Yeah? You keep missing her and you stay sober, or I will take you down. Am I talking clear enough? Or do you need another explanation?"

"You're being real clear, Frank." Donovan's voice was lower in his throat, almost a growl. Then it suddenly lifted back to its usual tones, and Pete forced a smile back onto his face. "You don't have nothin' to worry about. I learned my lesson."

"We'll see about that, won't we?" Frank stared long and hard at the younger man, and finally Donovan moved away to take a seat with the rest of his friends. They sat near, but not actually with, Lucas Brightman. The man's power over them was something to watch. The entire gang of overgrown punks was on its best behavior, and despite an almost frantic energy possessed by the group, none of them ever looked at Brightman. They looked everywhere else, but never at him.

With the exception of Peter Donovan, every last one of them worked at the textile mills. To a man they depended on Brightman for a job. While Frank had no proof, he knew where it counted that they were all doing extra work for the old bastard. The sort of work you don't get a paycheck for. The sort of job you got paid for in cash, and that you never told anyone else about. He didn't doubt that Donovan still worked for the man in that capacity, even if he no longer lived in the area.

The gym was filling quickly, and still more people were coming in through the doors. The smart ones came in carrying colas and beers. They would remain cooler than anyone else, at least as far as the temperature was concerned.

Burt Ditweiller came in with a sixpack of Busch in one hand and a sub sandwich in the other. Frank watched the disheveled man stumbling down the aisles between the fold-out chairs, until he finally managed to get to a seat in the front row. Burt was a good man, but a mean drunk. Until the fire swept across the docks, Burt had been the dock master. Now, he was likely unemployed. Frank couldn't really blame him for tossing back a few too many beers, but he still had to do his job and make sure all went well. Despite the man's sincere promise not to be bad, Frank took away the sixpack, promising to return it at the end of the meeting. Burt looked like he wanted to argue, but apparently he thought better of the idea when he saw the armored soldiers starting to file into the room. Clipboard passed by during the argument, asking if Frank needed any help. Right around then, Burt became Mister Cooperative. Frank hoped Burt's new disposition would last all the way through the meeting.

Twenty of the armored men came into the auditorium. Each soldier was armed. They took positions along the walls, surrounding the audience, and Frank thought of men surrounding a barrel of fish or a pen full of fowl. Not a one of them looked out of shape, though it was hard to tell through the heavy black armor covering most of their vital areas. Seeing them made Frank feel like he'd been invited to the wrong end of a turkey shoot.

From the door opposite the stage four more of the soldiers appeared. They walked slowly and deliberately up to the stage, where they were joined by the one Frank thought of as Clipboard. The people sitting in the audience began mumbling amongst themselves. None of the noises they made sounded very happy.

Clipboard checked the microphone on the podium set in the center of the platform. Frank wondered if the man was checking for bombs, and was tempted to point out that all was well, as he'd set the damned thing up all by himself. Just like a good little gofer.

Frank climbed back to his position on the stage and was joined by Milo Fitzwater a few minutes later. Milo was looking much better, and Frank was glad he'd decided to get some rest. When they made their usual greetings, Frank could smell the Rolaids on Milo's breath. Some things, at least, never changed.

The podium and microphone were finally given the Clipboard Inspector's Seal of Approval, and one of the men stepped forward. Frank could tell by the walk alone that Colonel Anderson was ready to speak.

Anderson stood in front of the audience, waiting for silence. He did not wait for very long. In a matter of seconds all eyes were focused on the Colonel. He lifted one finger, and the armored men on the stage moved in unison. Frank felt his stomach knot into a heated ball, and forced himself to breathe, though his body did not want to comply. As one, the men behind Colonel Anderson lifted their arms and then placed their hands on the sides of the necks. For one horribly irrational moment, Frank though they would pull their heads off, revealing something hideously alien. Scaly skin or maybe a face covered with slimy tentacles. He almost cried out. Instead, they simply removed their helmets, and then the faceplates secured under the metal hats.

Despite his worries, they were all human. He didn't know whether to be relieved or disappointed. Five sweaty human faces looked out at the audience. Each was topped with a military crew cut, and each looked exhausted. Two Caucasian faces, one Hispanic set of features and two African-American faces peered out at the audience. A murmur went through the crowd, and Frank could tell what most were thinking, even if they'd never say anything in public. Peter Donovan, or one of the men he was sitting with, didn't have any social worries about speaking his mind. Someone said: "Damn me, they got niggers mixed in with 'em." The voice honestly sounded shocked. Despite the differences in color and race, the men standing before the crowd could have been pressed from the same mold. Each and every one of them looked like killing a person was an old habit. They looked predatory.

Anderson looked like his voice sounded, cold and hard. His face beneath the graying hair on his head was angular and brooding. He was the kind of man Frank expected was just as comfortable in a battlefront trench as he was in front of the television at home.

Anderson took one sharp step forward and laid his helmet and mask on the podium. He placed on hand on either side of the lectern and leaned slightly forward before he spoke. "Good evening, Collier. I imagine you have a lot of questions. I am prepared to answer as many as I can, but I'd like to explain a few things first.

"Number one: Collier is now under martial law. We will be imposing a curfew that *will* be followed. Anyone caught outside after curfew will be taken into custody for an indefinite period of time.

"Number two: The men around me and on almost every street corner in Collier are under my command. My name is Colonel Anderson, and I am a soldier with the United States Government.

"Number three: It is my duty to secure the object resting in the center of Lake Oldman at any cost, and that is exactly what I intend to do.

"Number four: This matter is extremely sensitive. We are not certain exactly what the craft is, but we believe that the continued security of this nation depends on us finding out as quickly as we can." Anderson paused for a moment as voices started talking in the audience. A few were loud, but most were subdued. Frank swallowed, wondering just what was coming next.

"Number five: Most of you have relatives or friends who were injured. We are doing all we can to care for them. The medical team we brought with us is trained to handle crisis situations. You may rest assured that your friends and family are being well taken care of and well provided for." The people in the audience began to mumble again, and Anderson raised his voice to be heard over them. "No one is allowed to see the injured at this time. However, Doctors Morrisey and Johnson will be working with us and will be available to answer your questions. Additionally, I've made arrangements for Pastor William O'Rourke to pass your comments along to your loved ones. He will be available from nine a.m. to our p.m. for that very purpose. When possible, he will also convey your family's return comments. I know this isn't the best situation, but due to the severe nature of some of the burns, the fewer people around, the less the chance of severe infection setting in.

"Number six: While neither I nor my men wish any harm to any of you, we *will* defend ourselves against any potential threats. In order to make certain that everyone here remains safe, including us, we will be coming around to each and every one of your homes tonight. Groups of my men will come to your homes and knock on the door. If they are not answered, they will attempt to open the door. If the door is locked, they will break the door down. Once inside, these men will ask you to produce any weapons you might own. This includes hunting rifles, firearms of all sorts, bows and arrows and anything else they deem a possible threat to security. Do not argue with them. We do not have the time to discuss the matter, and we will not leave without the weapons."

The people of Collier spoke as one cacophonous unit, crying out against the orders they'd just been given. Several stood up, and a few looked ready to storm the stage. Frank stood up as well, raising his hands for silence.

"Folks, calm down please." Frank was ignored, and tried several more times before he could finally gain their attention. "Calm down... Hey! Sit down and can it! The Colonel's not done speaking yet!" Frank glared out at the people in the audience his face set in a stern scowl. "Nobody's happy about the situation here, least of all me, but screaming ain't gonna solve a damn thing! Sit down and hear the man out." It took a few moments, but finally everyone decided to listen.

Anderson spoke again. "As I said before, you are now under a state of martial law. For reasons of safety and security, we cannot allow anyone who is not an authorized servant of the law to carry any weapons. We do not want to cause any harm, but we will not leave your houses without the firearms we demand. Don't think about hiding the guns or ammunition, simply hand them over. We have a list of every registered weapon in Collier. We will also search the homes of anyone we believe is a threat to security. You can make this easy, or you can make this hard. Either way, we are prepared to handle the situation." Anderson paused for a moment, his eyes scanning everyone in the audience. "If you still have questions, I am now prepared to answer them."

Once again, voices erupted from the audience. Anderson called out with enough force to send feedback through the speakers. "One at a time, please! Raise your hands and I will point to each of you. Pretend you're back in school and that I'm your principal."

A wave of hands rose into the air. After looking for a few seconds, Anderson pointed to a woman in the fifth row, Myrna Louis. Myrna heaved her ponderous weight from the seat, and Frank was mildly amused to see she'd put on her Sunday best for the meeting. Seeing her dressed in finery for the event made him wonder if she thought they were dignitaries here for a social event. "Colonel Anderson? I just wanted to know why we can't use the phones?"

"Well, ma'am, some people might only want to check up on a few loved ones, but there are others who would do their best to make contact with any number of television stations or newspapers. While no one would believe what they read there anyway, we'd rather not wind up on the front page of the *Weekly World News*. Next?" Frank had to admire the man's style; almost everybody chuckled at his comment. Everybody except Myrna. Judging by the guilty look on her bovine face, she'd desperately wanted to reach the *Weekly World News* or some equally strange magazine. Of course, Myrna still claimed she'd dated Elvis Presley, so that was almost to be expected.

Dewett Hammil was next to stand. He had on his usual shy smile, but there was a little more steel behind his eyes than was normally seen. "How do. My name is Dewett Hammil, and I just wanted to know one thing. Beggin' your pardon. Just how long you think it's gonna be 'fore we can reopen our businesses? I ain't makin' a whole lot of money sittin' on my butt, and I got bills to pay."

Joe Ditweiller—the meaner younger brother of Burt—cupped his hands around his flabby mouth and called out "Sit down, nigger!" before Anderson had a chance to respond. Dewett glared venomously, and Frank nodded to Buck. Buck Landers didn't hesitate. He walked across the room and grabbed Joe in both of his hands, hauling the man out of his seat. When Joe started to protest, Buck shook him like a rag doll and all but threw him across the room. Buck was smaller than the man he rattled, but most agreed they didn't want to meet him in a bad mood. Buck was a dirty fighter. A scattering of applause mixed with a smaller number of boos and hisses as the younger Ditweiller was invited to leave. Some of the applause came from Anderson and, after he started, from a few in his lot.

Frank watched Lucas Brightman through the entire scuffle. Old Luke was looking far too innocent, especially when one considered the fact that Joe was always going on about how Brightman treated him and his family so well at the mill. That the man associated with Peter Donovan did nothing to convince Frank that he wasn't paid to make the comment. Lucas Brightman was testing the waters. He always was too nosy for his own good.

Clipboard came over to the Colonel and whispered in his ear. After a moment, Anderson nodded and then leaned over the mike again. "Thank you, Officer Landers. Good riddance to bad rubbish. To answer your question, Mister Hammil, I cannot guarantee just when you'll be able to work again. Right now we need the area where your bakery resides to remain free of civilians. The area is being used as a take-off zone for our helicopters. It's one of the few areas large enough to accommodate the craft. However, you have nothing to worry about regarding your bills. For the inconvenience, Uncle Sam will cover your expenses until you can go back to your regular schedule."

His words won Anderson a grateful smile from Dewett, and the older man sat down, content for the moment. Anderson nodded again, and this time Mike Summers stood up. His voice cracked when he spoke. "Yessir. I—My name's Mike Summers and I want to know why my mom and dad can't come back into Collier. They were visiting my Gramma when you blocked off the town."

Anderson's voice lost a bit of its edge as he looked at the boy. "Are you an only child, Mike?"

"Yessir."

"Do you have a place to stay?"

"Yessir."

"Mike, I'd like to let your parents back into town. I really would. But I can't right now. We're testing the air here, Mike. We're testing for radiation and we're testing for possible risks from unexpected biological hazards. That's the reason my people are wearing masks right now. There might be something in the air that could possibly make everyone in town sick."

Once more, the people in the audience started mumbling and crying out. This time he let them go on for several minutes before demanding silence again. "I said there *might* be something in the air. I don't think there is, because, as you can see, I've already taken my mask off. But that's because I wanted you to know who you're dealing with. Most of my soldiers are under strict orders not to take their masks off under any circumstances." Anderson took his time looking at virtually everyone in the audience. "So far, we've got no evidence that anything along the lines of poisonous gases or unknown viruses have been brought in with the aircraft in the lake. But I don't feel comfortable allowing anyone in at this point, just in case something does show up."

"Sir, my folks are really worried. They was on the TV talking about how they didn't know if I was okay." Mike looked about ready to cry, and Frank held his breath, waiting for what Anderson would say. By the looks of the crowd, most of them were holding their breath as well. Things could get very ugly very fast if the man blew this one off.

"I can't let you leave, Mike. And I can't let your family in here, but I can pass on any message you might want to give to them and send back their reply. How's that sound to you?"

Mike smiled weakly, glad to have at least a chance to let his folks know he was all right. After a few more questions, ranging from "When will you let us go?" (When we have retrieved the object in the lake) to "Are there aliens in that ship in the lake," (We don't know, but we intend to find out) the moment Frank had been dreading came to pass.

Lucas Brightman stood and spoke as clearly as he could. His eyes glittered wetly, and every eye in the place turned to him. "What if we refuse to surrender our weapons? We do, after all, have the constitutional right to bear arms."

"Then you will be placed in the custody of Captain Frank Osborn and his police force. You will be fed three square meals a day and ignored."

Brightman looked deeply offended by the comment. He wasn't used to being told what to do, and he certainly wasn't used to the idea of having his rights tampered with. "What gives you the right, Colonel Anderson, to treat us like criminals?"

"You are not being 'treated like criminals,' sir. If you were, I wouldn't be up here explaining matters to you. You would already be behind bars. As I said before, this town and its people are under martial law. Your constitutional rights have been suspended out of necessity. "

"With all due respect, Colonel," Brightman's voice was cold with artificial anger. He was trying to make something happen. He was doing his best to make sure that all the right buttons got pushed. "Letting us stay in our homes hardly constitutes freedom. We have to be in by a certain hour. We have to surrender our weapons. We can't speak to anyone outside the confines of Collier. I've been watching the news, Colonel Anderson. There are a few miles of razor wire surrounding Collier. What makes you any better than a Nazi concentration camp?"

Several voices, mostly the ones of Brightman's cohorts, started rising in volume, protesting the treatment the people of Collier were receiving. Through it all, Colonel Anderson stared coldly into the audience. When the level of protests had eased to a minor uproar, the man spoke again. "What makes me any better than a concentration camp? One thing and one thing only. If you play by my rules, you'll get to go free eventually. We have medical supplies and, if it should come to us being around that long, we have food supplies. There are no gas chambers here. But there is a very serious need to get a job done to ensure the continued security of these United States. If that means that a few people get restrained or even killed, then that's a price I'm willing to pay. You don't have to like the situation as it stands, Mister Brightman. You just have to deal with it."

Lucas Brightman smiled, an oily, easygoing grin that set Frank's nerves on edge. "So what you're saying, is that the Constitution of these very United States is useless at the present time?"

"That's exactly what I'm saying. You are now under the rules of martial law. For all intents and purposes you are in a war zone. That means you do what I say or you pay the price." There was a moment when the two men stared at each other, both wearing feral grimaces on their faces. During that suspended fraction of time, Frank felt an odd kinship with the both of them. He'd done his time in combat, he understood that the two men were assessing each other, taking the measure of a new foe.

For all intents and purposes you are in a war zone. Truer words had never been spoken. Anderson knew it, Brightman knew it, and so did Frank.

Brightman walked away from his seat, heading over to where Buck was once again waiting beside a few soldiers at the door. Before he left, he turned and faced his new enemy one last time. "I fought in WW Two, and I fought in Korea." Brightman's body language had changed from a simple polite stance to a combat-ready position that looked sadly comical on his old frame. "Call me old-fashioned, but I was raised to believe I was fighting to stop this sort of shit from ever happening on these shores." The wily old man raised his chin in challenge, once again gaining a slight grin on his angular face. "I can't speak for all the men and women here, Colonel Anderson. But I can speak for myself and I can certainly make a good guess on how a number of these folks feel. I don't own so much as a pellet gun, but if I did, the only way you'd get it from me would be to pry it from my cold, dead fingers, you son of a bitch. This here is still America, and I'd die to save her, even from people like you, who think you can run around and treat her like a whore, in the name of 'National Security.'"

Brightman turned on his heel and slid through the door before anyone could respond. The silence in the auditorium was almost complete. No one spoke for several heartbeats. Frank stared into the mass of people sitting in the audience, and did not like what he saw. The faces out there seemed largely to agree with every word Lucas Brightman had uttered. The difference was, a majority of the faces looking back towards the stage belonged to people who owned virtually every type of firearm.

Anderson spoke again, and Frank was almost relieved to hear a sound other than his own beating heart. "Are there any more questions?" He waited for an answer, but none came from the audience. "That being the case, good night."

Anderson and his entourage left the stage without ceremony. Baleful stares followed them the entire way out of the building.

Frank sat where he was for a while, watching as the people he'd known for most of his life left the gymnasium. Buck Landers said it before he did, but his mind was working on a similar sentiment. "We are in for a serious night of shit. Brightman riled them all up, and now we're gonna have to try to get them calm before anyone gets blown away."

Frank nodded his agreement, looking at the empty floor and the scattered chairs left behind. "I guess we better get to it then, huh? Damn, why can't it ever be easy?"

No one bothered to answer him.

3

The business of door-to-door gun collection did not go well. The first few houses were easily handled. Annie and Walt Groff gave over the shotguns and revolvers without question, only asking that they be returned when everything was over. The military men handed out receipts for everything they took, and no one got hurt. The next few homes were just as easily handled, even if Hugh Elberry did cuss up a blue streak over the violation of his rights. Not that he ever used the guns since his arthritis started getting really bad, it was just the principle of the matter.

Around the tenth house, things started getting messy. Albert Clark had no desire to hand over his weapons, and his three sons agreed with his sentiment. The man was forty-six years old, and his sons ranged from Tony, age twenty-two, to Mark, age seventeen, to Berry, age twelve. Albert and Evaughn had managed to raise three fine sons, and not a one of them had ever given Frank the least bit of grief. They were good people.

Albert collected firearms the way some people collect stamps. He had an arsenal of over four hundred rifles, shotguns and pistols. To Albert, the weapons were works of art, carefully crafted and meant to be appreciated. When Frank considered the sheer amount of money the man had spent in gathering his collection, he supposed he shouldn't have been surprised by Albert's refusal to hand the firearms over.

Clipboard and five other soldiers stood together behind Frank. They'd all agreed that having the regular police present could only help stop the people of Collier from getting foolish. Albert nodded amiably when he answered the door, and stepped to one side to allow the entourage into the house. "Y'all come on in. Make yourselves comfy."

Frank knew the place well enough, from the comfortable velvet covered couch and love seat to the wide screen TV set against the wall. He'd stopped by here on several occasions after one fool or another attempted to break past the security systems just to look at the collection of weapons Albert kept on display throughout the house. To his knowledge no one had ever tried to actually steal any of the pieces, but a few of the rowdies in town forgot common sense and tried to climb through windows after they'd had a few too many to drink. Albert never pressed charges, he just told them to come back the next day and have a look around at a decent hour. Frank stopped just past the threshold when he saw the empty corner where Albert kept his display of Civil War rifles.

"Dammit, Albert. Where did you hide the guns?" Frank's voice sounded frustrated, even to himself. It had all been going so well...

Albert beamed, and the bright glare from the track lighting over the empty corner fairly glowed against his balding head. "Where no one will find them, Frank. I'm not gonna let anyone take my collection. Hang on one second, and I'll get my shaving kit. I'll be ready to leave with you."

Frank sighed, looking back towards Clipboard. "He's not gonna be a problem, but I can tell you right now he's gonna be spending some time in the jail. I was afraid he'd do this."

"What the hell's his problem, Captain?"

"His problem is that he loves that collection like most teenage boys love looking at women. He's got muskets dating back to the Revolutionary War, and he ain't partin' with 'em." Frank shrugged. "Hell, he's probably got a better collection of guns than the Smithsonian does."

Clipboard looked around the room, the glare from the multiple lights making his lenses look more insectoid than ever. "Damn. How many does he own?" the man buzzed through his helmet. "I've got at least four pages of serial numbers here."

"Right around four hundred or so. If there's a gun that's been made that he doesn't have, it's just 'cause no one would sell him one."

"No way. There is no way I can leave without those weapons collected." There was a decidedly hostile edge in the man's voice. Frank felt the tension crawling back into his shoulders.

"Like as not, he's got 'em locked away where no one can get at them. Hell, he doesn't even have bullets for most of 'em."

"Yeah? Well somebody else might have bullets that will fit them. Those guns have got to come along with us."

"Give it a rest, will ya? Albert doesn't even fire those guns himself, he sure as hell isn't going to let anyone else fire them."

Clipboard pushed that button on the jawline of his mask again, and Frank could not hear what he said, but he suspected he was in communication with Colonel Anderson. Albert came down the stairs, an overnight bag in his hand and a fresh set of clothes on his body.

"Albert, is there any way I can talk you into giving up your collection? Maybe I can arrange for storage at the police station. I don't think these boys are gonna take no for an answer."

Albert shook his head, a tiny frown pulling at his too large mouth and the lines above his brow growing heavier. "Nope. Those weapons are mine. They're all registered nice and legal and I'm not surrendering them." He shrugged his shoulders. "I know the rules here, Frank, and I'm glad to spend the time in jail."

"I don't think that's gonna make these boys happy, Albert. They're afraid someone else might get to the guns."

Albert laughed and shook his head, an ornery grin taking ten years off his face. "Not a chance in hell, Frank. The safes for those guns are the best money can buy."

"How did you move them all? I've seen those vaults of yours, they must weigh in at, what, couple hundred pounds each?"

"Got me a big ol' dolly just for moving those things. Tony's truck took care of the rest."

"They aren't even on the premises?"

"Hell no, Frank. I'm not taking any chances."

"Well, let me see the bag, just so's we can make it official that you aren't carrying one."

Albert handed the overnight case to Frank with a grin. "I ain't that stupid, Frank."

"You an' me, we already know that. But these boys aren't the type to take chances." The most lethal thing Frank found in the kit was a toothbrush. A battered book on the history of the modern firearm was in the bag, but it proved to be too bulky to use as a weapon. He handed the bag back. "You know I'm going to have to cuff you, don't you?"

Albert obligingly turned himself around and presented his wrists. Frank pulled the cuffs and locked the metal circles around the man's hands, first his left and then his right. "All right then," Frank said. "Let's get this done."

He was just starting to lead Albert towards the convoy of cars outside, when Clipboard's black gloved hand came to a rest against his right shoulder. "I'm afraid not, Captain Osborn. The Colonel wants to know the location of those weapons."

"Albert's willing to go to jail. Makes everything okay in my book."

"Your book doesn't count. The Colonel wants to know where those guns are located, and he wants to know right now."

Albert started to speak, but Frank interrupted in a louder voice. "Look, at the meeting these people were given two options, they could hand over the weapons or they could fall into my custody. Albert's in my custody, so what is the problem?"

"The problem is that this man has three sons and a wife who might have loaded weapons in their possession. We need to retrieve the weapons now, as a safety precaution."

"What, I'm supposed to place all of them under house arrest as well?"

"No. But I'm supposed to retrieve those weapons." Clipboard turned to Albert. "Where are the weapons, Mr. Clark?"

"Where they can't do any harm."

"That's not a good enough answer. Do you want to try again, or do we start searching the premises?"

Albert shrugged, a slight smile of defiance on his face. "It's the only answer you're gonna get, mister."

"Albert, I don't know if this is a smart attitude..." Frank tried to warn him, but it was too late.

"Full search! Start at the top and work your way down!" The buzzed command had an instant effect on the other four soldiers. They'd been so quiet throughout the exchange that Frank had almost forgotten they were there. The men moved up the stairs with little noise.

Albert looked to Frank with a worried look on his face. "What are they gonna do?"

"What they have to in order to find the weapons, Mr. Clark." Clipboard shrugged. "I hope you have a damn good cleaning service." From above, the sound of heavy objects falling came. The ceiling above actually dropped a bit of plaster as something fell over.

"You can't do this!" Albert flexed his shoulders as he stepped towards Clipboard. His arms did not follow is commands, and he paused to look at them before remembering that he was under arrest. The handcuffs stopped what would have been a physical confrontation. "I know my rights! You can't do this!"

Clipboard turned around so fast that almost seemed to have grown another insect face. "Wrong! You don't have any rights, Mr. Clark. Those rights do not apply in times of martial law, and you are now in violation of the orders placed on this community in the interest of national security." With each word, the man leaned further into Albert Clark. His armored face was only inches away from Albert's, and his clipboard reached out to tap Albert lightly in the stomach in cadence with his words. "As of this time, you have the right to produce the weapons registered in your name. Failure to do so will result in my men having to tear this house apart in order to find them. If we do not find the firearms on the premises, we will move to your son's house and begin tearing that apart as well. Do I make myself clear?"

Albert must have finally decided he didn't like having a clipboard used on his belly like a cattle prod, because he lifted his left foot off the ground and slammed it into his tormentor's lower thigh with an inarticulate scream. Frank started moving forward right then and there.

Clipboard hopped backward, favoring his right leg. His metal board and attached pen went sailing as he dropped into a defensive combat stance. Albert tried stepping forward, but one solid yank on the cuffs knocked him off balance. Frank stepped between the two men, his hands held out towards each of them. Clipboard was just moving forward, apparently ready to retaliate. Frank's hand pressed against the armor on his chest.

"That's about enough out of the both of you." He did his best to stare down the bug eyes on the man's mask. Something large and porcelain, judging by the sound it made, shattered upstairs. "Mister, if you think I'm gonna let you take a swing at a man in cuffs, you better think again. I'm doing my best to keep the peace here, but I'll be damned before I let you start slapping around defenseless people."

Before Clipboard could respond, Frank turned to Albert and snapped. "Have you lost your stupid mind, Albert? You don't go around kickin' at men with guns, especially when your dumb ass is already in chains." Clark started to protest, but Frank pushed on. "You better figure out which is more important to you, Albert, you and your sons' houses or that gun collection. I'm here to make sure they don't get too enthusiastic about beating up your family. I can't stop them from tearing down your house."

"But Frank—"

"But nothing! I ain't here to protect your guns, Albert. I'm here to make sure you get out of this alive!" He stared hard into his neighbor's eyes. "I don't like it anymore than you do, Albert. But we've got no choices here. Now, are you gonna give up the damn guns or are you gonna lose all of your other possessions?" Something very heavy screeched across the floor upstairs. "You'd best decide now, 'cause I'm still about to haul your butt to jail, and I don't think these boys'll wait until later to finish what they've started. They'll still be tearin' this place up while I'm gone."

Albert Clark tried his best to stare Frank down, but it just didn't work. After almost a minute of silence—excepting the noises from upstairs—Albert told him where the weapons were. An old bomb shelter his father had built in the fifties was still airtight and functional. It rested beneath the ground, under the portable Sears and Roebuck tool shed in the back yard.

An hour later, the weapons were all accounted for and all secured in the back of the black truck the soldiers arrived in. Albert was given a very detailed receipt, just before Frank called in a squad car to take him away. There was no arrest being made properly, but a couple of days in the slammer were used anyway, just to make an example and to keep the soldiers from

getting mean. Albert didn't seem to mind. He took his overnight back and he remained uncuffed.

Frank climbed into his squad car and the soldiers into their
truck. After the armored men switched vehicles, leaving another group of soldiers to unload their burden, they were on
the way again.

Clipboard was all business, walking around like a bear with
a pinecone up its ass. Frank did his best to ignore the man.
The favor was returned. Seven houses later, the group ran
across something Frank had never actually expected. They
ran across gunfire.

George Harding was a bit of a recluse. He'd been a
friendly and open boy growing up, but two tours of Viet
Nam—courtesy of the United States Marine Corps—had
brought him home to Collier a very different man. He'd never
really recovered from whatever had happened to him during
those years. Not completely. They say a man's home is his
castle, and in George's case, the castle bore too many simi-
larities to the owner for that statement to be a lie. His house
was slowly disintegrating from years of neglect, and his lawn
looked as overgrown as the shaggy beard on George's baggy
face. He was a lifelong bachelor at fifty-five, which wasn't
too surprising when one considered that he liked his privacy
and he liked his peace. He was sometimes rude, almost always unkempt, and often intoxicated. But he was not what
most people would call violent. He still got out and he still
mingled with the other people around him; he just didn't par-
ticipate in very many community projects. The only time
most people spoke to George was when they ran across him
at the Piggly Wiggly. Most of the time he was on the Internet.
Somewhere along the way he'd apparently discovered that
he liked talking to lines of hastily written text on a computer
far more than he liked speaking directly with people. There
was a buffer that way.

No one ever really complained about him, because most
people didn't see him often enough to give him much

thought. So when the group stopped in front of George's house, Frank didn't expect the situation to be any different than it had elsewhere.

No one could have been more surprised than the captain of the Collier Police when George Harding came out of his house carrying an automatic rifle. Hell, the only thing old George had registered was a .22 pistol. Frank had about enough time to take in George's wild mane of black hair and the soiled pajamas the man was wearing before the rifle registered in his mind. He didn't even have time to call out to the man before Collier's local drunk opened fire.

The good news was simply that George was drunk enough to forget to aim first. The bad news was that George managed a few lucky shots. One of the soldiers, sadly not Clipboard, staggered back as three bullets punched him in the chest. The truck behind the soldier let out a whine of protest as a bullet bounced off the hood of the engine and another shattered the windshield. By the time the rest of the men had drawn their weapons, George had disappeared from sight. His front door slammed audibly.

Frank ran towards the downed soldier just in time to see the man get back to his feet. Three dents in his torso marked where the bullets had impacted. One of the slugs was still stuck against the body armor. Frank had assumed the pads were made of Kevlar, but looking closer he couldn't decide. Like as not, if the armor had been Kevlar, the man wouldn't be moving. He'd be down and out with several broken ribs. Impressive stuff, whatever it was. The light was too poor to make easy detection possible.

The soldier shrugged off Frank's offered help and moved forward. "Fuck you, too, asshole," Frank muttered. Two of the men moved in unison, returning to the truck. Fifteen seconds later, they pulled the battering ram from the back of the vehicle and moved towards the front door. They moved with machine-like precision, stepping in unison and cocking back the heavy steal tool as casually as most men would pop the

top on a beer can. Frank admired the result of the hours of
training the men had gone through. There was no way the unit
could work that smoothly without endless practice sessions.

One strike was all that was needed for the men to knock
the door from its hinges in a splintering explosion of rotted
wood. The decay in the door was not apparent from outside,
but was very evident in the way the door collapsed. The two
soldiers staggered a bit, apparently not prepared to meet with
so little resistance. Several popping noises came from inside
the house, and both men staggered back. Holes appeared in
the walls of George's house, and flinders of oak flew away
from the place.

Frank started running forward, cursing himself for his stupidity even as he moved. He knew before he took his first
step that it was already too late. George was a dead man. He
tried just the same.

By the time he'd covered half the distance to the door, the
two men had recovered from George's assault. They were
joined by the other three. For the first time, Clipboard was
indistinguishable from everyone else. He namesake lay in the
thick grass, discarded and replaced by the weapon normally
slung over his shoulder. Five muzzles flashed in unison and
part of George's house just sort of disappeared. Frank was
aware that he made a sound, but for all the world he had no
idea what that sound was. It could have been a laugh, a scream
or even a sigh of defeat.

He stopped moving. The soldiers continued on. No new
sounds came from inside the building. After a few moments,
Frank started towards the house again, resigned to the certain
knowledge that George Harding was already dead. He was
right. What was left of George painted the walls in crimson
and bled across the tan carpet in the man's living room.

Frank felt his stomach twist itself into knots. He wanted
to be angry. He wanted to take careful aim at the eyepiece on
Clipboard's mask and fire repeatedly into the glass. He wanted
a lot of things. Instead he could only stare at poor George

Harding's mortal remains and wonder just what the hell had gone wrong inside the man's head.

Clipboard moved into his field of vision. Judging by the direction in which his faceplate was pointed, he was wondering the very same thing. Frank noticed the very slight shake that had developed in the man's hands and felt a certain satisfaction: now he didn't feel quite so bad about the way his knees were jitterbugging all over the place. Clipboard spoke. It took Frank a few seconds to realize that the man was talking to him.

"I'm sorry. I didn't catch that."

"I said I'm sorry this had to happen. I really hoped we could get this done without any casualties."

Frank stared at the bug-eyed lenses, searching for even the faintest hint of the eyes behind the mask. In all the time the man had gone without a helmet, he'd never had a chance to study the soldier's face. "Well, I should have expected something like this. I just never expected it from old George."

"Why would you expect something like this?"

"'Cause this is the South. Damn near everybody in this town has a nasty independent streak, and almost everyone of legal age has at least one firearm."

"That's ridiculous." Clipboard crossed his arms. "Why in the name of God would the people of Collier all need to carry weapons?"

Frank shrugged. "Like I said, this is the South. Most of the people down this way still hold a grudge about losing the Civil War."

"That was a hundred and thirty-five years ago. I doubt anyone in this town was alive when that took place."

"Well, there's one other reason."

"Yeah? What's that?" The arrogant tone had snuck back into Clipboard's buzzing voice. Frank held off the urge to hit the man.

"You can never tell when a bunch of jack booted assholes are gonna come into your town and try to tell you that the

Constitution of the United States is worthless." Frank turned and walked out to his car before the man could reply.

The rest of the night fell into a simple routine. No one else was killed, but Frank arrested 17 more people before they were finished with the collections. He knew all of them, if not by name then certainly by face. Most compared him to the Nazis and some even made comments about his dubious lineage. He ignored the comments. What he could not disregard were the sullen looks and sad expressions that very clearly called out to him. Every last one marked him as a traitor.

Maybe it wouldn't have bothered him as much if he didn't feel like a turncoat inside. Logic told him that he was doing the right thing. His emotions disagreed.

He finally made it home just past midnight. When he fell onto the bed he closed his eyes immediately. His sleep was sound, and he did not remember any of his dreams. That was probably for the best. For the first time in his adult life, Frank Osborn cried in his sleep.

4

Frank did not wake easily. His alarm clock kept going off and he kept hitting the snooze button in the hopes of getting another precious ten minutes of peace. So, naturally, Buck called him at a quarter past nine to see where he was. "Hey there, Frank. I catch you gettin' in some beauty sleep?"

"No," he replied testily. "You caught me tryin' to play hooky."

"You wantin' to stay in today?" Buck's voice was softer than usual. Whenever Frank felt like being ill, Buck's voice changed to that of a mother hen. "I'll take care of things over here, if you need the time off." Frank hated that mother-hen voice; it made him feel guilty, and he suspected that Buck damn well knew it, too.

"I'll be there in twenty minutes." Frank thought about the situation for a second, then asked, "How the hell did you manage to get me on the phone, anyway?"

Buck chuckled on the other end of the line. "I'm real good at getting my way, Frank. Haven't you figured that out yet? I can handle things over here, Frank. It ain't like we're gonna get a lot of new stuff going on anyway."

"Make it forty minutes if that'll make you happier. I've got to go by the lake and talk to Colonel Anderson."

"Will do. Talk to you then."

Frank hung up the phone without any attempt at further conversation. He showered quickly, then shaved. The shaving took a little longer, as the minor burns on his face were still sensitive. The skin was peeling away from the area, leaving a fresh pink layer of flesh in its place.

Inside ten minutes from the time he got off the phone, Frank was on his way out of his house. Seven minutes later he'd reached what had once been Oldman's Lake. There was no water left in the lake's bed. Only dead fish, a lot of junk and the ship that was the cause of Collier's dilemma.

Once again he felt compelled to stare at the craft, almost mesmerized by the sheer size of the thing. It thrust from the rapidly drying mud like the fin of a shark frozen in time. Deep cracks in the ground around the ship were obvious even past the silt that had settled around the base. The damn thing had broken the earth beneath it even after slicing through the lake proper. From the way the curvature of the vessel ran—a perfect disc shape as far as he could tell—at least half of the saucer was still buried beneath the bottom of the lakebed. Looking right at the thing, Frank felt as if there was more to the shape than could be seen. Hidden dimensions of depth were hinted at in the somehow off-kilter line of the ship's edge. Despite the fact that the surface of the vessel was smooth and seamless, Frank sensed there was more just beneath the surface of the downed ship's metallic hide. A chill ran from his toes to the crown of his head, ignoring the ninety plus degree weather.

Frank heard the sound of boots behind him, but the voice of Colonel Anderson still gave his heart reason to double its normal pace and made him jump slightly. "It's an amazing sight, isn't it?" His voice buzzed and, without turning, Frank knew he was back in the environmental security of his mask.

"It doesn't feel real. You know what I mean?"

"Yes. It doesn't feel like it belongs here."

"That's exactly it."

Frank turned and faced the man. He was right; the helmet and breathing apparatus were back in place. Darth Vader Junior lived again. Frank had to squint to see the man completely. The sun was almost directly overhead, but the glare in the overcast sky was nearly blinding. "Is that thing as hot as it looks?"

Anderson laughed tinnily. "Hotter. If I wasn't breathing compressed air, I'd be melting. The oxygen in the tanks is cold and that makes it a little more tolerable."

Frank looked back the other way, once again staring at the massive blade cutting into the heart of the now dead lake. "You ought to have a great time when the rain hits. This here is southern Georgia. Like as not the roads'll be steaming after the rain stops."

"That bad, huh?"

"Not if you like being soaked through your clothes as soon as you leave your house." The Colonel laughed politely, and Frank screwed up enough courage to ask what he felt he had to ask. "What happens next, Mark?"

"We do a little analysis, we figure the best way to get this monster out of here, and we leave."

Yeah, he thought, *and my ass bears a powerful resemblance to Mother Teresa. No way in hell is it that easy.* "How do you imagine you're gonna get something that big out of here without being seen?"

"That's the biggest part of the problem. We might have to disassemble it here." Anderson paused for a minute, moving his entire head in a half-circle as he took in the ship without benefit of peripheral vision. "Provided we can find a way in."

"Tell me you boys didn't forget your saws..."

The man laughed again. "No. But I'm having doubts about how we're going to cut into anything that can survive the sort of impact that thing suffered when it hit the lake."

"How tough can it be? I mean, it landed in water."

"It landed in water, probably somewhere near terminal velocity. And Oldman's Lake isn't more than a hundred feet deep at best, lower in a lot of other parts of the lake. That thing should have blown a crater into the lake that was big enough to save us from draining it. I think it did something to actually absorb a lot of the impact itself. And the scariest thing about it is the structure is still sound from what I can see. An airplane would have been confetti after a wreck like that."

"When you gonna test it?"

"What? The ship?" Frank nodded. "In about three hours, if all goes well."

"Why so long?"

Anderson pointed to an area a good ways off, where several trucks were being unloaded. A sizable group of the armored soldiers moved large metal poles from the stacks on the back of the trucks. More of them stood closer to the edge of the lake, placing the beams on large pallets set near a small crane on the back of still another truck.

"We have to move all of that down into the lake bed. Then we have to build a scaffold."

"What the hell for?"

Anderson looked straight at him, and Frank was certain the man wore a stunned expression on the face beneath his respirator. "What for? Hell, Frank. Just how long do you think we have before some asshole in the media decides to break through the barrier we've got around this place?"

"Gotta hide your prize, hunh?"

"That, or lock away a stupid cameraman until this whole thing blows over."

Once again, Frank noticed a hesitation in the Colonel's voice. He'd have bet his life savings the man was lying through his teeth. Frank waved a quick good-bye, then turned towards his Mustang in the distance.

He felt it necessary to leave, before he could get stupid and ask a question or two that he really didn't want to have answered. Like just how the Colonel expected the people of Collier to keep quiet about everything happening around town, after he and his force of walking tanks took their leave.

Frank and his trusty old car moved through the streets slowly. He wanted to look around, to see what was going on and where. In less than three days, Collier had become a stranger. For as long as he could remember, Frank had always felt comfortable in his little slice of the world. Now, someone had made a mess of the entire place. The people on the streets, excepting the ominous black guards, all looked like the people he'd known for most of his life. The way they acted, on the other hand, was hardly normal. Nobody waved as he went past. A few people even turned away from him, as if to tell him that he was to blame, and they wanted nothing to do with a traitor to the community.

Frank went past the office where he worked and drove at a leisurely pace until he reached the true heart of Collier, the Square. The Collier Square was really little more than a shopping arena. Four roads intersecting and leaving a large green patch of grass with a statue of Our Town Founder plopped in the center. Around that statue of Henry Collier a dozen table and bench combinations rested. On almost any given day, the elderly retirees of Collier congregated on those benches, talking about the past and playing any number of games.

Today the benches were empty. The only people in the Square were wearing black armor and carrying assault rifles. Bobby Carlson was dead, and he'd practically been the leader of the bench-squatters. Without him, they had nothing to come around for, nothing to talk about. Frank sighed. Hell, he didn't even know how many others of the elderly were dead as a result of the dream-smasher sitting in the lake. Maybe all of them, and that was a sad thought. No old folks to tell stories about Collier to the little ones, like they used to when Frank was growing up.

His one attempt at a brief break from reality was wasted. He couldn't even watch the old folks and dream of a time when he used to visit them and hear stories about the Civil War and WWI. Now he could only stare at the sentinels who held his town at bay. Stare and hate.

Frank moved slowly around the square, noticed that almost every store was closed, and finally turned towards the office and the work waiting for him. The parking lot was full, save for the spot reserved for squad cars. He parked illegally, blocking in four of the cars parked in the reserved areas—none of which belonged in those spots—and made his way into the wing of the building reserved for him and his officers.

The chaos was already in full swing when he pushed past the frosted-glass doors. The waiting area was full of sullen-looking people, all of whom had a bone to pick with him. Oh yes, this would be a fine day indeed.

Buck Landers was sitting at his desk, a shit-eating grin on his face. He waved cheerily at Frank, and Frank seriously considered just hitting the man in the head on general principles. "Mornin', everybody," he said into the chorus of grumbles that greeted him. "Give me five minutes and I'll speak with you." He pushed past a few dozen people and made his way to his private office. After he closed the door, amidst the rumbles of an unhappy crowd, he checked his blood sugar, cursing himself for taking too large a shot, and ate a Kit Kat candy bar. They tasted worlds better than the glucose wafers ever could, and worked almost as well, so he kept a whole box of them stashed in his filing cabinet.

He smoked one last cigarette, and then he opened the door. The crowd of familiar faces gone sour was not quite as large as it had first seemed, but there were still a lot of people all crowded into one area. A lot of unhappy people.

"Okay," he said, taking time to look each and every person in the eyes. "How many of you are here to bitch me out about arresting your friends and family last night?"

Only one hand did not rise at the question. Reverend William O'Rourke simply smiled patiently. Frank looked directly at the man and smiled back. "Reverend, you have something I can help you with before the screaming match starts?"

Will spoke in a loud, clear voice. Years in front of the congregation had given him the sort of powerful voice even most opera singers would envy. "Yes, Frank. I'd like to see if you can pass the word around that we'll be having a mass service for our fallen loved ones tomorrow morning at ten o'clock. Not at any of the churches, but rather at the cemetery proper. All three of God's ministers will be present, handling the needs of the Lord's flock." Will's eyes moved around to capture everyone in the room. Almost to a one, they hung their heads as he spoke. "If the rest of you could aid me in this task, I'd be very grateful. Also, I'll be taking messages into our injured friends and family at noon, two and four today. You may bring messages until the time I go in, and if you care to wait, I'll bring out messages from those who are able to reply."

With his speech done, Will leaned back against the wall and crossed him arms. The crowd seemed much calmer as a result of his presence. Frank understood why. No one likes to make an ass of himself in front of a minister. Just one of the rules of nature, at least in the South. He nodded his gratitude to the older man, and Will responded with a knowing wink. God love him.

Frank cleared his throat. Everyone turned to face him again. "Now then, we're gonna do this nice and calm, or I'm gonna have to get testy. Don't think I won't either, 'cause me and the rest of the police here in Collier are all doing at least double duty. Not a one of us wants anyone yelling at him. We might have to throw a few more people in cells, if you see my meaning." A few voices started to growl again, and Frank raised his voice to be heard over them. "Any of you want to register a complaint about how I'm doing my duty, you can just walk your butts over to Milo's office and yell at him instead. He's the one with the power to fire me, and the power to hire another Chief of Police. Otherwise, y'all can raise your hands and I'll get to each of you in turn."

A few people actually did run off in an effort to find Milo. Frank wasn't too surprised by their actions, but he was mildly offended.

Steve Walters was the first to raise his hand. Frank was rather shocked to see Steve, as the man lived out on a farm well beyond the town's actual limits. Somewhere along the way he'd simply assumed the man wasn't in town. "Yeah, Steve. How can I help you today?"

"Frank, I gotta get back to the farm. Amy's gonna have a helluva time running the place by herself, and I can't afford to lose the revenue if she can't manage."

"I'm sorry, Steve. That's up to Colonel Anderson and his people. I can't do a thing about it."

Steve sighed mightily and turned away. "'Fraid you'd say that. See y'all later." The man left quietly, and Frank was grateful.

Albert Clark's sons, Tony and Mark, the eldest two, stepped forward. Tony seemed calm enough, buy Mark looked about ready to take a bite out of anything that came too close to his face. "What's up, fellas?"

"Wanted to see our dad, if it's all right with you, Captain Osborn." Tony spoke politely, while his brother tried to stare daggers through both of Frank's eyes.

"Don't see a problem with that. Buck, why don't you escort these two down to the holding cell where Albert's waiting?"

"Sure thing, Frank." Buck slid his butt away from the edge of his desk with practiced ease and moseyed in the direction of the jail cells. He gestured for the boys to follow, and they disappeared around the corner. Mark's eyes never left Frank until he walked into a wall. Frank managed not to laugh.

Myrna wanted to use the phone in his office, until she found out it didn't work either. Sam Peabody and a dozen others demanded to know what Frank was going to do about Buck and a group of the Colonel's forcing their way into people's houses and stealing their firearms. Frank explained everything they'd all had the chance to hear the night before and the whole group left after screaming at Frank for a good ten minutes. Only Will O'Rourke's presence, Frank was sure, prevented the group from trying to hang Frank by the neck until dead. Mandy Sterling wanted Frank to come out and arrest her husband for beating on her again—Buck left a few minutes later, as the bruises on her arms and stomach spoke much for Bryce Sterling's efficiency with his fists. The line of complaints and accusations took almost two hours to clear out. Long before it was over, Frank wished he had taken Buck up on the offer to let him stay home.

When that was done, Frank picked up his phone and calmly explained that he needed to talk with Colonel Anderson. The asshole on the other end tried to outlast him, but Frank got stubborn and was eventually patched through.

"Anderson."

"Colonel? This is Frank Osborn."

"What can I do for you, Frank?" The man sounded distracted, but Frank decided to bite his tongue on the nasty comment he felt building inside.

"Well sir, I was wondering if you could convince your operator on the phones to patch me up with all the homes in town."

"I think that could be done, Frank, but I'll need a good reason."

"How's this one: I'd like to pass on the information that we'll be holding funerals for our dead tomorrow morning. I can't afford to spare the manpower to pass the word on my own, or I wouldn't bother you." He tried to keep the anger from his voice, but it wasn't easy. Much like the Colonel, Frank was a man used to being obeyed. Having the man question his motives was about enough to send him off the deep end.

"I think I can arrange something, Frank. You should hear from me soon."

"Much thanks." He hung up the phone, and looked at Will leaning against the wall. "Will? How's Emily doing?"

Will looked at him with ancient eyes and Frank suddenly remembered that the man in front of him was almost sixty-five years old. He didn't look a day over fifty most of the time. His hair was still mostly brown, and he carried himself with the posture of a man half his age. If a person did not look too closely at the lines on his face, the years tended to fade away. At the present time, he was looking as old as he really was. His face was filled with worry, and the circles under his eyes spoke of the sleep he had not received.

Will sighed softly, shaking his head. "That she's alive at all amazes me." Will looked away from a moment, and Frank saw the man close his eyes. A single tear managed to escape before he got himself under control. "She's in a bad way, Frank. My poor Emma's in a lot of pain, and there's nothing I can do for her."

"Those doctors of hers treating her right?"

"I don't honestly know. They've got her in an oxygen tent, and I can't see her clearly through the plastic." Will turned away, walking towards the door. He stopped when his hand connected with the pull handle. When he looked at Frank again, his eyes were as haunted as any Frank had ever seen. "They won't let me see her, Frank. I can't even be there for her, to offer her even a little comfort." Will opened the door, stepping halfway through the threshold before he said his last on the subject. "But I can hear her scream, Frank. I can hear her scream every time she wakes up."

Frank let the door close behind the pastor. He thought about following, but was stopped by the ringing of the phone. In the empty silence of the room, the sound was remarkably like a shriek of pain. Frank ignored the goosebumps crawling over his flesh and put the receiver to his mouth and ear. "Captain Osborn here."

"Captain? The Colonel has granted your request. Tell me when you're ready, and I'll patch you through to everyone in town."

"Thank you. I wasn't really sure if you could do that or not, but I figured I had to try."

The man did not acknowledge his thanks. He simply disconnected the line. Never having met the operator, Frank wanted to smash his face through any convenient wall. Four minutes later, he made his call.

Twelve minutes after that, Mick Poundstone came from over at the Collier Memorial Cemetery to explain that the funeral would only be symbolic. The bodies of the dead were being kept by the Colonel and his men. In the interest of National Security.

5

Frank pulled as close to the lake as he could, astonished by the number of people he saw out and about on the streets. Most of them were children, and he supposed he shouldn't have been surprised. In all his time he'd long since come to understand that children can adapt to just about anything. There were kids gathered in clusters all around the dried-out lake. Seven or so of the ones around the right age for high school were tossing a Frisbee around in a large semicircle, wearing as little as they could to ward off the intense heat of the day. Not far away, Mike Summers and Marty Wander were playing a game of "smear the queer" with Tommy Thornton and the new kid in town, Joe Hubeny. Frank thought about Andy Newsome staring with dead eyes from the back of his patrol car, and the brief joy that had started to bloom in his mind wilted away. Andy was dead. He'd never play the game again. Somewhere in town Andy's little brother, Billy, was still trying to recover from the death of every living relative he'd ever known.

There comes a point where enough is simply enough. Frank Osborn was no longer in the mood for pat answers and ominous warnings when he stormed into the tent Colonel Mark Anderson called his command post. The guards let him pass, and he was angry enough that he never even wondered why.

Anderson sat at his desk, the glare from a florescent lamp reflecting of the lenses in his mask. He must have noticed Frank, because he held up a hand, palm outward, requesting silence. One hand was under his jaw line, apparently depressing the built in microphone in his faceplate. A moment later, he turned his head slightly and looked at Frank.

"Let me guess, you're upset about the bodies?"

"Very good. You get a gold star and a five point bonus on your next exam."

"Excuse me?"

"Never mind, it's an old joke. What the hell is going through your mind? Why are you keeping the bodies of our dead from us?"

"Because the bodies could potentially reveal what happened here, and that can't be allowed."

"Let me guess. 'National Security.'"

"Right the first time."

"All right. I've done my best to help you out, Colonel Anderson, but this is just going too damn far." Frank leaned across the desk, staring at his own reflection in the bug-eyed mask. "I helped you round up guns, I'm doing what I can to help with the curfew, and I've already had a few death threats thrown my way by people I've always been friendly with. But now you're trying to keep the bodies of my friends and the loved ones of this community. I need a better excuse than 'National Security' before I'll stand still for this nonsense."

"It's the only answer you're going to get, Frank." Anderson stood up and pushed away from the cheap metal desk where he kept his papers. "There are radiation burns and other bits of evidence on the bodies that would tell too much to a qualified medical examiner. I can't afford to take any chances on this. I thought I'd made that clear enough already."

"I'm starting not to give a damn about what chances you need to take and not take, Colonel. We're talking about a community here..."

"No." Colonel Anderson shook his head and Frank's reflection in the lenses shifted crazily. "We're talking about meat. What I've got in cold storage is not a community, it's a pile of corpses." Frank opened his mouth, ready to protest, but Anderson cut him off. "I understand that the bodies belong to your loved ones, but I don't honestly care. I've got more important things to deal with than this. I can't spare the time to placate you and your backwater town. I've got real problems to handle."

"'Backwater town?' It took every last bit of Frank's restraint to keep from just going postal all over the man he was looking at. Hell, Frank barely recognized his own voice when he spoke. "Fuck you, Colonel. And while you're at it, you can fuck your 'National Security.'"

Frank turned and started away. When he felt the Colonel's hand on his shoulder, he paused and slowly turned his head. The bug-eyes he had found so unsettling three days earlier had become so commonplace that he didn't even flinch. "You want to keep that hand, mister, you'll take it offa my shoulder."

Anderson withdrew his hand. "I'm sorry for my outburst, Frank. Try to understand my position here. I'm between a rock and a hard place. I cannot let the bodies of your people go. There are too many potential risks."

"Yeah? Now I want you to try and understand where I'm coming from. I've paid my taxes, I've served in the United States Armed Forces, and I've voted in every damned election in this country since I was eighteen years old." Frank started counting off points on his fingertips. "I've never once in that time done anything that could cause this country any sort of trouble. So where do you get off treating me and mine like common thugs, when we haven't even done anything? I know all about why you want to keep that thing in the lake a secret. Hell, I can't even blame you for that. But, damn it, I have to draw the line here.

Exasperated to the point of nearly crying, Frank tried to make his point as clear as he could. It drove him crazy that he couldn't see the man's face, couldn't see if any of what he said was getting through. "We're already hurtin', Colonel. We gave up our weapons with almost no complaint. We're accepting the curfew—and believe me, that ain't easy to swallow—and we're just trying to lick our wounds and start making our lives work again." Frank sighed and waved his arms, uncertain how to make his point known. "Look, in the last three days, we've lost over a hundred local people and at least that many strangers from out of town, had our basic rights taken away from us and even been refused the right to see our injured friends and family. Just how much more do you think you can take from these people before they start taking something back?"

"Is that a threat, Frank?" Anderson's voice took on a Clint Eastwood edge, soft and husky, like a predatory growl.

Frank almost laughed. *Nothing. The man understands nothing at all of what I'm trying to say. Might as well be talking to a chalkboard.* "Hellfire and brimstone, Anderson. You really don't get it, do you?"

"Get what?"

"The only reason the people of Collier are being so damned nice to you is because they agree with your basic demands. All in the name of National Security. We're a real patriotic lot down this way. But that's gonna come to a stop when they hear that they can't even give their dead a proper burial."

"Why should that bother them so much? I mean, people lose their loved ones all the time." Frank could hear the edge of exasperation in the man's buzzing voice, and part of him wanted to understand where the Colonel was coming from, but most of him just didn't care.

"Because the people of Collier are also real proud, Colonel. Down here we tend to think a dead person is entitled to a certain amount of dignity, same as when they were alive. That means they're supposed to have a decent burial and be allowed to have visitors from time to time."

"And no one wants to see them taken away."

"That's exactly right, Colonel. No one wants to think that their loved ones are sitting in a government vault somewhere, just rotting away or, worse, being examined by a bunch of pencil pushers."

"What if I told you my hands are tied in this matter?"

"Then I'd warn you to start watching your back. And no, that ain't a threat coming from me. That's a warning that the people here have taken about all the shit they care to swallow."

"Don't you think you're blowing this a bit out of proportion?"

"Nossir. I think *you're* taking an awful lot for granted. I don't think you're even beginning to understand just how serious the people here are about maintaining their freedom."

"I'll give your argument some consideration, Frank. That's the best I can do."

"Thank you. That's all I can ask of you."

Frank stared at the Colonel, as the man suddenly turned his head, listening to something that Frank could not hear. Once again the man gestured for silence, then he touched his helmet. He was apparently preoccupied, because he forgot to turn off his external speaker.

"No. Warn them back down. If they continue, fire one warning shot. If that doesn't work, bring them down... No. If you see a camera in action, just shoot them down. There are to be no leaks, do I make myself clear...? As a matter of fact, even if they agree to come down, you should make certain they come down in here, not out of our reach... That's right, but behind the church, or over at the town offices, not near the lake... What else? Arrest the morons. I don't give a rat's ass about their first amendment-rights! Just do it!"

Frank felt the wind kick up around the tent, and watched as all four tent walls tried to buckle inward. The sound of helicopter engines picking up speed came to him, even past the harsh voice of the Colonel. Without another thought, Frank walked to the entrance of the tent and stepped back out into the remains of his hometown.

All around him, the children of Collier, and those few adults brave enough to dare the heat and the dark militia surrounding them, stood looking towards the sky, squinting against the glare of the sun. Four helicopters lifted from the ground, sending a wave of air in all directions at once, and shattering the faint illusion that Collier was just another town.

It only took a few seconds to see what was causing all the commotion. A smaller helicopter was hovering over the town, its nose pointed towards the lake and the monolithic structure now hidden beneath a web of steel beams and heavy tarps. One of the teenagers—it sounded like Steve Boothe, but he couldn't say for sure—called out to his friends.

"Look at them sumbitches go! They're gonna eat that sucker for lunch!" To Frank's dismay, the boy sounded excited.

He could not hear what was said between the single news 'copter and the four large flying arsenals surrounding it, but the warnings were heeded. The smaller helicopter—owned by Channel Seven out of Stockon, unless his eyes were failing him—began to descend towards the parking lot confiscated for use as a landing zone, not far away. The four larger aircraft remained where they were, but all focused on the single interloper.

As the Channel Seven 'copter got lower, Frank could see not one but three figures with cameras on their shoulders. All were pointed in different directions; one at the tent behind him, one at the lake, and one towards what was left of Milo's hardware store. He recognized the face of the man sitting beside the pilot almost immediately; as he lived and breathed, it was Channel Two's own Ben Johnson all the way down from Atlanta. The plastic smile was gone from the man's face. He looked overheated and more than a touch worried. Considering the number of machine guns pointed at the craft, Frank couldn't blame him in the least.

Frank looked at the craft as it slowly settled in, but noticed that the little helicopter never actually touched the ground. It hovered perhaps an inch above the pavement as the pursuing vehicles slowly settled down.

Frank was still looking at the newscaster when the man's face suddenly changed expression. The fear faded and was replaced by a steely determination. One word came from the man's mouth, and even though he couldn't hear what was said, he knew that word was "Now."

How the boys in the military helicopters fell for the pilot's stunt was something Frank would never figure out. Perhaps they'd grown too confident in their ability to control everyone around them, perhaps those damned masks of their made it hard to see minor details. Whatever the case, the four had just settled and their blades were slowing, when the good old Channel Seven suddenly lifted from the ground and took off towards the lake.

All four black helicopters fairly erupted from their positions, lifting into the air with a speed and grace that their target could not hope to match. The smaller craft screamed and roared as it dove past the canvas and the men anchoring the heavy cloth around Collier's secret. The other four made scarcely a sound, almost as if they preferred to save their energy for more important matters.

Frank felt like an ant trying to catch all the action at a tennis match. He and damn near everyone else there ran as fast as their feet would take them, heading past the tents and over towards the edge of Oldman's lake. By the time they reached the sheer side of the lakebed, the helicopters were almost out of sight. Seeing the 'copters reduced to the size of HO-scale train accessories at the far end of the dead lake made Frank reevaluate just how large Oldman's really was. Small wonder he never worried about getting out to the ocean; he had one in his back yard.

The craft were coming back their way, and the closer they came, the harder it was to make out all the details. The starship—or whatever the hell it really was—blocked Frank's view of almost everything. But he saw enough. He saw the Channel Seven 'copter moving towards the ship at full tilt, apparently in an effort to use the thing as a shield or maybe to make the other helicopters smash themselves against it. If the latter was the case, the pilot had seen too many movies.

He also saw the missile leave the side of one of the black, wasp-like 'copters. How anything could move so damned fast was beyond him. One second there was a flash of light, the next, there was a streamer of smoke running from the attacking craft and tagging the closer helicopter's tail end.

Frank watched the Channel Seven traffic 'copter lose its backside to a fireball. It transformed from a smoothly flying machine into a blaze as bright as the sun, and then into a hurtling comet of fire and debris. Shrapnel flew through the air, arcing away from the explosion and leaving trails of smoke to mark where they had passed. The craft was still a good way off, and Frank was grateful for that. None of the flaming debris even came close to the shoreline. He was even more thankful for the massive alien structure sticking out of the ground: the smaller pieces fell short of the shore, but he had no doubt the actual helicopter would have made it all the way to where he was standing if not for the shrouded ship.

The manmade structure around the Unidentified Stranded Object rocked violently and then burst into flames. Several workers fell or jumped away from the skeletal framework, plummeting towards the hard-baked ground below. Heavy plastic tarpaulins caught fire and shriveled against the metal posts to which they were anchored. The crude structure fell apart as another explosion occurred on the far side of the vessel. Scaffoldings over a hundred feet tall fell towards the shore, carrying burning plastic and at least one man in black armor.

The four 'copters of the Apocalypse lifted back into the air, silently moving past the wreckage and back to their landing spots. A small army of Colonel Anderson's storm-troopers erupted from the tents, moving as quickly as their armor allowed. They stopped at the edge of the lake. Far below, several of their comrades lay broken on the ground. Despite the terrifying heights from which they'd fallen, a few of them were still moving.

Once again, Frank watched on as the soldiers did their thing. The crane setup they'd used earlier to lower materials into the lakebed was moved back into position. In less than five minutes, they had a squadron of men on the lakebed and moving towards their fallen brethren. At the same time, several of the soldiers strapped on massive backpacks with long hoses and moved to what was left of the Channel Seven heli-copter, blasting it with a thick white foam that extinguished the flames almost instantly.

Frank hunkered down and lit a cigarette, watching the show and ignoring the people around him. Part of him wanted to offer his aid, but he knew it would be refused. That and, while he hated to admit it, a part of him liked watching the bastards suffer.

Behind him, he heard the cold, efficient voice of Clip-board buzzing orders to the men below. He could not hear their replies, but he could hear the commands. He felt a heat bloom in his chest. Clipboard's voice irritated him more than he could ever hope to explain. The man was even more of an ass than Colonel Anderson, and everything about him made Frank angrier.

Down below, one of the soldiers was being lifted onto a canvas stretcher. Where he'd lain there was a pool of blood. Frank couldn't tell if the man was alive or dead. Suddenly the amusement he'd felt was gone, replaced by a strong sense of self-loathing. He turned to face Clipboard. The man was look-ing down towards the mess below.

Frank stood and stretched his legs for a second, forcing the blood back where it belonged. "Anything I can do to help?" He almost hated himself for asking, but it was a part of his nature that he simply couldn't deny. A part of why he'd become a cop in the first place.

Clipboard turned his helmet until the two glossy lenses
stared directly in his direction. "I appreciate the offer, Captain Osborn, but I believe we have the situation in hand." The
man's voice was still coldly efficient. Frank still hated him for
his attitude. "You might want to check on the civilians over
to my right, however. They shouldn't be standing that close to
the edge of the lake."

Frank nodded and turned away. He had known the offer
would be refused, so the attitude from Clipboard was about
what he expected. He walked the ten yards it took to reach
Mike Summers and the rest of the youngsters. "Y'all need to
get on back from the edge. Everything going on here, it might
collapse. Then those boys'd be dragging you out of that hole,
not other soldiers."

There must have been something in his attitude, because
the boys moved back without argument. All except Marty
Wander. He was still in the same spot, looking not at the
bodies below but at the spaceship.

"Marty." No response. "Marty!"

The boy looked at Frank for a few heartbeats before responding, his face showing surprise. "Huh? Oh, I'm sorry,
Officer Frank. Did you say something?"

"Yes I did. I said you need to get your butt away from the
edge before I drag it back to your daddy for a proper whuppin'."
Marty backpedaled as quickly as he could while he turned his
eyes back to the craft.

"Don't tell me you still haven't seen enough of that stupid
thing already, Marty."

"I...It's just I don't understand how it did that. That's all"

"Did what?" Frank felt a sudden chill settle into his backbone, and slowly turned to face the thing behind him.

"I don't understand how it changed its color."

The ship was still there, but it had changed. Just as Marty
said, the color was different. All the wet, oily markings floating

across the surface of the thing were gone. Where the ship had been dark before, it was now as clear and well-shined as the finest mirror. Somewhere along the way, the thing had decided to reflect back whatever light was thrown its way.

"Goddamn," he whispered. "The thing's like a chameleon. It's trying to hide itself."

Frank stared at the craft for a long time, contemplating a new aspect of the ship that he'd barely let himself ponder before. How had it changed color? Was that an automatic function of the ship? Or was it something done manually by whatever was inside the vessel? Was it possible that whatever had piloted the ship to Oldman's Lake was still *alive*?

He was still staring when the first of the bodies was removed from the lake.

Chapter Four

1

Frank waited until the chaos had died down before he tried talking to Anderson again. The man was obviously not happy—even with the environmental armor in place, Frank was learning to understand the Colonel's moods. Gestures and the way his body moved spoke volumes. Frank didn't care if the man was wallowing in shit or having a pizza just the way he liked it. He wanted a final answer, one way or the other.

He got his final answer, too. Not the one he wanted. Anderson did his best to explain that the bodies were a risk, but it didn't do him any good.

"You're under the impression that the people here would want the bodies of their families lifted out of the ground to prove that there was something in the lake," Frank retorted. "What you don't understand is that no one here gives a good fart about the ship. Weren't you paying attention earlier? You had kids playing in the park here, just like they've always done. They don't care that there's a goddamn alien spaceship sitting out there. They just want to get on with their lives."

"We had a few children playing out there. We also had four people with cameras and camcorders." The Colonel gestured to a large steel box at the edge of his desk. "They weren't out there to play games, Frank. They were out there to photograph the ship you say no one cares about. I know human nature, Captain. The people who are grieving today will be scheming in another few weeks. Money means more to most people than you think. So does fame. Don't think for an instant that Myrna Louis wouldn't give up a few night's sleep to get on *Sally Jesse Raphael*, because I know she would. So far,

I've confiscated two cameras and a tape recorder from her. I'm surprised she hasn't managed to wrangle up a Geiger counter."

Frank had to give him that one. "Myrna's the exception, not the rule. How can we be expected to leave those bodies with you and not protest, Colonel? Do you really think you'd take it as well if the men you lost today were stolen away from you and from their families?"

"You have a good argument, Frank, but I've got a better one. Acknowledging that my personal goal is complete protection of the national interests, which would you rather see: the bodies returned to the people of Collier? Or the Myrna Louises of this town executed because they can't be trusted? Those are pretty much my options here. I don't find the latter choice to be very viable, do you?"

"No. No, I suppose you're right on that one. I just don't think you're gonna convince the people of this town that you're in the right." Frank walked to the entrance of the tent just as the rain began to fall to the ground outside. The canvas of the tent took the drops of rain like a gentle tap on a drum. Soon the sound of a thousand beats filled the air. *The natives are getting restless, Bwana.* The thought crept into his skull with a life of its own. Frank bit the side of his mouth to avoid cracking into a smile. Somehow, Frank doubted Anderson would find the comment amusing. "I've done what I can to help you, Colonel, but I won't be the one to answer questions on your behalf about this one. You'd best appoint an answer man from your own ranks. I'll continue to do my best to keep the peace here, 'cause that's my job. But when it comes to the bodies we ain't gonna get to bury, I wash my hands of the matter."

Frank walked away, elated that he'd finally stood up to the Colonel, and simultaneously terrified that he'd hear a safety being released, followed by the gentle burping of the Colonel's rifle as the bullets tore through him. The fear was irrational, of course. So far, the Colonel had been very accommodating.

That didn't stop him from expecting the bullets to show up anyway. Probably nothing could do that. The bullets didn't riddle his body. He lived.

He made a brief stop at the office, explained the situation to Ricky Boggs, who was, for the present time, the night shift. Ricky nodded solemnly, and went back to watching the TV he'd rolled out of the evidence room. Frank went home.

A long shower helped work the tension from his body, at least until the warm water ran out. After that, a hasty retreat from the chilling stream of liquid testicle-shrinker was required. Frank turned on the TV and watched the news on CNN. He preferred to listen to the world's problem's today. Anything too close to home would be a disaster for his efforts to remain calm. After hearing the latest about the political chaos in Bosnia and the Middle East, the pretty blond anchorwoman went on to explain what little was known about the deaths of several cameramen, a pilot and a reporter who had tried to get pictures of the quarantined town of Collier, Georgia. Frank promptly changed the channel, settling for a syndicated episode of *Cheers*. Carla was verbally slamming Cliff, and Norm was moaning about his wife Vera. Sam was flirting with Rebecca and Woody was dressed as Mark Twain. Life was as it should be in the *Cheers* universe: stable. Frank fell asleep before the show was over.

2

The day started off sullen and overcast. That seemed woefully appropriate to Frank. One hundred and fifty-nine funeral services, all being performed at once. He stared at the long line of grave markers—made from wood and bearing the names of the dead in carefully burnt letters, as there were not enough markers at the local funeral home to accommodate a tenth of the victims—and sighed. So many dead.

If the number of markers was intimidating, the long list of mourners was truly phenomenal. If there was anyone from all of Collier who did not attend the ceremony, it was because they were locked away in the makeshift hospital. Even the least friendly members of the town's society were present, dressed in their Sunday best and listening to the words of the three men of God who handled the services. Separated from everyone else were all the townsfolk who were officially under arrest. Frank knew the Colonel would be pissed off, but he just didn't give a damn. *Let him be pissed. He'll get a taste of his own medicine for a change of pace.* All of Frank's small police force—those still alive after the wreck—were there with him. They looked as tired as he felt. There were a number of tourists and visitors there, too, over two hundred faces he did not recognize, standing amongst the faces he'd known for his entire life. They were trapped in Collier, same as everyone else.

Surrounding the area, at a discreet distance, were the soldiers who enforced Anderson's law. They were as still as statues. Frank moved his eyes around the area, ignoring the words of the ministers and the sounds of the mourners alike. He tried not to dwell on the faces that were not in attendance at the funeral, but it was difficult.

For no good reason, as it was wont to do, his mind moved away from where he was to dwell on Kathy. Somewhere in California she was likely with another man. Frank felt a sting of tears in his eyes and blinked them away. He'd be damned before he'd cry for her again. He looked up towards the cloud-painted heavens, and then back to the row of wooden headstones. Bethany Harper's name was etched on the one directly before him. Right next to the little girl's marker was one for her mother, Suzanne. Both of them dead, and old Wade Harper was locked away in the high school-*cum*-hospital. Frank wondered if he even knew he'd lost both of the girls in his life. Bobby Carlson, the entire Habersham family, the Newsomes, poor, demented George Harding, Alan Macafee, Edna Carter, Tom Walden...The list just went on and on, a list of people who'd never again be a part of Collier and of people who never even had a chance to become a part of the town.

Not far away, Linda Arminter held Billy Newsome in her
arms. The boy was sobbing, loud hiccuping bellows of grief,
for the loss of his entire family. Both of his parents and his
older brother, all killed in one fell swoop. When that much of
a family died in a traffic wreck, the newspapers and broad-
casts for half the continent mentioned the loss and let the
world mourn right alongside the survivors. Here in Collier,
poor Billy's overwhelming loss was swept under the carpet by
the Colonel and his people: a dirty little secret that no one
wanted shared.

The slow-burning anger in Frank's soul increased its intensity by a few thousand degrees. Linda Arminter was a good
woman, but she could not replace Billy's family. No boy that
age should suffer grief so intense. The boy should be playing
hide-and-seek with his friends, or going to the community pool
and swimming. He shouldn't be so alone. Even if he was
being cared for, his soul had to be hurting more than anyone's
ever should. Frank was feeling sorry for himself because his
wife had left him. Billy was feeling sorry because a freak disaster had torn away every reason he had for living.

Frank turned to look at the soldiers standing around the
gathering. He wasn't really surprised to see a lot of the
townsfolk were doing exactly the same thing. The rain finally
started to fall in Collier, and when it struck the ground it left
behind an outraged puff of steam with every drop that fell.
Somehow, that just felt right.

3

Frank's predictions about Collier's response to the imprisoned
bodies of the dead proved true. There was only so much grief
and aggravation that the people of Collier were willing to take.
For someone, that limit had finally been reached.

Frank was at home, doing what he could to relax—which
was not much—when the call came. The sound of the phone
was rapidly becoming an alien thing, and he actually let out a

squawk of surprise when the shrill ring erupted from the end-table. After collecting himself, he snatched the headset from its cradle. "This is Frank Osborn. How can I help you?"

"Frank?" It was Buck's voice, but he didn't sound his normal calm self. "Man, I'm glad I caught you. You need to get your ass down to the Miller's farm right damn now."

"Good to hear from you, too, Buck." He couldn't help the sarcasm. It just slipped out whenever he was caught off-guard. "What's the matter?"

"Frank, somebody killed one of Anderson's men."

Frank felt his blood turn to slush in his veins, and tried to collect his thoughts. "Shit. This ain't gonna be good."

"'Ain't gonna be' my ass" Buck snorted. "It's already a mess. Anderson's fit to be tied."

"They're out at the Miller farm?"

"Yeah, just past the back field. Must be a dozen soldiers, plus Anderson and his second-in-command."

"I'm there." Frank hung up the phone, marveling that Buck had managed to get him the information via the phone lines. So far he was the only one who'd had any semblance of luck with getting phone access. Frank pulled on the shoes he'd left near the door, and then he ran to the kitchen and slapped together a peanut butter and jelly sandwich. Doc Morrisey would be unhappy about his choice of meals, but Frank would worry about that later. Right now he had to get out to the farm before the shit really hit the fan.

Lights flashing and siren screaming through the night, Frank made his way to Walter Miller's farm in record time. Thanks to the curfew enforced by the soldiers, there was no one to get in his way. The long line of trees that surrounded the narrow dirt road leading to the farm was partially obscured by the heavy orange dust where someone had just passed. When he could see past the last of the oaks, he spotted a small gathering of Jeeps and Humvees painted to match the armored men who drove them. He pulled in behind three of the black vehicles, blocking the exit for two of them. Up ahead, he could see the armored silhouettes of a dozen or more men. Their lights were all concentrated in one area.

Frank walked to join the gathering, feeling like the only person wearing jeans at a black-tie party. He shouldn't have felt alone. The figure strapped into the razor-wire fencing put up by Anderson's men was dressed only in his underwear and blood.

The man had probably been handsome once, but the crimson stains and the gaping wound where his neck should have been marred his young, classic features. His mouse-brown hair was matted to his scalp by drying perspiration, and there were creases on his face from the environmental gear that Anderson insisted all his men wear. Despite the lowered angle of the man's head, Frank could still see the pained rictus that marred the cadaver's features even more. His bare legs were spread far apart, and deep lacerations ran from his ankles to the middle of his thighs, where he had been planted deep in the razor-wire. Both of his hands had also been buried in the tangles of steel and blades. Despite the lacerations running down to the bones of his fingers, there was little blood.

Carved into the dead man's chest were four simple words: GET OUT OF TOWN.

Frank continued to stare at the corpse, until Anderson blocked his view. "You have any ideas about who might have done this, Captain?" All pretenses at pleasantry were gone from the man's voice. Frank's first name had been forgotten, and he'd been placed back into his role as police chief.

"My guess is about three quarters of Collier probably wanted to, especially after today. But I can't even begin to guess who actually committed the crime."

Anderson sighed. "I know all about how you feel regarding the funeral. My question is, do you know who did this?"

Frank looked at his own reflection in the smoky glass lenses covering the man's eyes. "No. I don't."

"Do you know who was capable?"

Frank looked at the dead man again, studying the ground around him. There were numerous footprints, but not all of them were wearing combat boots. "I'm guessing that he wasn't killed here. Where was he stationed?"

"About a mile down the road. We've got people looking there for signs of a struggle." The Colonel paused for only a moment, then he asked another question. "What makes you sure he wasn't killed here?"

"There ain't nearly enough blood around his wounds. His arms and legs are cut to hell and back, but there ain't a puddle growing under his body. Also, his armor's gone. I don't know how long it takes you to get into that shit, but I'd guess it took about fifteen minutes to peel him out of it. A lot of your stuff dowsn't have the usual buckles and latches."

"So who around town has the necessary skills to manage what was done here?"

"Damn near every person over the age of ten."

"Excuse me?'

"This is a small town, Colonel. The laws don't quite work the same way down here that they do in places like Atlanta or New York. Every kid over the age of nine has at least one knife, and most of them have been on a hunting trip or two." Frank paused and reached for the cigarettes in his shirt pocket, cursing silently when he remembered that they were on the coffee table in front of his TV. "About half the girls in town go hunting too. It's part of what we do here in the autumn. Ain't many kids above nine or ten years old who can't gut a fish or skin a squirrel in under a minute."

"It had to be someone with experience," interjected the Colonel.

"Why?"

"They knew just where to strike. There aren't a lot of vulnerable spots on these suits of ours."

"Bullshit."

"What?"

"I said, 'Bullshit.'" Frank looked the Colonel over, shrugging. "I can count about ten vulnerable spots just with a glance. Your suits ain't all that special."

"How do you figure?"

"You got joints. Every joint on your body is covered by...what? Heavy denim and a little rubber? Whatever it is, it ain't armor. Seems pretty obvious to me that someone just snuck up behind your soldier over there and drove a knife into his throat. It's what I would have done in the same situation. What any decent soldier would have done if all he had to use as a weapon was a knife."

The Colonel was silent, and his stance rigid, but he slowly nodded his head. "How many people in town have worked in the military?"

"Anderson, there's about five boys in all of Collier over the age of eighteen that haven't been in the Army or Marines. We still believe in doing a tour of duty around these parts. The only ones that didn't serve are the ones the military wouldn't take."

Anderson remained silent. Frank spoke up. "You want me to do a formal investigation into this matter?"

"No. Thank you just the same. This is a matter for my own investigators."

"Yeah. I figured it was something like that." Frank moved back towards his car. "If I can help, just say the word."

"That I will, Captain. That I will."

Frank drove away, stopping at the Piggly Wiggly to buy a carton of cigarettes and a new four-pack of Bic lighters. The store was open, despite the curfew, and there were a few people shopping. Frank almost reminded them that they were in violation of the Colonel's martial law, but shrugged the idea away. They knew. Why insult their intelligence?

In the line behind him, Peter Donovan was purchasing what had to be every single bottle of bleach in the entire store. Frank knew the man wasn't a fanatic for cleaning, but he was simply too tired to care what Donovan was up to. He paid for his

groceries and then he drove home. Morning would be soon
enough to deal with any of the troubles around town.

Frank Osborn was tired. He was tired of trying to keep
the peace, and he was tired of Anderson's condescending attitude. Mostly though, he was tired in his heart and in his mind.
Frank smoked two cigarettes down to the filter and then he
passed out. When the sun came up again, his whole world was
busily working its way into a downward spiral to hell.

Interlude

1

Life in Collier changed very quickly. On the Fourth of July, the city was celebrating. On the fifth the people were confused and stunned into silence. Even the most volatile citizens in town could hardly make a noise above a whisper. It had more to do with shock than it did with fear. On the sixth of July, the people started recovering. By the seventh almost everyone was once again capable of thinking rationally and most were thoroughly enraged by their situation.

Still, the town was mostly quiet. The anger they felt remained bottled within, a storm that was starting to build but one not quite ready to break. The signs were there, but the air was still too calm for any real explosions.

The death of Corporal Dean Henderson, late of Alabama, did not calm the tensions in the air. It only made matters worse. For the first time since the soldiers had arrived, they were actually on guard. Despite the overwhelming heat of the day, they stood taller in their dark armored suits. Their rifles were held a little tighter in their hands. Most importantly, their once almost frozen forms moved with a current of barely contained anxiety. They had learned the hard way that the people of Collier could bite back.

While the men from Project ONYX were learning that lesson in the early hours of July seventh, most of the people in Collier were asleep. There were exceptions, of course.

Marty Wander and his best friend, Mike Summers, were sneaking away from the Wanders' home, all but carrying their bikes until they were well away from the house. Marty's dad would surely have skinned them alive if he'd known what they were up to. They were lucky, however, and the man slept through the night. Marty's dad was one of those people whose business was mostly unaffected by the thing in the lake. Grass still grew and the people of Collier still wanted their lawns maintained. Wander Landscaping had gone back into full swing just after the funerals ended the day before. As owner of the company, Jack Wander led by example: he only got home around eight thirty in the evening. By ten he was asleep.

Marty and Mike rode the dark streets and slipped between the shadows with the confidence and ease of early youth. They weren't afraid of the guards posted everywhere. The soldiers were just another obstacle to sneak past. Though the trek was arduous, they managed to reach their destination after only half an hour of stop-and-start riding. The close calls with the soldiers only added to their combined sense of excitement.

The boys came to a stop in the woods on the far side of what remained of the docks. From where they stood, they could see the Colonel's tent and the massive blade of the ship resting in the lake's bed. Just as they were arriving, the Colonel and about fifty of his soldiers ran from the tent to the row of Jeeps parked on Roswell Avenue not far away.

"Whaddaya think they're doin'?" Marty asked as the boys crouched low.

"Probably going off to bust a few heads. Seems like that's all they're good for." Mike sounded bitter, and Marty couldn't blame him. After all, Mike was separated from his family as a result of the Colonel and his soldiers. That was really why Mike was here tonight, to rectify that situation.

The unofficial competition between Mike and Marty had escalated to its greatest levels ever. Mike was going to try to escape the boundaries of Collier and find his folks. Marty was going after a different goal. Marty wanted to see the UFO. Not at a distance either, he wanted to touch the thing.

All his life, Marty'd held a special fascination for UFOs and all the myths surrounding them. If a show about strange lights in the sky came on, he was glued to the area in front of the television. The only books he didn't have on the subject were the ones printed before his eighth birthday—and then only if he couldn't track them down. Simply put, Marty Wander knew more about UFOs than just about any kid on the planet. It was one of the great disappointments of his life that he'd never managed to get himself abducted by aliens.

He also knew that he could rectify that error. The ship out in Oldman's Lake was enough to convince him of that. The ship was a sign, his destiny in action. William Woody, a lifelong resident of Roswell, New Mexico, had stated more than once that he actually saw the UFO they'd found out there before it crashed. He'd seen it on July Fourth, 1947. Fifty years to the day before the ship crashed in Lake Oldman. And what was the name of the street closest to where the UFO had landed? Why, it was Roswell Avenue. That was simply too much to be a coincidence in Marty's mind. That was a sign. His time had come. Surely the aliens were here to pick him up. They just hadn't landed as well as they might have hoped.

Mike thought Marty was nuts. The feeling was mutual. Mike was going to have to get past not only the guards, but the razorwire fence. All Marty had to do was get past the guards, a feat he'd already accomplished. Now it was just a simple ride down the dried banks of the lake—which were, thankfully, not as steep here as they were near the Colonel's tent—and he'd be home free. Mike had miles to go before he could hope to be free of the Colonel and his men.

They'd gone out after the funerals and they'd looked around for the best possible trail to take. What they had discovered was that there was no trail. There was only a long list of obstacles to be avoided. The scariest one for Mike was the razorwire, which stood taller than he was and was densely packed enough to give a squirrel a hard time. The blades on the wire seemed to grin brightly in the daylight hours, inviting all to touch its pretty edges, while waiting to carve through flesh. When they'd reached the endless fence of wire, Marty pulled his battered old leather wallet from his back pocket and ran the folded edge across one of the blades. He'd used very little pressure, but the blade had cleaved the leather it touched in half with no effort. Now Mike was carrying wire cutters, and he had a sweatshirt wrapped around his waist and gardening gloves tucked into his pants. Marty doubted these extra precautions would be enough.

"Looks like now's the best chance we'll have." Mike's voice was soft, almost sad. The tone of his friend's words brought Marty back to the here and now.

"Listen, you better be safe out there. Don't let none of them guards take you down."

Mike smiled, and for a second Marty understood how Tom Thornton seemed to feel whenever he looked at the two of them together. For one brief instant, Mike looked like a god. Untouchable and unstoppable. "Ain't nothin' gonna happen to me, Marty. Just you be careful if you run into any of them aliens."

"Hell. They're probably all jelly inside of that ship. Way that sucker hit, I don't much think anything could have lived."

"'Less they started out thataway. Then they're gonna be jelly with an attitude."

"Tell your mom and dad hey for me."

Mike smiled again, and reached out to punch Marty on the shoulder. Marty felt a heavy dread, knew in his heart that the two of them would never be together again. He resisted the urge to give his best friend a hug. Last thing he wanted was Mike thinking he'd gone faggot on him or something.

"Be careful." He returned Mike's shoulder punch.

"Like hell." Mike snorted, then mounted his bike and wheeled off towards the far side of the lake. Away from the town and all the soldiers.

Marty waited until Mike was completely out of sight, then climbed aboard his own bike. The Huffy was in great condition; he'd checked it earlier that day to make sure the tires were inflated and the chain was properly oiled. Just the same, the ride down into the lake's bed was far rougher than he'd expected. The bike bucked and jumped, trying to throw him, but Marty held on. He stood tall on the pedals of the dirt bike, never letting his body connect with the seat. Long years of practice had taught the best way to avoid busting your balls while traveling at high speed was to make sure that nothing got near them. The speed of the trip was not as exhilarating as it usually was; the thought that Mike might get himself killed toned down Marty's usual enthusiasm.

Up ahead of him, the monolithic ship towered higher than any building in the entire town. From this distance, and actually lower than the rim of the thing, the ship's size was mind-boggling.

Marty stopped while he was still a good hundred yards away. From where he was, the straight climb of the lake's side up to the trench where the fused sand had been—what should have been the water's edge—completely blocked his view of the Colonel's command post. If anyone was up there watching him, he could see no sign of them. The ground was hard and sun-baked. It was rough, but he could walk across the surface with no real difficulty. The overcast night made his eyes work harder, but there was really no concern about seeing where he was going. Marty's eyes had long since adjusted to the darkness.

As he walked closer to the ship, Marty encountered the debris from the helicopter that had crashed. There was little to find; most of it had been picked up by the soldiers as soon as they had finished carrying away their companions who'd fallen to their deaths or broken their bodies inside the hard armor they wore. A few pieces of melted plastic and bent metal were all he saw. But they did not interest him. Marty approached the ship with a reverence at least as great as that he held for church. He was stunned by the size of the craft and mesmerized by its proximity.

How many stars had the ship passed on its way to earth? Had it run across other life forms in its travels? Did the creatures flying the vessel come in peace, or were they prepared for war? Those thoughts and a thousand more ran through Marty's mind as he moved closer and closer to the gigantic structure.

From almost a hundred feet away, he could feel the air
around him change as he approached. There was a physical
aura of energy, not unlike the static charge surrounding a TV
screen, that pushed against him. He stepped over and past a
dozen buckled girders, feeling no real remorse for the men
who had died while trying to hide the starcraft. For the moment, the burnt smell of plastic and the ruined metal beams
were of no consequence. After years of dreaming about seeing a UFO in person, Marty was finally about to touch one.

Marty stepped forward, pushing his way into the field of
power he felt around the ship. Instantly the air around him
became almost painfully dry, even as his hair stood on end.
He was uncomfortably hot, but did not care. Nothing was as
important as the confirmation of his beliefs. From barely a
dozen feet away, he looked at the edge of the metallic wall
where it drove deep into the ground. There were no flaws to
show that the ship had ever suffered a heavy impact. The
seamless, mirrored hide of the craft ran flush with the baked
silt of the lake, as it if had grown from the center of the earth
all the way to the lake's edge.

Marty, uncomfortable and aware that the freshly healing
burns on his face were beginning to sting again, walked along
the side of the structure looking for any indication that an
entrance into the craft existed. When he could find none, he
finally gathered his courage and reached out to touch the metal,
fully prepared to feel his flesh crisp as a result of the ship's
heat. Instead he felt an intense cold, strong enough to bring a
shiver to him. The glistening surface of the ship was as cool
as the interior of the meat freezer in his family's garage and as
smooth as a freshly washed windowpane.

Marty had expected to see pit-marks where a thousand
different rocks had smashed into the ship as it traveled between worlds. There was not a single scratch to mar the
perfect surface of the craft. A deep vibration ran from his
hand into the rest of his body, a constant hum that almost
masked a secondary vibration. An oscillation not unlike the

pulse of a heart. After several seconds of merely touching the metal, Marty lifted his hand and rapped smartly on the surface. He could hear no ringing echo, could feel not the slightest hint that he had made any impact on the vessel. He had almost expected the ship to be built from metal as thin as a piece of paper. Too many science fiction movies had led him to believe that the alien technology would make a thick hull unnecessary. To reconfirm that the exterior was extremely thick, or at least very dense, Marty placed his left hand against the metal and struck the surface again, as hard as his hand would allow, exactly five times. No vibration reached his left hand.

Marty felt a wave of disappointment run through his system. There was nothing magical about the craft, except for the crash landing itself. There were no hidden truths etched into the hull of the ship, nor any markings of any type that he could copy down and try to translate. His depression couldn't have been greater if he'd found a MADE IN TAIWAN tag on the underbelly of the ship.

Worst of all, there was no fragment of the ship that he could take with him as a souvenir. He had no evidence that he'd touched the ship, no trophy to show to Tom Thornton, or Mike if—*no*, he scolded himself, *when*—he came back. Marty started to turn away from the spaceship, but stopped when something caught his eye. Where he'd been standing before, where his hand had rested on the craft, there was a small line that had not been there a moment ago. Marty approached the mark as if it might try to bite him. The line was not merely a scratch across the surface, however. Marty could plainly see that the perfect line was a seam.

Eagerly he ran his fingers across the slight indentation. His heart pounded as he felt along the seam's edge, and touched the precision of the magical flaw in the previously perfect metal. He struck the metal again, just at the edge of the seam. Still he heard no echo, felt no vibration. Disappointed, he turned away again. They'd just have to believe him, that was all.

Marty had only taken a few steps when the light suddenly flared to life behind him. One instant he was lifting his foot and stretching his leg beyond a ruined girder, the next his shadow appeared on the ground, surrounded by a yellow-green glow.

Heart thundering in his chest, Marty turned to face the spacecraft again. Eyes no longer used to any illumination protested as he stared at the light, which seemed almost as bright as the sun. Nearly blinded, Marty stumbled towards the source of the light.

A few moments later, the dogs in the area began to bark frantically, and birds erupted from their nests, desperate to escape the sounds they heard. The flaring green light that painted the area where Marty had been a moment ago faded disappeared as suddenly as it had come into existence.

2

Dewett Hammil moved as quietly as his old body would let him, which was not as silently as he had moved in his youth. In his time he'd been able to sneak just about anywhere he wanted, with little fear of being heard or seen, despite his size. He'd been limber enough to crouch almost to the ground, and strong enough to maintain the awkward position for a very long time.

Those days were long in his past. Now his knees popped like firecrackers whenever he stood up or sat down, and his legs didn't have the sort of stamina they'd had when he was fit and ready for combat duty. The night was on his side at least. Night or day had never made any difference to Dewett. Collier was an old and trusted friend, and one that had never let him down, regardless of how late the hour. Old age, he knew, had taken a harsh toll on his ability to sneak past anything at all. Still, he was a man with a mission, and he knew exactly what he had to do.

Despite his own misgivings about his physical abilities, Dewett managed to slip past the line of sawhorses with no effort at all. Hell, his knees only popped once, and his bad left knee had the decency not to go sour on him, which it was wont to do ever since Korea. After the wooden barrier, it was only a few hundred feet to his store. He made it all the way inside without a single joint betraying him.

Once inside—a task made easier by the fact that them military bastards hadn't fixed the broken glass door, thank you Uncle Sam—Dewett moved to the back room, where he kept the dry goods. The soldiers must have been doing something right, because the foodstuffs he stored there were untouched. Moving around in the darkened kitchen was hardly an effort. For over thirty years, Dewett had baked and sweated every morning away back here, making bread and cakes and sweets for a good portion of Collier's population. When his eye had started going bad on him, he'd just pretended everything was fine, and started working the area by memory. It wasn't until he failed his driver,s license renewal that he finally broke down and got himself a pair of spectacles. That meant about three years he'd gone with eyes bad enough to make a bat happy with its own sight.

He found the chocolate chips on the first try, and used his massive hands to scoop a good ten pounds of the semi-sweet morsels into a heavy-duty garbage bag. That done, he located the crushed pecans and did the same thing again. Lastly he hit the walnuts, which were a fine complement to the pecans. He only took around five pounds of walnuts, though, because this batch was a little on the bitter side.

Dewett grasped all three bags in his right hand, and flicked his wrist a few times, until the bags had spun together into one large bundle. He ignored the pain in his arm and swung the package Santa Claus-style over his shoulder. With a last look around the darkened kitchen, he slipped back towards the front of the bakery, ready to head home and start baking.

The problem was simply that he could not sleep. He hadn't been able to get a good night's rest since the satellite smashed into the lake. Fifty-five years of bending his back to hard labor every day except Christmas was a hard thing to get away from, and not doing anything was starting to make Dewett fidgety. Since he'd given up drinking a long time ago and he couldn't stand the idea of using any of those crazy sleep pills, he only had one option. He had to work, or he'd go insane. Just a few sheets of cookies a night, that would surely be enough to handle the problem. At least he hoped they would. He'd give the cookies to Frank Osborn and them paramedics. They'd certainly earned the chance to munch on a few sweets, what with everything they'd done since the whole mess started.

So he'd waited until late in the night before sneaking away from his house, and then he'd walked the entire mile and a half from his place to the bakery, praying to God Almighty that his knee would not betray him halfway there. Now, he was on ready to head home, and he prayed that his bum knee would not decide to crumble under him on the way back.

Dewett wondered if Angela had noticed his absence yet. She was a sweet woman, his Angela, but she could get mighty angry if the situation warranted. He hoped she was still asleep and not waiting for him like she had when they first got married. Back then, he'd been a damned fool, set in his ways and unwilling to give as much as an inch. (Not that he was much better these days, but where Angela was concerned, he'd wised up a good forty years ago.) He'd go out to the Whittaker farm and suck back the hooch along with a few of the other men in town and drink most of the night away. Nine times out of ten, Angela was awake and waiting when he came home.

She'd never say a word when he actually stumbled through the door. She just sat there, drinking down a glass of iced tea, or another cup of coffee with about ten spoons too many of sugar. She'd just sit there and watch him with lovely dark eyes grown even darker, and then she'd go to bed. The few times he tried getting frisky in that state, she'd walloped him upside his fool head and moved off to sleep on the couch. Or if she was feeling particularly bitter about his attitude, sent him to sleep on the couch.

It was always the next morning when she made her displeasure known. Just as soon as the sun was up, she'd be there with a frying pan in one hand and a metal spoon in the other, banging the two together in a loud ringing racket. For the rest of the day, so long as he was in the house at least, she would berate him endlessly, making every imaginable noise to get his attention. More than half the time, she'd make comments about his family history, and about how foolish she'd been to marry a man who had no good sense.

Dewett had avoided that sort of confrontation for almost four decades now, and he intended to keep it that way. Angela might not believe in violence, but she could surely make him suffer if she saw fit to do so. Old Herbert Whittaker used to make fun of him, called him a fool for letting his wife treat him that way. Dewett wasn't a fool, though, and he knew it. After all, it wasn't his wife that left when things went sour at the farm, it was Herb's wife. Besides which, he'd been raised by his mother and his mother alone, after the local white boys had decided they didn't like the way his father looked. Marcus Hammil had been hog-tied and dragged behind a horse until he died, his sin being that he owned land. After his daddy's death, his mother made sure to raise him properly, and in his momma's eyes that meant he wasn't ever to strike a woman in anger. He had learned the lesson well.

In all their years as a couple, Dewett had never raised a hand to Angela. A good thing too, 'cause she'd likely have waited for him to go to sleep and then cut his manhood away from him for his trouble. Back then there was so much wood near Lake Oldman that she could have dumped his body and never fretted it being found. Provided she could have moved his oversized corpse.

He was almost home and that was a good thing, because his knee was making more and more threats that it might give out on him. Even from two blocks away, he could see the porch light was lit in front of the small house he'd bought outright three years after he opened the bakery. Angela was up, and he could fairly well see her sitting at the kitchen table, reading one of her romance novels and sipping away at her iced tea. No way she'd choose coffee this time of year; it was just too damned hot, even this late at night.

Dewett sighed mightily, prepared to face a night of silence and a day of harping. He deserved it. He should have left a note.

He needn't have worried himself over the matter. The man in the black armor saw fit to stop him from reaching the door. One second the street was clear, and the next there was a dark form with glittering bug eyes standing in front of him. Dewett's eyes had long since adjusted to the night, and he could see that it was one of them soldiers who'd come to town. He could even make out the weapon in the man's hands. A lethal-looking thing it was, too. Dewett suspected the war overseas would have ended a lot faster if he'd been armed with one of those nasty looking rifles. He surely would have never had but one run-in with the local Klansmen, and he would have bet on that.

Around the same time the barrel of the soldier's weapon pointed at Dewett's face, he realized he was in a bit of trouble. The soldier's words just helped to confirm his suspicions. "It's well past curfew. What are you doing out here?"

"I surely didn't mean no trouble, sir. I just needed a few things from my bakery." Dewett flinched as a powerful beam of light washed over his face.

"What's your name?"

"My name is Dewett Hammil, sir. I just live right over there, in the green house with the porch light on."

"Mister Hammil, are you aware that you are violating the curfew imposed under the martial law placed on Collier?"

"Yes sir. I just wanted to get some things from my bakery."

"You couldn't handle that matter during daylight hours?"

Dewett smiled sheepishly, shaking his head. He was embarrassed and more than a touch nervous. "Nossir. I ain't been allowed into the bakery since that thing fell in the lake."

"Why did you feel it necessary to go there now?"

"I just felt the need to bake some cookies, sir. And I didn't figure I'd have the money to go to the store for the ingredients."

"What's in the bag, Mister Hammil?"

Dewett swung the bundle off his shoulder without a second's hesitation, letting the spun together ends of the bags unweave and separate. "I got some chocolate chips, some pecans and some walnuts. Can't make my special cookies without 'em."

"Set the bags down and step back."

Dewett did as he was told. A moment later, the barrel of the man's rifle was lifting the edge of one bag and the light that had settled on his face was moved to examine the contents. While Dewett waited, the man repeated the examination into each of the bags.

Eventually the soldier grew tired of looking around inside the bags. He stepped back and retrained his rifle on Dewett, along with the bright light. Dewett felt his pulse slow down a bit, and realized he'd been holding his breath.

"Mister Hammil, I'm going to overlook this little incident. But for your own safety, do not leave your house after curfew again, do I make myself clear?"

"Yessir."

"My orders are to shoot first and ask questions later. Lucky for you I can't quite bring myself to do that. But I'm not always posted in the same place. If I were you, I'd stay inside from now on. Cookies aren't worth your life."

"Yessir. Thank you, sir." Dewett was as polite as the Queen of England herself. He reached down and grabbed his bags, wrapping them around one massive fist. He wanted to yell at the man in the armor for taking that tone with him.

He also wanted to kiss the man's feet for letting him live.

Dewett walked the rest of the way to his front porch without a single breath escaping his lips. During the part of the trip where he could see the soldier, Dewett also saw the barrel of the man's rifle tracking him. Any wrong move would make him one dead fool. His bum knee throbbed hotly beneath his skin, threatening to pop out of place and send him falling to the ground. Dewett Hammil had no doubt in his mind that even something as simple as tripping would be enough to make certain that he never got up again. His heart thundered in his chest, and he prayed to God Almighty that his ticker wasn't going to give out on him. Every step was an exercise in self-control like few he'd ever endured. Because every step closer to his home and his wife seemed far too slow, and he didn't dare run. Sweat fell into his eyes, and clammy perspiration painted a mustache over his trembling lips.

Dewett opened the door to his house and slipped past the threshold at a speed that, under other circumstances, might have changed his mind about not being able to move as quickly as in his youth. No sooner did he close the door than his bad knee finally decided to go south. Dewett fell to the floor with a thud that shook his wife's collection of knickknacks half off the shelves. He lay there for what seemed a very long time, sucking in great heaving breaths of air and reveling in the familiar smells of Angela's cooking.

When he dared look up, Angela's legs filled his field of vision. Behind the *Just Where The Hell Have You Been* look she cast his way, he could see the deep love and concern she had for him. Dewett stood up, and behind his wife he could see the mostly empty glass of iced tea sitting on the table in a puddle of its own sweat.

"Dewett Alexander Hammil," Angela started, her voice shaking with suppressed emotion. "I thought I'd broke you of staying out to all hours a long time ago. You had me worried near to death."

Dewett smiled, the fear in his soul replaced by the love he felt for Angela. His long, thick arms snaked around her, and he rested his mouth and nose against the top of her head, breathing in her scent and reveling in her presence. "God love ya, Angie, you did. I just forgot for a little while."

She pulled away a little, looking into his eyes and seeing something that made her smile. "You know that if I catch you sneaking out again I'm gonna whomp you on top of your old fool head, don't you?"

"Angie, darlin', I wouldn't have it any other way."

That night Dewett slept as well as he ever had. When he awoke the next day, he started baking cookies. He never told anyone about how deeply the ingredients for making those cookies had affected his life, but Dewett never again snuck out of the house. Somewhere along the journey, he'd decided that Collier was still an old and dear friend, but one he preferred to encounter in the daylight hours.

3

Peter Donovan sat in the massive entertainment room of Lucas Brightman's house and sucked down another mouthful of beer. His left hand rested on the massive oak table in front of his plush chair, and his right hand cradled his bottle of Samuel Adams with easy familiarity. (Let the Yankees call it ale, the shit still tasted like beer to him. Gave him the same sort of pleasant buzz, too.)

The room spanned the entire length and width of Brightman's oversized mansion, taking the entire basement as its domain. Dark wood paneling and a crimson carpet seemed to swallow most of the light, leaving the place in a sort of perpetual twilight. Off towards the back of the room a full-size billiards table demanded a great deal of space. The built-in bar that covered one wall made the immense area seem smaller. At present only one of the three large tables in the room was occupied. Pete and his buddies were playing poker there, leaving the overstuffed couch and chairs ignored by everyone. The room was quiet, but the feeling was casual.

Across the table from him, Joe Ditweiller was still concentrating on the hand of cards wavering before his face. Joe was about a bottle shy of sliding his fat ass to the floor and passing out. He never could hold his liquor, and Pete always felt that was the first sign of a weak man.

Judd Fitzwater was to Pete's left, smiling like the cat that swallowed the canary. That was a sure sign Judd was bluffing the hand he held. The man couldn't bluff any better than his father, the Honorable Asshole In Charge of The Town. You could just barely see a family resemblance if you were drunk enough and squinted your eyes, assuming that father and son were in a poorly lit room and at least ten feet apart. Judd was damn huge in comparison to his dad. Easily a full foot taller, and built like a man instead of a donut. Where his father's head was mostly bald, Judd had a full mane he kept a little too long and slicked against his skull. Damn near looked like Dracula that way, but no one ever told his as much. Where old Milo's face was as round a fat girl's butt, Judd's looked like it was roughly carved from granite. Pete still figured ol' Judd's mom must have been getting her satisfaction on the side. No way did the runt they called mayor have anything to do with Judd's gene pool. Pete had even said as much to Judd once, after drinking a few too many. Judd had settled the matter by taking one of his size-fourteen shitkickers and planting it firmly in Pete's testicles. Just after that, he'd mopped the floor with Pete for about an hour and left a few scars under Pete's hair-line. They'd been best friends ever since. Funny how that shit worked out. They had nothing in common, not even their political views, but they were as tight as brothers.

Burt Ditweiller was a lost cause. He was fast asleep and snoring loud enough to wake the dead. That was okay; Herb Cambridge had taken his place at the poker table and was winning everybody's earnings.

Pete looked at his own cards and decided the time had come to fold. He'd lost enough money for one night, and he was a man who knew when to cut his losses.

"That's it for me, boys. I'm gonna go crash." Pete stood and drank down the last drops of his fancy Yankee beer. The guest room was just through the doors on the right, past the two pool tables Brightman had set up for when he wanted to have the boys over.

Judd looked away from his cards and nodded, Joe might have nodded, but if he did Pete couldn't tell the difference from what the fool's head had been doing for the last ten minutes. Herb Cambridge lowered his cards, looking very serious and just a little pale. Tonight had been a first for him. "You think they found the body yet, Pete?"

"If they didn't, I don't guess they're tryin' very hard. We left it where it could be found."

"I don't want to know any more about whatever you assholes are talkin' about." Judd's voice rumbled from his chest, a full two octaves lower than it normally was. "I'm here to play some goddamn poker, not to hear what you dumb fucks did to anyone. You understand me?" Judd had not been involved in the killing. Despite his size and the violence he'd done in his youth, he did not believe in hurting anyone. He sure as hell didn't condone murder.

"Not a problem, buddy. We didn't do shit and you ain't heard a damn thing." Pete's voice was calm. He knew Judd would never tell anyone what he'd heard. Judd knew all about most of what the group did. He knew where every body was buried. He just never spoke of the matters and expected not to hear about them. Never failed, soon as one of the boys started drinking, Judd heard about everything anyway. He always said the same thing, and after that everyone shut the hell up. Judd was too damn mean to be a pacifist for long and he really did his best to remain neutral where his friends' illegal hobbies were concerned. By Judd's philosophy, what he didn't know couldn't come back to haunt anyone. The boys all respected that.

"That's damn right. I don't know shit. Keep it that way."

"You got it, Judd." Pete smiled and nodded again before going off to the bed that called to him with a siren's song. He was tired, and he needed his rest. Tomorrow the boys had a few more things to set right, and Pete intended to be rested when the slaughter began anew.

4

Major Steve Hawthorne sat down on one of the collapsible chairs in the command tent and listened. He listened to Mark Anderson's silence, and he waited for the explosion.

There would be an explosion; of that he was certain. Mark was a good commander, certainly one of the best, but he was only human. Steve knew how much the operation pained his friend, and knew that sooner or later Mark would go a little crazy, would vent steam just to keep his sanity. Hawthorne looked over to where his helmet and clipboard rested, contemplating again how best to escape before Anderson blew his top.

They were cowardly thoughts, but he couldn't avoid them. Just as he understood that he really had no choice but to wait for the tirade and endure it. It came with the territory.

"I can't believe these assholes." Anderson's voice was tightly controlled, a bare whisper. The remaining fuse for his temper began to burn.

"How's that, Mark?" Innocence in his voice, like he didn't know what was coming. He could taste his stomach acids in the back of his throat.

"I've done everything I could to avoid having to hurt anyone. Anyone. And these backwater little redneck bastards kill one of my men." Anderson's voice was a little louder now, and his teeth were clenched behind bared lips.

"It almost had to happen, Mark. We were warned by Calloway that there would likely be heavy resistance."

"I expected resistance, Steve. Not cold-blooded murder." Mark ran his hand across his silvery burr-cut. His eyes stared out into nowhere, and the color in his face slowly started darkening. "I didn't expect them to cut a man apart. That's where I made my first mistake."

"So the question is, what are we gonna do about it?"

Mark looked at him like he'd look at a pile of feces on the ground. Steve decided it was a good time to keep his mouth shut. "Increase the curfew limitations. No one found walking the streets after sunset gets to play anymore. Only Osborn and his men get to move around at night. Anyone else is dead. I don't care if it's an old lady walking her poodle. Shoot to kill, ask questions later. No excuses this time. I know they've been going shopping after curfew. No more. Close down the stores, and if they don't want to close, chain the doors on them."

Steve grabbed his clipboard, immediately scratching down notes to himself. Anderson continued. "I want a list of known troublemakers from Osborn. I want it ASAP." Anderson walked away from the desk, his hands moving constantly and his whole body wound tight. "This shit stops now. No more friendly behavior to the locals, and no more bending over backwards to make them feel comfy. They want to kill my men? Fine. I can return the favor."

"Anything else, Colonel?"

"Yeah. One more thing. Get some sleep. I'm not taking out my anger on you today, Steve. I don't have the time to get angry."

Steve smiled and nodded, reaching for his helmet. Sometimes life was good.

5

Daylight came into Collier with a heavy, warm sigh. The air was too thick and already the temperature had passed the eighty-degree mark. The only people unaffected by the intense heat were the children, who, through the miracle of childhood, always seemed capable of ignoring blistering heat and intense cold alike in the pursuit of a good time.

On Bud Markle's farm, even his champion pit bulls were lazy and panting. The most any of them would manage when he called to them was a wag of the tail and apologetic eyes that said "Sorry, Bud, but it's too damned hot and I'm having trouble with mustering enthusiasm. Perhaps you could try me later?" Bud himself was stewing in his own sweat, and doing his best to ignore that he needed to take a shower, if only so he'd stop offending his own senses.

Bud sat at the top of his porch stairs, staring out at the road beyond his front yard. There were a lot of soldiers in their spiffy black uniforms over on the other side of the road, where Jesse Miller's boy now did his best to keep up with growing peaches. None of the soldiers had so much as looked over towards Bud and that suited him just fine.

Bud figured the men in those black uniforms were probably nice enough folk, but they were nice folk with too many weapons and a license to kill. That, and he just plain resented being told what he could or could not do by anybody. Hadn't liked being told what to do when he was a young 'un, and he hated it now.

The soldiers were also bad for business. It was damned hard to make extra money selling a little weed or powder to the kids in town when they couldn't leave their houses late at night and sneak over. Hell, most of the folk in town probably needed repairs on their cars by now, but they weren't likely to come out to Bud's garage to get them, not since that damned Texaco up and sprouted a garage last year. He scratched at his belly, contemplating how best to handle the problem. Bud didn't sell a lot of the stuff, and never to anyone who wasn't of age, but the extra income sure came in handy at the end of the month.

Bud did not look at himself as a bad person. He'd never killed anyone, never robbed a bank, never even had his way with a woman who was unwilling, though he'd considered it a few times. He didn't steal, nor did he beg. He just found creative ways to make ends meet. Supply and demand: that was the ticket to Bud's success. He supplied what others wanted, and he demanded his fair price. Pure ambition for a comfortable life sometimes led Bud to sell things that were not exactly legal, but only to people old enough to know better.

Truth be told, Bud's belief in the capitalistic dream was the only thing stopping him from reporting that he'd seen the people responsible for the dead soldier they were still going on about on the other side of the street. He reached down into the oversized box of Milk-Bones dog biscuits at his feet and drew one forth for his pit bulls to see. They failed to gather any serious enthusiasm for the treats. It was just too damned hot for them to manage an appetite. When he called for Caesar by name, the dog sighed and finally struggled to stand up and walk over to his master. Bud smiled and rubbed the dog behind the ears. "Maybe I better get your pool set up, huh ol' boy? Give yall somethin' to cool off with." Bud looked at the cheap plastic wading pool, leaning against the side of his house, and decided he'd go ahead and fill it. The dogs needed a break from the heat, what with the fur coats God had stuck on their bodies.

Bud heaved himself away from his perch and waddled over to the wading pool with its interior of dancing cherubic mermaids and smiling starfish, knocking it to the ground more than actually setting it in place. It took him a few minutes to locate the pliers he used for turning the exterior spigot for water—the metallic wheel which should have been there had long since broken into fragments and Bud never seemed to get around to replacing it—but he soon had the pool half-filled with tepid water and a small army of dogs barking enthusiastically as he sprayed them with the stream.

For a moment he drowned out the sound of the dogs, his mind and eyes focusing on the group of soldiers who were still giving Walter Miller and his family a world of grief. He thought about the townsfolk he had seen creeping through the woods behind his own place and the commotion the dogs set up when they came too close. Awful lot of angry people in town and not a gun for any of them to defend themselves with.

Bud contemplated the firearms he had buried under the floorboards in his kitchen. They just might be the answer to all of his problems, financially speaking. Lucas Brightman had money to burn, and it was his boys were out doing the killing last night. He contemplated the potential returns on his five-year-old investment—he'd grabbed up all the firearms he could at a few pawnshops when he heard about the possible new legislation against firearm sales a few years back. Maybe he'd finally get beyond breaking even. That would be nice.

His decision to speak with Brightman made, Bud went back to hosing down the dogs. After a shift in the wind made him catch a whiff of his own body, he decided he'd go ahead and take a shower himself. Enough was enough; he just plain should have worn deodorant.

6

Artie Carlson lay in his bed and tried to block out the sounds of Emily's screams. Emily O'Rourke was in the next bed, and even through the sounds of oxygen hissing into her tent and the heart monitor beeping and pinging, he could hear her labored breaths. Despite the drugs the doctors kept pumping into her, the poor woman could not remain unconscious for long. Despite the drugs in his own system, her screams whenever she came awake kept him from the solace of sleep.

Emily O'Rourke was the wife of Pastor O'Rourke, and a good friend of Artie's mother. That did not stop him from growing to dread the idea that she might awaken. The screams she made were almost entirely inhuman. Raw wails of agony ripped from her mouth, past the tubes they'd forced into her to help her breathe. He had actually heard one of the men in the white suits say to another that there was no physical way she should have been able to scream. But she managed just the same.

Artie'd had a crush on Emily when he was a teenager and she was in her mid-thirties. Despite the age difference, he'd still felt the thrill of first love—or at least that's what he'd always assumed it was, until he met his future wife—every time he'd seen her smile. He'd never told her, or anyone else for that matter. She was a married woman, and he wasn't stupid enough to think she could have feelings for him. At least not when he was away from his fantasies. Emily was always so energetic, and filled with enough smiles to make the worst of days brighten up. When he and Carla had split up—his fault, he was a jealous man and a mean drunk—he'd thought of Emily often, wondering if Pastor William O'Rourke had any idea how lucky he was. Only recently had he realized that somewhere along the way she'd gone and grown old on him when he wasn't looking. Her bright eyes weren't quite as lovely a shade of blue, and her strawberry blond hair had lost its luster to a wave of gray and silver that hadn't been there only a few years earlier. Liver spots crept across her hands and, worst of all, the smile lines around her eyes had magically transformed into crow's feet.

Dreams weren't supposed to grow old. Maybe that was what drove him to drinking like a fool; too many aging dreams left unfulfilled.

Emily's daughter, Karen, was almost exactly like her mother in appearance, but she wasn't quite as quick with a smile. Not since that asshole Peter Donovan had married her and made the 'love taps' Artie used to give Carla look like playful rough-housing. The difference was that Artie knew he'd made mistakes. He'd have bet the use of his legs that good ol' Pete never figured out he was to blame. Having that thought brought a short chuckle from his mouth. After all, he had already lost the use of his legs, at least temporarily. Even through the painkillers they fed him every four hours he could feel the angry flashes of pain from burnt nerve-endings.

He could still remember Pete talking about how he'd had to "put Karen in her place again," almost every time the bastard showed himself at Toby's Bar and Grill. He could also remember seeing Karen walking with a limp on a few occasions. Despite the fact that Artie did not believe in interfering in another person's business, he was glad he'd called the cops on Pete. It was worth the shit-kicking he'd received when Pete got out of jail, just to know that he'd done something for Emily. She'd even come over and thanked him, told him he'd probably saved Karen's life that night, because Karen was in bad shape.

About two months later, Karen and Pete had split up. Just around the same time, Pete had decided to beat Artie's ass into the ground again. Would have done it too, if Buck Landers hadn't come along and run interference. That had been a scary sight; even through the blood welling in one eye, he'd seen Buck make his move. He had seen Pete pull a knife on Buck and then he'd seen good ol' Pete kiss the asphalt. Buck whupped Donavan's ass in under a minute, which made a total of two fights Pete had ever lost. Artie was about the only person on the planet who'd seen both of those fights. He considered that a badge of honor.

From behind the tent, Emily O'Rourke screamed in pain and Artie watched her silhouette lift off the bed in an arch of agony. He closed his eyes and tried not to think of his secret love for Emily. He tried not to match the burnt wreck in the next bed with the woman he'd worshipped from afar for as long as he could recall. He failed.

His legs were healing just fine, and Artie was glad of that. Maybe soon he'd be able to leave this nightmare behind him. A good bottle of his old pal, Jack Daniel's, and he'd be able to forget just about anything he wanted. He shifted his weight as Emily screamed again. Most of the blisters on his legs were drained now, and there was an awful lot of pain involved in moving.

Deep in the back of his mind, Artie contemplated murder. The thought of Emily had helped Artie keep himself from going over the edge on any number of occasions. Despite the fact that the love was unrequited, he still felt he owed her more than he could ever repay. Might be that some night soon, when the doctors were done making their rounds and everyone was asleep again, he'd have to visit Emily and help ease her pain in the only way that would ever really work.

But for now he listened and, in the darkness, he wept for the love he'd never truly known and the pain she was enduring.

Karen's Story

Chapter Five

1

Karen awoke to the mixed smells of frying bacon and maple syrup. Her stomach reminded her that she was hungry. On the bed beside her, despite her numerous orders to stay off the furniture, Roughie was still lying flat. The Mastiff-and-German-Shepherd-mixed dog opened one eye and looked Karen in the face. His tail wagged three times and he went back to sleep.

Maurice and Joan Dansky had proved to be one of the few bright points in her life since the space ship crashed in Oldman. Both were excellent cooks and both insisted on doing all of the housework in exchange for her letting the two of them stay with her. While the gesture was completely unnecessary—she'd have made the offer anyway, it was the way she'd been raised—Karen wasn't about to complain about their cooking talents.

Somewhere in town, her other two unexpected guests were running around and staying out of house as much as possible. Dutch Armbruster was not happy about being stuck in Collier, and neither was his girlfriend. Considering that Dutch was in his forties, and Becka was—if Dutch could be believed—all of nineteen, Karen wasn't overly surprised that they wanted to get on their way. If Karen was right about Becka's real age, Dutch was probably a bit afraid of her father coming down to find him and shove a shotgun where the sun don't shine before pulling the trigger. Karen was willing to bet money the girl wasn't a day over sixteen, and likely a bit younger. She had them sleeping in separate rooms, a move that neither of them seemed to like, under the pretense that she wouldn't have unmarried lovers committing sins under her roof. It was only a pretense, but she was a minister's daughter and they needed a place to stay. The mismatched lovers agreed to her terms. She was still contemplating calling on Chief Osborn and having him look into the matter of the girl's age, but the police were already busy enough.

Karen ran her fingers through her hair and decided the shower could wait a few hours. In a matter of minutes she was dressed in a new pair of jeans and an oversized tee shirt. She paused long enough to brush her teeth, and then she bolted down the stairs to see exactly what the Danskys had cooked up for her this time. Maurice smiled, and gestured for her to have a seat as he flipped something over in the frying pan. "Good morning, Karen! I hope you're in the mood for omelets." His Northern accent was rapidly becoming as familiar to Karen as the sound of Joan's nasal voice raised in what passed for singing. Joan was always singing, but at least Karen knew how to block out that particular noise.

"If you're cookin' them, Maurice, I'm always in the mood." Maurice smiled, bowing to reveal the sunburnt top of his balding head.

"You better believe he's cooking today, honey. This heat has made me into a limp noodle." Joan smiled as she spoke, making the cigarette in her mouth move in patterns that were as complex as human genetic codes. Joan was a constant source of amazement for Karen. One moment the woman was humming and happy, the next she was raising her voice in complaint about the weather, her physical condition, or even about Maurice. How Maurice could take the abuse with a smile was something Karen doubted she would ever understand.

Maurice set a coffee cup down in front of her and filled it almost to the rim, just barely leaving enough room for Karen to add cream and Equal. Karen smiled her thanks and tried to convince her stomach to remain calm for a few more minutes. She needn't have bothered. By the time she'd finished stirring her coffee, Maurice had set a piping hot western-style omelet in front of her, along with French toast and maple syrup. "Maurice, I'm gonna get fat if you keep cooking like this." The protest was half-hearted at best.

"Karen, you could not get fat if you had to. My daughter should be so skinny."

"What he said," added Joan. "You should see how that girl puts on weight. She's like an elevator; one minute she's up in weight, the next she's down."

"So who can blame her with that husband of hers?" Maurice piped in a complaint about his son-in-law, which was the only subject he ever complained about. "The no-good bum couldn't hold down a decent job if his very life depended. She only loses the weight because he can't afford to put bread on her table."

In an effort to change the subject, Karen brought up the bacon she now tasted in her omelet. "I hope you folks didn't buy this bacon just for me, I don't want to inconvenience you."

"Inconvenience us?" Joan piped up. "Darling, without you we'd be living in the streets right now. You couldn't inconvenience us if you demanded a song and dance number with every meal."

"Besides," Maurice added. "It's turkey bacon. The miracles of modern science never cease. Guilt-free bacon, be still my heart." He clutched at his heavy chest and looked to the heavens with a lopsided grin. Karen couldn't help but smile.

"I was glad to take you folks into my house. It's certainly big enough, and with all the people on the streets and the soldiers with their guns, I'm glad for the company."

"A girl your age doesn't need company. She needs to get herself a good husband instead." Joan crushed out her cigarette and shook her head, he mouth once again set in a slightly hostile frown. "If we were in New York right now, I'd introduce you to my nephew, Richie. He's a wonderful boy and a fabulous provider. You'd like him." She beamed with pride as she continued. "He's a medical malpractice lawyer. Lives in Manhattan."

Karen feared they'd pull out another picture to prove that
Richie was perfect for her, but apparently Joan's purse was out
of reach for the moment.

"Joan, darling, you've got to stop pushing men at Karen.
She'll find one when she's ready."

"I'm not pushing! How can I push when there's no one
around to push in her direction? What? I'm not allowed to be
proud of my family? Since when is a little family pride against
the law?"

Karen was exceptionally glad the two of them could cook
and clean. As much as she adored the Danskys, their constant
griping could tend to become annoying. It wouldn't be a problem, really, if she had a full-time job. But there were times
when being a schoolteacher could become a true pain. Two or
more months of vacation every year was a fine concept, but
not when one was stuck at home.

She was supposed to be on a cruise right now, escaping from
Collier and enjoying the Caribbean Islands. The soldiers had
decided otherwise. Instead of enjoying her first real vacation in
five years, Karen was playing landlord to four strangers.

She was also spending an immense amount of time every
day with her father, doing her best to keep him calm and lend
him moral support in his time of need. July Fourth had marked
the end of her father's happy times. Since that day she'd only
seen him smile twice, and both times the expression looked
more like a wince of pain than of joy.

Karen forced her mind away from dour thoughts and concentrated on enjoying the exceedingly good omelet that
Maurice had prepared for her. She deserved to enjoy her
breakfast, as she was almost certain she'd hate the rest of
the day. The Danskys made idle chitchat with Karen, and
she answered appropriately for the next half-hour before ex-
cusing herself. It was time for a shower and then off to get
the day started properly.

The shower was an elaborate affair, involving skin conditioners, special treatments for her hair and at least half of

the hot water supply. The daily shower was the one luxury Karen afforded herself. When she was done, she felt ready to face the world again. The tension was gone from her shoulders and neck, and she no longer felt as stiff as Frankenstein's Monster when she moved. Her hair she pulled back in a still wet but efficient ponytail. The day would be hot enough without trying to do anything special to what she referred to as her mop. Her outfit was a short-sleeved blouse and matching light blue pants.

By the time she was finished with dressing, it was time for her to go. Her father would be entering the "hospital" soon. She liked to see him before he went in. He liked for her to be there, and Karen hated to disappoint him, especially in light of recent events. Besides, she wanted him to pass on a message to her mother, even if the woman couldn't hear her words. Karen and her mother had never been exactly close, but that didn't stop the pain when she thought of Emily O'Rourke lying blistered and withered in the high school gym.

Even in the worst of times, traveling from one side of Collier to the other was hardly difficult. With the martial law imposed by the government, the pace was leisurely. Not a single car was encountered on the road, except for a few parked jeeps and the armored soldiers who stood by the dark vehicles. Karen gave little thought to the soldiers. They had not stopped her from doing anything save go out after dark, and Karen seldom did that in the first place. Still, as the heat of the morning began rising into the furnace of afternoon, she almost pitied them. They were locked in outfits that had to be about as comfortable as miniature ovens.

Karen stopped at the intersection of Fourth Street and Allburn Avenue, more out of habit than because it was necessary. The stop sign—complete with red flashers and a STOP ENFORCED DURING SCHOOL HOURS sign above it— at the corner of the high school was only enforced during the school year. As she pulled into the parking lot, she aimed for the front of the building where the teachers normally parked.

Most of the spots were filled, including the one she thought of as hers, simply because she always parked there. She managed to settle into a spot between Herb Cambridge's battered old pickup and an oversized Cadillac that had long ago seen its glory days.

The crowd waiting outside the school was smaller today than it had been initially. More and more of the folk in town were avoiding the school, because they knew there was nothing they could do. They could not see their loved ones, nor could they be near them. The guards saw to that. She guessed that, after a while, most people just couldn't stand the limitations imposed by the soldiers. She couldn't blame them.

The soldiers were in no short supply today, either. There were far more than she was used to seeing—the idea of being used to them had not fully registered, but when it did, Karen would suffer a bad case of the shivers—and they all seemed more agitated than usual. That was not a good sign of how well things were progressing, at least not in Karen's eyes.

She caught up with her father as the crowd was dispersing, just before he entered the building. One look at his face was all she needed to know that he hadn't slept. The smile lines around his eyes had become full-scale crow's feet. The crow's feet were overshadowed by the dark rings under his eyes. William O'Rourke tried to smile when he saw her, but even from a few feet away she saw that the effort was another failure. He moved over to her and hugged her briefly, and she felt his arms, which seemed somehow to have grown weaker and thinner over the last week. *Older*, she thought. *He's getting older by the day.*

"How are you, Daddy?" She did her best to keep the sadness she felt from overwhelming her calm voice.

"I'm fine, sweetheart." He smiled, and she saw the affection he felt for her in his exhausted eyes.

"You didn't sleep again." Her voice was accusatory, but she couldn't help that.

"I slept a little, but it's not the same without your mother next to me." His eyes moved away from hers as he spoke, and she knew he was lying. He hadn't slept a wink. William O'Rourke was a poor liar on a good day. At present he couldn't stop his eyes from roaming. He never could look a person in the face when he lied.

"Would you like me to come over tonight and stay with you? Or maybe you could come over to my place?"

"No, Kari. That wouldn't work. Between the two of us we have enough extra guests to fill the Holiday Inn over in Macon. Somebody has to be at both places to make sure everything's okay."

Karen hated when he used logic to end an argument. Logic always won over passion where her father was concerned. "Well, I don't think the people over at my place would be a problem to leave alone. Besides, you always say we're supposed to have a little faith in our fellow man."

Once again, he tried to smile. "A little faith. Not too much."

They hugged again and he turned to go inside. Karen called out for him to wish her mother love, and he nodded. A moment later he was gone and she was alone in a crowd of familiar faces.

Her father would remain inside for at least two hours. In the meantime, she decided to pay Laurie Johnson a visit. They hadn't seen each other in over a week, and that was rather unusual for the two of them. The Hav-A-Feast diner was a fair hike from the school. Despite the atrocious heat, she walked it. Several other people decided that food was a good concept and drove the distance instead. By the time she reached the old white building a heavy layer of sweat was staining her clothes and dampening her hair. She wished she'd had the sense to drive.

The diner was busy, but that wasn't too surprising. Despite a few days of almost no real business, directly after the UFO crashed, Hav-A-Feast was almost always jam-packed with customers. The only strange thing about it was not knowing who most of them were. Laurie was moving like a blur through the place, carrying more plates than should have been humanly possible, all stacked on one arm, and passing out meals with a quick, distracted smile. When someone asked for water, or another Coke, Laurie nodded and kept going. Without missing a beat, Karen grabbed two empty pitchers and filled them with ice, A moment later one was brimming over with cola and the other with water.

Laurie saw what she was doing, mouthed a quick thank you, and grabbed another stack of plates. Between the two of them, the chaos was manageable again in a matter of minutes. Laurie pulled a couple of plastic glasses from under the counter, and filled the oversized containers with more ice and Diet Coke. Then the two of them slid back into the cubbyhole between the swinging kitchen doors and the pickup station. The small alcove was less noisy than everywhere else, and the closest thing to a private spot in the entire area, excluding the rest rooms.

"Thanks, Karen. You're a life-saver." Laurie drank down half of her cola in two oversized gulps, gasping for air when she was done.

Karen took a sip of her own drink, smiling with affection at the skinny woman next to her. They'd been the best of friends for the last ten years, ever since they'd gone to work together at the Pizza Inn before it burned down. The little Middle Easterner who had built the place never tried setting up a business in town again, and had moved shortly thereafter. While working together, the two young women from different cliques—Karen was a cheerleader, Laurie was a hellraiser—discovered they had a lot in common. Not the least of which was a penchant for picking the wrong men in their lives. They'd been friends long enough to be each other's maid of honor. Hell, Laurie was one of the few people in town close enough to Karen to remember that before Peter Donovan, Karen had almost married Jack Calloway. Aside from Karen herself, Laurie and her father were the only people who knew about Karen's abortion after Jack's parents were killed in a car accident and he'd had to move in with his grandparents in New Jersey. They had no secrets from each other. "You know I can't resist a chance to save the day. It comes with being a minister's daughter."

"Really? I suppose you drinking me under the table in high school comes as a result of being a socialite's daughter?"

"Kiss my butt."

"It'd take too long."

"My mother is not a socialite..." Karen started

"We're too poor for that." Laurie finished the statement with her.

"Besides, I haven't had a drink in over four years."

"Yeah. I know. And I still don't see how you can manage that one." Laurie seldom drank herself, but when she did it was normally too much in too short a span of time.

The two sat in comfortable silence for a minute. From time to time Laurie stuck her head around the corner, looking for any sign that a customer needed something or, worse still, was trying to skip out without paying the tab. There were no pressing matters to attend to, so she stayed with Karen.

"You want something to eat?" Laurie always asked, and only about half of the time got a positive response.

"Oh, not just now, sweetie. I ate an omelet this morning that must have had five eggs in it. The folk staying with me are gonna get me spoiled. When this is all over, I'm gonna have to cook for myself, and I won't know how."

"Looks like you might be keeping them for a while." Laurie refilled her soda before coming back over to the cubbyhole. Nothing made Laurie happier than knowing she had a captive audience waiting for her to return.

"What do you mean?"

"Somebody killed one of the soldier boys last night. I don't reckon anyone's getting out of town anytime soon." Laurie's voice was nonchalant about the matter, but that was to be expected. Other than Arnetta at the mayor's office, she was practically the central gossip post in the area. Blasé was her specialty.

"How'd you hear about that? They can't be making it public." Karen wasn't overly surprised to hear that one of the armored men was dead. It was only a matter of time, in her opinion, before at least a few people in town got antsy about having their freedom revoked. She and Laurie had been discussing the matter only yesterday.

"How else?" Laurie raised one eyebrow and her face switched to a sly grin. "Arnetta Wilcox came by for a late breakfast and told me all the details."

Karen tsked a few times, a grin on her face. "I don't know why Milo keeps her on the payroll. He's got to know she's talking about this sort of thing."

Laurie smiled and nodded. "Sure he knows. But no one else is willing to work for what the town can afford to pay." She shrugged and then winked conspiratorially. "Besides, if she was gone, I'd just have to train a new one to tell me everything. Milo knows I wouldn't be happy about that."

"Milo still chasing all his meals with Maalox?"

"Oh, yeah. Some things never change."

"Did Arnetta tell you the asshole's back in town?"

"You mean Pete?"

"The very same."

Laurie got that *just-swallowed-a-bug-and-it's-still-squirming-in-my-throat* look on her face and replied. "She didn't have to tell me, Karen. I could smell him when he came in for breakfast."

"He came here?"

"Yep. But I sent him packin'. I don't want or need his business. And I told him as much."

"Long as he stays away from me, I'm happy."

"You still carrying that pepper spray you bought when he started his macho shit last time?"

"Hell yes. Long as Frank Osborn says I can, I'll continue to carry it."

"Good. He gets in visual range, you shoot him in the eyes."
Laurie slipped a piece of gum into her mouth and offered one
to Karen. Karen declined with a shake of her head. "Oh, and
make sure you stay upwind this time, too."

"You're about as funny as a heart attack, Laurie." When
Karen first purchased the spray, she'd carefully followed the
instructions and test sprayed the substance into the air, making certain that the nozzle pointed away from her. Everything
worked fine, except for a stray breeze bringing the stinging
droplets back through the window she'd aimed out of and right
into Karen's face. Laurie was the only person who knew about
the incident. It was Laurie who found Karen an hour later,
lying on the couch with a wet towel over her face and ugly red
marks wherever the stuff had touched skin. Despite keeping
quiet about the incident, Laurie couldn't resist poking fun at
her from time to time.

"Oh, you still offend too easy. I'm just funnin' with you."

"How's your dad holding up?"

"Not quite as bad as yours, but he isn't sleeping worth a
spit."

"My dad is too set in his ways. I don't think he's had any
sleep since mom got hurt."

"I don't doubt it. How's your mom doing?"

"I don't know, but I don't think there's been any real im-
provement." The two were silent for a few moments, lost in
their own thoughts. Or at least Karen was. Laurie was likely
just being respectful.

"I'm keeping my fingers crossed for her, Kari. You know
I am."

"I know." Laurie reached out with a callused hand and
gave Karen's hand a quick squeeze. Overcome with thoughts
about her mother's condition, Karen reached out and took
comfort from her friend's wiry arms. For such a skinny little
thing, Laurie always seemed to be the stronger of the two.
Karen tried to stop the waterworks from getting the better
of her, but she failed. For the next few minutes she clung

desperately to Laurie, silently sobbing while her friend made comforting noises and rocked her gently.

2

Karen had just returned to the high school when her father came back out of the building. He looked far worse than when he'd entered. Beside him was Laurie's father, Doctor Alan Johnson. Doc Johnson was doing his best to console Karen's father, but it obviously wasn't working very well.

Karen waited at a distance while her father composed himself and passed out messages to the few people who had come back. There were very few messages to be had. A moment later, Doc Johnson was joined by John Morrisey, the only other town doctor permitted into the building. Between the two of them, they answered as many questions as they could about the condition of individual patients. Very few were recovering. Most seemed to be suffering from that universal danger that all hospital patients dread: complications. Edward Armbruster, no relation to Dutch, was added to the growing list of patients who had died while under the care of the military's "specialists." As with all the recent dead in Collier, his body was claimed by the soldiers.

Karen had been feeling better after her long-overdue crying jag. Now the freedom she felt as a result of the catharsis was fading in the afternoon sun, just as surely as if her feelings were nothing but dry ice left to evaporate. She waited patiently as the doctors finished their brief summary of the numerous injureds' conditions, and then she waited some more as her father answered a few more questions and the small crowd dispersed.

Not long after the questioners went away, the doctors too fled the scene. Only she and her father were left behind. She joined him and took his heavy hand into her own, far smaller hand. They walked slowly, and Karen felt the silence as if it were a physical barrier.

When she could take it no longer, she broke the uncomfortable quiet. "How's Mom doing?"

Her father looked towards her with haunted eyes. In a barely audible voice he answered. "She's dying, Karen. It's only a matter of time before the Lord takes her away."

They walked in silence again, as Karen tried to think of what to say and her father fell deeper into his private torment. The heat of the day was hideous, and Karen did not doubt they'd reach or break the hundred-degree mark. Despite the summer inferno, her father's hand felt like a block of ice. His stride was wooden, and he kept his gaze locked on the ground.

"I wish I could make her better, Dad. I really do."

"I know, sweetie. I know."

"Why won't you tell me what else is bothering you? I can see it in your eyes. You've never been like this before." She hated prying into his business. Her father was a very private man in many ways. Still, someone had to make him talk, before the strain inside his soul started doing permanent damage to his earthly shell. She could, perhaps, survive the loss of one parent, but losing both would devastate her.

William O'Rourke sighed heavily. His eyes never left the concrete before him, but he slowly tugged at Karen's arm, and they steered towards the football field behind the school. The sun was moving towards the west, and the two of them were able to find a small pool of shade where they could at least escape the extra heat caused by the sunlight.

Karen wanted to ask her question again, as the silence grew longer and deeper. But she knew her father well enough to understand that he would speak when he had finished composing his thoughts.

Fully another ten minutes crawled past before he decided to answer her. "All of my life I've believed that God is in Heaven and that Jesus Christ died for our sins. I've known that, whatever happened in this lifetime, no matter who I lost, I could find them again someday, in a world far better than this one." He looked towards her, and Karen felt her heart break for the agony written on his face. "I've known that I would likely outlive your mother. Her health has been going for a few years now, and she's not been as energetic or as quick to catch her breath as she was only a few months ago.

"I hate to see your mother in pain, Karen, but in my soul I've known that we would be together in perfect health, for all eternity. I've never loved anyone but your mother. Not in any real sense of the word. I've loved you, and I've loved God, but the biggest part of my heart has always been set aside for Emily."

Her father reached out to touch Karen's hand, and clutched her fingers in his own with all the desperate strength of a drowning man. "I could accept her being in pain, because I knew that the Lord would provide for her in the next world. In Heaven or whatever you might want to call it. I knew that someday she'd be better. I've answered other people's questions of faith without any trouble, because I always knew in my heart that God was real and He would provide for us all. I have always had my faith, no matter what happened or how bad it was for anyone I knew, I've always had my faith."

William O'Rourke sucked in a breath and held it for a second before speaking again. His voice trembled as he talked, and the tears began to run across his lower eyelids, threatening to spill from him as surely as hers had earlier.

"But I don't know anymore, Karen. I truly don't know." The words came from his mouth in an increasing torrent, a tide of emotions that would not be denied any longer.

"There's a thing sitting in the lake that defies everything I've ever believed, and I can't seem to see around that anymore. No matter what happened in the past, I always had my faith in God Almighty. But I can't seem to find that faith now that I need it the most. How could God exist and allow a thing like that to smash into the lake and kill so many people? How could He make my poor Emily to suffer so much torment and not have the decency to end her pain? Your mother is the one saving grace I've always known, and now I am denied even the comfort of her voice." The tears came then, and for the first time in her life, Karen saw the strongest man she'd ever known crumble into despair. "How can I believe in God when He'd do a thing like this? Where is His mercy?" He continued to speak, but his voice broke apart and the words were lost in a fading cry of anguish.

As Laurie had done for her earlier, Karen now did for her father. She held him in her arms, rocking him softly and letting him cry his sorrows to the world. After a time the tears stopped, and he was able to compose himself.

Karen stared at her father for several moments before she responded to what he'd said. "Daddy. When I was a little girl I used to ask you a hundred different questions about the Bible. We'd talk about the miracles of the past, and I'd ask you why there were no miracles anymore." She paused to make certain he was listening. He was. "At first you always said that miracles do still happen, like when a man in a coma for a dozen years wakes up alert and hungry, happy to be with his family. You also used to say that every life is a miracle, and that should be enough. But later, you always had the same answer for me, no matter what the question I had might be. If I found a discrepancy in the writings of the Bible, you didn't chalk it up to human error, or even the fact that the Bible has been translated a hundred different ways. You just sighed and said 'Karen, you have to have faith.' Sometimes you'd add in that the Lord tends to work in mysterious ways."

Karen made her father look her in the eyes, and smiled as best she could under the circumstances. "Dad. Sometimes it is not our place to know what goes through God's mind, or even to understand the machinations of His will. Sometimes, you just have to have faith."

They sat a short while longer, and then they rose and walked to their cars. Karen had some chores she needed to handle, like shopping for a house suddenly filled with too many people—they bought food and it disappeared at a speed that astonished Karen. She'd never known so much food could go away so quickly. Though they never spoke of the matter again, her father walked a little taller when they left the field. Karen believed that she had done him some good, and that made her feel better than she might have expected.

3

Karen entered the Piggly Wiggly with a smile as the air conditioning blasted away the sweat trying to cover her entire body. The smile did not last long. In addition to the fact that over half the store's shelves were empty, Peter O' Rourke was inside the store. Worse still, he'd seen her.

With a big, easygoing grin on his face, he nodded in Karen's direction. He was still a handsome man, but somewhere along the way he'd stopped being an object of desire for her. Perhaps it was around the same time he started using his fists to settle all of his arguments. She chose not to nod back. Instead, Karen grabbed a cart and very deliberately moved to keep a solid distance between the two of them. She'd already had a talk with Frank Osborn, and he'd promised to haul Peter into jail at the first sign of trouble. Any trouble at all. She felt good knowing that a single call could get the bastard put away indefinitely.

Karen kept her eyes straight forward and her right hand in the depths of her purse. It only took a moment to find the pepper spray, and about the same amount of time to disengage the safety. If he tried anything...

"Hey, Karen! How are you today?" It took a concentrated effort not to just pull the spray out and fire. She recognized that the voice was not Pete's—sometime after her heart skipped a few beats—but she was tempted just the same. Beth Thornton's was close to the last voice she wanted to hear. After the last dozen or so Parent-Teacher Meetings, the large woman was properly on Karen's private shit list.

Karen eased the pressure on the pepper spray and forced herself to smile. She turned to face Beth Thornton. "Hi, Beth. I'm as well as can be expected. How are you?"

"Oh, I'm just fine," the woman chirped. "Joe's stuck at home all the time, what with him having that accounting job in Stockton these days, and I'm afraid he's gonna drive me crazy with all the gardening he's doing. But we're making out okay."

Beth Thornton was never fine. Every sentence from her mouth that involved her family was a statement on how difficult life was when you were raising three kids and a husband, all of whom were, if she could be believed, lost when she was not present. To hear the woman talk about her family, they were all as helpless as newborn babies and completely dependent on her for even the simplest functions. Karen had stopped herself from asking Beth if she had to wipe their asses too, on more than one occasion. "Well, at least he's trying to keep busy."

"Thank God for that." Beth waved one hand frantically and pressed the other to her ample bosom. "If he was inside all the time, I'd have to tie him to a chair."

"Well, look, Beth, I have really got to get my shopping done. There's almost nothing left in the house..."

"Oh, I don't mean to keep you, Karen." The saccharine in the woman's voice could be interpreted as an argument against that statement, but Karen knew better. The woman always sounded that sickeningly sweet. "I'm just passing around some flyers. I thought I should get one into your hands, since you see so many people at the school every day."

Before Karen could respond, Beth had shoved a bright pink piece of paper into her hand and waddled away. It was only as she saw the woman leaving, that she realized Tom Thornton was with his mother. The boy held his hands out in supplication, mouthing the words "Save me" as he walked away. Karen smiled. Tom Thornton was one of the class cutups, and normally a thorn in her side. But at twelve years of

age, Tom likely hated his mother almost as much as Karen
did. At least he didn't get nasty about having to go to the
store with his mom. At least he didn't throw fits in public, if
he did hate it. Not at all like Karen was at his age.

The flyer held simple, typed information with two badly
reproduced faces of children. It read:

Dear Everyone.

*As you may have heard, Marty Wander and Mike Summers
have disappeared. It looks like they might have gone off on their
own, as their bikes are missing. But they weren't home this morning
and they haven't shown themselves by Noon today. Under the circumstances, that makes us worried. If you have seen these too boys,
please pick up the phone and ask the operater to let you contact us.
He should put you right thru, as we have special permission from the
Colonel in charge.*

Thank You,
Andrew Wander

Below the poorly written request were the two black-
and-white pictures—black and pink, actually, thanks to
Beth's choice of colors. The quality was such that, if one
stared very hard at the images, one could almost imagine
that they were actually more than woodcuts. Karen resisted
the urge to pull out a red pen for correcting the text, and
tried to remember if she'd seen the two anywhere during
the day. Despite her best efforts, she could not recall seeing either of them. That in itself was unusual. Almost as
unusual as Marty Wander not being home on time. Andrew
could be a bit of a stickler for harsh punishment when it
came to disobeying his orders. Many people saw that as a
flaw, but Karen wished there were a few more parents who
would follow his lead. The Lord knew that most twelve-
year-olds were unmanageable.

The biggest problem wasn't the guards surrounding the city; it was the small army of tourists in town. At least that's how Karen had it figured. The guards would follow orders. The tourists might not. Two twelve-year-old boys missing from town were not a good sign. She folded the pink paper into eighths and then slipped it into her back pocket. Later, after she'd finished shopping, she'd have to jot down a list of places to look for them. Jolene Wander was probably beside herself with worry.

As she moved down the canned vegetables aisle—a very depleted area, but not nearly as bad as the canned pastas—Karen reached for an industrial-size can of early peas and found that someone else already had a hand on the object of her attention. She knew the hand immediately, knew, all too well, the swastika tattooed above that hand. Karen released the peas as if she'd been stung, and sucked in a shocked breath.

"Sorry 'bout that, Karen. Didn't mean to scare you. But a man's got to eat." Pete held the can of early peas in his hand, held it out to Karen, as if to apologize.

"You can keep the damned peas! And while you're at it, you can keep away from me!" Her ex-husband was almost as surprised by the venom in her voice as she was. "You get one warning, Pete, and this is it. If you get near me again, I'll have your sorry butt thrown into the jail until this whole mess is settled."

Despite her harsh words, Karen could hear the old tremble in her voice. She wasn't certain if the shake in her speech was from fear or just from seeing him again. Either way, she truly hated it.

Pete put down the peas and held up his hands in mock surrender. She loathed the smile on his face, so filled with humor and maybe even a little contempt. She despised him even more. Hell, when it came to Pete Donovan, she hated just about everything. The old saying about there being a fine line between love and hate was true, and Karen had long since crossed over that line where her ex-husband was concerned. Any hint of love that had ever been in her heart for him had been destroyed when he attacked her that last time.

"You've got an attitude problem, Kari. That's what you've got. Best be careful, or someone's gonna come along and adjust it for you." Pete said the words with an innocent smile centered on his smarmy face. It was the same sort of smile she used to find so attractive, back in the days before he came back from his stint in the Marines.

"Don't you dare threaten me, Peter Alexander Donovan. I swear I'll go to the police straight away if you threaten me again." There was a lie. She was calling Frank the second she was certain Pete wasn't going to be there to stop her from calling him. But she had no intention of advertising that fact. Her hand dug around in her purse and Karen cursed herself for never getting around to cleaning the excess contents from the bag.

"Who's threatening who here, Kari? I'm not threatening to call the cops every time you breathe, now am I? No, little missy, that'd be you makin' the threats. Not me." Peter's voice had shifted down into a low purr, a certain sign that he was now paying her attention. From past experience, Karen knew that was not a good sign.

"What are you doing in town, anyway? You're not supposed to get anywhere near me. Not after what you did to me before."

"A little argument gets out of hand and you have a restraining order put on me. Big surprise that our marriage failed with you acting that way." Karen wanted to scream; every word from his mouth was another in a long list of reasons for her to hate him. Every word was a twisting of the truth or an out-and-out lie. The problem was that most people tended to think of Pete as an upstanding citizen. Most never saw the photographs taken after the serious beatings. Pete was good. He never left a single mark on Karen that couldn't be hidden beneath clothes. Everyone in town knew he'd beat on her—that wasn't the sort of thing you could keep quiet in a town the size of Collier—but only a few knew how badly he'd hurt her.

"I don't call three broken ribs and internal bleeding a 'little argument,' you sonuvabitch. I call them assault. Lucky me, the police agreed."

Peter started moving towards her when she finished her statement. He moved on the balls of his feet, and fairly flowed across the ground. One second he was a good twenty feet away, the next he was looming over her. Flashing memories of how he'd hit her and kicked her again and again during their six years of marriage blasted through Karen's head. Her hands turned to ice, even as she finally managed to locate the pepper spray in her purse. Pete's eyes pinned her in place, much like a cobra paralyzes a bird. A deep, sinking feeling spun through Karen's stomach, even as her knees threatened to buckle. Her throat constricted and, despite her desire to do so, Karen could not find the breath to scream.

Then a new voice entered the conversation. It was deep and low, a rumble of thunder on the horizon. It took Karen a second to recognize the voice as it spoke out. "This guy ain't givin' you any trouble, is he Karen?"

Dutch Armbruster was an ugly man. His nose was wide and crooked from too many fights. His skin was pockmarked by old acne scars and highlighted by a few scars that could well have been made by knives slicing into his skin. His straggly hair was dark brown shot with gray, and ran down half the length of his back. Thick eyebrows overshadowed his small brown eyes. The mutton-chop sideburns and mustache on his face partially hid the excessively thick, wormy lips of his mouth, which often hid his chipped teeth. Right now those teeth were bared in a feral smile. His hairy chest and over-sized gut were only partially obscured by the greasy, sleeveless denim jacket on his back. The jacket left fully exposed his massive arms, which were covered with crudely carved tattoos. From his hips to his ankles, his body hid beneath Levi's blue jeans that had long ago lost their shape. Heavy, scuffed boots covered his size-fourteen feet.

Karen had never seen a man look so handsome.

Dutch took a step forward, and the odor of tobacco and stale beer wafted over Karen. Pete took three steps back, eyes scanning over Dutch as if they'd just seen something that should not exist.

Karen opened her mouth to speak, but Pete beat her to it. "What goes on between me and her ain't none of your business. Why don't you just leave it be, son, before you end up gettin' hurt."

Dutch's grin grew wider. "I'm making it my business, college boy. Karen here's been nice enough to take me in until the assholes in uniform decide I can go my own way. That means she's my business. Get the idea?"

Pete looked from Dutch to Karen, and then he repeated the process several times. His face grew redder and redder as he made his examination. "You think you're tough, huh, asshole?"

"Don't think it, I know it."

"Well, this ain't the time or place for this little talk. There's people trying to buy food, and they don't need to see any violence." Pete backed away, never taking his eyes off Dutch. "We can discuss this later." He turned to look at Karen, his eyes promising retribution. "And when that's all taken care of, you and me can have a talk, Karen. For old times' sake."

Pete faded around the corner of the aisle, and Karen was quite content to let him. Adrenaline was making her feel weak as a kitten, and her knees were shaking. "Thanks, Dutch. Thanks very much."

"No problem, Karen." The man seemed to deflate somehow, without actually shrinking in size. The combat grin he'd had on his face was replaced by a friendly smile. "That's what friends are for."

A moment later, Becka came around the corner pushing a grocery cart filled to overflowing with every imaginable sort of food. She was a lanky girl who had only just started blossoming into a woman, and her body was lean enough that Karen almost felt a twinge of envy every time she saw her. Her red hair was pulled back in a pony tail and her small breasts were covered by a shirt that was two sizes too small. But her pretty face was smiling brightly when she saw Karen. "Oh," the girl said. "I thought it was our turn to buy the groceries."

Karen smiled affectionately at the girl. "I think maybe we can finish the shopping together, if that's okay with the two of you."

"Sure. Cool," was Becka's response.

"No problem," responded Dutch.

When the group got home half an hour later, they brought enough food to feed a small army. They also found that the Danskys had apparently felt the need to go shopping as well.

Karen took the time to report Pete to Frank, despite having to argue with the operator on the phone before she could get patched through to his office. He promised he'd get on it immediately.

Between the cooking, the cleaning and the unexpected bonus of having Dutch volunteer to act as her personal bodyguard, Karen decided the new living arrangements weren't so bad after all.

4

Dinner that night was spaghetti and canned sauce. While Maurice had done all that he could to doctor the sauce, it still tasted slightly tinny. The best staples at the store were long gone and beggars couldn't be choosers. Dutch certainly had no difficulty with the aftertaste. Three helpings after he had begun his meal, he was finally slowing down.

The group had spent the last few hours talking about any number of subjects, but one of the most prominent topics was Peter Donovan. Despite Karen's desire to forget that the man had ever existed, some things simply weren't meant to

be. By the time everyone had finished eating, the small group
knew everything about Karen's ex-husband. More than she
was honestly comfortable with them knowing. Still, Dutch
had pretty much saved her from whatever twisted thoughts
went through Pete's mind, and she felt she owed him at least
that much.

Becka was helping Joan with the dishes—and listening to
Joan's makeover tips—when the doorbell rang. Roughie came
silently from Karen's bedroom, his tail wagging and his tongue
trying to match the pace. Dutch started to get up from his
place at the recliner he'd claimed as his own territory, but Karen
waved him down with a smile.

Karen faced the door, half-expecting to see Pete once she'd
finished opening the heavy oak obstacle. Her mind flashed
past a dozen different slasher movies where the killer waits
politely at the door. She thought of calling Dutch over after
all, but forced herself to remain calm. With a slightly shaky
hand, she turned the knob and pulled the door open, cursing
herself for never getting a spy-hole put in.

Frank Osborn stood outside, sweat making his dour face
glisten in the light pouring from the open door. "Hi there,
Karen. Can I come in?"

"Hi Frank." Karen felt her face crease into a smile, and
let out the breath she hadn't even realized she'd been holding. "Yeah, come on in." The man slipped past her with an
unconscious grace that always surprised her. The effect was
ruined by Roughie when the dog promptly rose from the
ground and put his paws on Frank's shoulders. Frank took
the over-enthusiastic face-licking better than most people,
even going so far as to scratch Roughie behind the ears.
"Would you like something to drink? We've still got a few
Cokes left, and there's plenty of iced tea."

"I'd love an iced tea, unsweetened. Thanks."

Karen rushed off and poured him one in a large plastic
Jurassic Park cup she'd picked up a few years back. By the time
she'd returned, Frank was sitting on the loveseat, across from

Dutch. Dutch seemed worried, and Frank was giving him a look that made it very clear he'd be watching the man from now on.

"Here you are, Frank. I see you've met Dutch. He's staying here since that thing fell into the lake. He's also my hero of the day." Frank took the tea and nodded his thanks. "Dutch was there at the store when Pete decided to let me know he was in town."

"That so?" Frank gave the man the eyeball again, and Dutch nodded emphatically to agree with Karen's statement. "Well, that's very good of you." He turned back to Karen. "Well, speaking of Pete, I've got a APB out on him. He gets spotted, he goes to jail. I won't let him out again until this whole thing has blown over." Frank looked at her, his eyes showing the anger he felt inside. He'd never liked Pete, and she knew that. It was one of the reasons she liked him so much. He was a good cop and he knew a snake when he saw one. "Problem is, he could be almost anywhere. Like as not he's holed up at one of his buddies' houses. We're looking into it as best we can." He grimaced apologetically. "I've only got four officers left including me. I have to be honest, it could take a while to find him."

She nodded, hating to hear those words. "I understand. I just hope you nab him soon."

"I'll do my best, Karen. Now, the main reason I'm here. I've been trying to find out if anyone in town has seen Mike Summers or Marty Wander. Them two boys snuck off in the middle of the night and no one's seen or heard from them since." Frank gulped down half the glass of tea and continued on. "Jolene is worried sick about them, and Andrew wants to tan both of their butts. I'm just praying they didn't get themselves into too much trouble." Frank's face had shadows of exhaustion where she'd never seen any before. He, like so many of the people in Collier, looked older than he should. Even when he was supposed to be sitting comfortably, his entire body was ramrod straight.

Karen thought about the two boys. Both had been in her class this last year, and she remembered them all too well. While they both managed good grades, they were the class cut-ups and almost always in trouble. They were two of the only children she knew whose parents had granted Principal McCullough permission to use a paddle at his discretion. Frankly, it seemed the best way to keep them both from getting suspended. Still, they were decent kids, if a little too enthusiastic for their own good. She could not recall seeing them.

"Are they maybe ten or eleven years old?" Dutch's voice came as a surprise. Both Karen and the police chief looked his way.

"Yes. Actually, they're twelve." Karen felt a sinking sense of dread go through her as she spoke.

"Were they on bikes, maybe?"

This time it was Frank who answered the question. "They were both on bikes. If they came by here, they'd have probably come from the north."

"I think I saw 'em last night."

"What were you doing out after curfew?"

Dutch blushed. "I was talking with Becka. She's my girlfriend."

Frank nodded, leaving the subject alone. "Did you see which way they went, Dutch?"

"Yeah. They were headed for the lake." Dutch shrugged. "I didn't say nothin' about it 'cause I didn't want to get them in any trouble. I mean, I know about the curfew and all, but a kid's got to be a kid, if you know what I mean." The more Dutch spoke, the stronger his Yankee accent became. She was thinking somewhere in Pennsylvania was his home, but it was only a guess.

Frank scowled at the man and reached for his cigarettes. He then realized where he was and began to put them away. Karen fairly ran across the room and grabbed an ashtray. A happy Chief Osborn was less likely to nail her hero of the day to the wall. "Here you are, Frank. You can smoke if you want."

Frank smiled his gratitude and lit up. After the first exhale, he pinned Dutch to the wall with his eyes. "Can you tell me when they went past?"

"Musta been after midnight. One in the morning, maybe."

"Did they have anything with them that you could see? Sleeping bags or knapsacks?"

"Nope. Nothin' like that. They was just riding along towards the lake. Oh. One of 'em had a sweatshirt on his shoulders, like a cape. I thought that was a little strange."

Frank scratched his head about that one, apparently uncertain as to whether or not it was significant. After a moment more, he shrugged his shoulders and turned to look at Karen with a dark stare. "Okay. Next subject. Details on what happened with Pete, just so I've got it clear in my head."

Karen stared at the police chief for a long time before answering. "I ran across him at the store. He was starting to make noises about old times and me needing an attitude adjustment, when Dutch came along and suggested that he leave me be."

"Dammit! I'll slap his butt in cuffs the next time I see him. He won't be a bother after that."

Karen smiled her relief. Other people in town might not think Frank Osborn was very effective, but she knew better. He was the sort of cop other cops should strive to be like. He was effective and he didn't play games. "I really appreciate this, Frank. I don't need to be looking over my shoulder for him. Not right now. I've got enough to worry about."

Frank smiled tightly and nodded his head. "Just have to find him first, Karen. Proves he isn't very smart, if you ask me. I told him if I even thought he'd been close to you I'd put him in a cell." Frank stood up, straightening the sharp creases on his uniform pants. "I hoped you'd side with me on that one, Karen. I don't think he's all there anymore. Hasn't been since he joined the Marines."

"Do you know where he's staying?"

"No. But I don't figure there's too many places he could be holed up. Maybe with Judd Fitzwater, but I don't think so. Him and Judd's wife, Carmen, ain't never got along too well. Heck, maybe I'll just ask Carmen and she can tell me."

"She probably will if she knows. All I know is he's been going by the diner every morning."

"Then maybe that's where I'll wait for him." Frank scratched Roughie's backside, and the dog made ecstatic faces while stretching his entire body. "One more thing. If you folks have the time tomorrow, Jolene and Stan are trying to get together a search party for the two boys. They're all meeting near the lake, right across the street from Colonel Anderson's tents. Buck Landers will be there too, making sure no one gets stupid." With the last comment, Frank stared at Karen and winked. She started to blush a bit and wished she were somewhere else. She and Buck had gone on several dates. He was a nice guy, and completely smitten with her by what she could figure. Unfortunately, she tended to think of him only as a friend. She disliked herself for that attitude, but there was no spark of romance. She felt nothing special when he came around.

"We'll see if we can make it, Frank. Thanks again."

"Thanks for the tea. Y'all have a good night."

Frank left, and Roughie spent the next half-hour pouting about the disappearance of his new back-scratcher. For a while everyone watched TV, sticking mostly to the sitcoms. Then Maurice and Joan went to bed and Dutch and Becka went outside, despite the curfew.

A little after ten, Karen retired to her room. Despite her best efforts to break him of the habit, Roughie soon followed suit. She idly scratched behind Roughie's ears as she thought about her failed marriage. As so often happened, Karen found herself playing the game "What If" before sleep came to her. What if Jack Calloway had never moved away? Would she have kept the child she had aborted? The Lord knew how often she found herself wondering if the child would have been a boy or a girl. Would she and Jack have married? She liked to think so. Imagining that they would have married helped her imagine a life in which she and Pete had never tied the knot. She even imagined what life would have been like if Pete had stayed away from the Marines and lived in town before they married. A life where he was not the foul-tempered monster that came back to her after four years of military service. A life where he was still the man she wrote letters to while he was overseas, still the dreamer who had left and not the harsh realist who came back from his time in the military.

Karen forced her mind away from such silly notions and embraced the idea of sleeping. After only a short while of tossing and turning in the dark, she managed to drift away. By morning Roughie had managed to fall asleep across her feet. She didn't have the heart to yell at him.

Chapter Six

1

Karen and her entire crew of houseguests were up bright and early the next morning. They, like a good number of Collier's people, were at the edge of the lake at the appointed time. Over five hundred members of Collier's community showed up for the search of the woods. Being a bit more cynical of late than perhaps was healthy, she couldn't help wondering if most had simply shown up for something to do. With the soldiers having closed down the business district, very few people were actually working at the present time.

Karen was one of those close enough to hear the shouting match between Colonel Mark Anderson and Chief Frank Osborn. Anderson's face could not be seen past the helmet and mask he wore over his face. In contrast, Frank's face was very visible and very red. He looked ready to take a large bite out of Anderson's neck.

"For the last time, Captain Osborn, I cannot allow this many people to move through the woods. For all I know there are camera crews waiting on the other side of the razorwire to take pictures of everyone and ask all the wrong questions."

"And for the last damn time, Colonel, I don't much give a damn. We've got two kids missing out here, and I don't see you or your men doing anything about the situation. Now what the hell do you expect me to do? Go on about my business and pretend that two little boys are not important enough to look for?"

"You've got two choices here. One, you can cull this search party of yours down to fifty people. Two, you can leave the search to me and my men."

"Fifty people ain't enough. There's hundreds of acres of woods out there, and those trees are pretty well packed together. As for you and your men handling the matter, I don't see that you've done much so far."

Both men stood in rigid positions, their muscles obviously drawn tight from tension. The Colonel pointed with one finger, aiming at the silvery disc in the lakebed. "I can't very well release all of my men from their duties just to look for two kids too damned stupid to obey the curfew. It doesn't work that way."

It was obvious the man intended to continue talking, but Andrew Wander decided he'd had about enough, and interrupted the argument. The Colonel's assistant, the one who always carried a clipboard, tried to stop him, but Andrew bulldozed past him with an angry shrug.

Andrew Wander was hardly a giant of a man. He was only of average height, but his long hours of handling his landscaping business ensured that his lean frame was nothing but muscle. He always looked *wrong* to Karen. Andrew's sun-bleached, almost white halo of hair—he was balding on top, and the halo had a big brown spot in its center—in opposition to his skin made him look like a sepia-toned negative of a person. Darkly tanned, the man looked almost bronzed as he reached for the Colonel. Anderson tried to avoid the hands, but was not fast enough. One second the soldier was standing on his own two feet, the next he was flying through the air.

Frank stepped forward, reaching for Andrew, but the landscaper turned and stared with murderous eyes into Frank's face. "You keep the hell out of this, Frank. You've already done enough harm." Andrew was, apparently, one of the many people in Collier who felt that Frank had not handled the situation properly when the soldiers had taken control.

Andrew moved towards the Colonel as the man was rising to his feet. The one with the clipboard moved forward, but his commander held out a hand to stop him. Looking at the faces in the crowd, Karen felt that was a wise move.

Andrew Wander's face was contorted by emotions. Anger, fear for his son and frustration over the situation changed his face completely. What little hair Andrew had on his head was wild. Combined with the feral set of his lips, he did not look like the person who normally came once a week to mow Karen's lawn. He looked like a sociopath on a rampage.

The Colonel stood ready to fight, but Andrew stopped himself before combat began. "You sumbitch," he started, his voice trembling with anger. "You come into this town and you lock us all away. We cain't talk to no one, we cain't even see our friends in the hospital. You come into town and you make us stay inside." Andrew stood with fists ready and legs spread wide apart. Despite the unbridled fury on his face, tears were starting to spring forth from his narrowed eyes. He blinked angrily, as if to deny the tears. "All because you want that fucking thing over there. That's just fine. I don't give a good goddamn about that thing anyway." Andrew stepped forward, pointing with his right index finger while his arm shook with suppressed rage. "But I'm gonna look for my boy, and my friends are gonna help me. You want to try and stop me, you come on, right here and right now. I swear to God, I'll kick your fuckin' head in if you get in my way."

"I've about had it with you people. I'm trying to make this as painless as I can, and you still give me crap. You will not look for your son, Mister Wander. That option is gone." Despite the buzzing quality of his voice, Anderson's anger was still apparent. He turned to look at the crowd, taking his eyes off Andrew Wander. "You will return to your homes, all of you." He looked back at Andrew and, in spite of the mask that hid his features, Karen would have sworn he was gloating. "Effective immediately, the curfew in this town is full-time. Consider yourselves under house arrest."

Andrew Wander struck the Colonel with all the fury of an angry god. He did not walk or run to meet his enemy, he leaped. There was no battle cry from Andrew's lips, but half of the people there supplied one for him. The Colonel may have been prepared, but he was not prepared enough. Andrew reached out and slammed his fist into the faceplate covering the man's face, as if he had forgotten that the breathing apparatus was there. Something in Andrew's hand or the Colonel's armor made a dull snapping sound. Part of the Colonel's lower jaw slid into view, and Karen knew immediately that he could not see. The lenses on his faceplate were half-hidden beneath the edge of his helmet in an instant.

The landscaper didn't give his enemy a chance to recover. Andrew grabbed the man at crotch and throat and lifted him from the ground a second time. Karen clearly saw the rapidly swelling lump on Andrew's right hand as he hoisted the Colonel above his head. Instead of throwing his opponent, Andrew slammed the man into the ground with all of his might in a move he must have learned watching professional wrestling. The ground Colonel Anderson hit was much harder than the mats used by the pros. The mask that covered the Colonel's face was knocked away, along with the helmet that had protected his skull. As the man gasped for breath, Andrew dropped to his knees and began pistoning one fist after the other into the Colonel's face.

Karen felt sure that the Colonel was a goner. Neither Frank nor the soldier with the clipboard made any move to interfere. When other soldiers came rushing forward, the Colonel's second stopped them with a gesture. Anderson had made clear before that he'd handle it, and that was exactly the way it was going to be.

Then Anderson lifted one of his hands in a blurring chop that caught Andrew full in the throat. Andrew gasped for breath, falling away from his enemy and clutching at his neck. Both men spent a second or two on their knees, gasping and recovering. Then they rose and the fighting began again. Despite several lacerations on his face, the Colonel seemed composed and ready for anything. Andrew was still in a rage, and in the end that cost him dearly. He came at the Colonel with a wild swing and the man stepped back out of range before moving in again and landing several hard jabs to Andrew's ribs and stomach. The air left Andrew in an audible whoosh, and the fight went out of him. The Colonel either did not notice or did not care. He followed through with a savage elbow strike to the side of the Andrew's head, and then finished the fight for good by kicking him in the ribs with enough force to knock the landscaper off his feet. Several wet, popping sounds came from Andrew's side, and the man screamed as he went to the ground.

Karen and the rest of the crowd stared at Anderson. Finally, after a few silent seconds, Sam Morrisey and a man Karen had never seen before moved forward and started examining Andrew where he lay, unconscious, in the grass.

Anderson moved, slowly at first as if uncertain of his own balance. He walked over to where Frank Osborn was standing and stopped, looking first at the crowd and then at his men. "You have until seventeen hundred hours. You've got twenty of my men. One of my men will go with each group. Anything happens to any of my men, and I'll personally kill two civilians for each one who gets hurt. Do we have an understanding?"

Frank Osborn looked at him for a few seconds. Then he nodded. "Thank you, Colonel."

"Don't ask me for any more favors. Next time someone in this shithole town disappears, I *will* have everyone placed under house arrest. I've got enough problems without this bullshit." The Colonel spit a stream of bloody saliva from his mouth and walked back towards his tent, stopping once to pick up his helmet and mask. He looked over at his second and spoke briefly. Every word was perfectly clear in Karen's ears. "Twenty men. Anyone tries to escape, shoot 'em. Get me a fucking medic. My head hurts."

"Sir, yes sir."

Ten minutes later, after Sam Morrisey had come back with medical tape to patch up Andrew Wander's broken ribs, Frank Osborn and the man with the clipboard began dividing the volunteers into groups. Five minutes after that, the search parties began the arduous task of searching the woods.

2

The sun had reached its zenith and was beginning a slow arc towards the western horizon when Karen found Mike Summers. Lack of preparation, combined with the intense heat of the day, had forced over thirty people to retreat back into their homes. A few of them had to be carried, and that took still more people from the search for the missing boys.

Karen was hungry and frustrated, more than ready to call it quits herself. She was walking along the edge of the perimeter established by the soldiers. Her skin felt tight and hot, and her mouth refused to keep enough moisture to allow her to swallow. Despite the fact that she was supposed to be looking through the woods, her eyes stayed on the ground for the most part. Even lifting her head was proving an effort.

She'd cut herself a few minutes earlier. Forgetting that the barrier beside her was composed of wire and razor blades, she'd foolishly let herself get too close and was rewarded with a stinging wound on her right elbow. After that, she stayed a little farther away from the wire wall.

If she hadn't been looking down she might never have seen Mike's bicycle. The density of the razorwire made seeing though it almost impossible, and for that reason no one paid it much attention after the first few minutes. After a short time, everyone simply accepted that Mike could never have gotten tangled in that mess. It was easy to forget that the wire was, in fact, only solid in appearance. Despite the great loops of tightly woven material, there was still a substantial amount of open space in the center of the structure.

So when Karen saw the shredded remains of the bike tire, it came as something of a shock. Seeing anything disrupt the symmetry of the barrier was almost as unusual as seeing something pass partially through a brick wall. The tire was in ruins, with little but shreds of black rubber hanging loosely over the aluminum rim. Karen stared for a few moments, puzzled by the oddity before the implications finally sank in. After that she called out as loudly as her parched throat would permit and studied what she could see of the Schwinn. The bright red paint of the bike's frame could only be seen if she looked very carefully. From what she could make out, it looked for all the world as if Mike had rammed the bike into the barrier while popping a wheelie. The handlebars stopped at the height of her chest and the front wheel, equally shredded, was almost at the level of her eyes. The bicycle hung suspended within the network of wires like a fly trapped in a spider's web.

Even as she heard the sounds of several people responding to her call, Karen spotted Mike Summers. Or at least what was left of him. Somehow the boy had managed to get himself into the interior of the razorwire loops, and there he hung, his arms and legs snared by the blades of the barrier. From all appearances, he had almost managed to break through to the other side before he slipped. Heavy gloves on his hands had not stopped the blades from cutting through to the bones of his fingers. The sweatshirt he wore had only briefly prevented the razors from biting deeply into his skin. Worst of all, at least one blade had caught hold of Mike's face. The gash ran across his mouth and up to his cheek, lending an eerie, silent smile to the boy's once-handsome features. Both of his eyes were wide open, and Karen stared into the lifeless orbs for several seconds before remembering how to breathe.

She started to reach for the wire, desperate to help Mike before he bled to death. Despite the rational knowledge that he must have surely already expired, her mind demanded action. Every instinct she had cried out to make his pain go away.

Black gauntleted hands reached out and stopped her an instant before she would have caused permanent injury to herself. She struggled for a moment before realizing what she had almost done to herself. The strong hands pulled her back, and a buzzing voice spoke softly to her. "No, Karen. We can't have you hurting yourself, can we?" A second later she was handed to someone else. All she saw clearly was the back of the soldier's armored body as he pushed the wires apart and carefully crawled into the interior of the deadly barrier.

Several of the townsfolk watched helplessly as he gently pulled the murderous blades from the boy's body. Mike Summers did not slump when he was released from the wires. His body was as stiff as if it had been carved from wood. Extracting the corpse from the razorwire trap took a long time, and Karen could hear the man grunt with exertion as he finally backed out of the snare, protecting the dead body from further injury, despite the lacerations he received wherever his own body was not armored. A few moments later, he gently laid the body on the ground and stood up. Many of the people in the crowd wanted to blame someone for what had happened. Like as not, they wanted to blame the soldier who stood with them. Despite the anger they felt, no one said a word. They simply stared at the empty shell that once had been Mike Summers. Mike was known to all of them. He was a clown and a daredevil. More than one person there had commented that the boy's luck would run out one day, and he'd end up getting himself killed. Time had proved them right, but not a one of them felt the least bit smug about it.

Five, perhaps even ten minutes later, three more of the soldiers came through the woods. One of them produced a body bag. A few people mumbled or coughed as the boy was sealed from sight. No one spoke. The search party left the site just an hour before the Colonel's imposed curfew. They'd gone out to find two boys and returned with only one body. They'd left town a search party and come back a funeral procession.

It was only later that night, as she was preparing herself for bed, that Karen thought to wonder how the soldier had known her name. By then he was not available to answer her.

3

The next day they found Marty Wander's bike in the lakebed. From that point on everything just seemed to go straight to hell. Karen was at the high school *cum* hospital, waiting for her father to come back out from his first round with the injured folk in town, when she heard the news. Arnetta Wilcox came over to her, her hair a mess and sweat stains under her armpits. She was such a sight that it took Karen a moment to realize what she was talking about. She had to ask Arnetta to repeat herself.

"I said they found Marty Wander's bicycle. It's down at the lake, near that great big eyesore." Arnetta sounded exasperated and tired, but her eyes still held that secretive gloating light they had whenever she was first on the scene with the news. Despite everything going on, Karen knew the woman was enjoying herself. In that moment she hated the old woman.

"There's no sign of Marty?"

"No," Arnetta said. She then leaned forward and whispered conspiratorially. "And I don't think there'll be any news. If they could hide the wreck from that helicopter, I suspect they could hide a body."

"Oh, for God's sake, Arnetta. Tell me you haven't been saying that to other people." Karen felt her eyes bulge at the thought.

"I most certainly have. Everyone has a right to know, don't they?" The look on the woman's face said much more. It said she liked causing trouble. She didn't care to just tell the news; she enjoyed the chance to elaborate and explain her personal opinions.

"Did you ever think that people might go and do something stupid if they believed that, Arnetta? Did you think maybe they'd want to accuse the Colonel?" By the slowly dawning look of horror on Arnetta's face, Karen knew for a certainty that the thought had never been allowed to register. That the woman had considered the option had been a given in Karen's mind. But Arnetta hadn't let the thought catch on.

Karen thought about her father inside the high school, and then she thought about the potential mess at the lake. "Does Frank Osborn know about this?"

"Why, I don't think so. He wasn't in his office when I went by."

Karen moved away from the school, hoping her father would be all right without her. He'd looked much worse for the wear this morning and she was already feeling guilty about not being at his side the day before. Just the same, Frank had to be told about this before anything could get too ugly.

Frank was a creature of habit, and Karen hoped that was still the case. As she had two days before, Karen moved towards the Hav-A-Feast Diner, ignoring the heat beating down on her. Frank normally ate at the diner. It was close to his office and Laurie always gave the police a discount. While the day was technically a little too young for lunch, Frank was also the sort who preferred to eat his breakfast late. She'd heard plenty of stories about Frank's habits from Laurie, who she was convinced had a crush on the man, despite the twenty years separating them.

She was almost at the door when Frank Osborn came out of the faded chrome and glass diner with a look of pure desperation on his face. "Damn that stupid old cow to hell, Buck. Why can't she ever leave good enough alone?"

Buck Landers came out of the door half a foot behind him, looking about ready to shoot something. "It's just her nature, Frank. Arnetta don't mean to cause any harm. She's just too slow fer her own good."

"You heard what Arnetta's been saying?" Karen spoke out even as the police chief was preparing to snap a comment back at his second in command. Frank looked over at her, his eyebrows lowered and his nostrils flared like an angry bull's. After a few seconds his face softened just slightly and he nodded. "Good. I was just on my way to warn you."

Frank pointed a finger at Karen as he started walking towards his Mustang. She'd seen his cruiser at the office on her way over, but she figured he must surely have his reasons for not driving it. "You tell Arnetta that I had best not see her. I'll slap her in jail if this gets ugly. I'll find a reason."

Karen nodded as he yanked the driver's side door open, practically leaping into the car. Buck nodded to her as he climbed into his own squad car and in moments both of them were gone, heading towards the lake.

Karen stood for a few moments outside of the diner, contemplating what to do next. Then she moved towards her own car and started for the lake herself. Maybe she couldn't help, but she would at least know what was happening. Even as she moved in that direction she chastised herself for being only a little better than Arnetta Wilcox about the subject. At least she wasn't going around and spreading rumors.

4

The lake looked much the same as it had the day before. The biggest difference was that five hundred or so people were not there to watch as Frank and the Colonel began arguing again. That, and the Colonel was no longer wearing a helmet or a mask. Both were absent.

"That's fine. You don't have to listen to my warnings, Colonel. But I can feel a little better knowing that you have been warned."

"I have every intention of listening, Captain Osborn. I'm just not overly concerned."

"That's your option."

"I'm not concerned because I'm not going to play any more games. If anyone attempts any violence on me or my men, they will be killed."

"You're serious, aren't you?" Frank's face was pale, and he looked angry.

"Deadly serious. I've lost three men now, Osborn. I'm no longer playing games."

"Three?"

Three? What's happening to his men? Is it radiation? Karen felt her stomach tightening. If something was killing the soldiers in their armor, what was happening to the people of Collier?

"Oh. That's right. You weren't informed. Two of our men didn't report in last night. We found them in the same shape as the first one. It seems pairing them up has not been as effective as we'd hoped."

"I'm sorry about that, Colonel."

"Bullshit. You couldn't care less. I wouldn't in your position." The Colonel paused to take a sip of coffee from a dark blue mug he was carrying. "You have your job to do and I have mine. Yours involves keeping the peace. Mine involves that thing in the lake." He gestured with his head to the shiny mountain of metal reaching past the edge of what was Lake Oldman. "You've done your job admirably, Captain. I commend you." The man was handsome enough, in a military way, with his ramrod posture and his haircut even shorter than Frank's flattop. But the look on his face was almost too serene for the circumstances, and Karen found that more unsettling than the anger she'd seen on his face the day before. "Now it's time for me to handle my job. That includes defending myself from anyone stupid enough to attack me. We will defend ourselves, Frank. There will be no survivors if we are attacked."

Frank stood still, looking at the man with a face that could not settle on a single expression. "You're gonna gun down anyone who protests? Anyone who comes here wondering about the bike in the lake bed?"

"No. We're going to defend ourselves against anyone who decides to attack us. Questions that I can answer, I will answer. Accusations followed by fists will be answered only with violence."

Frank looked as if he wanted to say more, but his mind just didn't seem willing to aid him in his efforts. "I—"

"I've got a lot to do today, Frank. We're going to try digging that thing free. Pass the word around to any would-be mobs. No more mister nice guy. I mean it."

The soldier turned away, moving back towards his tent. Frank stood in the same spot, his glare drilling holes into Anderson's back, unmoving save for the bellows of his lungs gulping in air. After a moment, he slowly walked back towards his Mustang. Buck was leaning against his own car, looking as relaxed as ever. Sometimes Karen found herself wondering if Buck was even human. He almost never seemed fazed by anything.

Frank slumped against the hood of his car, his head low and his eyes staring at the asphalt. He reached into the shirt pocket of his khaki uniform and pulled out his cigarettes. After sticking the butt of one in his mouth and lighting it, he looked up again and locked his eyes with Buck's. "I want at least one officer out here from now on. Anyone wants to ask questions, that's just fine. They even look like they're gonna get into an argument about anything, I want it calmed down or I want that person in cuffs."

"What if it's more than one person?"

"Then I guess if we can't handle it, little Hitler over there can. All we can do is what we can do." Frank looked up at the sound of a car coming down the road, towards the soldiers' base of operations. The car belonged in a museum, not on the road. A massive Rolls Royce Silver Cloud, in mint condition. Lucas Brightman believed in traveling in style.

Lucas Brightman was always civil to Karen, but that did not mean she liked him in the least. Back when she and Pete were starting to fall apart, Brightman had offered her ex-husband a job. From the point when he accepted the man's offer, their rocky relationship had imploded. She'd always suspected Brightman was at least in part responsible.

When the car stopped, Brightman climbed slowly from the passenger's side and looked around the area with cold eyes. He nodded congenially to Karen, and then he moved over towards the police chief's Mustang.

"How are you today, Frank?" The words were friendly, but the smile that accompanied them made Karen think of a piranha.

"I've had better days, Lucas. Hell, I've had better months."

The old man laughed heartily, moving closer with an almost serpentine grace. For some reason, the sight of Brightman in such a cheerful mood made Karen's throat tighten. "We should talk, Frank." The man looked towards Karen and then towards Buck. He placed a companionly old hand on Frank Osborn's shoulder. "But we should talk in private."

Frank looked at the man, his mouth twitched with a nervous tic. His eyes, looking too old for his face and exhausted beyond any possibility of repair, rolled around the area once, and then locked onto Brightman's car. "So why don't we go for a ride, Lucas?"

"I think that's a fine idea, Frank. Let's go for a ride." Karen watched as the old man led the police chief towards the Silver Cloud. For all the world, Brightman looked like he was gently handling an invalid.

She and Buck watched as they entered the back of the car and continued to stare as the massive antique rolled away.

A few seconds later, Buck said the very words that she'd been thinking. "Why do I get the feeling that Frank's making a deal with the devil?"

"'Cause I think he's about to, Buck. God help us all, I think he's about to."

5

Though it took some prodding on her part, Karen was eventually able to get Buck to tell her what had happened to the Colonel's soldiers. They'd been killed and mutilated. While a part of her was surprised by the actions—one murder she'd heard about, but the mutilations were still a surprise—it took her almost no time at all to come up with a list of potential suspects.

The list was longer than she would have guessed before starting on her little project. One of the advantages of a small town was simply knowing everyone. Karen, a school teacher and regular at the Lutheran Church in town, knew more about most people than they would have ever guessed. Throughout the school year she overheard conversations between the children, tales of their daily lives that included knowledge of their families and their friends. Even her father, the pastor at the church, admitted that most of the regulars there were almost as gossipy as hens. Two twelve-year-olds couldn't share a first kiss without half the town knowing about it within a day.

So she knew just who had been in the military and who knew how best to hunt. She could guess at those in town who were most likely to chafe under Anderson's rule. She wrote their names in a neat, orderly script across three pages of green stationery. It wasn't very hard and, within an hour or so, she'd come up with what she considered the top one hundred most likely candidates in town. Pete was near the top of the list, not that she'd expected anything different. The scary part to her was that the list, long as it was, was nowhere near complete. It couldn't be complete when there were so many strangers in town. For all she knew, Maurice and Joan Dansky were international terrorists, and Dutch Armbruster and Becka were drug runners. Not that she believed any of that to be the case, but she couldn't tell for certain.

Still, it would have to do. Karen grabbed her purse, and moved towards the door, stopping only long enough to rub Roughie's belly. The mutt was a belly slut. He'd roll on his back and expose his stomach to perfect strangers, all in the hopes of getting a proper stomach scratch. If a burglar ever came into the house, Karen knew she was doomed. The dog would likely help the robber find his way around as long as there was a belly rub in the bargain. Not that burglars bothered her much in Collier. Not nearly as much as Pete did.

Thinking about Pete, Karen left the house, heading for the Hav-A-Feast Diner. Laurie Johnson would listen to her, and maybe even manage to talk her out of betraying the people of Collier. She hoped so. She truly hoped so. Even thinking about what she was giving serious consideration to doing with the list was enough to make her want to be ill. *Did Benedict Arnold think he was doing the right thing?* she asked herself. *Did Judas think he was handling matters in the best way?* Karen traveled slowly, her thoughts dark and worrisome. Was she doing what was best for everyone in town? Or was she being a coward and a traitor? Her mind said one thing; her heart had an entirely different opinion.

6

Laurie was puffing furiously at a Tarryton, wiping the stainless steel tables in the kitchen in a vain attempt to get them cleaner than they already were. Karen tried to help twice, and both times Laurie stopped her. "You eat when you're nervous, Karen. I clean when I'm nervous." After Laurie said that, Karen left it alone.

The Hav-A-Feast was closed for the night. Despite the fact that the sun was still up, Laurie closed early and went back to her trailer in the back of the place by eight PM on any given night. Her reasoning was solid. "I don't need any men in armor loading me with extra bullets on my way home. And even with my house right back there, some idiot would do it." Despite her cheerful smile for everyone, Laurie was a born pessimist. Karen never had quite figured out that aspect of her girlfriend's personality.

Laurie tossed the dirty rag over her shoulder. The discarded cloth landed in the garbage flawlessly. The cigarette butt she crushed into an ashtray already in danger of overflowing. Karen looked over at Martin Harper, the line cook and person actually in charge of cleaning the kitchen area. Martin was scrubbing furiously at the stainless-steel grill, scraping another day's worth of caked-on food from the surface with a spatula. From time to time he'd pause long enough to pour a few more ounces of soda water across the hot metal surface before starting again. He claimed the soda water lifted the grease and food, but Karen was certain he just liked watching the fluid boil and evaporate. Martin was one of the few men in town with hair long enough to put into a ponytail. He was also one of the meanest cooks in town. If the flabby cook hadn't been friends with the entire police force, someone would likely have helped him cut his hair a long time back.

Martin looked up and waved briefly before going back to his scrubbing. He did not offer a smile, and in all the time she'd known him, Karen couldn't recall the man ever smiling. He was an oddity, but he was a nice oddity.

"Are you listening to anything I'm saying?" Laurie's voice finally registered in Karen's ears.

"I'm sorry, Laurie. I was off in La-La Land again."

Laurie smiled tightly, another cigarette in her mouth and a broom in her hands. "Nothin' to apologize for. I just wanted to know if you'd heard about Arnetta."

"No, what about her?"

"Frank has her sitting behind bars."

"What?" Karen focused all of her attention on the present, forgetting for the moment that she wanted to discuss something with Laurie as soon as Martin left for the night. "What on earth for?"

"Flappin' her gums too much. He said with the way she's spreadin' rumors, it's only a matter of time before she incites a riot."

Karen thought about that for a moment and nodded. "She just might, too. I was at the lake with Buck when news of them finding Marty Wander's bike finally spread around town. Arnetta's darned lucky no one was angry enough to start anything. I think if it'd been Frank there, instead of Buck, there might have been some people getting themselves shot."

"It wasn't all that bad, was it?" Laurie sounded skeptical.

"No. There was only about ten people all together who showed up while I was there. I think they were more curious than angry. The bike's in perfect shape, and the government boys left it where they found it, just so people won't start blaming them for everything. That's my guess at least. I think the soldiers are afraid to touch it. Besides, they were mostly trying to dig around the edge of that ship out there."

"You're talkin' about too many subjects again. I don't see how you manage to teach anyone anything as a teacher if you're always talking about five things at the same time."

"My students learn. They just have to keep up with me, that's all." Karen hopped up on the edge of the table Laurie'd just finished cleaning to death, narrowly avoiding the broom that her friend used to attack the floor. There was no dirt to be found, but Laurie was sweeping again anyway.

"Anyway. Frank said he'd had enough of her blabbing mouth, so he locked her up. Said he'd think about letting her out after the soldiers clear out."

Karen stared hard at the floor beneath her feet, as if the broken tiles and browning grout might hold the answers to life's mysteries. "Do you think they'll just leave, Laurie? Do you think they'll dig up their ship and then just take off?"

"Want the truth?"

Karen nodded.

"Yeah, I think they will. I think they'll finish their job and leave."

"Why?"

"'Cause it'd be too much work to take us all with them, and too much work to hide all the bodies if they decided to kill us."

"I don't think they will." Karen frowned, feeling the muscles in her neck tense up as she prepared to speak. "I think they're being too secretive to let us go." Karen looked up as Laurie stopped working and turned to face her. The cigarette in Laurie's thin, hard mouth defied gravity, holding on to an ash that drooped away from the main tobacco stick as if the compressed soot were held in place by Krazy Glue.

"What do you think they're gonna do, Kari? Lock us all away for the rest of our lives?"

"I don't know. I just don't think we're all getting out of this alive."

"They got away in that town in New Mexico... Roswell, that's what it was called."

"I saw those specials too, Laurie. But this is different."

Laurie sighed, already growing impatient with Karen. She was fast to grow tired with any subject she didn't approve of. "All right, I'll take the bait. Why is this different?"

"Most of that town never saw anything. Most of this town has seen too much."

"Good point. But what can they do with us?"

"I'm not sure, but I think I can find out."

"How?" Now Laurie sounded weary.

Karen looked to Martin, who was now trying to clean out the grease traps without spilling the waste all over the floor. He was far too intent on his work to be eavesdropping. "I'm gonna give that Colonel a list of who I think is doing the killings. Maybe in exchange for that he'll find a way to keep us all alive."

Laurie coughed hard, hacking as if she'd swallowed the wrong way. "That might not be too smart, sweetie. What are you gonna do if somebody finds out? Somebody on that list, maybe?"

"I'm going tonight, after the curfew."

"Didn't they say they were gonna shoot violators of the curfew?"

"I'm counting on them being liars."

"Why don't you go now, or in the morning?" Laurie sounded genuinely concerned.

"'Cause if I do that, somebody might see me." She sighed, trying to find the right words to explain her logic. "Somebody might put two and two together."

"What if you get caught by the folks doing the killings?"

"Then I'm counting on me being a local as enough to keep me safe."

"Kari, honey? What if Pete's one of them?"

"Then I'm in deep trouble any way you want to look at it. But I've got to try, Laurie. I don't know, maybe if I take Roughie with me, he can warn me of trouble."

"And maybe that big ol' mutt of yours will see a cat and drag you halfway across town again."

"There is that risk," Karen admitted.

"So, it's settled then. I'll go with you."

"Oh, Laurie. I can't ask that of you."

"You ain't askin'. I'm tellin' you. There's a difference."

"But—"

"No buts. I figure you're less likely to get attacked if there are two of us. Besides, If it gets too nasty with anyone, it's best to have someone covering your butt."

Ten minutes later, those minutes spent in idle conversation that was forced and strained, Martin said his good-nights and went off towards his home. If he'd heard any of what they were talking about, he hid it well.

Despite several more protests on the part of Karen, Laurie went with her into the darkening night. She also made a point of showing Karen the knife she carried in her purse.

Somehow, they never got around to picking up Roughie before they left.

7

The sun set fast, and after that the biggest threats to Karen and Laurie were the mosquitoes. The little vampires were everywhere, and they seemed to find Karen's blood particularly flavorful.

The town was silent. Inside the houses they passed, Karen could hear conversation or the sound of televisions and canned laughter, but there were no cars on the road, and no people walking the streets. Normally, this time of year you couldn't walk down a street without someone waving or calling out your name. That was one of the best parts of living in Collier; no matter where you went, you almost always felt safe.

Right now that just wasn't the case. There were soldiers on the streets, silent black monitors with orders to kill. And there was Pete. Pete was in town, somewhere, and she knew her life would never be the same if he caught her out here by herself. Even having Laurie along added no comfort. Pete was normally the type to have backup if things didn't go the way he wanted them to go. Dutch was a nice man, and she was grateful for his help at the Piggly Wiggly, but he had been lucky that day. Pete hadn't planned on running across her. If he had, there'd have been nothing Dutch or anyone else could have done about it.

Laurie was breathing hard on her left, and, aside from the sound of a few nocturnal bugs, that was the only noise in the immediate vicinity. The lights in the closed houses did nothing to make Karen feel less exposed.

They walked down Providence Lane, which ran parallel to Millwater Street. Providence Lane was narrower and provided better cover. With four blocks to go until they reached Roswell Avenue and the Colonel's base of operations, they let themselves relax a little. They dared speak to each other, if only in whispers.

Laurie spoke first. "It's not too late to turn around, honey. We could go back to my place and get drunk instead of doing this." Her voice was a murmur, but might as well have been a scream. Karen nearly wet her underwear when her friend spoke. She clutched at her chest and gasped for breath.

"Are you trying to give me a stroke?" Karen demanded, her own voice an angry hiss. "I told you before, I'm fine doing this on my own. You don't have to be here, and you don't have to be involved in all of this nonsense."

"Sure I do. That's what friends are for."

"Well, then don't complain about it."

Laurie opened her mouth to speak. Someone else beat her to it. "Good evening, ladies. Please place your hands above your heads and turn around, slowly." The voice was a buzzing threat, and seemed thunderous in comparison to their own hushed tones.

Laurie said "Oh, shit on it," and raised her arms. Karen followed suit when she was certain her heart wasn't actually going to erupt from her throat.

When she turned, she saw the two armored men facing them. Both were completely in the shadows, and had not moved at all as she and Laurie walked past. How she'd missed the sounds of them swinging their rifles around was something she could not fathom. The soldiers moved forward and one of them moved his firearm off to the side as he came within touching distance. "If either of you move, my friend over there will shoot you. That's not a matter of choice; those are our orders." The soldier closest to them touched the jawline of his helmet and then turned his head slightly. After a moment in that position, he nodded and then turned towards them again.

The man patted his hands down Laurie's sides and then across her front and back. "Are you enjoying yourself?" Laurie's tone was one part relieved and one part shocked. The man did not answer. He grabbed her purse and began sorting through the contents without any hesitation. When he was done, he'd removed her steak knife, her lighter and the perfume she carried.

Karen steeled herself for whatever the man might do to her. He ran his hands lightly down her sides, and then down her front and back. He did not linger. He acted exactly the same as he would if he were frisking a man. When he was done he searched her bag and removed her perfume, her pepper spray and her hairspray. Her heart was pounding as if she'd just run three miles, and the inside of her mouth was completely dry.

"Ladies, we have orders to shoot anyone on the streets on sight. Technically, you should be dead." The buzzing tones of his voice could not hide a certain amount of amusement that crept out with his words. "Would you like to tell us what you're doing out here?"

"We were on our way to see the Colonel." Karen had always believed in telling the truth. She saw no reason to change that philosophy now.

"Well, that works out nicely. That exactly who we're taking you to see." He stepped behind Karen and grasped her right arm. "Please don't struggle, and you won't get hurt." In a matter of seconds, he had both of her hands behind her back. Something thin and cold held them in place when he removed his own hands. A moment later, he hauled Laurie's hands behind her back and used what looked like an oversized plastic garbage tie to lock her wrists together. "Now then, please walk carefully and quickly. I don't want you falling and hurting yourselves." She was reminded of that TV show, Cops, where the officers were always so polite after they'd managed to force the bad guys into cuffs.

The trip was uneventful. After walking for fifteen more minutes, the two of them were led into the canvas headquarters of Colonel Mark Anderson. The man did not look amused. "What is it with people in this town?"

"Huh?" Laurie scowled at the man, but her pale skin and shaky voice betrayed her false bravado. "What do you mean?"

"It seems simple enough. I say 'Don't go out after dark, or we'll be forced to shoot you.' What do you suppose that means?"

"That you're gonna kill us?" Karen didn't even try to hide her nervousness. Her voice was shaking and her knees felt like they were made from Jell-O.

"No. It means that I should have told my men to kill you on sight. Unfortunately, I'm a bit of a softy." Anderson was not wearing his mask. His strong face was set in a scowl, and his bruises from the day before had transformed themselves into ugly greenish-yellow blotches. "Would you please tell me what the hell you ladies are doing out after curfew?"

"Well, sir. We came here to try and make a deal with you." Karen was pleased with herself. She managed not to stammer as she spoke.

"A deal?" The man's face stiffened, and an almost smile came to his features. "What sort of 'deal' were you planning on offering me, Ms. Donovan?"

"How did you know my name?"

"I have a dossier on every person in this town, Ms. Donovan. I know names and faces in most cases. Sometimes I know a lot more." He shrugged. "Now please answer my question."

"I wanted to try helping you with finding the killers of your men," she stammered. "I—in exchange for your promise not to kill everyone in town." The tears started then. She didn't want them, but they came anyway. The idea that the man in front of her might know everything about her changed the stakes considerably. What if he decided she didn't deserve to live? What if he decided she should be with Peter, no matter what? True, it wasn't something he was likely to make her do, but he could if he wanted. His authority over her life was complete and his knowledge of her life worried Karen deeply. One little bit of knowledge had changed everything. He wasn't a stranger anymore. He had too much knowledge, and the information in his possession suddenly made him appear as a parent appears to a toddler: powerful and unstoppable. She blinked hard and sucked in a deep breath. No good, the waterworks wouldn't stop.

The Colonel looked at her for several seconds, confusion obvious on his face. Then his emotions disappeared behind a hard, expressionless surface, and he held out a tissue for her. She shook her head. "Can't."

"Can't what?"

"Can't move my arms. They're stuck."

"Sergeant, remove the restraints from these women, please."

One of the two soldiers stepped forward, pulling a knife from his belt as he came. He faded from her blurry view, and a moment later her hands were free. A wave of pins and needles moved into fingers that she had not realized were suffering from lack of blood. She took the offered tissue in her numb right hand and nodded her thanks.

"Get seats for these two ladies, Sergeant. And something for each of them to drink." The man disappeared, returning a moment later with two fold out chairs. After he'd set them down he left again, returning the second time with metal cups filled with cold water. The Colonel promptly dumped the water out of each and produced a bottle of bourbon. He poured a few ounces into the bottom of each cup. "Now then, sip on that and tell me what you had in mind."

Karen took a very large sip of the bourbon, feeling the liquid burn down her throat and blossom into a warm furnace in the pit of her stomach. The sensation was comforting. "Colonel, what is going to happen to the people in this town?"

The man hesitated, apparently trying to compose his answer. "That's hard to say at this point. If the murders of my men continue, the results will not be good."

"If I can help you stop the people responsible, can you guarantee the safety of the people here?"

"I cannot make promises at this point. A lot depends on the level of cooperation we receive." He paused for a moment, staring Karen in the eyes and then looking intensely at Laurie. "For what it's worth, it has never been my intention to kill everyone in town. I need to ensure privacy, and I need to make certain that the national interests are protected, but I do not plan on killing everyone."

"But you will if you have to, isn't that right?" Laurie's voice was soft and low, but her words were clear just the same.

The man looked back at her, his mouth set and his eyes unwavering. "Yes, Ms. Johnson. That is absolutely correct."

Laurie shrugged, reached for the bottle of bourbon and poured herself another shot. "At least you're honest about it."

"I see no reason to lie."

"I've got a list of names. Some even have addresses." Karen spoke up, sensing a building tension between her friend and the man in charge of Collier. "If you promise to do your best to avoid killing anyone, that list is yours."

"This list pertains to the killings?"

"It's a list of the people I think are probably responsible. Not all of them, just the ones most likely."

"Why should I trust your list, Ms Donovan?"

"Excuse me?"

"I said, why should I trust your list?" The Colonel stood up, walking a few paces to a small cooler and pulling a Pepsi from inside. "How do I know that your list is nothing more than a selection of people you don't like for whatever reason?"

"Well, I guess you'd just have to trust me."

"You ask a lot under the circumstances."

Laurie spoke then, her voice filled with venom. "So did you when you came into this town. You asked for everyone to trust you and obey you." Laurie smiled tightly, holding up a hand to prevent Karen from interrupting her. "You say the government's gonna pay all the bills for everyone who's out of work right now, and you say that what you're after is for the good of the country. Mister, I have yet to see anything on the armor you're wearing or even anything on your Jeeps that says you're with the U. S. For all we know, you're a goddamn Commie."

"I can assure you that I was born here in the U. S. and that I'm a citizen."

"I'm sure you can. I'm also sure you won't, just in case we remember something, like part of your Social Security Number. I don't think you work for the military. I think you work for the part of the government that doesn't exist on paper."

"You might be right."

"Kari here, she thinks there's a good chance you'll just bury all of us. Or lock us away in a prison that shouldn't be there. One that the taxpayers don't know nothin' about. Me? I'm an optimist. I think we'll get to live for as long as we don't sing." Laurie smiled again, a broad grin that had nothing at all to do with happiness. Karen desperately wanted her to just shut up, but knew that it was too late for that. "I figure we'll maybe get new names and new jobs set up somewhere else. Which one of us is right, Colonel?"

Karen turned to look at the Colonel. He wasn't smiling. "Maybe you're both right. Maybe the ones I like will get to live, and the ones who annoy me will end up in a shallow grave. Or maybe we brought a bomb with us for when we leave. One that will vaporize everyone in town, and be attributed to a terrorist who doesn't really exist." The man leaned in closer, locking eyes with Laurie and returning her feral grimace. "Maybe it'll be done with a short-lived killer virus, one that was custom-built by the U. S. of A. to take care of problems of civil unrest. Maybe we'll just line up the whole damned town and thank them for their cooperation before we pull the triggers."

Karen reached into her purse and pulled free the three sheets of paper with names written on them. She set them on the desk and stood up. "I think we should leave now, Laurie. I think we're bothering this man." *Oooh,* she added to herself. *With a line like that I might even make it to the door before they shoot.* Her heart was making unpleasant motions in her chest as she started walking.

"Not so fast, Ms. Donovan." Anderson's voice was a steel whip cracking in the air. She turned slowly to look at him, conscious of the sweat dotting her skin.

The Colonel looked at her for a moment, and then gestured for her to sit again. Walking on legs that refused to move without making odd jerking motions, she did so. The Colonel looked at the sheets of paper she'd left behind, scanning the names and occasionally looking over in her direction.

"What made you decide to write this up?"

"I don't want to die, and I don't want my friends to die. I figured if we cooperate, maybe things will go better."

"Peter Donovan is on this list. Your ex-husband, if I remember correctly."

"That's right."

"Is he on this list because he's your ex-husband?"

"No. He's on that list 'cause I've seen him hunt and I've heard tales of what he did while he was in the Special Forces."

Anderson looked at her for a long while, and Karen wanted to scream at him. She wanted to yell and hit and throw things. Mostly, she wanted to go home and hide beneath the comfort of her covers. And never get out of bed again. Coming here had been a mistake. She should have known better. In one simple action she'd turned her back on a hundred people that she knew, that she'd known for years, for her whole life. Every part of her body wanted desperately to grab up the three green pages and run as fast as she could from the man sitting across the desk from her. His eyes were cold and menacing, even when he was trying to smile, and she just knew that before it was all said and done at least a few of those people would likely be behind bars or far, far worse. *Oh God, what have I done?*

"Thank you for your help, Ms. Donovan." He smiled thinly. "And thank you as well, Ms. Johnson. I'll keep you posted of any events that come from this." He turned to the two soldiers still waiting in the background. "Escort these ladies home. Be discreet. They don't need any added grief."

Ten minutes later, Karen was at her home, wondering if she'd made a deal with her own devil, and wondering how Frank Osborn was dealing with his. She went directly to her room and, for once, did not scold Roughie when he came in. She held him tightly and cried silent tears for the sins she had certainly just committed.

Chapter Seven

1

The following morning the situation in Collier went from bad to worse. By the time Karen had finished her morning rituals of kicking Roughie off the bed and showering, the town was in an uproar.

Karen came down to find that neither Joan nor Maurice had cooked breakfast that morning. Soon after she finished preparing herself a bowl of Special K, she found out why. Maurice and Joan came in from their bedroom, and let her know all the details.

The Colonel had wasted no time in trying to gather as many of the people on Karen's list as possible. Maurice Dansky had gone to the Piggly Wiggly to purchase coffee, and heard about everything going on. The Thomerson family was gone, gathered together by ten of the armored men and dragged from their home. Even the children were taken. Arlo Walton and Sam Chastain had been taken from their homes as well.

"I was just hearing about Sam Chastain when the soldiers came into the store." Maurice was still pale and shaken, but he was calm and speaking with the voice of a natural storyteller. "I've never seen anything like it in all my days, as God is my witness. They just came through the doors, marching in unison and carrying their rifles at the ready. My father used to tell me tales of how the stormtroopers in Germany looked when they came searching for someone. I used to think he was exaggerating about how big they seemed when they were on the hunt. He'd say 'Maury, those soldiers were men I'd known all my life. They were just people, and many of them had come into my bakery every day for as long as I could remember. But when they came in looking for Ute Goldberg, they were strangers. I didn't even recognize them at first. They were like giants.' I know what he meant now. I don't doubt him anymore.

"At first I thought they were just going to start shooting, and all I could think about was how I didn't want to die in that store, looking for coffee that wasn't there anymore. I didn't want to die without at least a cup of coffee in my stomach. I know that sounds stupid, but that's all I could think. But they didn't shoot. They just came down the aisle and went straight towards the offices behind that big two-way mirror. I turned and watched them go. I don't think I've ever been that afraid in my entire life."

Maurice paused for a moment, sipping at the hot coffee that Joan kept refilling. The two sometimes argued—even in less than a week Karen had grown accustomed to the sounds of them yelling—but right then it was obvious how much they loved each other. The man's voice grew more animated as he spoke, but there was an underlying note of fear that would not leave him.

"The manager came out of his office, and he looked terrified, not that I could blame him. One of the soldiers, he grabbed the man by the front of his shirt and pushed him against the wall. I swear to you, I thought that man was going to die then and there. But the soldier just asked him a question, and he answered, pointing his finger towards the back room, the one that says 'Employees Only.'

"As soon as the manager pointed, Joe Ditweiller and Herb came flying out of the back room. I've never seen two men look so scared in all my years. The tall one, Herb Cambridge is his name, I think. He came out of the storage area with his hands held high and his eyes as wide as plates. Joe Ditweiller came out behind him, with his shirt unbuttoned and his hands crossed over his chest. He looked like he wanted a fight, as God is my witness.

"The soldiers moved in and grabbed the both of them, demanding to know if they'd committed the murders. Cambridge, he made a sound like a teapot getting ready to start whistling, and the other one, he reached for the back of his pants and pulled out a gun."

"He must have been crazy, that's all I can say. Cambridge shoved the gun up against one of the soldiers holding him, and he pulled the trigger. Right up against his side, I tell you. Cambridge got him where the armor doesn't cover him up. He fired the gun and all I could think was 'He's just going to make them angry.' Then the man's side exploded. What do I know from guns? I've never owned one and I never will. But I didn't think a little pistol like he had could make such a hole. The soldier never even screamed. He just hit the ground and started bleeding all over the magazine racks.

"Then the soldiers returned the favor. Those two men. They may have done something wrong, but nobody should die that way. When the shooting was over, I couldn't tell where one of them ended and the other one began. I never knew a man could bleed so much. Even the wall behind them is gone. The doors were destroyed by the bullets, and the wall where the doors were hanging looks like Swiss cheese. Holes as big as my fist, and some even bigger." He made a fist to illustrate the size of the holes, and Karen blanched.

Karen listened in silence. She heard Maurice's words, but could not respond to them. A deep chill penetrated her soul as she thought of Joe and Herb. Despite being the sort of trashy men Pete found to be good company, she did not feel they had deserved to die.

As she poured herself another cup of coffee, Karen couldn't help thinking about the list she'd written at this very table. The list in Colonel Anderson's hands. The list that bore the names of both the men.

And for the briefest moment, she felt she understood the actions of Judas Iscariot and Benedict Arnold.

For a time she went upstairs, back to her room, where she watched a dozen different shows about nothing in particular, paying them not the least bit of attention. She stared at the images on the screen, thinking only of the list. Despite her feelings of guilt, she hoped Pete would put up as much resistance as his friends had.

2

The day kept growing worse from there. When Karen went to see her father at the high school, she arrived ten minutes too late. Aside from herself and her two companions, no one was anywhere around, except for the nearly motionless guards. Dutch and Becka were with her. Dutch had decided that she needed protection from Pete, and had appointed himself as her bodyguard. She'd managed to give him the slip the day before, but he'd caught up with her, and apparently had no intention of letting her slip away a second time.

The three of them went over to the diner, and were surprised to find that the place was almost empty. Laurie was sitting at the counter, reading Cosmopolitan Magazine. She smiled when she saw them and immediately grabbed menus. "Hey, everyone! Come on in and make yourselves at home."

"Laurie, did you do something to the food yesterday? I've just about never seen this place so empty." Karen had trouble grasping the idea that the booths and tables in the diner were not overrun by customers. It was just barely ten thirty in the morning, and with the hours most people in town were used to after the last week, the Hav-A-Feast should have been standing room only.

Laurie grinned, a smile that was partially a scowl on her narrow face. "I blame Lucas Brightman." She pointed to the distant area of town where Brightman's factory sat. "He decided everyone was getting too lazy, so he reopened the textile mill and called everyone in. Had ten of his guys running across town yesterday to let everyone know."

"Why on earth did he do that?"

Laurie looked at her, her face puzzled. "I think he did it to keep the peace." Karen must have made a face, because Laurie raised her hands in a gesture to ward off reprimands for saying something stupid. "I'm as serious as a heart attack, sweetie. Him and Frank Osborn had a chat yesterday, as I gather it, and old Lucas suggested opening the mill so everyone would have something to do, something to stop them all from going stir crazy." She snorted. "It's all conjecture, of course. My main source for city gossip is still in Frank's jail. But I actually think he did it to keep the peace around here. I think maybe he's scared someone will be stupid and get themselves hurt in a bad way."

"That's mighty nice of Lucas, but I can't see how it's gonna do him any good. He's already got more carpet and tile set aside than he knows what to do with."

"Karen, sweetie, it ain't like he's got to worry about the money he'll lose. He's got more money than God." 'More money that God' was one of Laurie's favorite ways to poke fun at Karen. It was the sort of term that was almost but not quite offensive in Karen's mind, and Laurie used that knowledge to her best advantage. Karen made a face in return, and Laurie winked at her.

"What d'you folks want to eat today?"

The three of them scanned the menus and finally decided on what they would have. Laurie took the order and went off to tell Martin. On a day like this, Karen was almost surprised to see Martin working.

Dutch started up the conversation. "Noticed you were out after curfew, Karen. Is everything okay?"

Karen started, feeling like a convict despite the fact that she'd done nothing wrong. *Well,* she amended, *nothing besides getting two men killed and maybe half the decent folks I know thrown in jail along the way.* She forced her mind to stop with the traitorous thoughts, but it wasn't easy. Maybe there would be a few more people alive when it was all said and done. That was how she had to look at it if she wanted to avoid breaking into hysterical tears. "Oh, yeah. I was over here with Laurie, and we lost track of the time. She offered to let me stay at her place, but I wanted to make sure Roughie wasn't doing anything wrong. He tends to mess up the bedclothes if I leave him in for too long."

"Heck, I'd have taken care of him," Becka chirped in her nasal tones. "He's a cutie."

Dutch smiled. "You'd take in every stray animal on the planet if you could."

"Well," Becka responded, with a sheepish grin on her face. "Somebody's got to look out for them. Too many people forget that it's their world too."

"You aren't starting with that again, are you?"

"I wouldn't say a word if you'd stop going hunting."

"Am I doing any hunting right now, Becka?" Dutch's voice dropped by a full octave, and the tension between the two of them was almost visible in the air.

"No. But only because you can't."

"Leave it be." The look Dutch shot at his girlfriend ended the argument. Karen chose not to say anything about the incident. Before the tension got too thick, she asked them if they'd heard about what happened at the Piggly Wiggly.

"I don't normally like to say much about the government, but that was just wrong. Maybe the one guy had it coming, but they shot both of them." Dutch shook his head, pausing long enough to suck down a gulp of his Coke. "There's no cause for that. None at all."

"He said they'd kill two of us for every soldier who got shot." Becka spoke softly, her eyes wide and her bottom lip pooched out in a pout. "I guess they meant it this time."

Karen shook her head, patting the girl's hand. "Don't you worry about it. They won't be coming after anyone who follows the laws they set up. Stay away from them and you won't get hurt."

Dutch sneered unconsciously, his eyes looking past the distance wall. "Don't kid yourself, Karen. If one person does the crime and two people get punished for it, that means an awful lot of innocent people get hurt. Any one of us could be in the wrong place at the wrong time and get our heads taken off for our trouble." For all the world, he barely looked as if he even knew he was talking.

"I hope you're wrong, Dutch. I really do."

Laurie came back with their meals, and all three of them ate. There was nothing more to say for a while, and Karen was happy for the silence.

3

For the last two days, Karen had not seen her father. When at last she did see him, she could not believe the changes that had come over him. He wore blue jeans and a wrinkled button down shirt, instead of the usual dress pants and pressed, starched shirt he normally wore while away from the church. His usually squared shoulders were slumped, making him seem smaller than he actually was. Worst of all, his handsome face seemed to have aged by another decade. William O'Rourke looked horrible.

"Daddy? Are you okay?" Karen spoke softly, as if using her usual voice might shatter him. Her heart seemed to flutter, and she wondered if the heat was finally getting to her.

Her father looked up, and, past the dark circles under his eyes, she could see the same light brown eyes she had always loved. But the strength of conviction was gone from them. The color was right, the shape was right, but staring into those eyes was like staring into the eyes of a mannequin. "Hello, Kari. How are you, my dear?"

"I—I'm fine, Daddy. But how are you?"

For just a second, the old, wonderful smile she knew so well came back into his face. It disappeared so quickly that she felt she must have imagined it. "I'm just tired. I haven't slept well."

"Then that's it. You're coming with me and I'm taking you to my place." He started to protest, but Karen placed her hand over his mouth, gently, as he used to do to her when she protested too much. "No arguments. You're coming home with me, and I'll take care of you. Just like you take care of Mom." She almost cringed at how dry and hot his skin felt.

William O'Rourke smiled again, closing his eyes and sighing. "There's no point in arguing with you on this one, Karen. I know you too well, and I am too tired." She moved him towards her car, and he followed docilely. By way of thanks, he squeezed her hand after they were both seated and buckled in. His hands seemed to have no strength. Karen could have wept, but forced herself not to. He had enough troubles already.

4

Dinner was fairly quiet, subdued. Maury had once again worked his magic, this time on a box of Hamburger Helper. By the time he was finished, the stuff actually had flavor and texture, two things Karen always felt were missing when she cooked up a box. Perhaps it was simply that she never followed the instructions, but she doubted it.

Dutch and Becka still weren't speaking to each other, and Karen began to think that the silence went far beyond the argument they'd had over animal rights. Both managed to be friendly, but it was obviously an effort. For his part, Dutch smiled and nodded, even laughed at the right times, but his mind was very obviously elsewhere. Becka was a different story. She, too, managed to be civil, but she was almost constantly glaring at Dutch. If looks could kill Karen had no doubt that Dutch would be a burnt crisp sitting in a pool of his own body fat.

The Danskys were still shaken by what Maury had witnessed earlier in the day. The man's usual exuberance was sadly lacking, and Karen hoped it would return soon. Joan doted on her husband, making certain that he was comfortable and touching him constantly as if to reassure herself that he was still alive. The house sounded lonely without the two of them constantly bickering, and Karen was amused at how quickly the sounds had become commonplace.

Her father ate in silence, smiling softly once when he looked at her, and concentrated on his food with the same intensity as she felt a prisoner on Death Row would use to finish his last meal.

Even Roughie noticed the tension in the air. He sat away from the table, eyes planted on Karen, and pouted in that way dogs have. Roughie's dark brown eyes seemed to hold the weight of the world, and he was obviously not happy. Eyes that expressive on a member of the opposite sex were probably the cause of many romantic trysts.

Despite the gathering darkness, Karen desperately wanted to escape from her own home. These people, even her father, were an added burden on her mind. Already she felt her stomach churning at the thought of Pete. No word had come from Frank Osborn, and that likely meant the man was still on the loose. Holed up where he could wait for the right time to act. Frank was a considerate man. He'd have called if anyone had her ex-husband in custody.

Mostly her thoughts were on Joe Ditweiller and Herb Cambridge. Neither of them were good men. Certainly not the sort she preferred to hang around and chat with. They'd known about how Pete treated her, had probably encouraged him in his abusive manners. But she'd never wished either of them dead. She'd never wanted any harm to come to anyone as a result of her list.

They were dead just the same, and her hand might as well have pointed the guns that shot them down. She thought of Herb's family, most of whom she knew at least in passing, and hated herself. She thought of Burt Ditweiller, who was a drunk and a oaf, but one of the nicer men in town. He associated with the same crowd as his brother, but was a nicer person, less likely to actually be mean for the sake of being mean. Now he was all alone, no family to turn to with his grief and anger.

The night slipped away. Before she realized the time had come, everyone was in bed. Karen sat in her kitchen a while longer, sipping at the coffee that cost Maurice Dansky more than he'd ever bargained for. From time to time she heard the faint sounds of screams. Sometimes the noises were angry, sometimes they wailed a distant grief.

Karen tried to sleep, but rest was not meant for her that night.

The following morning Karen arose early, determined to make the best of her situation, despite her feelings of guilt. She showered and started breakfast before anyone else in the house was awake. Pancakes and scrambled eggs would have to be enough for her guests. She was still tired, and had never really liked cooking. While the coffee was percolating, she set the table and let Roughie out to run around in the back yard. The oafish dog promptly tripped over himself and started rolling around in the grass, reveling in the early morning sunshine.

Maury and Joan arrived first, protesting her desire to do any work at all. She hushed them and served them breakfast. "It's only fair I cook at least one meal while you folks are here. I mean, this is supposed to be your vacation."

Dutch and Becka were next down. Though there was still some lingering tension between them, they both seemed in better spirits than the night before. When her father finally joined them, even he managed a weak smile. He looked better rested than he had the day before, and Karen was grateful for the change in his appearance. He was clean and tidy again, and the dark circles beneath his eyes were less pronounced than they had been. His eyes seemed less feverish.

They ate in silence, save for a few compliments thrown Karen's way. When they had finished their meal, Becka and Dutch started on the dishes. William O'Rourke looked across the table at Karen and smiled. "Feel like visiting your mother today?"

"Well, I surely am not letting you go over there on your own." She smiled. "You might decide you don't like my place

and try sneaking on over to your house when you're finished. I
can't have that."

"I would never do any such thing." Her father's voice had
an echo of the wry humor she was used to, and he managed a
smile that did not look entirely plastic.

"You most certainly would. I would too, in the same situation, and I got all my bad habits from you."

"Impossible. I don't have any bad habits." To prove his
point, the reverend promptly belched, patting his stomach.

Karen laughed more for his benefit than because she actually wanted to express amusement. He was trying too hard,
but at least he was trying. Joan and Maurice looked on, both
looking shocked. The laugh became a little more real when
she saw their faces. "Daddy, you are impossible."

"That I am, Kari. That I am. Now, let's go see if we can't
sneak you in to see your mother, shall we?"

"Oh, Daddy, I don't know if they'll let me..."

"I've been wearing them down. I think it would do your
mother a world of good to see you."

"We'll see." Karen left the kitchen table and walked over
to where her purse hung on the closet door near the front entrance of the house. Even with four strangers in the house
she hadn't been able to break that habit. She had quickly
learned that she had nothing to fear from her guests. Everything was exactly where it belonged each time she checked it.
She was sure today would be no different.

Together she and her father headed towards the high
school. After a few moments of silence, Will asked her to
make a quick stop at the lake.

"Well, we have time, I don't see why not." She used her
turn signal and followed all the rules, despite the lack of any
heavy traffic. "Why did you want to go over there, Dad?"

William O'Rourke was silent for a moment, his eyes focused out the windshield. Then he turned to look at Karen
with a sad smile on his face. "It's something I have to do,
Karen. Something I have to face. I haven't seen the thing

since it crashed." He looked away, as if caught red-handed with a dirty little secret. "I have to see it, to make sure I'm not...misremembering what it looks like."

Karen remembered his words from a few days past. His fears that the sight of the UFO removed all possibilities of God and Heaven. Somewhere along the way, she'd managed to forget what he'd said. Now she contemplated the words carefully, chilled by the implications for the first time.

"Do you still feel the same way, Daddy?"

"What way, Kari?"

"That that thing invalidates God?"

"I don't know, sweetheart. I just know I've got to see it again. I—I've got to know if it's real in my heart, the same way I know it's real in my head. Does that make any sense?"

"Yeah. I suppose it does." Karen turned down Millwater Street, dreading the steep hill leading down to the lake, as she felt her car's suspension groan with every bump and dip. At the bottom of the hill was the vast parking lot for the shops at the edge of Oldman's Lake. To the left of the lot the burnt remains of the docks hung slightly over the empty lakebed. To the right, Roswell Avenue stretched off, slowly winding around until it crawled towards the center of town. Directly ahead the command tents of the armed men who now controlled Collier sat, almost hiding the main mass of the ship. Even with all of the obstacles, Karen could see the exposed cavity where the lake used to be. She wondered what they had done with all the water they drained away, wondered how they could remove the water from so large a lake and simply make it disappear.

Beside her Karen's father inhaled sharply, a gasp of air that almost seemed to hiss as it entered his lungs. Karen rode the rest of the way down, weaving through the military jeeps and civilian vehicles that littered both sides of the road. Even from a block away, she could see the rigid stances of the soldiers. She could feel their anger like a physical wave undulating away from their inner turmoils. She did not envy them their tasks. She did not like them, true enough, and she wouldn't have traded places with them for anything at all.

The bright morning sun was blocked out by another cluster of gathering clouds. From the oppressive weight of the air and the look of the dark underbellies of the growing puffs in the air, Karen knew another storm was brewing.

She parked as close as she could to the main parking lot, stopping only when she reached the barriers erected by Collier's own little Nazi brigade. The engine in her faithful little Taurus rattled for a few seconds after she killed it. She made a mental note to see about getting the old beast a tune-up.

By the time she'd stepped out of the car, her father was halfway to his destination at the edge of the lake. The guards looked at him as he passed, but made no effort to stop him from heading towards the massive ship. From where she was now, she could see that the scaffolding—with its mezzanine grating and thick couplings—the soldiers had built around the gigantic disc was almost completely rebuilt. None of the old, scorched metal from before had been used in the reconstruction. Karen thought about just how much money that metallic framework must have cost the people trying to protect their precious secret and then decided it was probably best not to know. William O'Rourke stared at the spacecraft. Karen stopped a few feet to his left, wavering between the need to look upon the unearthly vessel and the need to make certain her father was okay. The man who'd helped raise her, who was always so strong and unshakable in his faith, focused on the ship. His eyes did not so much as flicker. Karen couldn't tell what he was thinking, but by the strained expression on his suddenly pale face, she could guess he wasn't happy about what he saw.

Karen had done her best not to think too much about the thing half-buried in the lakebed. She hadn't actively avoided being near it, but she certainly hadn't taken the time to give it much thought. She looked now. The gleaming hull of the thing reflected back the darkening sky, distorting the image and warping her perspective. It had no texture of its own, and Karen found that almost as unsettling as the idea that it had fallen from the stars. *How can such a thing exist?* she thought. *It doesn't make any sense.* The longer she stared, the more she thought she understood what was going through her father's head. There was nothing to prepare her for the possibility of life on other planets. The Bible made mention of Heaven and Hell—even if it didn't use those exact names—and it spoke of demons and angels. It never made mention of alien beings from other worlds. Or, if it did, the references were too vague.

She continued to look at the thing, watching the clouds reflected on its surface as they gathered and darkened. The scaffolding and the soldiers building the structure around the ship ceased to exist for her. There was only the gigantic, distorted mirror and the secrets it held. Her own reflection was a pinpoint, but the sky above seemed to grow larger and larger as she watched.

Karen tore her eyes away from the hypnotic ship when she heard her father's gasp. William O'Rourke still stared where he had before, but his breath came in deep hitching sobs. Though his eyes did not move, his head turned slowly from side to side, a denial of what his traitorous eyes continued to observe. His breathing was ragged, and tears were doing their best to obscure his vision. Her father looked angry, filled with a rage the likes of which she'd never seen on his face.

Karen reached out to comfort him. He never even noticed her. His hands worried at the cross around his neck, playing with the cross and clutching at it as if desperate to find strength within the symbol.

"Daddy? Are you all right?"

Her father gave no answer.

"Daddy? Come on. It's time to see Momma." Karen watched her father. A hard lump formed in her throat, and all the swallowing in the world didn't seem enough to make that lump move. Karen reached for him with her hands, but couldn't quite bring herself to touch him. He was scaring the life from her. Despite her fear, she needed to comfort him, if only she could find a way.

It was like a light switch being thrown. One moment her father's face was a twisted, ugly mask of fury. The next instant the tension flowed away, replaced by a sadness that was painful to observe. His right hand held tight to the cross, and then he pulled down on the delicate gold chain that held the symbol of God close to his heart. The chain snapped. Karen had never seen her father without his cross, not in all the years she'd been alive.

With a single flick of his wrist, William O'Rourke sent the golden cross sailing through the air. The metal gleamed in the light of the sun where it broke from between the clouds, then winked away into darkness again. It sailed past the edge of Lake Oldman and disappeared into the pit where the waters should have been.

Karen wanted to catch it before it fell, but there was no way. She stared at her father with wide eyes and felt a deep wrenching sensation in the pit of her stomach.

William O'Rourke turned to his daughter and smiled sickly. "Let's go see to your mother, shall we?"

"Daddy, what have you done?"

"It's nothing I feel like talking about just now, Karen. Let's just be on our way, okay?"

Karen wanted to say more, but her father turned his back to her, walking towards her car in the distance. She started to follow him when the world went mad around her.

The ground vibrated. That was the first sign of trouble. From the heels of her feet to the middle of her thighs, Karen felt the strange, angry tremors run through her body. She lost her balance, falling to the ground even as the noise began. It started as a deep hum, so low that she was barely aware of it. Then the sound began to grow, increasing in volume as it ran the range of octaves. Her ears hurt and the sound drove spikes of pain into her head. Karen heard herself cry out, and looked at the ground before her as her vision began to waver. The vibrations grew so intense that she could feel her scalp shaking on her skull. Despite her best efforts, she could not control her eyes in their sockets. They seemed intent on looking at everything at once, which made it impossible for her to focus on anything at all.

The thunder faded from her ears, but her teeth still shook in their sockets and her vision was still as screwy as a TV set with a bad vertical and a messed up horizontal. She heard the sound of dogs in the distance going into a frenzy, and guessed that the sound was no longer audible to humans. The ground actually bucked beneath her, and Karen was thrown down as she tried to stand again.

Then the heat came. Just a hint of what it had been on the Fourth of July, but still very intense. Karen felt as if she were a bug under a magnifying glass. Somewhere behind her, a giant child with a malicious heart had set the lens just so, pinning her in a beam of focused light. Karen turned around, despite the warnings her own mind was giving her.

Behind her, the giant silvery mass of the ship was trying to rise from the ground. The scaffolding around the craft bucked and screamed in protest. The men standing on the structure held on to anything they could grab, clinging with desperation. Even from a distance she could hear many of them screaming in primal fear.

Karen tried to stand, tried to get as far away from the ship as she could. Each effort to rise ended in failure. Finally she scrabbled across the ground, half crawling and half slithering to get away from the rising silver blade. She was finally making decent progress when the great vibration suddenly stopped.

The abrupt end to the earth dancing beneath her sent Karen face-first into the ground. After hugging the scorched grass for a few more seconds, Karen turned around to face the massive ship. It looked exactly as it had before. Nothing had changed, except that the gantry around the alien monolith was now in disarray. As far as she could tell, all of the workers were still there, though a few held on precariously.

"What happened?" It took Karen a moment to realize she was the one who'd asked the question. Her heart still thundered in her chest, and her vision, though no longer jumping, seemed thoroughly off kilter. Her mind screamed back in a panicky voice: *It's alive! Whatever that thing is, it's alive!* She shut the thoughts away, refusing to accept the possibility.

Her father's voice answered her query, even as he reached down to help her stand. "I asked a question of God. This was his answer." Karen stared into her father's eyes. All signs of serenity and peace were gone. The man before her might as well have been a stranger. He bore her father's face, but the soul she knew and loved so well seemed to have disappeared.

William O'Rourke ran a callused thumb across her forehead. She felt a stinging pain where his finger had touched. "You're bleeding, Karen. Let's get you to the hospital.

5

Karen drove slowly, nervous and still disoriented after the mini-quake that had knocked her to the ground. A constant stinging sensation ran across her forehead, and Karen looked at herself in the rearview mirror, studying the spot where the wound lay beneath thin cotton. It wasn't a very long cut, but it was deep enough to be bothersome. The only thing stopping the blood from running into her eyes was a kerchief from her purse that was now working as a headband and tourniquet.

Despite her careful pace, Karen and her father reached the hospital in under ten minutes. It would have been faster, but already people were heading towards the dried remains of Lake Oldman, eager to discover the source of the vibrations. Commotion aside, the high school still looked like the same building where she'd gone to school and cheered at the football games. She expected to see old Mr. Tatum standing in the hallway, not another man in black armor and black clothes. Not another entity without a face, staring straight ahead.

Karen had grown so accustomed to the guards here staring in silence, that she was almost surprised when this one moved. "I'm sorry, Ma'am. No unauthorized personnel beyond this point." That buzzing quality still unsettled Karen. She felt like she should be used to it by now, but she wasn't.

Before Karen could respond, her father did it for her. "Karen's my daughter. She's injured. Like as not she needs stitches."

The guard stood unmoving for a few seconds. "One moment, Pastor O'Rourke." The man touched a spot on his helmet and spoke, but the noises Karen heard were muffled and too soft to understand. After a few seconds, the man nodded and stepped to the side. "You're free to pass."

"Thank you." If the man heard Karen, he gave no indication. She and her father walked on.

For the first time since the whole mess had started, Karen walked the halls of her old high school. They hadn't changed. But the classrooms were a different story. Beyond each open door was a series of beds packed closely together. Each bed was occupied, but Karen couldn't see the faces of the occupants, or even their bodies. Thin cotton screens separated the beds, a modicum of privacy for the wounded. Looking around, Karen finally realized that more than one helicopter must have been carrying the medical supplies for the field hospital. Beyond each door at least one attendant stood in a white bodysuit as all-encompassing as the ones on the soldiers. These even bore nametags, which was another surprise after the lack of identifying features on the men in black.

Karen wanted to stop, to examine the people in the rooms and see if she could match them to any of the people she hadn't seen around town. Paul Cullins, a who lived only a few houses down from her, who was as much a part of her neighborhood as the trees running in front of every house, was one such person. Karen hadn't seen him since the Fourth of July. Just as she was passing the fifth door on her right, it dawned on her that she didn't even know if her neighbor was dead or alive.

Her father turned towards the right, heading in the direction of the cafeteria, and Karen followed automatically. Out of habit long forgotten by her conscious mind, her stomach growled. A second later the old habit was crushed by the smell of sickness wafting from one of the rooms. From off to her left, Karen heard a loud scream. She started, but her father seemed unaffected by the sound.

Once in the cafeteria, Karen's father led her by the hand to where more people in white environment suits were sitting. One of the figures stood, smiling as Karen's father spoke. "Doctor Hendridge? I'm sorry to bother you, but my daughter was injured a few moments ago. I was wondering if you'd be good enough to take a look."

Up close, Karen realized that the person in the shapeless suit was female. The woman had dark skin and heavy crow's feet. She also wore very thick glasses. Just the same, the woman walked with confidence and extended her gloved hand in welcome. "Hi, Karen. Your father's told me a lot about you. I'm Doctor Hendridge. I'm in charge of patient relations, whatever that's supposed to mean." The woman had a midwestern accent, and her grip was like steel.

Karen nodded in recognition of the doctor. "I really feel fine. I just don't like the way the blood is flowing. Could you just check and see if I need stitches or anything?"

Hendridge smiled again, her voice warm and friendly. "Oh, I think we can do a little better than that." She led Karen gently to one of the hard plastic chairs in the cafeteria and pulled one over for herself. With gentle hands, she removed the kerchief from her brow and began probing the wound. "Nasty, but not bad enough for stitches. You wait right here and I'll get that mess cleaned up."

The woman had a comforting voice, and Karen felt herself starting to like the woman, despite herself. She didn't want to like the invaders in her home town. She didn't want to know them at all. But having a face and a name for this gentle woman with her easy charm made it hard for Karen to feel aloof. Off in the distance, a high, shrill scream echoed through the air.

Doctor Hendridge returned with a metallic tray loaded down with gauze and medical supplies. Nothing on the tray was more intimidating than a mild antiseptic. Karen sat patiently as the woman began cleaning the wound, wincing a few times but otherwise remaining perfectly still. After a few moments, the doctor looked at her and frowned. "Looks like I was wrong about the stitches, Karen. This is deeper than I thought. Hang on for just a minute longer, while I go get my sewing kit."

Her father stood nearby, looking around the room without really seeing anything. "Are you okay, Daddy?"

"I'm fine, sweetheart. I'm just going to check on your mother." Another scream erupted from the area beyond the cafeteria, and Karen looked on as her father headed towards the noise.

Hendridge returned again, and Karen looked the older woman in the eye. "So, how did you cut yourself, Karen?"

"That thing in the lake tried lifting itself out of the ground, least that's all I can figure."

"You were there when it happened?"

"We were just leaving, heading over here when it started. I thought I was a goner for sure. You don't expect earthquakes in southern Georgia." The woman laughed politely. Karen built her nerve and asked the question that'd been haunting her since she'd entered the makeshift hospital. "Who's screaming?"

Hendridge looked at her for a moment, her face impassive, then looked away. "I don't know."

"Doctor Hendridge, I can't help but think you're not telling me the truth." Karen sat perfectly still as the woman brought a syringe towards her forehead and warned her that there would be a sting.

"I'm not telling you the truth, Karen. I know exactly who's screaming. But I'm really not at liberty to tell you about any of our cases."

Karen felt a sharp pain in her scalp, followed almost immediately by a cold numbness. "See, the thing is, I know that voice, Doctor. I know it real well, and I want to know if it's who I think it is."

"I can't tell you. How's your head feel? Can you feel this?" Karen was vaguely aware of a light thump on her forehead, but she felt it from a distance.

"Barely felt a thing." Karen heard her own pulse thundering through her body, but it never touched the cold void where she knew she was wounded. A wash of light red liquid spilled down her face, and Karen closed her eyes instinctively as she felt the doctor cover her eyes and nose with a cotton cloth.

"Sorry about that."

"Is my mother the one who's screaming, Doctor?"

"I—I'm not at liberty to discuss that, Karen." The woman's voice sounded weak, softer than before.

"If our situations were reversed, Doctor Hendridge, would you want me to answer the same way?"

"No. No, I wouldn't. But I'd understand why you were doing it."

"I do understand, Doctor. I just don't agree. I haven't seen my mother since the early part of Independence Day." Karen paused as the doctor deftly moved competent hands across her scalp. "I know that she's hurt. I know that she's hurt real bad." Karen tried to remain calm, but the more she thought about the situation, the angrier she felt herself grow. "I just don't know how bad. Put yourself in my shoes, Doctor. Would you accept silence when you were closer than ever before to the answer of your mother's condition?"

The doctor was silent for several seconds. Then she brought scissors forward and snipped at the air above Karen's eyes. She came back with a pair of tweezers and black thread, along with the scissors. Next she lifted some gauze and held it to Karen's head. Moments later Karen felt the gentle pressure as the woman's hands pressed the tape into place.

"Three stitches total. Could have probably done it with two, but I like to be safe."

Finally the doctor's dark brown eyes met with her own. "Yes, Karen. That's your mother." Her voice was very soft, scarcely above a whisper. "She's not doing any better and she should be. You didn't hear a thing from me. Do we understand each other?"

"Very clearly. Thank you, Doctor Hendridge."

The older woman was about to reply when a new scream added into the sound of her mother's tired shriek. Even as Karen rose from the seat, a third voice joined in the cacophony. Then came the sound of something heavy hitting the ground.

Karen moved towards the noise as Doctor Hendridge ran in that direction. A wave of vertigo and nausea washed through Karen, sending her veering off course and delaying her. For a panicky moment she thought she'd lost her way as the room began spinning. Whatever the good doctor had pumped into her scalp was not reacting properly with her system.

It took a great deal of effort, but Karen finally worked her way down the corridor, staggering past numerous open doors and occupied cots. She needn't have worried about finding her way; the gathering of white-suited forms blocking one of the doors saw to that. Karen watched as more and more of the medical staff pushed into the room beyond the doorway. From inside she heard the sound of her father screaming hoarsely. Another voice joined in, and several cries of outrage came to her ears, though they were muffled by the thin plastic hoods that protected the medical staff from any possible foreign bodies.

Beyond the mass of bodies, she saw her father's face. His skin was red and his eyes seemed to burn with an inner light. In all the years she'd been alive, she'd never seen her father look more terrifying. Twice in one day, he'd become a madman with cold, hate-filled features. She hoped it never happened again. His face was a contorted mask of anger, marred by a line of blood running from his split lower lip.

Adrenaline spilled into Karen's system and goosed her pulse into overdrive. The confusion and dizziness that had assaulted her vanished as her senses grew more acute. She heard a man sobbing, heard the sound of flesh slamming against flesh, and then heard the sudden silence as the masculine voice stopped spilling its grief. She was distantly aware of the sound of her own breathing, and in the otherwise still air, she heard the continuous faint screech of a heart monitor warning the world that the person it was attached to had stopped having a pulse.

The semi-quiet lasted for three heartbeats, then the chaos began again. A dozen voices talking at once; a voice screaming out louder than the rest, demanding a shock cart. Calls for units of this and cc's of that. The madness lasted longer than she ever would have expected, and all through it, Karen felt the adrenaline roar through her system, forcing her knees to shake and her hands to quiver. When she couldn't stand it anymore, she forced her way into the room.

Karen's father leaned against the wall, his anger replaced once again by that blank passionless expression he'd so recently adopted. Tears spilled from his eyes and mingled with blood from his right nostril and his lip. On the ground at his feet, Artie Carlson lay prone, unconscious, on the floor. Off to his right, a living wall of flesh encased in hazard suits surrounded a bed.

And on that bed, her mother's ruined corpse jolted as a medic applied paddles to the burnt flesh of her chest after screaming "Clear!" loud enough to drown out everyone else.

Karen stared at her mother's face. She'd been a beautiful woman, but whatever beauty she'd possessed was buried beneath a heavy layer of blistered flesh and medicated gauze. Emily O'Rourke's eyes were open, but they saw nothing at all. The light that had always shone in her blue eyes was gone, replaced by a thick caul of medicine and pus.

Those dead eyes stared at Karen, accusing her silently of betrayal.

The room spun. Karen stepped forward, trying to reach her mother. The floor leapt forward and knocked her down, keeping her from her task.

Then there was darkness, and the only thing Karen heard was the sound of her own silent screams mingling with the panicked call of the heart monitor.

Chapter 8

1

Karen woke in her own bed, uncertain how she'd gotten there. She had vague recollections of screaming, and recalled too well that her mother was dead, but that was all. There was nothing else to remember. Except her scalp, which stung with a frustrating heat and forced away her ability to focus on anything.

Rain was falling heavily outside, dropping torrents of water on the roof of her small house. Downstairs there was only silence. Roughie looked at her from the foot of the bed, his soulful brown eyes seeming to say, "I understand your grief. I'm here for you." Karen crawled across the bed and wrapped her arms around the mutt's neck. His tail thumped twice, heavily, on the bed.

A distant part of her wondered why she couldn't cry. Karen and her mother had never really gotten along all that well. She'd always been "daddy's little girl," and deep inside she knew her mother had resented their closeness. Still, the tears should have come.

Eventually, she released the tolerant mutt from her embrace. She began to relax, letting her mind ease into consciousness. Karen started and the room shook as a blast of thunder roared close by. Even Roughie was upset by the sound, and he normally ignored thunderstorms with the very best of them.

Having heard that lightning could fry a person while in the shower, Karen decided to play it safe and wait for later to wash her hair. She dressed herself in jeans and a T-shirt then went down stairs to let Roughie out. Roughie took one look out the door decided to answer nature's call a little later.

Karen stumbled into the kitchen, where she found the Danksys eating lunch.

"How are you, Karen?" Joan Danksy looked at her with genuine concern. "How's that head of yours doing?"

"Hi, Joan. I'm all right. Just tired." Karen's voice sounded faded and weak, even to herself. "Good morning, Maurice."

"It's afternoon, but good morning to you as well." Maurice smiled his same old sad smile, and promptly stood up, pulling out a chair for Karen. "Sit down. You should eat something."

"Oh, I'm not really hungry," Karen protested.

"Nonsense! You just don't know you're hungry. I'm gonna fix you a couple of grilled cheese sandwiches. Joan, darling, would you warm up the tomato soup for me?" Joan rose immediately, and reached for the pot on the stove. "You'll like the soup, Karen. It's homemade. I got some tomatoes from that nice Mister Feltzer down the road."

Karen thought about protesting again, but Maurice was already halfway done with the task of putting cheese on rye bread, and the butter was already melting in her battered old frying pan. Before Karen could decide whether or not to risk hurting their feelings, Joan had already placed a fresh cup of coffee in front of her and promised soup within a couple of minutes. Despite her earlier proclamation, Karen felt her stomach begin to growl as the smell of toasting bread came her way.

The winds outside picked up, sending a barrage of small tapping sounds against the house as the rain shifted course. "So," Joan said, speaking with the soft tones of compassion. "Would you like to talk about what happened yesterday?"

"What's to talk about? My mother was murdered." Karen was almost surprised at how simple she made that sound. Almost appalled by the apparent lack of caring in her voice. She felt drained; an empty vessel that could never properly be filled again.

Joan sighed, and Maurice set a warm bowl of cream of tomato soup in front of Karen, following it immediately with a perfectly scorched grilled cheese sandwich. He made a "tut

tut" noise as he brushed past her. His face was set in a scowl of disapproval. "So now we're supposed to believe you have no feelings, Karen?" Thunder from the south rattled the windows, emphasized Maurice's question.

"What do you mean?"

Maurice shook his head. "You act like your mother's death is just another day in your life. We know better than that. You're a good person, a *mensch*. Why do you act like her death means nothing?"

"It does mean something. It means that my mother was murdered by the town drunk. I just don't know how I'm supposed to feel about that, that's all." Karen felt old barriers she'd thought long gone begin building themselves around her feelings. The same barriers she'd erected when she and Pete were married. The ones she used to let the world at large know that everything was just fine, even when her beloved husband kneed her in the ribcage or forced himself on her like an animal. She seemed powerless to stop them from going up. Old habits die hard.

Joan smiled and ran her hands across Karen's shoulders, lightly massaging at the tension Karen hadn't even realized was squeezing her muscles into knots. Maurice sat across the table from her, reaching out with his warm, soft hands and wrapping her own hands within them. "Karen. Don't do this. Don't hide your feelings away. It's not healthy. I haven't even known you a week, and I can tell already that this is a bad thing for you to do." He smiled sadly, an expression his face seemed perfectly suited for, and continued. "When I was a young man I lost both of my parents to a drunk driver. They died horribly, pinned in a burning car and screaming for everyone around them to hear. I wasn't even there for them. We'd had a fight over me dating a young Catholic girl. My last words to my father were that he could go to hell for all I cared." Outside a flash of bright light flickered, followed a second later by a loud boom like the wrath of an angry god. The only sort of deity Karen could believe in at that moment.

The smile left the old man's face, and Karen saw, for the first time, that he was much older than she'd thought. He was usually so active and happy, and that always made him seem like a man in his forties. Now she realized that he was at least in his late fifties, probably older. He spoke again, even as Karen was wondering if he too would die before the bastards in control of the town were done with them. "I can never take back those words, Karen. As long as I live I can never take back those horrible words.

"I didn't think it was right that I should cry. I was a man, after all, and I had my brothers and sisters to look after. I was the oldest, and that was my responsibility. So I went on my way, and I got myself a job. I worked hard and I paid the bills. I spent all of my waking hours making money and listening to all the problems my family had to endure. I didn't cry when my parents were buried, and I never shed a tear when I had to sell the family home and move us to a smaller place."

Karen listened patiently, working over what her boarder said. It meant nothing, had no connection to what she was going through. "I'm sorry, Maurice. I don't get your point."

Maurice did that little half smile he was so fond of, the one that seemed to ask God above for patience. On most people it was an expression that seemed condescending. On Maurice it seemed somehow appropriate. "My point is that I held all my grief and anger inside for almost ten years. For this I got an ulcer and I got gray hairs years before I should have." Maurice shrugged. "Those things never bothered me. I ate less mustard and I wore a few more hats."

He clasped Karen's hands more tightly and she was surprised by his strength; he normally seemed so soft and gentle. When she looked into his eyes again, she saw more than she expected. She saw his grief, and the sorrow he claimed he never showed in public. "I was wrong to do these things, Karen. That's what my point is. Not because of the hair or the stomach pains, but because I shut off everything. You can't just ignore the bad things in life and accept the good

ones. It isn't that easy. God did not make us to live with
pleasure and forget the pain. He made us in His image, and
that means we must suffer to understand that others suffer
as well."

Karen pulled her hands away, crossing her arms under her
breasts. "I don't want to suffer, Maurice. I've suffered enough
already." She felt hot stinging flashes at her eyes and knew she
was on the verge of tears. "I don't want to feel anything,
because it all hurts too goddamned much." Her voice cracked,
and Karen rose from the table. She was damned if she'd share
her grief with people she barely knew.

Joan Dansky blocked her way, and Karen tried to push
past her without actually causing the woman to fall. It wasn't
meant to be. As Karen shifted to her left, Joan countered,
continued to bar her from leaving. When she dodged to the
right she found the older lady still blocked her path. Frustrated, ready to lash out, Karen threw her hands up in exasperation. That was when Joan made her move. Before she
knew what was happening, the older woman had wrapped her
own arms around Karen's ribs and pulled her closer.

Karen stood ramrod stiff, refusing to move, refusing to
give in. Joan pulled her closer still, until their faces were
against each other, cheek to cheek as if they were caught in
a dance. Karen felt her body sway, compelled by Joan's movements, and then she felt the burning at her eyes become a
flood of hot grief.

She tried again to force the tears away, but this time she
failed. Her mother's face came to her, unbidden and unwanted.
She thought of the times they'd spent together, the good times
and the bad. She remembered her mother holding her in much
the same way Joan did, comforting her after she'd gone through
with the abortion. She remembered her mother's anger with
Pete, and the list of names the woman had called him during
the divorce. Mostly she thought of her mother's gentle smile
and cheerful laughter. She remembered them and realized she'd
never experience them again.

And the tears flowed, and the storm locked within Karen O'Rourke's heart and soul finally broke free, raging as surely as the wind and rain that assaulted her tiny home and carving trenches of agony across her very being with the same intensity as the lightning that raped the heavens above.

In time both storms calmed and faded. Maurice and Joan led Karen back to her room, settling her into her bed just as her parents had done when she was younger. Exhausted from her crying fit, Karen fast fell into slumber. She dreamed of vengeful gods and burnt women; her sleeping mind conjured up ships that rose from dead lakes and struck her parents down. Her mother died again, caught by a powerful light that incinerated her very soul. Her father died as well, crushed by the hand of the God he'd forsaken.

And while she slept, her father died seeking vengeance against the new god he'd found and come to idolize in his own bizarre fashion. From there on, Karen's life only grew worse.

Interlude

1

The storm over Collier only faded for a short time before coming back with a vengeance. The winds tore at the trees with the force of a small hurricane, and the rain fell in sheets, spraying the sides of houses and cars, swept by the wind hard enough to wash through open windows, drenching furniture and unsuspecting people. Those who dared the weather and were close enough to see the fallen starship saw the bottom of the lake's bed fill with water as the torrential downpour continued. Certainly there wasn't enough falling to fill Lake Oldman again, but there was enough to soak the cracked, blistered dirt at the bottom, and to soften the dry pan back into mud.

Most people sought shelter from the storm, especially those who actually lived in the town under normal circumstances. Only a year ago they'd lost four people to lightning strikes in less than a month—Kyle Waters, who'd been fishing on Lake Oldman when the weather turned sour; Tommy Prescott, who'd just plain been in the wrong place when the storm broke and managed to fry him even before the actual rain started; and Louise Finnegan and her boyfriend Mark Walton, who'd been trying to get intimate when the lightning struck and fused them together at the hips—and even with all that happened in the span between, the memories were fresh enough to keep Collier's citizens wary.

There was only one victim of lightning during the storm. Corporal Rick Carlisle learned the hard way that Kevlar weave over ceramic pads and steel-toed boots don't make a person indestructible. The hard rubber soles of his boots might have afforded him some protection, but the thoroughly wet socks on his feet couldn't possibly have helped him out. He was calling in to command center to report that all was clear when the fork of electricity tore through his right foot and leaped towards the heavens by way of the top of his helmet. All command heard was "This is Corpor-" before the shriek of feedback half-deafened two of the radio technicians. A few moments later, the very shaken voice of Private Lance Monteleone reported that Carlisle was dead and called for help as he couldn't, at the moment, convince his legs to work. Monteleone was fine by the time a detail came out to the site, across from the Hav-A-Feast Diner. When the soldiers and medics arrived, they found Monteleone walking around in a dazed fashion. Carlisle was a differently story entirely. The soldier's helmet only came away from his skull by taking a sizable chuck of crisped flesh with it. The oxygen tank built into his armor had opted to explode along the way, so the soldiers knew there was no chance of reviving him. Several broke regulations and tore off their helmets before losing their last meal across the lawn in the Town Square.

Colonel Anderson took the breach of protocol personally, verbally tearing every last one of the "weak-stomached pansies" a new asshole for their troubles. Ever since the ship decided to half haul itself out of the ground the day before, his orders were very strict about any of his people removing any part of their gear without prior permission. True, the radiation in the area had only increased while the cause of all their recent grief was trying to move, but the surge in the energy readings was nasty enough to present a serious risk down the line, if it should happen again.

None of the men were happy about the tongue-lashing they received, but they took it anyway. It was just plain foolish to piss off Anderson these days. He was acting absolutely manic.

2

Mark Anderson listened to the voice on the other end of the phone line. He'd heard the same deep, rich voice for the last twelve years. He'd never had a face to go with the voice. As time went on, he'd simply come to imagine a tall, stocky man in an immaculately tailored three-piece suit. The sort of man one would expect to wield substantial power on Wall Street. The only name he had for the voice was Hardaway.

At the present moment, Anderson was dreaming about his hands around the neck of his imaginary businessman. He was dreaming about how red that pampered face would grow, and the feeling of a heart thundering between his hands. At times like this, he understood why the man preferred to remain anonymous.

"I understand your trepidation, Colonel, I truly do. Nonetheless, you have your orders."

Mark sighed. "When are these...'conditioning experts' of yours due in, Hardaway?"

There was a slight hesitation, and Mark imagined the cultured mouth of his direct supervisor scowling at the lack of a "Mister" before his last name. The idea brought a smile to the Colonel's face. "They should be there by twelve hundred hours. You are to give them any assistance they require, Colonel. Do I make myself clear?"

"Yes, sir. I understand."

"Colonel?"

"Sir?" Mark hated when Hardaway added a note at the end of their conversations. It was never a positive thing when the bastard wanted to continue talking. Bad things happened to people when Hardaway felt the need to elaborate, especially after he'd confirmed that Mark understood who was in charge. Anderson felt his stomach churn, and felt the vise grip of pain around his temples tighten another notch.

"This is the last recourse open to you. I know that doesn't make you happy, but if the conditioning experts should fail to accomplish their goals, the people of Collier are to be taken out of the equation."

"Yes, sir. I understand, sir."

He half-expected another response from Hardaway. Instead he got a dial tone. Mark Anderson very calmly set the headset back into its cradle and walked away from the desk he all but called home, before he started his rant of profanities. Steve Hawthorne made a point of looking unaffected by the tirade, an expression that had taken him years to perfect.

When Mark finished, Steve poured him a cup of decaf coffee and sat down in the chair facing the Colonel's. A few moments later, Mark sat down as well.

"What's up with Hardaway?"

Mark snorted. "The fucker wants to bring in a group of 'conditioning experts.' If they can't get the job done, everyone in this town is as good as dead."

Steve whistled a long, low note. "Guess he hasn't liked the reports too much, hunh?"

"No. He says we've had 'unacceptable losses.'" Mark slurped down half his coffee, looking at the only man he could trust in the entire town. "How the hell would he know about our losses, Steve? What gives him the right to just decide what's acceptable when he hasn't looked the area over, when he hasn't seen the faces of the people here?"

Hawthorne shrugged, reaching for his own coffee. "He's the big guy. He's the one who arranges our finances and makes sure we have what we need. That's all the right he needs, Mark."

"Yeah. Well, I don't know if he'd feel the same way if he had to meet with people like Frank Osborn, or even that little candy-ass, Fitzwater."

"Mark," Hawthorne set down his cup and shook his head. "There's a reason the man hasn't met with you personally. There's a reason you've never spoken except over a secured line."

"Yeah? Why?"

"Because he's just as human as you are. If he met you in person, he might hesitate to have you removed from the scene in a permanent way, if he decided you were expendable."

Anderson looked over at his second-in-command. He scowled and shook his head. "I hate it when you say that stuff, Steve. You know why?"

"Probably, but tell me anyway."

"Because I know you're right."

The two men stared across the desk at each other for several seconds. Neither spoke and neither needed to in order to understand what was next on the agenda. A group of specialists was due in only a few hours, and those unique talents would decide what happened to every single soul in the entire town.

"I sure hope those fuckers are good at what they do." Steve spoke out loud, but he didn't really direct the comment towards Mark. "If they aren't, this is going to get very messy."

Anderson snorted. "Yeah, and it's been such a neat operation until now."

"In comparison to what it will be? Yes. Yes it has." Hawthorne rose from his seat and reached for his helmet and face mask. Anderson couldn't help but notice the black gear's resemblance to a modified executioner's hood.

3

Peter Donovan sat in what he'd come to think of as his seat in Lucas Brightman's rec room and smoked another cigarette. Not far from him the owner of the house was playing at watching the grass grow through a window that was as spotless as everything else in his house. No matter what had happened

the day and night before, Brightman's maids always had everything back in order within a few hours. That was what Luke
wanted, and he almost always got what he wanted.

Brightman looked away from the window and moved over
to the bar, pouring himself a shot of Scotch whisky that was
older than Pete was by a decade or two. He looked at his
houseguest with eyes that were sharp enough to cut through
wood, and Pete stared back.

"I think it's fair to say things have gotten worse, don't
you?" Lucas spoke with the same refined Southern drawl he'd
always had—fair became *fay-uh*, and summer became *summah*,
bringing back to Pete's mind the image of an old plantation
owner in a white suit, and just possibly wearing a short-
brimmed white hat to go with it—and Pete reflected briefly
on how much he liked the sound of that particular dialect. It
spoke of breeding and money, both of which were things
that he respected.

"I imagine it would have been worse if you'd left the damn
mill shut down." Pete was still angry about that. He hadn't
wanted the mill reopened. The mill was where he'd been handling a lot of the munitions he and the boys were making—
the boys that were left after the Black Guard came through
town and locked about half of them away, thanks very fucking
much—and he was still worried that somebody would stumble
across their stash and make things even worse.

"I had my reasons for opening the mill again, Peter
Donovan. Don't you forget that."

Pete crushed out his cigarette and lit another, blowing a
cloud of smoke across the room. "Yeah? Like what?"

Lucas Brightman's eyes narrowed into a squint, and he
looked at Donovan long enough to make the guest in his house
feel decidedly unwelcome. "I live in Collier, boy. I know these
people. I might not always agree with them, but they're still
my neighbors. You watch out for your own, Peter. If you don't,
no one else will."

"I don't get what you're saying, Lucas."

"Now why doesn't that surprise me any?" Brightman looked at him for a second and then continued. Pete decided not to take offense to the old man's attitude. He was used to it by now. "Just because you and some of the boys decided to play terrorist doesn't mean I feel like watching others take the flack for it. Everyone in town is getting restless, and that is decidedly not good. You and the others, you know how to work quietly. You know how to avoid a mob scene."

Pete nodded to show he was getting the idea. "You're actually trying to stop them from following my lead?"

"You're damned right I am. You get two hundred angry people together without something to do that's constructive and they're going to get *de*structive. You know it and so do I. Normally I wouldn't give a good goddamn about that. But these aren't normal times, now are they? It is not Frank Osborn who'd be breaking up a mob scene right now. It's those bug-eyed walking tanks out there. And they don't much care if we live or die. It's all the same to them."

Pete nodded again, considering that. "Maybe I'll keep it quiet for a few days."

"Might not be a bad idea. Let them think they got the ones causing the troubles...or at least that they got the leaders."

Pete smiled. "I can do that. Besides, I have a few more things to fix up before we get started in earnest."

Brightman looked over at Pete and nodded slowly. "Just you be damn certain you know what you're doing, boy. I don't want the people of this town dead, I want them free. Am I clear?"

"Perfectly, sir."

The two men sat in silence for a while. It was a comfortable enough silence, but Pete wasn't feeling comfortable at all. His unfinished business would help keep some of the rowdier boys from getting too itchy. He left a few minutes later, ready to get the gang together for a little party.

4

Later the same afternoon, long after the rain had stopped again and the ground was once more dry and baking hot, Rebecca Susan Thomerson, better known to the people of Collier as "Becka," was wondering if she'd ever be able to get back home. Wondering if she'd ever see her family again. At first running off with Dutch seemed like a grand idea, but that was when she could still call her mother and tell her everything was okay,

Back when she could ask if her mother's new boyfriend was still there.

when she could make sure her mom was still doing all right and still hanging around with her latest boyfriend, Bobby

hands

Dallas, better know to Becka as Mr. Hands. The sick bastard couldn't keep his hands to himself, and kept trying his best to get into her pants. Becka felt it best to leave before she did something stupid, like beat his head in with a hammer, or he did something worse, like rape her and dump her body somewhere.

Bobby gave off the sort of vibes that said he could do something like that. Becka trusted her instincts enough to leave before he could cross that line. Oh, her mom had thrown all sorts of fits at first, screaming up a blue streak on the phone and calling Becka a liar when she finally told the woman why she'd left. She changed her tune about a month later, and Becka could only guess why.

Because it's a trap. Because he made her say all the right things so I could go home and he could get his filthy paws on me again. Because my momma loves his sick ass and I'm just a means to keep him. Because...

She had her suspicions, but they weren't anything solid. They were just guesswork.

Dutch was supposed to give Becka a lift back home; that had been the deal when they left Allentown, and it was still the deal now that they were supposed to be on their way back. Her fault, she was the one who wanted to see the fireworks in

Collier. Dutch, big teddy bear that he was, had never tried to use that fact against her. He just kept doing his own thing, and did his best to keep smiling through it all.

Becka knew what Karen thought, but it wasn't like that at all. They hardly ever had sex; Dutch was more like an uncle than a boyfriend. Mostly they talked. Mostly Dutch told stories about his time in Viet Nam and Karen listened like a rapt pupil, eager to learn as much as she could. It wasn't that she much cared about the war, it was more that she loved to hear him tell his tales. He was a perfect example of what Becka thought an uncle or grandfather should be. She'd never had either, but she'd always imagined what one would be like. All she'd ever had was her mom and, on rare occasions, one of her mother's boyfriends who was willing to talk to her when she was just a little kid. Most of them never stayed around long enough to give a damn about what Becka had to say. A lot of 'em just stayed for a few hours, or a few weeks if Mom was on a roll, then hit the road, never to be seen again.

Dutch was different. He was Becka's friend, not her mom's. In his own way he cared for her, too, and that was really something special. If he wasn't so much older, she'd maybe have thought about becoming more than just friends with him. But he was old enough to be her father, and smart enough to know he was being used by Becka. They had an understanding, and while they fought from time to time, both of them respected the established boundaries of their relationship.

Becka rolled over, looking around the area and wondering where Dutch had gone off to this time. They were in a patch of woods not too far from the edge of the lake, and pretty close to where the farmhouses started. Dutch hated being cooped up all the time, so Becka'd decided to make them a picnic lunch—peanut better and jelly on rye bread. The white bread was all gone and there was no mayonnaise left to go with the remaining tuna fish, but the sandwiches weren't too bad—just so he could get some space away from the house. They'd done some heavy petting after eating, and Dutch went off to slip on a condom, something he always did, as if putting one on in front of her was rude or something. That had been a good fifteen minutes ago. While he'd wandered off before, he'd normally waited until after they'd had sex on the occasions when they'd gone beyond groping and dry-humping.

The shade was good in this area, and the breeze was actually strong enough to help cool her body despite the humidity. Becka closed her eyes and just listened to the world around her. Occasionally, a cowbell would ring in the distance. The sound reminded her of when she was just a little girl, before her father left. She couldn't remember where they'd been living, but she remembered the smell of cows and the sound of the cowbells. The noise was comforting.

She'd almost drifted to sleep when she heard the noises. Flesh on flesh, a violent slapping sound that was all too familiar from the last few years in the Thomerson household. Becka's eyes popped open of their own volition, and the sun above nearly blinded her. Perhaps she *had* gone to sleep, after all. The sun was in a different position than she remembered.

She heard angry voices in the distance and moved slowly into a sitting position. Her skin felt hot and flushed. She could taste salty sweat on her upper lip as she ran her tongue there. Her body was stiff, but only a little. She moved around until her circulation was back where it was supposed to be and then she slipped into the shadows of the trees.

The voices were coming closer. A cold seed bloomed into full-blown fear when she heard Dutch's voice added to the chorus approaching her. Dutch didn't sound angry. He sounded hurt. Bad hurt. Becka looked around for something, anything, she could use as a weapon. She spotted a decent-sized rock near her right foot, and her peripheral vision caught the picnic sack where they'd gathered the leftovers from their meal at the same time. Becka'd moved herself into the shade. She'd left their mess behind. Even as she noticed that, she noticed the shadows moving across the ground, like a wave across an angry sea, heading directly towards the bag.

Part of the shadow broke away, stumbling and flailing as it went. The shadow raced forward, and Becka looked up to where the shadow joined with Dutch's feet. She heard laughter from farther back, and saw her friend fall to his knees not far from the remains of their lunch. Becka stifled a scream when she saw what they'd done to him.

Dutch Armbruster hadn't ever been a handsome man, but at present he was positively hideous. His face was bloodied and swollen, and his bottom lip was split so badly he seemed to drool blood. His already crooked nose was mashed and pulped; it leaned heavily to left side of his face. His right eye was puffed into a slit, and the other eye looked like someone had rubbed the white and cornea with coarse-grade sandpaper. His arms were bruised and blackened. Becka guessed he'd tried to stop the damage to his face until he had trouble moving his arms any longer. The black shirt across his belly was partially missing, and an angry red weal ran from his navel to his right hip. A thin line of crimson ran down and stained his blue jeans black from his hip to his crotch.

Dutch crashed to the ground with a grunt, resting on his hands and his knees. His graying hair blocked Becka's view of his face. Then, slowly, his head turned until he saw the lunch bag. Despite his obviously weakened condition, Dutch's hand and arm blurred as he slapped the sack away from where it was and sent it streaking deeper into the woods. He looked up just as the other shadows began to catch up with his. Dutch's bloodied left eye made contact with her own, sleep-mussed eyes, and he spoke in a voice that was barely above a whisper. "Hiee, Bega, hie!" It took her a second to translate what he said into *Hide, Becka, hide*, but she did as he said. She slid farther into the shadows, even as her knees began to quake and her blood pressure leapt towards the heavens.

Becka slid as far into the shadows as she could, willing herself invisible and hoping that her wish was strong enough to make it happen. Most of the men she saw were strangers to her, same as the vast majority of people in Collier, but one of the was very familiar; Karen had shown a picture of him to Becka as a warning. Peter Donovan.

Becka felt her skin draw into gooseflesh as she remembered the man. Seeing him that one time after he left the grocery store was enough to make sure she didn't forget him. He was handsome enough, but there was something about him that gave her the willies just the same. His smile was cruel, and never quite made it to his eyes. His short, red hair looked too perfect, like he'd spent hours making sure every hair was exactly the same length. Every move he made seemed to threaten impending violence. Donovan was wearing what Becka'd come to think of as the formal uniform for redneck assholes: he had on a black T-shirt, well-faded jeans that were a touch snug but held up by a wide black leather belt just the same—naturally, the belt's buckle was a brass representation of the rebel flag—and a pair of combat boots that showed a great deal of wear. In his back left pocket was a circular object about the size of a hockey puck. She guessed it was probably chewing tobacco. In his left hand he carried a new addition to the wardrobe: the wide handle of an ax, minus the head. The hard wood was dark and wet on one end. She could guess what caused the change in color from the bleeding wounds on Dutch's body.

Becka very much wanted to be somewhere else.

Donovan wasn't alone, either. He had two other men with him. They were bigger than he was, one of them almost as big as Dutch, but they weren't in the same shape as Karen's ex. They were softer, less like a walking coil of muscle. Somehow that didn't make them seem any less threatening. *Maybe it's the bloody baseball bats that make 'em look so mean. Yeah, I bet they're just sweeties without 'em.* Becka bit her lip to stop from giggling hysterically.

Peter Donovan moved over to where Dutch was trying to regain his footing. Dutch looked over towards the man's figure and shook his head from side to side. "No-oo. Preashe, no morah." *No. Please, no more.*

"I cain't understand you, Bubba. You gotta speak up."
The thick Southern accent in the man's voice didn't hide his
obvious satisfaction. As Becka looked on, Peter Donovan
hauled back one of his heavy combat-style boots and kicked
it forward into Dutch's ribcage. Becka heard something snap
even over her boyfriend's grunt of pain.

Dutch raised an arm and mumbled again. Donovan brought
the ax handle down in a savage arc, connecting with the bone
in her boyfriend's scarred wrist. Nothing broke that time, but
Dutch let out a full-scale scream as he went down.

"That didn't sound like an apology to me, buddy." Donovan
sounded casual and friendly, as if he were talking about the
Braves and their chances of winning the World Series. "That
didn't sound anything like 'I'm real sorry I messed with you
back at the Piggly Wiggly.' Hell, that sounded more like an
insult." He turned to face his two associates. "Ain't that what
it sounded like to you boys?"

The shorter of the two, a man in his late thirties, with little
hair left on top of his head and a great abundance of hair
sticking out of the collar of his T-shirt, looked uncomfortable. "Judd's gonna be sore pissed off if he hears about this,
Pete." The man had an accent even thicker than Donovan's,
and he looked like he was about ready to make a run for it.

"Then I guess he better not hear about it, Billy. You
unnerstand me?" Donovan's voice was harsh, filled with threat.

The one called Billy looked away and then down to the
ground. "I reckon so."

"Get your sorry ass over here, Billy."

Billy looked up sharply, a wary expression on his pudgy
face. "What for?"

"'Cause I figure the only way to keep you shut up is if
you're part of it all."

"I don't want to, Pete. I'm already on parole."

"Well, no shit, dickless." Donovan walked away from
Dutch, reaching out with one hand and grabbing Billy's shoulder. When he had a solid purchase, he shook Billy's entire

body, ripping the shirt on the fat man's arm in the process. "I know you're on parole, asshole. I was in there with you. It ain't like that's a problem anymore though, is it? It ain't like there's a chance of you going to jail for this." Donovan laughed, a short, harsh sound. "Hell, you might as well be in jail right now anyway." He waved his left arm, complete with bloody stick, wildly around them. "Ain't none of us gettin' out of here unless we work together. Them assholes in the black outfits ain't gonna let us walk. You know it and I know it. Now get your fat ass over there and break that fucker's head."

"You're the one's got a problem with him, Pete. I don't even know who he is."

"He's a stupid, Yankee fuck who thinks he can keep me from my wife, that's who. And you'll do it, 'cause if you don't, I'm gonna break this stick off onna side of your damn fool head!" As Peter Donovan spoke, he increased his volume and moved forward. Billy backed up just as fast, nodding his sweating, bald head as he went.

"I'll do it, Pete. But you better learn not to talk to me thattaway." If the man was trying to sound confident, he failed.

The third man with them watched the exchange with a bored expression. He scared the hell out of her, even worse than Pete. Becka suspected he'd have the same look on his face if he watched a woman get raped with a broken bottle. Despite the heat, he wasn't even sweating. He was very tall, but not really heavily muscled or anything. He was actually wearing a dress shirt, short-sleeved and white, with the button at his throat opened and the rest neatly in place. While he was also wearing jeans, his shoes were more appropriate for office work than anything else. The more she looked at him, the more he scared her. He wasn't anything spectacular. He didn't look like he regularly participated in this sort of beating, or like he did much beyond sit behind a desk and talk on a phone or dictate letters. But he still scared her. He worried her a lot.

The man spoke softly, but his words reached Becka even from where she hid a good thirty feet away, and both Pete and

Billy seemed to defer to him. "Hit the man, Billy. We got
work to do when ya'll are done playin' games."

Billy nodded nervously and raised his bat above Dutch's
head. Dutch didn't even seem to notice. Becka wanted to
scream. She wanted to cry out a warning or just run through
the woods and never look back. More than anything, she
wanted to stop the men from doing what they were doing
to Dutch Armbruster, who was, despite their constant arguments, the closest thing she'd ever had to a real friend in
her life.

Instead she stood perfectly still, practically rooted to the
spot. She watched the one called Billy swing the bat as hard
as he could and heard a sound like a cantaloupe smashing into
the ground. Dutch flopped on the dirt road near where they'd
been preparing to make love a short while earlier. His body
spasmed and where his head touched the sun-bleached clay, a
thick trail of red was left behind. Pete Donovan and his hairy
friend Billy continued their assault, breaking bones and bruis-
ing flesh long after Dutch had to be dead.

Becka watched it all in silence. The scary man watched it
too. She couldn't tell what was going on behind his dark eyes,
but in her own head, every blow to Dutch's body was another
reason for her mind to scream and scream again. The sounds
never reached her lips. That silence saved her life.

She stayed quiet all the way through the beating, and even
when the men gathered poor Dutch's body in their arms—the
quiet man never touched him, but he carried the weapons the
other two'd used—and hauled him away.

5

William O'Rourke stared at the saucer where it thrust from
the ground. In that gleaming, silver disc were the answers to
more questions about life and faith than he wanted answers
for. Did the inhabitants of that vessel believe in a god? Were
they the foundation of the modern religious beliefs, as so many

of the so-called New Agers believed? Why had they come to Earth in the first place? Did they seek peace? War? Universal trade with the planet?

He couldn't have cared less. A day ago, the questions he now shrugged off had bent William into a knot of anxiety. Now they were merely puzzles he no longer wished to solve. None of it mattered, not without Emily.

He closed his eyes, wanting to remember his wife's smile and her caress. Instead he only saw her burnt remains and the image of Artie Carlson with a pillow over her face, sobbing to himself as he extinguished her life.

He shook his head and gulped air. He wanted to be angry with Artie, but found he couldn't. The man had done exactly what he'd been toying with himself; he'd taken away Emily's pain. Both he and Emily had known that Artie carried a torch for William's wife. Both knew he'd never do anything about it. Now the man had done what William couldn't, and he was, in a way, grateful to Artie.

But the loss of Emily was still too big for him to completely accept. His main reason for believing in God had died. Despite all of his years as a minister, he'd always come back to the same reason for never really doubting God's existence: there had to be a God, because Emily was simply too perfect to be an act of random creation. As a result of Emily's existence he'd never had any trouble believing in a divine power. And just as soon as she was taken from his life, his belief fell apart. Maybe that wouldn't be the case if she'd died of natural causes, or not suffered for almost a week through the worst imaginable agonies. Looking at the ship in the lake, a part of him understood that the alien craft was simply an excuse, a place to focus his anger and his doubts. But most of him just didn't care to hear excuses. Most of him simply hurt too much to give a damn.

Emily was dead. Karen had grown into a fine woman, but having him around in his present state would simply be a burden.

So now he sat behind the wheel of his oversized Pontiac, looking down at the headquarters of Colonel Mark Anderson and beyond at the focus of all his rage. In his defense, William O'Rourke never even gave the notion any conscious thought. He simply turned the key in his ignition and backed out of his parking spot at the top of Millwater Street, across from the row of shops that hadn't been visited since the military came into town, and slid towards the edge of the hill. He never gave any conscious thought to why he waited for the black Humvee to pass before he started down the steep slope, his foot securely planted on top of the gas pedal.

The hand that rested on his car horn was placed there more as an instinctive warning than out of any fear for anyone's safety. Just the same, between that and the scream pouring from William's soul through his mouth, the people below saw him coming long before his car tore into the burnt grass of the Lakeside Park. His warning was just enough to get Mark Anderson and Steve Hawthorne out of the tent in time to avoid becoming fatalities. They cleared the way with less than a second to spare before O'Rourke's car tore through the tent, taking precious documents and a dozen confiscated cameras along for the ride.

Along with a dozen or so others, they were witness to William O'Rourke's last defiant cry of anguish as he and his car went sailing off the edge of the shoreline and slammed into the side of the ship stuck in the lake's bed. At that moment they had no idea who was behind the wheel of the car. All anyone saw was the massive steel structure tear into the canvas of the tent, taking the heavy fabric along like a funeral shroud. Then they saw car and tent alike disappear over the edge of the lake and heard the wrenching squeal of metal against metal as the entire mess slid to the base of the thing from the stars.

They saw the scaffolding set up by the men in black vibrate and then tilt as much as the ship allowed. (Later, when all was relatively calm again, Anderson would remark on the inability of the people in the area to leave his damned gantry alone, but by that point even Hawthorne couldn't be sure whether or not he was serious any longer.) They saw the two soldiers working near the top of the thing slip and fall, saved only by the network of safety cables they now wore, which attached to the metal framework as an added precaution. Then the witnesses heard another explosion and watched helplessly as William O'Rourke's body burned in the ruin of his car.

Through the entire process the ship remained motionless, a brooding silver monolith that resisted all attempts to harm it.

Karen Donovan simply stared at the wall when she found out about his death. Between that, and finding the body of Dutch Armbruster on her doorstep later the same night, she seemed incapable of reacting to anything. Only the Danskys knew better.

5

The fine, upstanding group of white supremacists who were now calling themselves the Collier Militia changed tactics the day after William O'Rourke killed himself in an act of defiance against his god and the alien ship. Because it was harder to sneak up and kill two heavily armed men when they couldn't use anything more violent than knives and baseball bats, they learned a new trick.

With the help of Paul Summerfield, a man who knew far more than he should have about terrorist activities, and whose cold demeanor had terrified Becka Thomerson even more than watching two other men beat her lover to death, they learned about the advantages of modern terrorist tactics.

The first thing the Militia did was break into the offices of Dr. Samuel Cumming and Dr. Arthur Trenton. They found what they were looking for with very little effort, especially since they had the permission of both doctors to take what they wanted. Under the present circumstances, neither man was doing much business in town; veterinary care was at an all time low in Collier, and both men were afraid of what the men in black had planned for the town.

The group's next move was riskier, but they managed just the same. They hit the Eckerd's pharmacy on Wilmington Street and they broke into the Phar-mor and Rexall drugstores on Main Street as well. Almost everything in the stores was left untouched, and in all three cases, the pharmacists explained that they couldn't be certain what was taken, because their inventory invoices had been stolen along with the missing drugs.

Then the cooking began. Distilled water was used in minimal doses to liquefy the digitalis pills they found. To add to the fun, several types of painkillers were dissolved in similar fashion, and mixed with the digitalis. The mixture was injected into bottles of Humulin R insulin, and that in turn was carefully loaded into the darts for the three tranquilizer guns the Militia had liberated from the veterinary offices. When that mixture ran low, additional darts were loaded with iodine laced with strychnine, simply because one can't be too careful.

Ping-Pong balls were filled with bleach, and then sealed with a small dab of Elmer's Glue. The glue would last just about long enough inside the gas tanks of the military vehicles to allow the person dropping the bleach filled packages into them to get clear before their contents mixed with the gasoline and started a nasty chain reaction. The idea wouldn't work on most modern vehicles: the Ping-Pong balls were too large to fit through the openings for nozzles, but they'd work just fine on the older model gas tanks. While the people working at the Brightman Textile Mill went about the business of making noise and producing stock that would likely never be used, the Militia worked quietly in a store room, concealed behind pallets of fabric that reached almost fifteen feet into the air. When the self-proclaimed defenders of Collier's freedom had finished with their lethal packages, they moved on to the next step and began making their special surprises for the hotels where the soldiers under Colonel Anderson rested when they weren't on duty.

The soldiers had to sleep some time, and even Billy Garner was smart enough to know that they couldn't possibly sleep with their breathing gear on. Or at least that was what they all hoped. Either way, the soldiers would soon discover that the hotels were off limits.

After several days of preparation, the Collier Militia was ready to up the ante of the war for Collier's independence. Tensions were high, true, but the excitement of finally fighting back on a large scale made up for their worries about life and death.

6

Frank Osborn was there when the helicopters came back in from their unexpected departure. What he saw coming off the choppers filled him with a sense of foreboding. Ten people in all, each with a single briefcase. Business people, some male, some female. Varying ages and physical conditions. None of them looked extraordinary, at least not from this range, but the way they moved, the way they gestured and walked, made him suspect otherwise.

Clipboard and Anderson were there too, but they were far closer than Frank. They actually went and greeted the people. Almost as a single unit, the people from the outside—that was how Frank had started to think of the world beyond Collier, though he wasn't consciously aware of the difference—nodded, spoke softly and moved away to where three waiting Humvees were idling. They didn't head towards the Dew Drop Inn and the Collier Motel where the soldiers were staying; instead they moved in the direction of the high school. For some reason that bothered Frank, but it was nothing he could focus on.

None of them wore survival suits. Not so much as a dust mask on any of them. Frank lit another cigarette, tossing aside the butt of one he'd lit only moments before.

He slid back into his patrol car, cursing the bad luck of having the transmission on his Mustang go bad on him as he did so. He watched the Humvees disappear over the hill leading away from the lake.

"Why the hell are you bastards goin' over to the hospital? That's what I want to know. What makes you so different from everyone else?" No one answered his questions, and Frank's mind refused to let them rest.

The sudden knocking at his car window made Frank half leap out of his seat. His heart pounded loudly in his ears, and he had to remind himself to breathe. He turned to see who was there and was rewarded by the sight of one of the Colonel's bug-eyed soldiers.

"What the hell are you trying to do? Give me a damned heart attack?" Frank's voice came out far higher in pitch than it usually did, and he felt himself flush with embarrassment.

"Sorry to bother you, Officer Frank, but we've found a body. We don't know if he's a local or not. He's not wearing any identification." The soldier paused for a moment, while Frank stared at him with blank eyes. "We were wondering if you could help identify him, sir."

Frank's brain finally fired all its pistons and he nodded. "Sure. Where's the body?"

"We haven't moved it yet. We're still investigating the area, and we thought you'd like to see the scene of the crime." The man waited passively for Frank to respond.

"You driving somethin'? Or do you need a lift?"

"I was about to ask if you wanted to take separate vehicles..." There was something in the way the man spoke, something in the way he moved that demanded Frank's attention. He couldn't place just what it was, and that annoyed him.

"I'll follow you."

The soldier nodded and moved off to yet another Humvee. A moment later, Frank was following the vehicle's taillights and moving off towards the residential area on the other side of the town square. He was about to light another cigarette when part of what was wrong with the soldier clicked into place. "Sonuvabitch.... He called me 'Officer Frank,' not Captain Osborn." The road went screwy in Frank's mind for a minute. The soldiers always called him Captain Osborn.

The only people in town who ever called him Officer Frank were the kids. That was the way it'd always been.

"What the hell's going on here?"

Book Three
Jack's Story

Chapter 9

1

Sergeant Jack Calloway sat behind the wheel of the Humvee and cursed himself for his stupidity. He'd done his best to be careful around the people of Collier, but he still caught himself using names he shouldn't and being almost familiar with the locals. By all rights, he shouldn't have even been here. Collier was once a place he had called home and, even if he hadn't been born here, there were still memories connected to the area. He should have asked to be left at Durango—Hell, they should have insisted he stay behind.

But everything'd happened so damned *fast;* nobody'd known about his connection to the town, and now it was too late. He was here, and there was no way to avoid seeing old, familiar faces. No way to escape the memories associated with the people of Collier.

First he'd called Karen O'Rourke by her first name, and now he'd just called the captain of Collier's police force *Officer Frank.* "Jesus Christ, it's like walking back in time." Oh yes, Jack was very angry with himself. He hated to think how Anderson would react if he heard about the incident. *Yeah, there's a great thought: my ass being ripped apart by Anderson's teeth.* He sucked in another lungful of cold, sterilized air though his mouthpiece and sighed heavily. This wasn't going the way he'd hoped it would, not by any stretch.

This was supposed to be a simple operation: locate the Bogie, retrieve the Bogie, and get the hell out of the area. So far ONYX had managed several such retrievals with great success. No problem, thanks for asking. But each collection mission was different. Normally the best they could hope for was a chunk of debris with strange writing on it, like the one they'd picked up in Utica, New York. The only other case where the government had actually found a ship was so well known that no one really gave it too much thought anymore, unless the press decided it was time to increase everyone's paranoia levels again.

So, naturally, the one damned time a retrieval goes wrong, it has to happen in his home town. *And could it go wrong in a small way? Oh, no. It had to be a BIG damn snafu, nothing small.* Quarantined town, media hounds sniffing around the edges of the razorwire barriers; half a dozen soldiers dead by violent means, and over two hundred civilians wiped out when the ship crashed into the ground, at least if you added the stragglers they'd had to kill since the unit had come to town. It just had to get better; it couldn't possibly get worse.

Famous last words.

He caught himself speeding along the residential street at just over fifty miles per hour, and slowed down when he realized he was leaving the police cruiser in the distance. This wasn't Sector 17, also known as East Bumblefuck, and he had to remember that there were still pedestrians walking along the streets of Collier. The differences went a lot further than merely the temperature. Here he had to worry about running down some little kid, or even mashing a dog's skull into the asphalt. There'd been enough stress between the soldiers and civilians without adding a few deaths to the stew.

A few minutes later, while still chastising himself for his slip-up, Calloway pulled up in front of a two-story house. The building was gray with red trim, and looked like virtually every other house in the subdivision, apart from the color scheme. He'd never understood why anyone in their right mind would willingly move into a neighborhood of cloned houses. It was like asking that your personality be leeched away. Of course he was wearing a uniform that looked exactly like all of the others in town to the naked eye, so who the hell was he to make comments?

A middle-aged man came waddling towards him, even as the sun began its final descent towards the western horizon. The man huffed as he climbed the slight incline from the driveway to Jack's vehicle. But he didn't think the old guy was winded. He looked afraid.

"You've got to come quickly! Three of your men, I—I think they're dead!" His accent said he wasn't local. Probably from the northeast, unless Jack was losing his ability to distinguish between regional dialects. The information was filed away, even as the meaning of the man's words sank like lead weights into his mind.

Jack shoved aside his earlier concerns for whether or not he'd revealed too much about himself, and grabbed his firearm from the passenger's seat. "Where are they?"

The man led him towards the side of the house. Jack pressed the SEND button near the right jaw of his facemask and spoke urgently. "This is Calloway. I've just returned to 1734 Glory Lane, where the body was found earlier. I've got Captain Osborn with me. Over."

"Affirmative, Sergeant. We're not receiving any responses from Pike, Williams or Hornsby. Is there a problem? Over."

"Possibly, Control. Man here says he thinks they're all dead." Jack saw two bodies in armor lying on the ground, with a little shifting, he could make out the third. The one big problem with the survival suits was still a lack of full peripheral vision. He studied the three armored forms lying on the ground and felt his blood pressure start a slow rise. "I can't tell for certain, but I'm guessing they must be. I need medical assistance immediately. Over."

"Medical is on the way. Secure the area. Out."

Osborn came up behind him, and Jack could hear the man muttering under his breath. Before Jack could tell him otherwise, Frank Osborn was down beside Hornsby's still form, reaching with his right hand, sliding it under the protective rubber of the connector between faceplate seal and torso seal, and placing his fingers against the soldier's neck. He paused for a moment and then went to the next one, Pike.

"Offi—Captain Osborn, you should stay away from them."
The man shook his head as if irritated by an annoying noise.
"Nope. Gotta see if any of 'em are alive."

"Captain, those men are—" *What? Not going anywhere? Armed and dangerous? Property of the U. S. Government?* "How are they, sir?"

"First two are dead," he stated as he moved to the third. "This one's still alive."

Jack breathed a small sigh of relief. Craig Williams was his regular patrol partner, an easy-going, talkative man with no more desire to hurt anyone in Collier than Jack himself possessed. Not like a few of the others running around in environmental armor. There were at least a dozen men on report for excessive use of force against the civilians. They took the deaths of the other soldiers personally, and wanted revenge. Jack couldn't blame them; he'd had similar feelings himself, initially, but they weren't here as an execution squad. At least not yet.

Osborn pulled the mask away from Williams' face, deftly moved his fingers along the sides of the man's armor, seeking a way to remove the ceramic breast plate. "How do I get this damned thing off him?"

Jack didn't speak. He walked forward and pushed his fingers into the two slots where the locking mechanisms hid under the flat black fabric covering the armor. Three seconds later, he was peeling the stiff shielding away from his friend's chest. Aside from a small puncture mark along Craig's ribcage, near his armpit where the armor didn't offer as much protection, the man didn't look hurt in the least.

Osborn spoke again. "You know CPR?"

"Huh? Oh, yeah."

"Then get your butt over here and start working on his chest. He ain't breathin' and his pulse just stopped."

Frank Osborn started blowing air into Williams' lungs, while Jack placed his two gauntleted hands against Craig's chest and started doing regular thrusts. Seeing how pale Craig was, Jack focused on his actions, avoiding the thought that Williams might well be dead or dying. The activity became the center of his world, until he felt Osborn shaking his shoulder hard enough to rock his whole body.

"What?" Jack realized that his arms were burning with fatigue, but continued his actions anyway.

"I said forget about it. He's dead. There's nothing we can do." Osborn was silent for a moment, looking at the dead man before them. Then he turned to Jack and sighed. "I'm sorry. I don't think anything could've helped him."

Jack closed his eyes for a moment, forcing thoughts of retaliation out of his head, right along side the thoughts of how fond he was of Craig Williams. They weren't exactly friends, but they'd been close to reaching that level.

The photosensitive lenses in his facemask activated, switching over to night vision amplification. Jack hadn't been consciously aware of the world growing darker around him until that moment. The goggles' ability to magnify the light faint light until it imitated full daylight was a blessing. When his vision readjusted itself, Jack leaned forward and scrutinized Williams' body. The small wound on the dead man's side caught his attention again—it looked like a nasty bee sting, but hardly fatal—and Calloway looked over the opened shirt, trying to find a spot where something could have caused the break in Craig's flesh. What he found was a small dart, the sort used for tranquilizing animals, sticking out of the fabric between the front and back armor plates.

Despite the best efforts to make a perfect suit of armor mesh with environmental gear, there were still areas left vulnerable. The heavy galvanized rubber over cotton hadn't managed to stop the dart anymore than it would a bullet or a knife. The sections where armor didn't protect the bodies inside the suits were necessary, at least if the person in the special uniform wished to move freely. Any more armor, and the suits became too cumbersome for combat situations. The best protection the military could design, and still it wasn't even enough to stop a dart from a tranquilizer gun.

"Looks like these fellas might've been done in with poison." The voice behind Jack startled him, but he didn't let it show. He turned to face Osborn, and saw him pointing to a spot on Pike's side, where another of the darts was still sticking through the heavy material. "Guess maybe I know what was stolen from the veterinary clinics now, don't I?"

Jack shook his head, irritated that no one, himself included, had considered the thefts worth a more careful investigation. Anderson was going to go ballistic. Jack couldn't blame him. Sloppiness was the only possible answer, and that was never a good excuse in the Colonel's eyes.

While Jack was contemplating just who was going to get reamed, Medical showed up, along with five more soldiers. With the lenses over his eyes, he could clearly see the name and rank of every person on the detail. Lieutenant Powell was on the scene, and Jack felt himself begin to relax. Powell could take over the investigation, and Jack could go back to just being a grunt again.

Powell looked at the bodies on the ground, looked at Jack, and shook his head. "You open the armor?" He asked, pointing to Williams' lifeless form. The voice came through on the private wavelength used for short range communications. No noise for anyone without a helmet to hear.

Jack responded using the same method. To anyone around them, it seemed the soldiers were simply standing around. "Yes, sir. Captain Osborn and I attempted CPR, sir. He was the only one still alive when we arrived on the scene."

The lieutenant stared in his direction and Jack realized how unsettling it was to have no idea what was going on behind the goggles they all wore. After several seconds, Jack looked away.

"Take the captain with you, go identify the civilian at the front of the house. You're a little too close to this particular scene." Jack nodded and turned to go. Powell, along with the other officers, didn't want salutes or any indication of who was in charge. With the shootings going on, Jack couldn't blame them. The entire reason their rank was printed in paints invisible to naked eye was to ensure that no one knew who to kill in order to cause the most damage to the unit. Only Anderson and Hawthorne broke that rule, and that was simply because they had to be available to the civilians. They were also the best-guarded of the soldiers, for obvious reasons.

Jack gestured to Osborn, and asked if he'd come around to the front of the building. He gestured to the older man as well, and the three of them started off. Despite the apparent freshness of the complex, the house they walked around was already starting to show signs of negligence. There were small flakes of paint peeling from the boards, and the grass hadn't been mowed in a long time. Up at the edge of the roof, just below the decorative trim around the gutter, a rather large wasps' nest brooded, like an oversized wad of wet paper. When he'd lived in Collier, no one would have let the minor details go for so long.

The New Yorker pointed to the spot on the front porch where the body lay, covered by a bright blue bed sheet with yellow sunflower patterns. "There he is. I think it's Dutch Armbruster. I didn't want to get close enough to find out, in case there's evidence you need to examine, and my eyes, they aren't so good anymore. He's been staying here ever since that thing crashed in the lake. His girlfriend is inside. She's a nervous wreck. I tried to ask her if she knew what happened, but she hasn't been up to talking. I...I think she's in shock, but I just don't know for certain." The man spoke a mile a minute, and his smile was a nervous one, almost as if he were embarrassed to mention anything at all about the dead man's private life. His thinning hair was stuck to the crown of his head by a heavy layer of sweat. Jack knew the weather had to be killing him; New York seldom got anywhere near as hot as it did in southern Georgia.

Frank Osborn moved the cotton sheet away, looking down at the battered form beneath the covering with a critical eye. Jack envied the man his detachment. Beneath his mask and helmet, he made a face as he studied the ruins of the man.

Osborn ran a finger across the man's neck, pausing to feel for a pulse. With a puzzled look on his face, he lifted one eyelid and then the other, looking at them closely as he did so. Lastly, after he'd checked the man's throat again, he held out a hand in front of the pulped nose on Armbruster's face.

Osborn looked over at Jack with a slight sneer on his face. Jack couldn't decide what caused the expression. Maybe it was just a bad day, or maybe he was questioning the competency of the person who'd covered Armbruster's body. "He's alive! You think, maybe, that you could convince one of your fine doctors to get the hell over here? This man's still alive, but he won't be for long if he doesn't get proper treatment. I can barely feel his pulse and he's hardly breathing at all."

Jack nodded, then he toggled the switch at his jawline, and spoke into the radio. A few minutes later, two of the medics came around the side of the house. The night felt like it would never end.

2

Contrary to his beliefs, Jack's shift eventually ended. Armbruster hung on, though there were still doubts about whether or not he'd live through the next twenty-four hours. Whoever'd beaten him had done a remarkable job of breaking most of the bones in his body. The only ones they'd left intact were the vertebrae around his spinal cord; if there were more undamaged, Jack was certain it was strictly an oversight on the part of the man's assailants. Unfortunately, Armbruster was is no shape to tell them anything.

Jack Calloway, and virtually every other person he'd spoken with during the last twelve hour shift, was convinced the same people who'd worked over Armbruster were responsible for the deaths of the men from ONYX. Simply put, they had to be stopped at any cost. Every soldier killed was another weapon potentially in the hands of their prisoners. Just as importantly, the deaths of the soldiers broke morale.

Despite what he suspected most of Collier felt about him and the other soldiers, none of them wanted to hurt anyone. The 'enemy' in this case wasn't a soldier from another land. The enemy was the population of a town caught in the wrong place at the wrong time. The people of Collier were near the end of their collective rope, and it didn't take a genius to know that the situation was about to go from bad to much worse.

He pulled up in front of the Collier House, an antebellum home that had long since been converted into a hotel. Since he'd left Collier, several additions had been added to the back. While the front lawn and the front of the house still retained the original style of the old place, complete with pillars and a second story verandah, the back looked much more like a Holiday Inn or a Ramada Inn. The rooms even had cable and HBO. Jack forced the thought of his night here with Karen O'Rourke from his mind. It wasn't easy.

Just a few hundred feet away, the Dew Drop Inn sat like a bloated frog in the darkness. Even from this distance, the place looked like an eyesore. Hard to believe the same people owned both of them. Hard to believe, for that matter, that anyone on the planet would actually think the name "Dew Drop Inn" was even remotely cute—but he'd seen several sleazy motels and even a few nice establishments with the same name. The Inn was being used to store equipment and supplies, and only housed a dozen or so guards. Jack was lucky; he didn't have to stay in the sleazy little dump. Evan Walotsky'd told him the place had cockroaches bigger than the local squirrels. Jack was inclined to believe him. He turned away from the eyesore and walked towards the Collier House.

On the bright side, the newcomers from a separate division, one not even connected with ONYX, were here to make matters worse. Oh, he had little doubt they'd manage to discover where all the weapons being used by the civilians came from. He had less doubt they'd do it quickly. But he'd heard about people like the "conditioning experts" who'd come in yesterday. They were normally saved for special situations, like when people witnessed something they shouldn't have and had to be silenced quickly. Or when the answers to questions were needed quickly and honestly.

Jack vaguely remembered going into a room full of such experts right after he was chosen for ONYX. There were three men and two women. He remembered that much. But he couldn't remember what they looked like to save his life.

Corporal Calloway, it is our job to make absolutely certain that you understand the gravity of the position you've been offered...

All he truly remembered was being cold, and leaving the same room a full day later. Jack shivered, despite the heat, as he checked in with his lieutenant, Evans, a man who had absolutely no sense of humor, and headed towards the Decontamination room.

The Decon room was a joke: once in the men's restroom, in the lobby of the Collier House, Jack took off his helmet and felt the air-conditioning attack the drops of sweat on his face. A few seconds later, two of the soldiers on duty sprayed him down with a yellow liquid and then hit him with a foul-tasting light blue liquid. After he'd dried himself off, he was allowed to go back to his room. Jack endured the same routine every day.

He stepped out of the Decon room and moved down the long hallway towards room 117, his home away from home.

Jack was lucky; he only had one roommate, as opposed to the four most of the soldiers had to deal with. *Rank hath its privileges, after all.* Ellison was already out on patrol, so Jack had the room to himself. He stripped out of the heavy survival suit and out of the sweaty garments underneath, as well. Despite his desire for a warm shower, he ignored the bathroom and fell straight onto his bed. The chemical showers in the morning would have to do; regulations didn't permit the use of local facilities for anything but answering the call of nature. Any water he consumed had to come from the canisters held in the kitchen, and there wasn't enough of that to allow for a shower.

Jack thought briefly about the time he'd spent living in Collier. He expected some sort of emotions to come through with the memories, but there was nothing. At least not until he came to Karen. There were plenty of feelings there, oh yes. Despite himself, he still wanted to be with her. The years hadn't changed that much.

Seeing her when she'd found the body of that kid stuck in the razorwire hadn't done him a lick of good. Just like that, he'd been a teenager again, weak in the knees at the sight of her, and feeling his own heartbeat thundering behind his ears. He'd wanted to wave to her, to see her recognize him, and to pull her into his arms. Naturally, the survival suit between them sort of slowed down that whole concept.

That, and she might not understand just why he was one of the people holding Collier at bay. Hell, he had trouble with that one himself. One minute he's off in the desert, living the life of any other grunt in the Army, and the next he's on a plane and cruising towards his old home town, carrying a gun and trained to kill in hand-to-hand combat. Aside from his face, and his feelings for Karen, there was little that he had in common with the Jack Calloway that she'd known so long ago.

He'd tried writing to her several times after he moved away, but he'd never received a response. He'd even tried calling once, but Karen's mother had simply stated that Karen was no longer interested in him. Jack wasn't too stupid to take a hint. Despite a very strong desire to see her, to talk to her, he understood that Karen was off limits.

Jack closed his eyes and started to drift towards sleep. It was a long time in coming.

3

Waking up took a lot less effort than finally convincing himself to rest. Jack suspected the explosions had something to do with that. The first rattling boom had Calloway rolling off his bed and reaching for his survival suit. Long years of practice paid off, and he managed to slip into the pants and torso of the outfit in less than a minute. When he realized his eyes were starting to water, the rebreather went straight over his face. Two plugs later, power and oxygen were making the mask do its stuff. Immediately, the lenses in the faceplate activated, adjusting to the lower level of light. Jack grabbed his boots and slid them over his feet, managing to shove his feet into his socks in the same motion. Clarion horns started screaming throughout the building, and he thought he heard gunfire.

Jack wrestled his second glove into place as he activated the radio-speakers in his helmet. The helmet slid over his head and worked on the clamps even as he listened...

"—umber of attackers unknown. Best estimate is at least seven, repeat, at least seven." Arlbuck was in the command center, barking orders and keeping everyone apprised of the situation at the same time. Jack grabbed his firearm and stepped closer to the window, spying what he could through the glass.

Several of the Humvees were on fire, burning as brightly as the noonday sun. There were already soldiers doing their best to put out the fires, but Jack could tell it was a lost cause. He switched his radio from Standard to Command and called out to Arlbuck. "Corporal, this is Sergeant Calloway. Get those men away from the vehicles and have them finish scoping out the area. The last thing we need is any of our boys caught watering the lawn by another asshole with a dart gun."

"Affirmative, Sergeant!"

Calloway was about to ask what the situation looked like when he got a first-hand serving of the local hospitality. From the corner of his peripheral vision, he saw the bottle sailing through the air. There was no wick, nor was there a flame, but he had the good sense to duck anyway.

The bottle shattered against his window, spilling down the side of the building. A second later, greenish smoke boiled across the wood and glass. Then the whole trail of liquid burst into flames, hungrily chewing into the aged wood.

Calloway kicked the window hard, breaking the glass from its frame. He climbed outside. There, in the distance, he could see the forms of half a dozen people darting behind a few of the Humvees that weren't yet burning. They were too far away to see clearly, but he could easily tell that they weren't in survival gear.

Everything was automatic. Jack was barely aware of his commands, toggling his radio switch instinctively and alerting the others to where the potential threats waited. Jack made certain none of his people were in the way and opened fire, moving forward as he did so. Several of the soldiers followed his lead, and Jack barked orders into the radio.

The people in the distance scattered, and one of them spun twice before falling to the ground. Another bottle came sailing through the air, clearly defined by the night vision lenses in his faceplate. Jack stepped out of the way, calling into his radio for the others to avoid the bottles. The heavy silhouette that threw the bottle went down in a hail of bullets from several of the soldiers. He must have been carrying more of the explosives, because his body went up in a spectacular fireball that swallowed the armored car he was trying to hide behind.

Calloway ordered Fitzpatrick and Walters to move to the sides and flank the retreating figures. Both men moved to follow his orders and took off at high speed. Two more of the silhouettes fell to their gunfire, but the others were breaking into the woods. A few more seconds and they'd be gone.

"Move it, people! I don't want those fuckers getting away! Fan out and cover the woods! Arlbuck! Get me air support, now. I want three 'copters in the sky and looking for these bastards!"

Arlbuck must have been ahead of him, because even as Jack spoke, he saw two of the black helicopters rising above the tree line. He wondered why he hadn't heard anyone else issuing commands, and called to Arlbuck to discover the reason.

The answer was all too simple: the first explosion he'd heard came from the other wing of the building. The place where the off-duty officers slept and ate.

"They're using some kind of poison gas, Sergeant. Not everybody over there's dead, but we've got a lot of incapacitated men."

"At least they ain't dead." Calloway's mind was whirling. Now that the initial threat was ended—at least he hoped it was—he had to give serious thought to what to do next. He was about to radio Colonel Anderson when the explosions came from the building next door.

He turned to look, and watched with eyes gone wide as the Dew Drop Inn exploded. Jack had just enough time to register what was happening before the shock wave hit him full in the chest. A hot wind like the fist of an angry god lifted him from his feet and threw him through the air. All around him, the other soldiers were experiencing the same difficulties. Jack held tightly to his firearm, praying for a soft landing. His prayers were rewarded with the hard thump of his ass and back bouncing off the top of an abandoned RV, right before he flopped to the ground.

Despite the breathing gear surrounding his face, Jack found he couldn't take in any air. His lungs adamantly refused to allow the fresh air in. He gasped like a fish out of water and tried to stand. His body flopped bonelessly on the ground and he groaned. *Fuck this*, he thought. *Maybe I'll just stay here for a spell. Hell, it ain't even my watch.*

After giving the matter a little more thought, Jack decided he could move after all. It was just a matter of convincing all his functioning parts to work together. He groaned and sucked in air. Despite being canned and recycled, it tasted sweet. The sound of ringing faded enough from his ears that he could acknowledge the screaming calls coming through his radio. He reached up and toggled the switch to SEND, and called out for order. After a few moments, the noise calmed down.

"Give me a status report, Corporal Arlbuck. What's the situation over at the storage dump?"

"There's nothing left, Sergeant. It's gone. Those bastards blew it sky-high."

Jack sighed, going over in his head just what the hell had happened. "Patch me through to Anderson, and while you're at it, get me a status report from the search teams working with the helicopters."

"I'm on it."

The radio was silent for a time, and Jack took a moment to assess the situation at the Collier House. Several soldiers were already putting out the fires that had started under numerous windows, but in one case a room towards the far end of the wing was burning ferociously.

"Arlbuck?"

"Yes, Sergeant?"

"Get the Collier Fire department down here. We're gonna need help to contain this mess. If there's no one there, have four of the boys in town commandeer a truck and bring it out here."

"Already taken care of, Sergeant."

Calloway smiled under his respirator. "Good man."

Arlbuck gave no response to that, and Jack went back to barking orders. Men were deployed to extinguish the fires where they could, and to move all supplies from the areas where the fire was already too large for them to handle. The good news was that the survival suits allowed them to attend to the matter with minimal risks.

Arlbuck's voice crackled in his ear. "Sergeant..." The man's voice was hesitant, almost but not quite fearful.

"Here, Corporal. What's up?"

"Colonel Anderson's on his way. The trucks should be with you in a few minutes."

"Affirmative." *Damn, this is gonna get nasty.* Jack prepared himself for the worst. Anderson wasn't going to like what he saw. No sir, he wasn't going to like it one little bit.

Four minutes later, Calloway was proved correct. Neither Colonel Anderson, nor his second, Major Hawthorne, were the least bit amused.

4

The firemen were still working on what was left of the Dew Drop Inn, which was little except a crater filled with smoldering debris.

The actual damage to the Collier House wasn't hideous, but it was bad enough. One full wing had been lost to the blaze, and almost half of the officers were out of commission; either wounded or dead. Every Humvee not out on patrol was ruined. In some cases the gas tanks were polluted with sugar, in others, the vehicles were burned beyond repair. The guards positioned to protect the vehicles were dead. Each and every one of them appeared to have died in extreme agony. Several still had the darts from their lethal injections sticking from their sides or, in three cases, from their necks. Total casualties for the night were at forty-three and counting. On the brighter side, they'd managed to capture or kill nine of their assailants. So far no one was talking.

Anderson was just shy of ballistic. He moved stiffly, as if in extreme pain. Calloway'd known his commanding officer long enough to understand that what could be interpreted as discomfort was actually a sign of extreme tension in his superior. He didn't need to see a face to know the truth: Anderson had now been pushed too far. The kid gloves were off, and now they'd be replaced by brass knuckles.

From behind his faceplate, Anderson coughed harshly once and pointed towards the hole where his supply station used to be. "This stops now, gentlemen. Right fucking now."

Hawthorne, God love him, took the hook and spared Calloway any more verbal explosions. Jack knew the anger wasn't meant for him, but he'd taken quite enough lumps for one night, without opening himself up to any more.

"How do you want this handled, Colonel?"

"Complete shutdown. Nobody leaves their homes from this point on. Anyone caught outside is to be shot on sight."

"I don't think they'll go for it, Colonel." Calloway couldn't believe he'd just spoken, but, in hindsight, he had to admit that'd been his own voice. "What I mean is, the people of Collier aren't going to sit still for this. They'll do everything they can to escape or get to the newsies."

Anderson turned his way, and Jack swore he could actually hear the man's teeth grinding through the hard shell of his faceplate. "And when they try, Sergeant Calloway, you and your men *will* to shoot to kill. We don't need any more people in the damned infirmary, so make sure you kill 'em right the first time."

"P—permission to speak freely, sir?"

"Granted."

"We've got less than three hundred soldiers left, and there're still over two thousand people in Collier." Jack shook his head and raised his shoulders in an effort to express the futility of the matter. "Colonel Anderson, we can't be every where at once."

Anderson turned towards him fully, and the spider-like lenses of his faceplate glittered coldly in the heat. "That won't be a problem for long, Jack. The reprogrammers have already begun their work."

"Reprogrammers, sir?"

"The 'conditioning experts.' They've already started making sure that we won't have problems for very much longer."

"How so, sir?"

"You captured four men alive tonight, Jack. They'll be talking over every detail of tonight's little encounter with our new friends from on high."

Jack grew cold just thinking about it. His mind flashed back to the faces he couldn't quite remember, and the

Corporal Calloway, it is our job to make absolutely certain that you understand the gravity of the position you've been offered...

voices which spoke coldly of his duties. He found himself shivering again, despite the heat.

"Sir? How does that help the problem with the townsfolk?"

"Simple. Every name those fine, upstanding citizens mentions is going to be executed."

Jack shook his head. "That'd be a mistake, Colonel. I don't think you want to do that."

Anderson leaned forward until their faceplates were almost touching. "Why not, Calloway? You think the rest of this town'll come hunting us down? You think maybe the police will arrest us?" The man's voice fairly dripped venom. "These are just ordinary people, Sergeant. They don't have many weapons left to them, and they'll have a good deal less once we've found out who the hell's been supplying them with the few pistols they did manage to gather."

"Um, sir?"

"Yes, Calloway?"

"They didn't use guns against us today, sir. They used tranquilizer darts and homemade explosives."

"Then I guess we'll gave to just do what we can with our assault rifles, Sergeant. Unless you'd rather take to carrying a baseball bat."

"Point made, sir."

"Hawthorne? You've been awfully quite throughout this little conversation. Anything you'd like to add?"

"We have control of their water, Colonel. Maybe we should start adding something to keep them calm."

Anderson stood stock still for several seconds. Hawthorne looked at Jack and shrugged as if to say 'this is just the way he thinks, it'll pass,' and then Anderson replied. "So do it. Talk to Hendridge over at the clinic. I want it taken care of."

Hawthorne nodded, and Jack breathed a heavy sigh of relief. At least there'd be fewer casualties if the people were too doped up to fight back.

Then Anderson spoke again, and sent more chilled water coursing through his veins. "Besides, the reprogrammers won't mind if we make their work a little easier. There's no way the people in this town can go on without being told to forget everything they've seen."

A few minutes later, Jack was dismissed and allowed to get the rest he so desperately needed. He slept in the same room as before, with the window open and the acrid smoke smell clinging to his nostrils. It was that or a tent near the command post, and he didn't have the energy to get set up. When he finally closed his eyes and fell into the soft darkness of sleep, his mind was filled with the images of faces half-seen and needles reaching for his arms. *Corporal Calloway, it is our job to make absolutely certain that you understand the gravity of the position you've been offered...* Jack understood what Anderson meant. Collier was as good as dead.

Chapter 10

1

In his dream, Jack was once again a teenager, barely old enough to shave. While a part of him understood on a primal level that he was only dreaming, most of him simply marveled at how little the town of Collier had changed. Over near the diner, the Williams Brothers' Barber Shop sat placidly, with half a dozen men waiting for their turn to get their crewcuts trimmed down again. He looked at the old brick building with a sort of heavy sadness, knowing that the place would be gone again when the dream ended. He'd always liked the Williams brothers; they always had a nice word for a passing kid, and often had a piece of licorice to offer with the friendly greeting.

Where the new municipal building stood in the town he'd gone to sleep in, a squat, two-story wooden house perched, the home of Martin Collier, the last remaining member of the town's founding family. Old Mister Martin was about twice as old as should have been possible, in Jack's eyes, but still managed a lazy wave and nod whenever anyone went past.

Down the road a stretch, the gravel trail leading to the lake was shimmering in the summer's heat, promising relief to any boy who could sneak past the construction workers who were building what would later be the docks. Mister Carlson was the foreman, and he always acted like a hard ass when any of the town officials were around. But all the kids knew if they waited until the mayor was out of sight, Carlson would let them pass.

But today he wasn't off to go swimming in Lake Oldman. He was on his way to see Karen, the girl he knew he'd marry someday. Karen didn't know it yet, but Jack did. They were meant to be together, just as sure as the sun would rise every morning.

Karen was a beauty, and no one in town could deny that. She was only fourteen, same age as he was, but she carried herself like one of those Miss America contestants. She was pretty enough to make grown men notice her, and she had a smile as sweet as the smell of honeysuckle carried by the August breeze. Just being around her made Jack's heart beat a little faster, and on those occasions when he managed to hold her hand, he felt certain that he'd found the finest pleasure life had to offer.

Down the road a ways, he heard the sound of Eric Mobley's Chevy Nova rumbling towards the road out of town. Eric worked over at the textile mill, same as just about everybody in Collier, but he often went on road trips for Mister Brightman. Eric was okay for a grownup; he treated the kids as they were real people instead of like they were five-year-olds with a hearing problem. Like just about everybody in Collier, Eric figured on living his life in town and dying there too. Somehow, the knowledge that Eric would die pinned beneath the wheels of a tractor trailer wormed its way into Jack's dream, and everything seemed a little darker for that knowledge.

He'd just managed to get to Karen's door when everything went wrong. As he lifted his index finger to push down on the doorbell, the sound of automatic gunfire exploded from behind the screen door, drowning out the sound of the football game that the reverend was watching. Jack stepped away from the door as he heard Missus O'Rourke screaming. He turned away from the house, his body shaking with adrenaline and fear, and ran towards his own home a few blocks to the east.

Jack only made a few paces before his world grew darker again, and his peripheral vision disappeared. He was suddenly taller than he should have been, and the smells of summer faded, replaced by the sterile, cold scent of recycled air.

Jack looked around, wondering for a second what could have gone wrong. Where the street had been almost empty a few seconds earlier, there was suddenly a crowd. He recognized all of them. They were people he'd spoken to every day when he was growing up. Even the black folk from the bad parts of Collier were there, looking towards him with grim frowns on their faces. He tried to remember how his father always told him not to be afraid of the niggers, 'cause they were just people too, but seeing their nasty expressions, and seeing the same looks on the faces of all the white folk in town, the lesson lost a bit of its impact.

The longer he watched, the more people showed themselves. Towards the back of the gathering crowd, Jack thought he saw his parents. (He knew they were dead, though they shouldn't be, not with him only fourteen years old, but there they were just the same.) They too looked disappointed in him. Karen O'Rourke was standing there, looking much as she had on the day they'd said their final goodbyes. She was crying, and her tears fell from her face, leaving crimson blood trails instead of the clear streaks he expected.

"We trusted you, Jack. We loved you. Why are you doing this?" Her words cut into him like lightning strikes. All around him, the people of Collier smoldered, their skin growing red and starting to blister. When Karen spoke again, her voice was surely as loud as the end of the world. "*I* loved you, Jack, and you let this happen." He looked towards her angelic face, and watched in dismay as the skin began to peel away from her skull and her hair caught fire.

Jack woke to the sound of his own whimpers. He sat up and sighed, feeling the muscles in his body quiver. Though he made the effort to sleep again, it wasn't meant to be. An hour later, he finally climbed from his bed and went to grab some breakfast. Though the food smelled good, he couldn't bring himself to eat. He kept seeing Karen, crying tears of blood as her face burned away.

2

Rotation time again. In an effort to make certain that no one grew too familiar with the local citizens, the soldiers working for ONYX were relocated every day. Today Jack had the dubious honor of working in Colonel Anderson's office. Despite the fact that he'd worked other locations around Collier, Jack knew he'd been assigned here for a reason. Hell, he'd requested it. There were too many names coming up in conversations, too many faces that were familiar enough to make him pause. Even if he hadn't asked for the relocation, Jack knew he'd have ended up here eventually anyway.

Anderson wanted Jack where he could keep an eye on him. Oh, he'd never say it out loud, but Jack knew what was going on. In Anderson's eyes, he was a weak link. Not because he couldn't perform his job well, but because he was from Collier. He knew too many people for the Colonel *not* to consider him a risk.

The whole idea was sort of funny, really. Jack might have known the people in town when he was younger, but most of them were just strangers with familiar faces. Almost twenty years had passed since he'd been a part of the community, and he had more in common with the people in ONYX than he had with the locals. Most of them wouldn't be able to even recognize him; years of harsh physical training and two decades of life away from the small town had long since removed any traces of the boy he once was, at least in his own eyes.

Still, Karen was in town. So was Pete. They were risks to his ability to function as effectively and, to be blunt, as ruthlessly as he might need to.

In the exact same position, Jack would have done the same thing Anderson had done. Or better still, he would have left Jack behind, made him stay at the base. There was good reason for that sort of decision, as Jack's nightmare the previous night had made abundantly clear. Even if it wasn't on a conscious level, there was some part of him that wasn't very happy about what was happening to his hometown.

Hell, even though the town had changed almost as much as Jack himself, he still had memories of the people in the area, still had feelings for a few of them. There was a small portion of his soul that was bleeding, weeping at the deaths of Joe Ditweiller and Herb Cambridge. He'd gone to school with them. They'd never been good friends, but he'd seen them every day, and they'd played a few games of baseball behind the church. They'd even had a few mutual friends, like Petey Donovan. There was a time when he and Pete had been inseparable. Hell, they'd been blood brothers. When Jack broke his arm at the age of twelve, it'd been Pete who half-dragged and half-carried him all the way to Doc Johnson's place. They'd even—

Jack forced his thoughts away from the past, doing his best to concentrate on the list of names the Colonel was reciting. "...Sam Williams, Peter Donovan"...Jack jumped a little at the name of his old blood brother—"...William Tidwell and Paul Summerfield. All five have been implicated by the rest of their good buddies. The big problem is all of them are either from out of town, or simply haven't been found at their residences. Does anyone here know anything at all about these people's whereabouts?"

Jack couldn't help but notice the Colonel's eyes looking his way when that last bit came out. He smiled beneath his breathing gear. "Colonel Anderson, sir. Has anyone looked into the textile mill?"

Anderson looked at him, his face set in an expressionless way. "No. But now that you mention it, that's not a bad idea. Brightman's been giving his people a lot of hours, especially when you consider that there's nothing in his mill that he can move." For the briefest moment, the man's face stretched into a semblance of a smile. Then he turned towards Hawthorne. "Get a squad out there. I want the place checked completely. Oh, and why don't you take Osborn with you? He's bound to know who belongs there and who doesn't."

"Other problems to deal with; Paul Summerfield has a record with the FBI. Seems he's wanted for several activities of a violent nature. He's a career protester. We don't have any idea what he's doing in town, but he's likely behind about half of the tactics the redneck brigade's been using against us." Anderson took the time to hold up a large, grainy picture of the man. It looked like a driver's license photo that had been enlarged substantially. "Also, we've got a food crisis on our hands, folks. The people in this town apparently don't believe in conserving their resources. We've got shipments coming in today, and we need to disperse the supplies to the houses in the area. No one's allowed outside of their homes, but we're going to make an exception to that rule.

"Lieutenant Powell. I want you and twenty men to handle dispersing the supplies. You are to go from block to block, allowing the people at each block to come out of their homes and gather the supplies. Each household gets one box of rations, unless there are more than five people living in the house. If there're more than five, give them a second one. Anybody gets antsy out there, shoot 'em. Is that clear?"

Powell nodded, saluted, and left the tent. Jack knew he'd be picking his men. So far, Jack was not among the chosen.

"I want to emphasize again, that any civilians found on the street are to be arrested." The Colonel looked towards Jack again, acknowledging, in his own way, the wisdom of Jack's earlier arguments. "But if anyone so much as belches the wrong way, you are to shoot to kill. We've lost too many people in this town, and I want it stopped.

"The good news along those lines is that we now know where the civilians have been getting their firearms. Just out of the town proper, across the street from the Miller farm, where the first of our boys ended up dead, there's a farm belonging to Victor 'Bud' Markle."

"Markle's been selling firearms to a few of the locals. He's been making a handsome profit, too." Jack jumped slightly in his seat. He'd known Bud Markle for years, and never would have suspected the man of trafficking illegal guns. The man'd always seemed content to raise his dogs and tend to his crops. Hell, Markle was one of the regulars in church, or at least he had been before Jack left town. "According to our most recent prisoners, Lucas Brightman's been financing the 'Collier Militia.' That's going to stop, immediately."

Anderson looked around the room for a moment, before nodding towards Lieutenant Evans. Evans was the only soldier Jack had ever met who never seemed to smile. He sometimes wondered if the man was a sociopath, for that reason alone. "Evans," the colonel continued. "I want you to pay a visit to Markle's place. I want every weapon there seized. When that's done, I want Brightman's textile mill gone over. I don't want so much as a pocketknife left behind. Any questions? No? Good. Get to it."

Calloway got chosen for the assignment. He didn't know which sounded worse, staying with Anderson or going out to face Markle and his dogs. Armor or no, he recalled the animals being very large and very mean. For the first time since he'd come to Collier, Jack felt comforted by the weight of his rifle.

3

Eric Pendleton looked over towards Jack and shook his head. "I hate dogs, Calloway. I always have."

Jack chuckled beneath his respirator. "Then you're gonna love Markle's place. I hear he's been raising pit bulls. Big, mean motherfuckers, who'd as soon chew your arm off as look at you."

"That's a nice thought." Pendleton's helmet rotated from side to side. With a sigh, the man climbed from the back of the truck they'd used to get to Markle's farm. The heat was already beyond unbearable, and the bad stretch of weather was showing signs of burning the peach trees, growing in neat, orderly rows along the roadside that led to the farmer's house. Everything looked withered and baked. Inside his survival

suit, Jack understood how the crops had to feel. He was practically ready to melt into a puddle himself.

Twelve men total walked along the dusty trail between the
trees. All of them worked for ONYX. They'd hoped to have
Frank Osborn along for the show, simply because they wanted
everything to end as quickly and peacefully as possible. No
luck. Officer Frank wasn't to be found. *C'est la vie.*

Each soldier was armed with an assault rifle and plenty of
ammunition. They were wearing high-impact armor, capable
of stopping almost any bullet, and they were well-versed in the
art of war. And every one of them let out a whimper when they
saw the dogs coming at them like a swarm of rats. Jack lost
count at twenty of the beasts. Perhaps it was simply a primal
reaction to the low-slung, muscular forms darting towards them
from the farmhouse. Maybe it was just an automatic response
to the low, deadly rumbles that came from the dogs.

For Jack, it was the sudden realization that, despite his
years of training and war games, he'd never once had to fight
against anything that wasn't human. Humans tended to run
from people dressed in armor and carrying serious firepower.
The dogs couldn't have cared less. Humans could be reasoned
with. The pit bulls didn't seem the least bit interested in listening to reason.

The dogs just wanted meat.

Off in the distance, a short movement caught Jack's attention. Markle was standing near his house, his legs wide
spread and his pondulous belly peering from beneath his stained,
yellow T-shirt. As Jack looked on, the man started waddle-
running towards the barn on the other end of the property.

Before Jack could react, the dogs were there. The armor
was a blessing, but the impacts from the two monsters running into his body sent Calloway sprawling to the ground. He
was chagrined and terrified at the same time. All around him
the sounds of rifles firing started, a series of gentle pops that
couldn't compare to the devastation the weapons caused. Jack
shot the first of the dogs trying to chew through his armor,

making sure to aim away from his body, and feeling the surprising pressure of the animal's teeth as they worried the edge
of his shin guard. The dog practically exploded as the hail of
bullets tore through its rear flanks.

He both thanked God for the gun and cursed himself for
leaving it on fully-automatic. Even with armor, he could have
blown his leg off too easily for him to want to consider.

Beside him, Wenkowsky cut loose with a scream of epic
proportions as one of the dogs managed to slip past the armor
on his belly and tear into his side. He fired on the dog even as
it chomped into the raw flesh of his hip. The dog stopped
biting, but the damage was done. The man would likely bleed
to death if someone didn't get to work on him and soon.

For a time the air was filled with the sounds of men and
dogs screaming and growling, as well as the chatter of rifle
fire. Then there was silence, save for heavy breathing and the
gentle noise of blood flowing from carcasses. The dogs, while
fearsome and ferocious, never really had a chance. They died
in pain and violence.

Then a new sound came to Jack, even as he was helping
Pendleton put a few pressure bandages on Wenkowsky. It
sounded like a low rolling thunder at first, then it became the
clear sound of a diesel engine roaring into life.

Jack looked in the direction of the sound and saw a sight
that was enough to make his stomach drop out. Markle came
spilling from the darkness of his barn riding on a tractor. The
damned thing looked big enough to knock down the trees between the farmer and the men from ONYX. Just to make
matters worse, the oversized farmer was wearing the armor
from one of the dead soldiers.

The survival gear didn't fit him well. Markle looked like a
sausage half-erupting from its casing, but he knew all too well
how solid that armor was. Despite the effective use of animal
darts, in the soft patches between the armor plates, that the
Collier Militia had adopted, the damn stuff was bulletproof.
There wasn't a man among the soldiers who wasn't a marks-

man, but the tractor's cage wasn't going to make hitting him any easier.

Calloway had doubts the armor could withstand a tractor running it down.

Pendleton cursed as he reached into the ammo pocket hanging against his thigh. "That motherfucker's wearing Brian's suit."

Brian Henry Brooks. The first of the soldiers murdered in Collier. Jack had heard about what they'd done to Brooks, but he hadn't seen the body. He'd been just as angry as everyone else when he heard about it. Brian'd been a fun, amiable guy. He was also one of the few soldiers at ONYX who was married. Anita Brooks was a widow, and from what Brian had been speaking about just before they took off for Collier, she was also expecting a child in a few months.

Somehow, the idea of running lost its appeal. There was some vengeance to take care of, and he aimed to handle the matter. Evans' voice cut through the thunder of the tractor's engine revving hard, and charged into the eardrums of every single soldier there. Only Wenkowsky failed to respond when the order to "Hammer him" went out. No one even noticed. As a unit, the soldiers turned and focused on the tractor coming their way.

Fingers squeezed triggers, and the bullets cut through the air, heading towards Markle on his John Deere. This time there were new noises as well. The scream of metal bouncing off steel and punching through the tractor's engine; plus the screams of fear and pain from Markle. Markle learned the hard way what the soldiers already knew. Bullets tend to find a way to do damage.

The tractor moved forward for a few more seconds, then veered into a tree, sputtered, and died. Markle bled to death before anyone could reach him. No one tried too hard to get there in a hurry.

After searching the grounds and all of the buildings, the men came up with two shotguns and a battered, rusty

.22-caliber pistol. Following the Colonel's radioed orders, the tractor, the farm and the house were all set ablaze. The dead farmer was packed into a body bag and dragged away from his burning property.

Wenkowsky was handled more carefully. He was alive, after all, and he'd never killed a family man. Or if he had, the man hadn't been a part of their family. Not like Brian Brooks.

Chapter 11

1

By the time Jack's unit had placed Wenkowsky in the care of the medical staff, four new men had been added to the group. These guys even brought along a few new toys: grenades and tear gas canisters. Then, just for fun, another dozen men joined them. Evans spoke to the group for a few minutes, making certain that everyone understood the plan of attack. Everyone did.

The Brightman Textile Mill rested on the side of town farthest from the lakebed. It was a large, gray brick building which could easily have been mistaken for a penitentiary if there'd been bars on the windows. Jack had not seen the building since he was very young. It'd always scared the hell out of him, especially when they were manufacturing the rubber matting for some of the outdoor carpets and the stench from the place seemed to belch forth across the entire town. Back when he was living in the town, his father had often come home from working at the mill with a strained smile on his face. Often, late at night after he though Jack was asleep, Richard Calloway would tell his wife stories of how bad it was at the mill. He'd regale her with bitter anecdotes about Brightman and the working conditions. When he was a young man and his father thought him safely out of earshot, he'd heard tales of people losing fingers and arms to the machines inside. Once he'd even heard about Dewett Hammil's son, Arthur, getting himself caught in some sort of cutting machine and getting shredded like so much wheat. He'd also heard rumors that Brightman arranged to have the boy *pushed* into the industrial monster. Remembering the old man's passionate tirades about how the niggers were destroying the country and ruining the youth of America, Calloway could just about believe it, too. There was a time when Jack knew he'd end up working in the mill, same as everyone else in town. As he stared at the bloated hulk, he thanked God that things hadn't worked out quite the way he'd anticipated.

The parking lot was empty, but that didn't mean the building itself was unoccupied. Just to be certain there were no surprises this time, no more dead bodies with poisonous darts protruding from a soft spot on the armor, the soldiers took the time to break a few windows and let loose a barrage of tear gas canisters into the mill. Every single one of the soldiers double-checked the pressure seals on their breathing apparatus. That damned stuff burned when it touched any membrane, and each and every one of them had been forced to breathe the gases in on at least three occasions, for the sake of training. None of them ever wanted to go through feeling that again.

When the white cloud began spilling evenly through the entire building, the soldiers moved forward. Jack held his breath for a few seconds after entering the chemical fog. He needn't have bothered; his outfit was properly air tight, even where the dog had tried chewing his shin to pieces earlier.

They checked every room, pushing aside bundles of cloth and rolls of carpeting when they found access blocked. While they found no people, Jack and three of the others managed to locate a nest built in one of the back storage rooms. The nest had a large collection of empty bleach bottles, ammonia bottles, and cooking pots. There were boxes for candle wax and empty crates that had once held jam jars. Four jars remained, half filled with bleach, and then sealed with wax. Filling the top half with ammonia would make a wonderful little mustard gas bomb, and Jack suspected that was what had hit his room the night before. That was what had started the fires. Quick, efficient, and deadly, but God help the fool who got clumsy when carrying them.

There were also a few bits and pieces of armor from the other victims who'd been cut by knives, before the Collier Militia had come across the handguns and dart guns that had made them a serious threat. Evans whistled long and low, apparently forgetting that his mike was on, until everyone around him winced at the sudden feedback. He mumbled an apology and then spoke out. "These guys are good. They've got enough medical supplies here to start their own hospital."

Jack looked over at the piled pill bottles and vials that had once held various drugs. He shook his head. "No wonder we've been dropping like flies. There's enough shit there to kill a bull elephant. Hell, a whole herd of 'em."

Evans touched his jawline, but Jack heard nothing from him. Private line to Anderson. He waited, dreading what the orders from the commanding officer might be.

A moment later, he found out. "Burn it down, boys. Colonel Anderson says he doesn't want these freaks to have any place left to hide."

"Sir? That's just crazy. What are we gonna do if the fire spreads?" A slightly-built sergeant named Wilson Piddock beat Jack to the punch with that particular question.

Evans shook his head. "I already talked to the Colonel about that, Piddock. He wants five men left here to make sure the fire stays where he wants it. You just got elected. You, Ordover, Davilla, Spivy and Hanson just became firemen. There's a couple or three fire hydrants around the perimeter, and there're hoses on the walls inside. Set up the hoses and then torch it."

Piddock said something, but his mike was off and no one was close enough to him to hear what he said. Evans overlooked the breach of protocol, or just plain didn't hear it. Jack opted not to point it out to the Lieutenant, just in case.

"As for the rest of you. We've got another target on our agenda today. We're going to visit Lucas Brightman's little palace and see what there is to see."

As Evans spoke those words, Calloway was filled with a sense of dread. Brightman was well known and respected in the community, even if he wasn't very well liked. He was quite literally the main source of income for most of the people living in Collier, just as his father before him had once been. If Brightman was involved in this mess, Jack had a nasty suspicion he'd have made arrangements to see his house well protected.

Interlude

While Jack Calloway and his patrol were out handling the dangerous business of removing the potential risks of the Collier Militia, Walter J. Powell was trying to remain calm. The people of Collier were hardly grateful for the food they were given. Most of them were quiet, but enough made gestures or foulmouthed comments to set Powell's teeth on edge.

Powell was a career man. Even if he hadn't been chosen for ONYX, he knew he'd have eagerly spent his life in service to his country. He thrived on the structure of the military lifestyle. More importantly, he understood the ways of the military. Discipline, that was what made a country great.

So here he was, doing his job and making sure the ignorant rednecks in this backwater town were given their food and supplies—not the standard shit served out in the Army, either, but name-brand foods and even Coca-Cola for God's sake—and his thanks for this task was to hear the little shits call him names and curse his existence. The soldiers with him were getting just as fed up with the attitudes of the locals. He could tell by the way they moved, and by how brusque they'd become when handing out the food supplies. They'd all started off with "Have a nice day" as their way of dismissing a person who'd received supplies. They'd even taken the time to answer questions when they could, about the current state of affairs in the job of removing the bogey from the lake. (Things were looking much better, ever since the ship had tried to extricate itself and had loosened the hard crust around its base.) Now, they handed out their food and nodded a dismissal, or shrugged in answer to questions asked by the citizens of Shithole, Georgia, if they bothered with any sort of gesture at all.

That suited Powell just fine. These morons didn't want the food, they didn't have to come out of their houses. They wanted companionship, they should have thought about that before hand, and stayed somewhere else. He'd had it up to his eye teeth with listening to the whining locals go on and on about how hard their lives were. Enough already.

When the last house of Market Street had received its supplies, Powell ordered them on to Beaver Ride Road. The names around here were laughable, but then again, so was the entire town. *Mayberry RFD* with an attitude problem.

Powell picked up his megaphone and explained the situation to the closed doors around him. Just as he was starting to give his speech about how one person from each house could come out into the street and receive a supply package, the local version of Andy Taylor showed up. Captain Frank Osborn pulled up behind the supply truck in his old Mustang. At least the man had good taste in cars. One of the other soldiers went over to speak to the man, and Powell went back to the business of telling the pissants how to behave themselves.

When he was finished, the doors of the houses on the street opened, and a small group of people walked towards the truck. None of them looked friendly, and most were likely the sort who'd say something just to piss him off. A short man with red hair and a cheesy mustache nodded amiably and grabbed his package. The man was wearing blue jeans and an oversized white T-shirt that billowed around him almost like a miniskirt. There was something about him that was familiar, but Powell couldn't place him.

A massive black man stepped forward, grinning sheepishly, and asked one of the soldiers how his day was going. The soldier responded with a friendly tone, and Powell understood why. Dewett Hammil was a nice old man and the local baker. Still, something about the short man bothered him.

Hammil took the large box of supplies the soldier handed to him, and Powell smiled. Every one of them had heard about the Great Cookie Incident, when the old fart had just about gotten himself killed so he could bake a few dozen cookies. It was one of the few little moments of their time in town that had actually been lighter in nature. The soldiers had taken the liberty of adding chocolate chips, pecans and walnuts to the man's supplies. They'd come from his own store, and they suspected he wouldn't mind.

Hammill looked a little stressed under the load, his limp became more pronounced, and the short man turned immediately to him, offering to help. As the two men switched packages, Powell saw the butt of a pistol sticking out the backside of Shorty's pants.

There was no hesitation: Powell swung the business end of his rifle towards the short man and screamed. "Stop where you are!"

Both men stopped, and turned their heads slowly to face Powell. The lieutenant felt his pulse rate increase, as he thought about the risks involved in trying to stop the would-be terrorist. His mind raced at a hundred miles an hour, and his senses sharpened, even as they focused almost exclusively on the short man.

Behind him, Powell heard the sounds of Frank Osborn calling out. He couldn't hear what the man said. Even as Osborn's voice came his way, Dewett Hammil was suddenly falling to the ground, crying out in pain. The short man dropped Hammil's package and started to turn towards the fallen giant. The rational part of Powell's mind understood that Hammill was injured.

The emotional side of his brain, however, only saw that Shorty was moving, his hand coming dangerously close to the small of his back and the firearm that rested there. All around him, the soldiers tried talking at the same time, and the people on the street moved away from Shorty, or in a few cases, towards Hammil.

Perhaps it was simply paranoia. Maybe it was too much stress and too much time spent in the survival suit and in the blazing heat of the day. Whatever it was, it made Powell pull the trigger on his rifle. Three bullets shot towards their target, and Officer Richard "Buck" Landers of the Collier Police Department died as they penetrated his chest and neck. Around the same time the bullets hit, Powell finally made the connection with the policeman he'd only ever seen in uniform.

Frank Osborn's cry of rage was buried beneath the panicked screams of the people living on Beaver Ride Road. Powell never heard them. But he felt the hand that grabbed his shoulder, and he had just enough time to register the barrel of a gun shoved against his neck before Osborn pulled the trigger. The helmet was well-designed, and the bullet that blew a hole through the top of Lieutenant Walter J. Powell's skull bounced around like a pinball, making mincemeat of the dead man's face and brains.

Like Powell before him, Frank Osborn had just enough time to realize that he'd made a hideous mistake before his life ended in a swarm of hot lead. Nineteen well-trained men with automatic rifles turned and fired at Osborn before they even gave the idea any conscious thought.

And that was how the final battle for Collier really started.

Chapter 11

2

Someplace behind them, the Brightman Textile Mill was dying in a fire strong enough to melt steel and ignite concrete. Somewhere ahead of them, just around the next bend in the road, Lucas Brightman's palatial home stood waiting, brooding as they came towards it.

Brightman's house should have been beautiful. Jack could look at the classic lines of the Victorian manor and appreciate the craftsmanship that had gone into building the place. It was three stories tall, and sitting on its perfectly manicured lawn, the dark brown mansion looked like it was just waiting for a chance to be photographed for *Better Homes and Gardens*. It was the sort of house he'd once dreamed about owning, sometime before he'd lost his hopes of ever being more than a grunt in a secret military operation.

Still, the place terrified him. Jack Calloway could feel his pulse racing, and was breaking out in a hard sweat, despite the natural cooling effects the canned oxygen he breathed had on his body.

Damn, I just know this gonna blow up in our faces. I can feel it. The words went through his mind again and again; a private mantra that he desperately hoped would somehow protect him from the coming devastation.

The usual chatter from the other soldiers was missing, and Calloway suspected they felt some of what he felt. He knew what part of the problem was: despite the captured people the day before, they'd never managed to get their hands on the damned tranquilizer guns used in most of the slayings. Someone, somewhere, had a weapon that was perfectly designed to kill a soldier, even one in a suit specifically made to keep people safe. All they had to do was get a clean shot at the softer parts of the armor, even behind the knee, and it would all be over for one more of Uncle Sam's boys in black. He didn't know what even half the drugs he'd seen packages for were supposed to do, but he was willing to bet there wasn't a cure for the shit if it got into a person's system.

There was no sign of activity from the house. Jack didn't find that very comforting. He was having trouble catching his breath, and he knew it wasn't because his oxygen supply was running low; they'd all changed tanks before coming over here.

The group broke apart into four smaller squads, each taking a separate part of the perimeter. Jack and his men, including Pendelton and three men he'd barely ever worked with, moved towards the eastern section of the house, covering the front end of the building. Evans and his squad took the northern area, where the long wraparound porch was likely to be a problem. Walker and his squad took the western part of the house and Chadwick's squad covered the southern portion.

The idea was simple enough: each squad would start at the edge of the heavy woods around the house and move carefully towards the building itself, checking for any potential threats and eliminating them. Once at the house, they'd do the same thing they'd done at the textile mill. A little tear gas, a little patience and then a full sweep of the interior.

It shouldn't have been a problem. Naturally, it didn't work out the way they'd hoped it would.

The four leaders stayed in constant communication, using the separate band held aside for just such situations. Because there were only two radio bands available to them, they were privy to what was happening in Collier. They got to hear all about the deaths of Buck Landers, Walter J. Powell and Frank Osborn.

Maybe if they hadn't been so stunned, they could have predicted what happened next.

Corporal Leonard Walker stepped on a homemade land mine. Whoever designed the damned thing knew what he was doing. The entire grounds of the building shook from the impact of the mine going off. Walker never knew what hit him. Nails and steel shavings penetrated every part of his body that wasn't armored, and the impact was sufficient to divorce his right leg from the rest of his body. Even though they were on the private band, the soldiers could hear the screams from Walker's squad as they cut through the air.

Jack Calloway switched over to the standard radio band and called for his men to stay where they were. If there was one land mine, there might well be others. They were close to the house, but Jack didn't feel safe backtracking just yet and he couldn't be certain what was ahead of him.

"Pendleton," Jack said, as his initial adrenaline rush started to fade to a tolerable level. "How many spare clips do you have?"

"I've got an additional hundred and twenty rounds, Sergeant."

"Good, we might need them. How about those grenades? How many does the squad have?"

"Three, Sergeant."

"Beautiful. Throw one to me."

"Excuse me?"

The panic in Pendleton's voice made Jack laugh nervously. "With the pin still in place, Pendleton. I'm not quite ready to die just yet."

Jack turned and waited patiently until Pendleton's nerves were good enough to let him make the throw. Just the same, the man's aim was off and Jack felt himself tense up as the small bomb bounced and rolled across the lawn. Ten feet between him and the explosive, just lovely.

"I want everyone on the ground and prone. If I'm gonna do something stupid, no one gets hurt but me. Understood?" They all voiced their agreement and carefully lowered to the ground, waiting patiently.

Jack switched his rifle from fully automatic fire to single action, then fired a bullet into the ground six inches from where he was standing. He wanted to scream, but held it in. When nothing exploded, he did it again at roughly the twelve-inch mark. Then at eighteen inches, then at twenty-four inches. Nothing blew up, so he moved two feet closer to his prize. Again and again he fired into the ground. Again and again, nothing went kablooey.

When he finally reached the grenade, his entire body was shaking. "O-okay, guys. This is the routine. I'm gonna throw this bad little boy, and we're all going to duck low. Make sure the soft areas on your suits are covered as best you can."

"What are you doing, Sergeant Calloway?" Pendleton sounded ready to wet his pants. Jack couldn't blame him, but felt obligated to do his best to at least appear like he felt confident.

"If the mines are pressure sensitive, then the grenade ought to set them off without blowing us to hell and back. Get it?"

Before Pendleton could respond, Evans' voice came through his head set. "Calloway, give me a status report."

"All's well here, so far, Lieutenant. I'm gonna set off a grenade over here in a few seconds, see if I can't detonate any prizes waiting for us in the ground."

Evans was silent for a moment. Then, "Good idea. Glad I thought of it. I'm gonna do the same thing over here."

"Anything from Walker's squad?"

"Them that ain't dead are wishing they were."

"How about Chadwick?"

"All well so far. I'm gonna suggest he try your grenade method. Why don't we handle this with a countdown."

"Sounds like a deal, sir."

"I'll get back with you in a second."

Calloway switched bands again, back to the regular communication frequency, and ordered his men to "think small thoughts" while they squatted. By the time his men responded to the order, Evans was back on the radio. "At zero, gentlemen. Ten...nine...eight...seven..." Jack waited as patiently as he could, and when the Lieutenant reached zero, he pulled the pin from the grenade, rolled it to a spot about halfway to the house, and pulled himself into a standing fetal position.

The grenade went off with a resounding BOOM, and then the ground ten feet away, on Calloway's right hand side, disappeared in a lightning-strike explosion. He felt the nails and pennies as they slapped against his side. He also felt the shock wave lift him from the ground and launch him through the air like a tennis ball going up against Andre Aggasi.

About half a minute later, he realized that his head was still attached to his neck. The ringing in his ears made the sounds coming from his helmet little more than garbled squawks. "I don't know what you're saying," Jack mumbled, "but it's damned nice to hear you."

A few seconds later, Pendleton grabbed his shoulders and started shaking him. Since the motion made the world want to spin, Jack slapped the man's hands away.

"...aid, 'can you hear me, Sergeant Calloway?" The voice in his ears was concerned, almost frantic.

"I've got you, Lieutenant. Sorry about that. I guess I was a little close to the land mine."

Pendleton's voice broke in. "I'd say. I've never seen anyone thrown like that before. Are you sure you're okay?"

"Yeah. At least I think so. Everything moves, and I'm only seeing one of you, so I guess that's a good sign." He knew there was something he wanted to ask, but it took him a little while to remember just what it was. "Is everyone else okay, Lieutenant?"

"All's well over here. Count your blessings and give yourself a pat on the back. Chadwick's side of the building had three mines. No one hurt, but everyone's good and shaken."

Jack nodded, then stopped that when he realized it only made things start spinning again. "What's next, sir?"

"Next? Grab another grenade and make your own door in this shithole. I don't trust the ones we already have. Better still, do the tear gas, then the grenades. Maybe we'll get lucky and the place will blow sky high. Then we wouldn't have a problem."

"Pendleton."

"Yes, Sergeant?"

"Smoke the place. And don't miss this time, dammit."

"Yes, Sergeant!"

Calloway watched the bomb bounce off the side of the house, got up himself and threw the canister through the closest window. Thirty seconds later, the tear gas started spilling out again. In the meantime, he took the liberty of yelling at Pendleton, and questioning the man's heritage.

"Pendleton?"

"Yes, Sergeant?"

"Walk your skinny ass over here and hand me a grenade."

After telling everyone to drop again, Calloway tossed the second grenade and watched the east wall of Chateau Brightman explode into toothpick-sized flinders of wood and shards of glass. "All clear over here, Lieutenant. Orders?"

"Wait just a minute..." The building shook twice, then Evans spoke again. "Move 'em in, people. Let's catch us some bad guys."

There were no more mines in the house. But there was trouble just the same.

Interlude

Colonel Mark Anderson ordered the helicopters off the ground right after somebody decided to roll a burning car down the hill towards his tent. Fortunately for him, the car veered to the right and joined with the remains of Pastor William O'Rourke's vehicle at the bottom of the lake's bed.

Unfortunately for the would-be car bombers, they only managed a few hundred yards in their getaway vehicle before the soldiers returned the favor. Two more citizens of Collier lay dead in the front of a battered white pickup truck that had last seen a fresh paint job sometime before Carter was elected President of the United States. Their blood mingled with the radiator fluid spilling across the asphalt.

Anderson sighed and reemphasized his orders to the pilots and their flight crews. Shoot to kill; ask questions later. Hawthorne sat nearby, looking worn and frazzled. He'd aged a decade in the last week. Anderson didn't want to think about what he himself must be looking like by now.

Frank Osborn was dead less than two hours, and already everything had gone to Hell. How the news got out was anyone's guess, but the vast majority of the people in town were now making their dissatisfaction well known. An elderly man on Second Avenue was arrested when he mooned two of the soldiers. They couldn't quite bring themselves to shoot the moron, and Anderson couldn't blame them. Mayor Milo Fitzwater was fit to be tied. He'd torn into the Colonel's tent like a Baptist minister into a brothel.

The short man even managed to look scary when he got truly angry. Fitzwater ripped into Anderson verbally for fifteen minutes, and through it all, he let the man have his say. Even the soldiers who'd actually been on the scene said it was Powell who fired the first shot.

Thanks to one of his trusted lieutenants, two officers of the law were dead. Worse, those two men were the closest thing Anderson'd had to allies in the city. They were the force that kept everyone in Collier from going bugshit crazy.

Fitzwater actually having made it to the tent was a sign that everyone in the town must have gone insane. He would never have made it anywhere near the command post if the soldiers out there didn't already have their hands full.

He was doing his best, God knew he was trying not to let them get hurt. But every fool who walked away from the protection of his home was begging for grief. An hour after Osborn's death, Mark Anderson sent out patrols with loudspeakers, warning everyone back into their homes. That was his last effort on their behalf.

So the car going over the side of the lake was just one step too many. Anyone not in uniform who was caught outside would get one warning. If they didn't come peacefully, they'd just have to accept the consequences.

And if the 'copters caught sight of anyone out of a uniform, they were to shoot to kill.

So far, over a hundred people had surrendered. Twice as many were already dead, and Mark suspected the worst was yet to come.

Thinking about the long list of people his soldiers had arrested, and reflecting on the abilities of the conditioning experts, he wondered who was getting off easiest. The people sent here weren't supposed to make his life easier. They were here to clean up any details he might miss. Little details, like what to do with an entire town of eyewitnesses. He'd spoken with the man in charge of the reconditioning project. He understood exactly what the ten painfully mundane people were all about.

The man in charge of the group, who went by the stunningly original name of 'Mr. Smith,' agreed with him on one aspect: the fewer people killed, the better. Anderson wanted to see the people left alone, left to pick up their lives and, if necessary, compensated for their vast inconvenience. At worst, he wanted them relocated and given new identities. The Witness Protection Program had worked along those lines in the past—albeit with willing participants—and he couldn't see why it shouldn't be done again. With a little work, their records could be altered and the names they'd had in the past could be erased from existence.

Mr. Smith didn't quite agree. There would be no compensation. There would be no hopes that the people of Collier could keep a secret. Instead, they were going to get a special treatment created in the interest of, oh, and this part just plain *hurt*, 'National Security.'

As he thought about the situation, as he sat back down at his desk and poured himself another cup of tepid coffee, Colonel Mark Anderson knew what was happening to the people being held in the Collier jail and at a few of the houses they'd been forced to commandeer.

They were being reprogrammed. Their entire recollections of everything that'd occurred since the Fourth of July were being erased and replaced with all-new memories, custom-designed by Mr. Smith and his cohorts. The people from out of town who were now being held in Collier against their will were also getting special treatment. They'd remember all the gory details of being held hostage by a fictitious mad man with a life-threatening nuclear device hidden somewhere in the town, and for fun they'd also have crystal-clear recollections of the threat of a plague hanging over their heads.

The world's most wanted international terrorist, Amir Hal Densalid, was nothing but a sham. A ghost created to point the blame at someone else when the government needed to hide a secret.

He was also a great excuse. If things went any farther than they already had, the government was fully prepared to detonate a small warhead with a very short half-life. The area would be clean of radiation within a week. That was all the time ONYX would need to clean up all the details of a situation gone hideously wrong. All evidence would be destroyed, and there would be no witnesses left.

Mister Smith and his friends had an answer for that problem, too. Because, with a little extra time, they could erase the entire history of every citizen of Collier. The people would still live, safe and secure, well fed and well taken care of for the rest of their lives. They'd just be someone else entirely. Someone very much like the person each of them had been before the transformation. The major differences would simply be a new name, and new faces to replace the ones that were so important to them right now. The United States of America was a big country; losing a few thousand people all over the nation wouldn't take any effort at all.

The people would still be alive, but their lives would be lies generated to make them forget what had been stolen from them. Techniques perfected over the last fifteen years made the re-creation of a person as easy for the conditioning experts as it was for a master chess player to trounce a novice opponent. Chemicals and suggestions, with a little torture thrown in on the side: in its own way, the entire idea was just as bad as murder, but sounded kinder to the people in charge of the ONYX Project.

Personally, Anderson thought he'd prefer death to what the prisoners were enduring. Death seemed less terrifying.

Chapter 11

3

Crawling past the ruined walls wasn't all that difficult. Jack'd had plenty of practice moving over rough terrain, as had every other member of ONYX. The efficiency with which they tore through the house was testament to the extensive training each of them had endured for the privilege of being a part of the elite fighting force. There was no remorse for the damage to the house. There was no regret for the destruction of the numerous rare and even priceless antiques that decorated the palatial home. There was only the urgency to find the threat to ONYX and eliminate it.

While Jack preferred the idea of doing his work without any bloodshed, he understood that there might well be a need to kill. They soldiers moved through the building, each squad taking a different level of the mansion. They were a little short-handed; the death of Corporal Walker and the severe injuries to his squad made the job more time-consuming, but otherwise didn't hinder them. One man from each of the remaining squads was left outside to tend to the wounded. In Jack's case, he left Pendleton. The man was simply too shaken to work as an effective soldier at the present time.

Given a choice in the matter, he'd have stayed behind himself. Despite the ability to function well under stress, Jack kept thinking about the names Colonel Anderson had mentioned earlier. One name in particular: Peter Donovan.

Seeing Karen had been awkward, but it was something he could survive. Seeing Pete wouldn't be too bad, but what if Pete decided to fight back? What if Pete was one of the men who'd been killing his companions? What if Pete drew a weapon on him? Would he be able to do what he had to do in order to survive?

Jack just didn't know, and he wasn't looking forward to finding out.

Jack and his two remaining squad members checked every room of the third floor. They were cautious and they were thorough. Jack even had the forethought to check the attic, but found that there was nothing in the narrow area save pink fiberglass insulation. They were professional and efficient, just as they'd been trained to be. There was no one home, no sign of a hasty departure.

Jack breathed a sigh of relief and reported to Evans. Evans, for his part, acknowledged the success and then ordered them down to the basement.

The momentary relaxation that had crept into Jack disappeared again, replaced by that same sense of dread he'd had since first seeing the house. He acknowledged his orders and the trio moved down the stairs, going to the one place on the property that hadn't been covered yet.

Never one to shirk his responsibilities, Jack led the way down into the bowels of the house. His lenses compensated for the darkness, and in less than a second, he could see clearly, despite the lack of any illumination. The stairs were solid, made of hardwood. He checked each one as he went, making certain that no tripwires were waiting to set off another unpleasant surprise.

Two doors greeted him at the bottom of the long staircase; one to the left and one to the right of the oak-paneled wall that faced him. Jack took the one to the right, ordering the other two men to handle the one on the left. There was no attempt to simply turn the knobs on the doors. Steel-toed boots cracked wood and finally broke locks. All three men drew back from the entrances to the rooms, fearful that an explosion might come their way. When nothing happened, they entered their respective areas.

Jack got lucky. In the room beyond the door he'd chosen, five men and one woman sat in plush furniture or stood around a pool table. He recognized Lucas Brightman immediately. Despite the fifteen-plus years since he'd last seen the man, there were few changes in the way he looked. He was old, withered and bitter, the very picture of Ebenezer Scrooge. The only things missing to make him fit the part were the sagging nightgown and cap, they'd been replaced by an expensive looking summer suit. Brightman was sitting in a leather chair that fairly swallowed his slight body whole.

Jack scanned the rest of the room, taking in each of the people there. In the seat next to Brightman was a portly woman with silver hair and too much makeup. Like Brightman, she wore clothes that spoke of money. Her face was tear-stained, and her overly dressed lips trembled on the verge of a scream. Like as not, she was the old man's wife.

Sitting across from the elderly couple, a very large man stared at him with eyes as cold and dark as a winter night. His face was lined, but his features seemed almost young despite that fact. His dark hair was slicked back, and for all the world he looked like he belonged behind the desk of some small business, or perhaps on the road selling vacuum cleaners. This face he knew, but not from town. Paul Summerfield looked exactly like the picture of him that Anderson had held out for all of them to see earlier that day.

A greasy looking man with long, even greasier looking hair looked his way. The man's facial expression switched from a sneer of annoyance to a look of uncertain, watery fear even as Jack took him in. He'd known the man once upon a time. He used to be an occasional player during the summer time baseball games behind the church. Sam Williams had changed from a crew-cut bearing kid with freckles and pimples into wasted life. He had the look of a burnout, the sort of person one tended to cross the street to avoid having to see too clearly. Worst of all, his freckles were gone but the zits still remained.

Billy Tidwell was next. Aside from growing about a foot in height and losing some of his hair, he looked just like he had as a kid, down to the dusty tennis shoes on his feet. Billy was one of the few kids in town that everyone picked on. There was something about the way he ducked his head and avoided looking directly at anybody that just demanded mistreatment. That too had not changed. Billy stood perfectly still, except for the head bobbing, with one hand on a pool cue, and the other picking at the crack of his butt. Well, one other thing about him had changed; his gut was even larger than when he was the local fat kid.

Lastly, Jack saw the face he'd dreaded seeing. Peter Donovan was leaning over the billiards table, braced for a shot. He looked at Jack too, but his look of annoyance didn't change when he saw who'd entered the room.

His crew cut hair was the same. Pete's face was still strong and handsome. Everything else about him was different. His lean body was hard, wiry and well-tanned. Tattoos ran across both of his forearms, including a swastika. He wore a black T-shirt and tight, black jeans. The frozen snarl on his face was an expression Jack would never have believed his blood-brother capable of producing.

Jack's throat went dry, and he looked at the gathering before him with absolutely no idea of what he was supposed to be doing. He should have known, he *had* known, but all of his orders just went away as soon as he looked at Pete.

Pete made it a little easier for him by goosing his memory. "Well," he demanded, "are you gonna just stand there all fuckin' day, or was there somethin' on your mind?"

Jack reeled inside. He thought about long past baseball games, about the way Pete used to have of smiling, like his goofy grin said there couldn't possibly be anything wrong with the world. He thought about the two of them sitting in the diner as kids, scraping up the money to share a banana split, and about how they used to camp out in the backyard and pretend that they were explorers, or soldiers, or castaways stranded on a desert island. He closed his eyes and then he shook his head.

It was like a light switch went off in his skull. One second Jack was reeling from the sudden onslaught of childhood memories and glimpses of the past; the next his emotions seemed to shut down. All the anxiety was gone, and his path of action was clear. Whatever doubts he'd had about how to face Pete Donovan evaporated.

"All of you. Up against the walls." One hand leveled his firearm at Pete's chest, the other flicked the toggle on his jaw line. "Get the hell over here. I've got six people in here."

The other two didn't bother to respond verbally. He heard them come up behind him, and felt himself relax the smallest amount. It only took a few minutes to round them up.

Jack took care of frisking the group while his two companions kept them well behaved. Peter Donovan had a tranquilizer gun strapped to his ankle and buried inside his boot. Jack removed the weapon, and pulled a set of ten rubber-tipped darts from a small package taped to the inside of his other boot. Donovan called him several names while he quietly did his duty. He accused him being a nigger, a nigger lover, a sonuvawhore, a kike bastard, a wop, and finally a pig. Jack removed a pistol from Sam Williams' pants, and a large knife from Billy's belt. He told himself he felt nothing, and remained calm.

Lucas Brightman carried nothing more lethal than a money clip. The same went for his wife, unless you counted the diamonds that glittered from her earlobes. Jack suspected those could do some serious harm if thrown—the weight alone might just be lethal. Paul Summerfield carried the other dart gun. He also had over thirty of the loaded darts in his pants and strapped to his ankles. Unlike Peter, Summerfield said nothing at all. He simply stared with his dead eyes, and made Jack want to run screaming from the room.

Instead of fleeing, Jack carefully unloaded each of the weapons. He removed the clips from the pistols and then took the bullets from the clips and emptied the chambers of each weapon. He took removed the gas cartridges from the tranquilizer guns, and he slid the knife into his own belt.

Then, while all eyes were on him, he reported to Evans that there were six prisoners in their custody.

And while he waited for Evans and the rest of the soldiers to show up, Jack Calloway spent a few minutes beating Peter Donovan within an inch of his life. He broke Pete's nose and jaw with one well-placed roundhouse kick to his face, and then he got down and dirty all over the man. He cried while he did it, silently mourning the death of his youth. It took three men to pull him off Donovan's bloodied form. It took five minutes to calm him down.

4

The war for dominance in Collier ended very abruptly. The last of the Collier Militia was paraded through town in handcuffs, dragged down each residential street, while Colonel Anderson walked alongside them, explaining the new rules to everyone who cared to listen.

In truth the battles had all been fought by that point. Once the aerial support started shooting anyone outside of their homes, the vast majority of Collier's citizens and extended guests beat a hasty retreat. Anger is a powerful weapon; it can drive a person to amazing acts of courage and stupidity. Mortal fear is a great defense against anger, however, especially when anger is literally the only weapon available.

Or, in other words, anger can't stop automatic rifle fire. Most of the people clued into that in record time. The few who didn't catch the general drift got added to a list of the dead that was already far too long for anyone's comfort.

While Peter Donovan and his associates were marched through town, Colonel Mark Anderson explained that they would not be killed. He also explained that the people receiving medical aid in the high school would not be killed.

Then he clarified those statements, adding that he could and would change his mind if anyone at all acted out. Just to make sure his point got across, he left the bodies of those killed during the riots brought on by Frank Osborn's death exactly where they fell. For forty-eight hours, the people of Collier got to watch their friends and loved ones bloat and roast in the summer sun.

Speaking with Anderson later the same afternoon, Jack Calloway learned how much the Colonel hated doing that. There just wasn't any choice left. Jack had never seen a man look more haunted.

During the two days of silence, Jack watched several people taken away by other soldiers. He also saw two cars and several tons of dirt removed from the lake's dry bed. He even helped with the removal of the dirt.

A week behind schedule on what was supposed to be a rush-job retrieval, the people from Project ONYX were finally getting down to business. Jack told himself he just couldn't be happier. Life was finally going back to normal.

He probably could have believed the lie too, except for a single piece of paper. Dirt-stained and scorched around the edged, the pale green page was covered in a feminine script. At the bottom of each page was a name and an address. The name was Karen O'Rourke Donovan.

He stared at the paper for several minutes before letting it drop from his fingers. He went back to work, scraping the dirt away from the base of the silvery disc thrusting upward from the lake, and did his best not to think about Karen.

He avoided wondering if she had disappeared from her house yet. He didn't let himself wonder if she'd been killed during the fighting in town. He didn't acknowledge the last name of Donovan that had been added to her own, and he most certainly didn't think about how beautiful she'd looked when he saw her the day he found that boy's dead body tangled in the razor wire.

He worked mighty hard at staying away from thoughts of Karen, but she kept popping into his mind just the same.

So, later that night, he went over to Karen's house. He didn't think about it much when he knocked on the door, either.

He never said his name. He never gave her any reason to believe she might know him. He simply waited until her saw her sleepy, cautious eyes peering from the narrow crack she opened in her door, and asked her if she was any good at keeping secrets.

Two hours later, Karen Donovan and all of her houseguests left her house. They never returned.

5

Getting the group out of town was easier than he'd have ever guessed. The main reason no one managed to get in or out of Collier was the razor wire. It was reason enough, God knew, but with the number of injured and dead soldiers in town, the guards of the perimeter weren't quite what they should have been. At least not on this side of the barrier. How many soldiers wearing regular uniforms were on the other side of the perimeter was anyone's guess.

Jack took the time to carefully cut the wire in the same area where Mike Summers' body was found. It took him all of forty minutes. He pulled back the thorn bush of lethal razors just enough to let a person slip through if that person was careful. He then slipped through and scanned the area on the other side of the border. He could see no guards, and with his night-vision lenses in place, he was fairly certain he would have spotted them.

Jack slipped back the way he'd come. He gestured the four people and the dog closer to him. The dog only listened because Karen dragged him closer.

"I'm saying this exactly once. I won't repeat myself. I'm taking a very big risk here, and I'm trusting you." He turned to face each of them as individuals, forcing himself to look away from Karen when she started looking uncomfortable. "If any of you ever mention Collier, Georgia to anyone beyond that fencing, I'm a dead man. Please, believe me when I say that."

The man he'd spoken to before, the one from New York, nodded emphatically. "Never a word from my lips, sir. Not to anyone."

The others nodded.

Jack held the razor wire in his gauntleted hand, grateful for the heavy padding that protected him. "Get out. Don't look back. Don't ever mention this to another soul."

They moved carefully past the barrier, and the older woman cried out softly as her arm brushed one of the blades. In a few moments, they were gone from his sight.

Jack sealed the mesh as best he could. It would take a person hours of looking to find the spot, and then they'd have to be looking in the right general area. The coarse layers of wire were too tangled to make it an easy task.

Jack allowed himself to think of Karen one last time, and smiled. At least he'd managed to save her. At least he'd done that much right. He'd only just started back to camp when he heard the chatter of rifle fire from the other side of the lethal barrier. He heard an inhuman scream, and knew Karen's dog had been hit.

Jack left the area. He slunk back to his bed and fell into a deep, troubled sleep.

He spent all of the next day wondering when they would come for him, when the other soldiers would show up and escort him to Colonel Anderson.

If anyone suspected him of any wrongdoing, they hid it remarkably well.

Chapter 12

1

Over the course of the next week, the men from ONYX managed to excavate most of the ship from its point of impact. They couldn't find a single scratch anywhere on the surface of the vessel, but they found quite a few substantial ruptures to the hull of the thing. Sadly, every one of the tears in the metal failed to provide anything but more questions. They quickly learned that the exterior layer was at least a foot thick, but found no point where the damage allowed even a fiber-optic camera access to the interior.

The people of Collier remained locked in their homes, and, on three separate occasions, violators of the forced house arrest learned the hard way that the Colonel wasn't playing nicely anymore. Three names were added to the list of fatalities: Andrew Wander and Wade Harper, both of Collier, and Tom Fitzroy, of Selma, Alabama. It didn't take long for the rumors to start regarding Andrew Wander's death. Whispered speculation soon maintained that he was killed in cold blood as a result of his fight with Colonel Anderson.

Had Anderson heard the rumors, he'd have laughed until he cried. Wander was the last thing on his mind; he had enough to deal with already. The reprogramming of Collier's citizens had already begun, and over a third of the population was no longer aware of the situation that held their town at bay. At present, they were unaware of anything at all, as most were being kept doped up beyond the ability to reason. The same was true of those injured in the initial landing of the bogey. Those capable of recovery, who were actually up to the rigors of the reprogramming, were carefully examined for radiation damage on a cellular level and then treated to the same battery of conditioning that everyone else in town endured.

The few who were beyond modern medical help were taken away, flown back to the Durango base and kept alive for study. In each of those rare cases, the victims had suffered extreme damage, and careful examination of their DNA showed dramatic changes were taking place. Anderson and Hawthorne both did their very best not to think about what was happening to them. Sometimes, it was best to leave a situation alone, especially if there was absolutely nothing you could do to change matters. Time would reveal what was meant to happen.

Ten people, working what seemed like impossible hours, were in the process of erasing a moment in history. Mark Anderson couldn't help but feel terrified by the notion.

While Anderson kept himself busy with the daily tasks of running the town, Major Stephen Hawthorne spent his days actively working on the mysteries of the alien craft. Hawthorne took measurements, photographs and video footage of the vessel, all the while cursing the fact that nothing they'd tried had managed to even dent the hull. The situation was even more frustrating than dealing with the interrogation he endured every night when he and Anderson got together to discuss the day's events.

Worse still, the damned thing was making noises again. Nothing as substantial as the massive rumbles that had sent people sprawling, but enough to make him worry about just what was going on inside the thing. Ultrasound, Magnetic Resonance Imaging and even good old fashioned X-rays had failed to provide any useful information: all three methods of examination proved that the thing was solid.

Most frightening of all, as far as Hawthorne was concerned, the breaches in the ship's exterior seemed to be getting smaller. Every careful measurement he'd taken and triple-checked was now inaccurate.

For the soldiers working in the ONYX Project, the hectic, exhausting pace they'd been forced to keep continued unabated. Those who could were returned to duty as soon as their injuries allowed.

None of the soldiers showed any signs of cellular mutation. Those too injured to come back to work were flown to Durango, along with the dead citizens of Collier and the soldiers who didn't live through their tour of the sleepy little town. All records of the dead were meticulously copied down, and then all electronic information on their existence was removed. The hard, physical files were being removed as well, but the process was taking a little longer.

Collier, Georgia was being erased, one piece at a time. The process was slow and painful, but the memories of that agony would fade soon enough. At least for the people who lived in Collier. Both Anderson and Hawthorne, the only people who knew all of the details of the operation and who were also present in the town, almost wished they could find the same solace as the townsfolk. Almost. Neither of them would have willingly submitted to what the conditioning experts were doing to Collier's people. They'd heard too many of the screams coming from Lucas Brightman's house, where the ten people were working their dark magic.

To the world outside of Collier, the situation in the small town had become a footnote. After the "unfortunate incident" where several of the reporters had managed to have a fatal "accident," after defying the governmental orders to stay away, very little information was released on a day-to-day basis. The situation remained unchanged, and the scandals involving this week's celebrity of the hour made for juicier reporting. The phone calls and visits made to over one hundred executives from the national news stations, the local radio and television companies and all of the newspapers and magazines worth noticing, ensured the situation remained little more than a footnote. Journalistic integrity was important to reporters, but not always as significant to the people who paid their bills. Also, it's much easier to help put a spin on a story when the lives of family members are at stake. Threaten a man and he might bristle: show the same man how easily his wife or his child can be made to suffer, and the story changes. When all was said and done, the press would get the homogenized story of ONYX's choice, and numerous important people in the industry would be paid off or receive back the incriminating evidence that could have destroyed their careers and lives.

ONYX was a fairly small organization, but one with far-reaching hands. No one who met with them knew who they were or who they represented, but everyone who met them learned quickly that they were living on borrowed time as far as ONYX was concerned. In the modern information age, no one was safe from ONYX's hackers, who were some of the very best the world had to offer. The people who ensured the integrity of the Fourth Estate learned that integrity is a luxury. When it was all over, they'd be grateful for the scraps ONYX gave them.

2

Fifteen days after the ship had landed in Collier, the excavation was complete. The eight cranes it took to gently lower the vessel from its upright position, and down onto what they soldiers assumed was the ship's base, strained and protested under the weight. Two of the powerful winches failed before the ship was in the proper position, but the fall caused no apparent damage—not too surprising when one considered the incredible impact the vessel had already survived.

There were no obvious points of entry into the craft, and both Hawthorne and Anderson were flummoxed. The ship was larger than three football fields. It weighed too damned much to carry out by means of any known vehicle, and there was no way in hell they could move the damned thing all the way to Durango without half the nation noticing.

After careful thought and consideration—along with several heated exchanges with Mister Hardaway—the decision was made. Collier had to die. There would be no explosion; the ship remaining here ensured that, but there was always the plague to fall back on. Names would be reinserted into the appropriate computer files, bodies would officially be confiscated by the CDC, "for the safety of everyone," and the survivors would be completely reprogrammed. Along with the locals, Sergeant Jack Calloway had the misfortune of meeting with the conditioning experts. Anderson waited a full week before deciding to pull Calloway from active duty. Those people he'd set free had been captured within moments of their escape. The dog found with them was being treated for gunshot wounds to the left hip and buttock.

Anderson hated himself. He loathed what he had to do, but knew of no other recourse. On the brighter side, many of the impoverished people in Collier—and there were quite a few who barely managed life at the national poverty level—would come out of the incident with well-paying jobs and exceptional benefits. The press would also be ecstatic, as they would get their juicy story after all. One mad Middle Eastern fanatic and a vial of biological stew confiscated from Libya several years earlier would explain away much of what happened. The United States of America, always looking after her own, would take care of all the relocation expenses for the unfortunate souls locked out of their beloved hometown before the hideous incident occurred. The esteemed President, completely unaware of the actual events in the town, would likely garner a great deal of the popular vote for the successor of his choice in the near future.

The plans were made and the surgical excision of Collier, Georgia from the map of the United States began in earnest.

Two days later, it was all for nothing.

The twenty-first day of July started out like every other day for last week or more. Everyone did what they had to do. The reprogrammers handled a caseload that would surely have given any mental hospital a fiscal stroke, and the soldiers cleaned up the mess left from the entire fiasco.

Then the ship took off. Hawthorne and Anderson were standing at the edge of the lake's bed, looking at the damned thing when it happened. One moment they were trying to decide the best place to put the alien craft, and the next minute the monstrous ship was lifting itself out of the cavernous pit with barely a whisper.

There was no light to give them warning. No heat assailed them as it had the people of Collier. The gigantic disc simply lifted itself into the air and hovered for a moment. Then the feedback came. White noise loud enough to cause physical agony erupted from every radio and headset within ten miles. Every engine shut down, and all of the watches stopped working. Just before the sound would have ruptured eardrums, the headsets in the survival suits of ONYX's people cut off. Hawthorne was still reeling in pain when the leviathan in front of him started moving again. Anderson screamed.

The shadow from the ship blocked out the sky as it moved overhead. One soldier, determined to keep the prize they'd struggled so hard to capture, was actually foolish enough to try hanging on to the monstrous disc. It was a lost cause, and Corporal Eric Pendleton broke both of his legs and his right arm when he fell the fifty-seven feet back to the ground. He'd spend several months recovering from the damage.

The ship hovered for several seconds, waiting for God-only-knew-what to happen, then launched itself out of the atmosphere, moving from a sun-blotting disc to a minute dot to a speck and then to nothing in less than a second. There was no hideous wind, nor even an implosion of air to let people know it had gone away.

Anderson screamed a second time, and then he sat on the ground and had what could only be called a full-scale temper tantrum. Hawthorne couldn't blame him. After a time, the necessary calls were made and the situation was explained.

And while Anderson did his work, Hawthorne contemplated the ship he'd seen, the miracle he'd actually touched. Life on other planets? Oh, my, yes. Was it friendly? Did it come seeking war? Did the life forms within the craft seek knowledge of the Earth's dominant race? Were they anything at all like the unfortunates seized so long ago in Roswell, New Mexico?

He hadn't a clue. One thought kept slipping through his mind whenever he let his guard down momentarily. One simple idea that just wouldn't let him alone. *What if they come back? What the Hell will we do if they come back, and they take the way we treated them and the way we treated our own as a hostile sign?*

Major Stephen Hawthorne resumed his duties as the second-in-command to Colonel Mark Anderson. He did his work with the same enthusiasm he had always employed, and he made notes on everything that occurred. He was, in short, the same man he'd always been. At least as far as the rest of the world was concerned.

Hawthorne had his own apartment at the Durango Military Installation. No one had the place bugged, and no one knew his dirty little secrets, despite his own convictions that someone, somewhere, knew every move he made and how many bowel movements he had a day.

So no one ever guessed that Hawthorne never slept another full, restful night again. His nightmares of invading fleets were a private matter. In a way, he was luckier than most. In other ways, he was far less fortunate.

Epilogue

Collier died. The death was painful, as predicted, and the media had a field day with the entire situation. The few people from Collier who were not home when the "plague" wiped out the town were celebrities for a time, and each and every one of them had a dozen stories to tell. For three years, Collier was looked upon as the worst case of terrorism ever to strike American soil. Naturally, someone else came along and had to outdo the statistics, but that is another story for a different time.

The lake was refilled, and the bodies were removed. Every shell casing was accounted for and the places which suffered damage during the incident were demolished. There was a story for each building destroyed. The media thrived on the excitement for over a month.

To make the story even more thrilling, Amir Hal Densalid, the most dangerous terrorist in the world, managed to escape. The U. S. Government had egg on its face, but the mad genius had done the same thing to other countries before. The United States of America joined a growing list of nations that swore the man would be brought to justice.

Anne Marie Greenberg was married to Sergeant Jack Calloway. They lived together at the Durango Military Installation and both understood that the security of their nation came before everything else. From time to time, Anne had dreams that she'd been married to another man, one far crueler than her Jack, and some nights she awoke with tears in her eyes. On those occasions, her loving husband would comfort her in his strong arms and rock her gently back to sleep. The dreams made her avoid the Whitmore Gas 'n Go, over on Baker Street: the creepy guy who owned the place looked a little too much like her imaginary ex-husband for her own comfort. This man's hair was longer, and he had a mustache thick enough to grow potatoes in, but otherwise he could have been the spitting image of her dream enemy.

Anne taught school at the base, taking care of the young children and teaching them to love God and Country above all else. She had a good life. Her parents were good to her. The retired couple lived at the installation as well, and her father served as the base's Rabbi. It never bothered her that her parents had a strong New York accent and she had spoke with a slight Southern drawl; she'd been raised in Florida, and it was only to be expected.

But sometimes she worried about her little sister. Lucy was a little flighty from time to time, and she was an insatiable flirt, a dangerous habit when living on a military base. Still, with her folks in town and Jack to help her watch after the little minx, she knew it would all work out in the long run.

Anne loved the little community that was growing around her in Durango. It was like she'd always hoped her life would be. Almost something out of a fairy tale. She had her handsome prince, she had her family, and she had twins on the way in a few months. Life was good. She wouldn't have traded it for anything in the world.

Serenity Falls
by James A. Moore
(Meisha Merlin Summer 2002)

Interlude: New York City

Jonathan Crowley watched from the shadows, taking his time in assessing the situation. Two boys, probably in their late teens, and one girl around the same age. One of the young men was unconscious, or doing a good job of faking it. The other was doing his best to tie the girl onto his makeshift altar, a wooden contraption designed to look like an inverted crucifix. He'd gone all out and set it up to swivel, so the victims would actually be suspended upside-down when he committed the deed. She was fighting back very vigorously, taking it personally that the punk was trying to take the clothes off her struggling form. Crowley couldn't blame her, it was barely in the fifties and the air had a distinct nip.

Three weeks ago he'd received a phone call. Just the usual, from someone he hadn't seen or even much thought of in over a decade. A girl, Elisa Merriwether, from Connecticut, quite pretty as he recalled. He'd taught her when he was at NYU. She had never done anything wrong, but one of her sorority sisters had decided the best way to get good grades was to sell her soul. The sheer volume of stupid people he ran across never ceased to amaze him. It had been a minor affair; the demon riding her back was barely even dangerous to her, really, but he'd handled it just the same.

Then, out of the blue, the girl had called, "just to shoot the breeze." She'd been thinking about him and tried the old number. What a surprise; it still worked. And then the conversation about the murders: seven of them so far; grisly affairs...He'd ended the conversation with a promise to look into the matter, and that had been the start of the latest little mess.

Two days ago, after many, many patient days of research and numerous walks through the crime scenes, he'd finally made a connection. The boy down there was part of what had once been a fledgling Satanic cult. Drugs and excesses had taken the cult apart bit by bit. Most of them had probably been in it for the free cocaine and sex anyway. That was usually as far as most of them cared to go, and for that reason they were harmless. Naturally, there were always exceptions, like the moron on the other roof.

Crowley allowed himself a small grin as he watched the boy try to force the girl's legs into the proper place on his homemade altar. He hadn't designed the damned thing well at all. It was hardly conducive to getting her pretty legs locked down, and her struggles only made the matter worse. She was a fighter, which was why Crowley was taking his time. He liked a good fight. And, judging by the setup, the dork struggling with her was a rank amateur. The amateurs always got elaborate. *Probably*, he mused, *to make up for their lack of any really original ideas.*

The kid had finally managed to strip her clothes away. Like as not he'd want to rape her before making her his latest sacrifice. Still, credit where it was due, he'd been smart enough to use condoms if that was the case. None of the other three obvious sacrifice victims had shown any evidence of semen, though all had been violated before their hearts ha been cut out.

Crowley watched as the young lady—a cheerleader if he was making out the cast-off clothes properly—planted her foot on the side of her abductor's head and sent him reeling back, spitting profanities like a scalded cat. The geek's mouth was bleeding, and he looked a bit dazed, but not so stunned that he couldn't get inventive with his obscenities.

Crowley took a running start and cleared the distance between the two rooftops with ease. He landed on the tarpapered surface without gaining the moron's notice. He was good at not being heard when he set his mind to it.

As he moved closer, the heavy in the little play he was watching wiped the blood from his lip, staining his pimple-covered face. Crowley couldn't decide which seemed angrier, the would-be killer or the rampaging acne that covered his skin from chin to forehead.

The boy shook his mop of greasy brown hair and made several promises as to what he was going to do to his victim. For her part she kept mostly silent, the gag in her mouth preventing her from really getting into a verbal conflict at that time.

Crowley admired her body almost as much as he admired her feistiness. Still, she was a bit too young for his tastes, so he decided it was time to get down to business, even as she cut loose with a volley of kicks that kept the Pimple King of New York from managing to get her feet pinned in place.

She stopped kicking when she saw Crowley moving behind her captor, who was now panting heavily from the exertion of fighting her off. Her lovely brown eyes grew wide in a silent plea. Crowley winked at her and smiled broadly.

"Personally, I don't think she's in the mood to be sacrificed to any dark gods today." The kid almost wet himself as he spun around to face Crowley. "Maybe you ought to call it a night before she manages to get you a good one in your balls."

"Who are you?" He tried to sound tough, but the way his voice cracked took any possible threat from the scowl on his face. Still, Crowley gave him points for effort.

"I'm the good guy. The one who's here to stop you from killing the nice cheerleader." Crowley came closer, his smile growing wider as he approached. He added a little extra saccharine to his tone when he spoke again, just to get under the twerp's skin. "What's your name, little boy?"

The kid bristled. "None of your fucking business! Why don't you get the hell out of here, before I cut your heart out?" To give his words some semblance of a threat, he pulled a very long and very effective looking dagger from his belt.

Crowley's smile grew a little wider, and a lot meaner. "Or instead, I could just shove that knife of yours right down your throat. Whattaya say?"

The kid moved forward, the ancient weapon held skillfully in his hand. Crowley sidestepped and planted his foot in the small of his assailant's back, sending him halfway across the roof before an air-conditioning unit stopped his forward motion. The dagger went flying and landed even farther away with a loud clatter.

"Clumsy, clumsy, clumsy. Who the hell taught you how to fight, sunshine?"

The mocking tone in Crowley's voice only served to make the cultist even angrier as he climbed back to his feet. Crowley let him get up without making any further attacks.

"I'll kill you!"

"Oh, that's an original threat. Try this one on for size: First, I'm going to break both of your kneecaps. Then, because I can, I'm going to hurt you. When I'm done and I grow bored, I'm going to snap your miserable little neck and send you straight to hell."

No words this time. Instead, the boy made a few quick gestures, and smiled directly at Crowley. "I have friends you can't even begin to imagine." The punk walked forward confidently, his smile broad and sadistic. It rather reminded Jonathan Crowley of his own smile when he looked in the mirror. That would never do. He preferred being unique.

Crowley was about to speak when the hair on his neck rose, lifting as if touched by a heavy breeze. His eyes narrowed, and his heart thudded just a little faster. "What did you call, boy? What did you summon to do your dirty work?"

Zit-face smiled even wider, and behind him the girl screamed as best she could past the gag in her mouth. "A special friend. He takes care of me and all I have to do is give him bitches like her." His gesture was casual, barely acknowledging that the girl he'd been attacking earlier was anything more than an object.

Crowley let his eyes slide over to the boy's victims again. The jock, who had doubtless been with the cheerleader and on her side, was still out cold, possibly dead. The cheerleader was looking above her, struggling to get her arms free from their bonds. He let his own attention rise to meet whatever it was she found so fascinating.

There was nothing to see. No shadowy menace, no tentacled creature, not even a stereotypical imp. He hated when that happened. Because he knew *something* was there and now he'd have to work for it.

The boy touched him. Actually put a hand on his shoulder, preparing to swing at his face. When it came to telegraphing his moves, the kid was a pro. Crowley turned to look at the twerp, looked at the hand on his shoulder and looked at the kid again. Then he smiled. "Now that, was a bad, bad mistake."

Apparently the kid felt the same way. He started backing up, his eyes growing wide as he looked at Crowley. "I—I have *friends*! They'll help me!" His voice cracked on that last and the boy looked around desperately for his elusive allies.

Something BIG knocked Crowley off his feet. The impact felt like a luxury sedan slamming into him at high speed. He saw the fear fade from the boy's face, replaced by triumph, just before he was lifted from the ground by the impact.

Crowley felt the tarpapered roof smash into his face, and the hard, hot grip of something very strong holding the back of his head, pushing him across the ground. He was glad he'd taken off his glasses before coming here, but less enthusiastic about the feel of his skin peeling back under the force of the attack. And the taste of the tarpaper and grit wasn't doing much for his mood either. He closed his eyes and pushed back with all of his might, struggling to free himself from the grip.

The Acne King's voice crowed cheerfully. "Oh, there he is..."

Whatever had him, had him good. It slammed Crowley's face into the ground a second time, pushing hard enough to make his nose creak and his teeth lose enamel. He closed his eyes and swung an arm awkwardly behind him. His hands having to see for him as he reached for the thing that held him in place.

Braille for the terminally dense. He touched wet, scaly skin, his hand moving lower...that felt like a ribcage...that could just possibly be a hip...His hand slid lower, touching a muscular thigh as thick as a tree stump.

The thing hissed and pushed harder on his face, its strength much greater than he'd expected. He struggled, felt his lip pop open and start bleeding, and decided to end this quickly, before he really lost his temper. Crowley reached lower and found exactly what he'd hoped to find: male anatomy. That the penis was erect was not a promising aspect of the scenario, but he could live with it.

He found the testicles beneath the main body of the creature and looked up at the snot-nosed little punk who'd summoned the thing in the first place. Then he squeezed as hard as he could, while grinning savagely at the boy.

The pressure on his skull eased up, and Crowley looked to see what was attacking him. There was nothing there, just the massive weight on his body and the strange squeaking noise from where he figured a mouth would be. He whispered a few words and nodded with satisfaction as the illusion that hid the thing shattered like a porcelain plate dropped from the top of a house. It was big, with little by way of flesh around its face. It rather looked like someone had stripped the skin away from a Mr. Universe contender and slapped snake-scale bandages over parts of its body. The shredded face looked down in shock, the glowing orbs where its eyes should have been going wider, and then it roared in pain.

The beast bucked and thrashed above him, trying to get away, but to no avail. Crowley's grip was like steel. The kid wasn't smiling any more, and neither was the thing he was doing his best to make a eunuch. But Crowley was smiling a lot.

"You have absolutely no idea how badly I'm going to hurt you..." To emphasize his words, he twisted his handful of monster-flesh and squeezed even harder. The thing squeaked this time, and Crowley finally managed to push it off of his body. His face felt raw and burned. But that didn't stop the smile. The taste of blood running into his mouth was hardly new and, as always, amused him.

He looked down at the mess on the ground, and his grin grew even larger. "I'll get back to you, cupcake..."

He looked at the boy. The boy looked back, terrified. "Y—You can't do that!"

"Why not? I didn't see that in the rules anywhere..." He stepped towards the nervous teen. "And I should know. I always play by the rules."

The kid backed up again, and Crowley came forward, his face getting nastier and nastier with the grin. Then he reached out for the frightened cowering boy in front of him. There was no kindness on his face. "Rule number one: If you want to play with nasty monsters from other planes of existence, expect me to take it personally. This is my world, and I expect a certain amount of order."

"K—Keep away from me," squawked the nerd.

"No."

"I mean it! Keep away! That was just the warmup!"

Jonathan Crowley laughed then. And the girl blanched right along with her would-be killer. Something about the way he laughed had that effect on people. Made them want to hide under the covers and stay hidden for a long, long time. It was something he dealt with.

"That was the best you had, punkin. Now it's my turn."

Being of mostly sound mind, and limited courage, the boy turned and tried to bolt. Crowley let him get a whole two feet away before he made his move. One step, two, and then he reached out with his hand and wrapped his fingers into the loser's greasy hair. Pulled him backwards hard enough to lift him from the ground. The punk screamed very nicely.

"Come on, now, you're hurting my feelings. Here I go out of my way, I spend weeks looking you up, and all you want to do is run away." He added a little extra pout to his voice, a mocking noise that he knew would only make matters worse. "Is that anyway to treat a guest in your fair town?"

He dragged his new friend closer before shoving him to the ground. When the kid tried to scramble away, Crowley brought his foot down on the boy's kneecap and pressed until he heard something break. All the color drained from the ex-cultist's face and he gasped faintly, the shock and pain taking away his ability to scream.

"Remember what I said I was going to do to you?" Crowley's voice was a purr, his smile almost serene. "That's one kneecap. Should I go for the other one too?"

The kid started crying then, faint little hiccuping sounds breaking apart his words. "No. Oh, God, please, no."

Crowley leaned in closer. "Did the other ones beg you the same way? The ones you fed to your friend?" Crowley pulled back for a second, checking on the creature. It was still curled up and moaning. He nodded, satisfied for the moment. "You think about how you're going to answer that, kid. I'll be back in a minute." He turned away, heading towards the thing on the ground. "Oh, and if you even think about moving, I'll cut your balls off." The boy froze like as a statue.

Crowley walked past the girl, who was doing her best to get herself untied from the ropes that wound tightly around her wrists. "Stop that," he chided. "You'll only hurt yourself. I'll be there in a minute." The cheerleader stopped, her pretty face puzzled by the humor in his voice.

He looked down at his supernatural victim and smiled. "I don't think I've met you before, I would know. What, exactly, are you?"

It didn't respond, save to glare at him hatefully as it started to recover from his earlier assault.

"You *can* speak, can't you?" He walked a slow circuit around the thing as it started to rise, its face wrinkling with anger.

Its mouth opened and it spoke in a guttural, barely understandable voice. "I'm the girl who's gonna rip your head off!"

Crowley blinked. *Girl?* Then he smiled. "You know something? I've met a lot of weird shit in my life, but never, not ever, a demon with a New York accent."

The creature's eyes bulged just a bit, and it made a hard swallowing motion that left Jonathan Crowley feeling good about himself. The musculature over its eyes wiggling down and back up as it tried to regain its composure was a display that was, frankly, disgusting to watch. "I *am* a demon...I am a *very powerful* demon..."

"From what I've seen, eight of the nine members of the Dark Light Cult—a *very* original name, I can assure you; I haven't run across it more than a dozen times, honest—died in the last year. Way I figure it, laughing boy over there decided to bring one of you back. Which one?"

The thing did its best to look puzzled, which, considering the lack of actual flesh over the body, was pretty damned impressive. "I-I don't know what you mean."

"Sure you do. You're not a demon. You just managed to hitch a ride here from wherever the hell you went when you died. So, let me ask you again. Who are you?"

"I'm Satan! Lord of the Underworld!" it roared as it rose to its full height of almost seven feet, the blaze of its eyes glowing more fiercely as it declared its name.

Crowley stood completely still for a good three heartbeats and then broke into laughter that left him nearly incapable of doing anything else. The sort of deep belly laugh that leaves a person aching afterwards. The skinned monster looked on, slack-jawed by the shock of the laughing fit.

When he had himself under control, Crowley wiped his eyes with a finger, pushing the unexpected tears away. "Oh...Thank you. I needed that." He chuckled. "'I'm Satan, Lord of the Underworld'...heh heh heh...That's rich."

"What are you laughing about?" He watched as the creature planted it's massive arms on its hips, in a decidedly feminine way.

"Toots, Satan wouldn't give you the time of day. Which one are you, Leslie Monroe, Amelia Dankins, Suzanne Comer or Brandy Sinclaire?"

"Amelia Dankins," it confessed, its voice numbed by the discovery of its secret. "How did you know?"

"Trade secret. Let me see if I have this right. Zit-boy over there wanted to bring you back from the dead, and you needed fresh kills to come back properly, only it didn't work out the way you'd planned. Am I right so far?"

The Amelia demon nodded.

"So you decided to find a new body. Only it hasn't been easy finding the right one, the one that could accept your energies?"

The creature stared at him blankly, its raw face expressionless. Crowley shrugged. "Close enough for me, I suppose." That said, he drove his thumbs into the monster's eyes. What had once been a young woman who fell in with the wrong crowd and did many stupid things before overdosing on bad heroin shrieked, falling backwards as he blinded her.

"You really are stupid, Amelia. You tried to deal with a devil. Devils lie. You never had a chance." He ducked a wild swing that lifted his hair with its passage. "You've been building a body, hoping to come back from the dead in a form that would be strong enough to withstand anything." Crowley talked on, even as he moved the few feet he needed in order to snatch up the dagger that the Acne Kid had lost in their earlier scuffle. "The thing is, even if you do make a good deal with a devil, they always end up shafting you. It's nothing personal; it's just what they do. The best you'd have gotten is what you are now." He shrugged. "Consider this a mercy killing, if that makes it any easier."

He threw the blade at the wretch's chest, burying it to the hilt in the exposed muscles. It screamed again—he really couldn't bring himself to think of the beast as a her, as the pretty, sad face he'd seen on her high-school picture—and watched it twitch and falter, slumping to the ground before it breathed its last. The body decomposed in a matter of seconds, leaving behind only a thick black smoke that drifted away in the faint wind.

Crowley walked over and plucked the dagger from the ground where the creature had been' then walked back over to the boy that had started all of this insanity. The boy looked at him with wide, terrified eyes. "Your girlfriend won't be coming back. She shouldn't have come back in the first place." He leaned in close, his face inches from the shocky eyes of his prey. "That just leaves you and me. And buddy, I don't think your chances are good."

The boy broke down. He closed his eyes and started crying quietly to himself. Crowley sneered in disgust. "Is this where I'm supposed to feel sorry for you? Where I realize that you were just a pawn in a game you didn't understand?" Instead of answering, the boy turned his face away. The tears kept coming.

Crowley reflected that perhaps, that would have bought mercy from some. He was, after all, a sad sight to behold. If Jonathan Crowley felt anything other than cold, sadistic pleasure from the boy's dilemma, he hid it very well indeed.

"I just can't do it, kid. I'd like to, but I keep thinking about the people you and your pet freak killed in order to bring her back. And every time I do that, you come out on the losing end of the scenario."

Crowley walked over to the cheerleader, who was looking at him much the same way a paraplegic might look at a train speeding towards the wheelchair that was pinned in the rails. Her pretty brown eyes were as wide as saucers, and she looked ready to run, bound hands and all. He walked behind her, and rested his hand on the ropes binding her wrists. As he untied her, he looked back to his new friend on the rooftop, the one with the shattered knee.

"I mean, how the hell am I supposed to feel sorry for you, when you were about to kill this girl for your own pleasure?" The girl moved her hands as the ropes fell away. She moaned softly at the pain of blood flowing into starved fingertips. "Am I supposed to look at your tears and think you've learned your lesson?"

The boy looked up and, through the tears in his eyes and the snot running down his face, he nodded. Crowley had seldom seen anyone looking so forlorn and genuinely pathetic. He reached behind him and handed the girl her clothes. Disheveled as they were, they were better than nothing.

Crowley looked at the girl and studied her face for a moment as she got dressed. "What do you think, sweet heart? Should I call the cops and let you deal with him that way?"

She looked from Crowley's face to the boy on the ground, her face a study in careful concentration and maybe just a touch of shock.

"I don't know..." she said.

"Really? Do you think he'll never try this again? Or something just as nasty? Anything he can in order to make his life a little better, even from behind bars?"

She looked at the quietly crying boy again, at the shabby clothes he wore, and the way his leg sat awkwardly from the knee down. He looked harmless enough.

Then she thought about the words he's said when he was trying to strap her onto his altar.

"Keep your promise." Her voice was as cold as the wind that crossed her flesh as she dressed. "Send him to hell."

Crowley smiled. "Not a problem."

It took a long, long time for Crowley to get bored. At least it seemed that way to his victim.

Afterwards, the man who smiled far too often for the comfort of those around him got to the business of the last person on the rooftop. The young man who'd been lying unconscious since he first ran across his prey. He touched the teenager's form and felt that the skin was cold. He moved the boy's head. Wet redness welled up in a pool beneath the ruined skull. He was dead.

Jonathan Crowley turned away from him, and looked at the cheerleader where she sat, facing the street far below. "If he was your friend, I'm very sorry. He's dead." His voice was soft, and as close to caring as he ever really managed. "For what it's worth, I don't think he suffered."

The girl turned towards him, her face looking more lost and distraught than even when her assailant was struggling to strap her to the altar. Her tears were genuine, and in his way, he felt for her. But he offered no comfort. He was not the sort who could make such gestures with ease. They always felt like a lie.

"Do you need a ride home?" The words were out of his mouth before he knew just what he was going to say. She looked at him with that same weird blend of relief and fear and sorrow that he should have been used to a long, long time ago, but that still always made him feel just the least bit confused. Her emotions were at war, and Crowley very rarely had that problem. He always knew what it was he wanted. He seldom had enough doubt in his system to let the emotions go that crazy. "Or, if you prefer, I could just call you a cab."

Her expression switched over from fear to a touch of relief. He reached into his coat and pulled out his cellular phone. Despite what he'd been through, it still worked. He dialed quickly, and spoke into the mouthpiece even as his ruptured lip began healing itself. The process itched like mad, but was very, very handy after fighting the occasional damned soul come back from the dead.

Jonathan Crowley waited on the rooftop until the cab came and picked the girl up. The fifty-dollar bill he'd slipped her would cover the cost of the ride home. Seeing as he'd taken it from the ex-Pimple King of New York, he felt he could afford to let her have it.

She would, no doubt, be puzzled about exactly why she had bruises on her wrists, but her mind would make up a story before she got all the way home. Maybe an attempted mugging during which her valiant boyfriend managed to save her but died in the process. Maybe something else that was just as plausible, but not the truth. She would forget about Crowley and she would forget about the demon-thing. At least for now. Later, if she needed to, she'd remember the number for contacting him. Just in case something a little past the mundane ever came into her life again.

It was a small magic, a little thing that hid the truth from her, and it was a mercy as far as he was concerned. Sometimes he could be merciful, but only ever with the people he suspected were truly innocent of any wrongdoings. They were few and far between.

Most of the time he left the memories intact as a warning not to ever do anything even remotely stupid again. Little offended Jonathan Crowley as much as stupid people.

He made a call to the 911 Emergency number from a payphone nearby. "Yeah, I got a problem! Some stupid bastard is making too much noise on the roof, and I can't get any sleep! Would you maybe like to send a few cops over here? Before I have to do something everyone will regret later?" He gave the address for the building and hung up the phone. The bodies would be found; that was the important part.

Crowley had just started down the street when he heard the voice call out to him. He looked up to find the source of the voice and saw the dead jock looking down from the rooftop. He'd looked better. Whatever was trying to possess him—it wasn't Amelia, he knew that much at least—was too strong for the form to hold. "I see you, Hunter! I see you and I know you!" The jock pointed with a hand that was rapidly blistering, smoldering from the strain of holding an uninvited guest.

Crowley smiled. Maybe this would get interesting after all. "Yeah? Well big fat hairy deal, sports fan, I see you, too."

"You will be mine! Do you hear me? We have unfinished business!"

Before Crowley could respond, the jock's form slumped forward, plummeting down to the sidewalk below. Crowley watched until it hit the ground and broke. Terminal velocity was never pretty.

"Should have left me an address, pal. I'd have come looking for you." The body didn't respond, not that he'd expected it to. Crowley left the scene. He didn't really feel like putting up with the NYPD and any questions they might have. Besides, if they tried to restrain him, things would get ugly.

He always tried to save the really nasty business for the ones who honestly deserved it. In his own way, he could be merciful. Not that many others agreed with his personal definition of mercy.

Author's Biography

James A. Moore has been writing professionally for almost 10 years. During that time he has written and sold six novels including the novel *Under the Overtree*. He has worked in the comics field and on numerous role playing games. He's been both the Secretary and the Vice-President of the Horror Writers Association.

James A. Moore lives in the suburbs of Atlanta, GA.

ISBN 1-892065-19-3
$16.00

Praise for James A. Moore's
first novel from Meisha Merlin,
Under the Overtree

"The woods around Lake Overtree, near the small town of Summitville, CO., hold dark and ancient secrets, and the Folk of the woods have chosen teenager Mark Howell as their emissary of vengeance and fulfillment. Moore's dark version of a young man's coming of age resonates with psychological tension and supernatural overtones that form a vivid contrast to the minutiae of everyday small-town life. The author's ability to depict scenes of graphic violence as well as moments of quiet horror make this title a strong candidate for most horror and dark fantasy collections."—*Library Journal*, March 2000

"A gawky and impatient young teenager yearning for acceptance from his stepfather and romantic affection from a female classmate undergoes a bodily transformation that enables him to realize his dreams in James A Moore's *Under The Overtree*. Mark soon learns that his metamorphosis comes with a devilish price in this creepy novel recalling vintage Stephen King."
—*Publisher's Weekly*, February 28, 2000

"*Under The Overtree* is full of complex plot twists, and gets deliciously creepy at times. Unfortunately we're going to have to wait until spring [2000] before the book sees general release. I hope that when this book does hit, it hits with its feet running. In an age where horror fiction is enjoying a bit of a renaissance, there is still a lot of "crap" out there. This is one book that deserves to be picked up and enjoyed. Don't miss it!"
—Kevin Kovalasic at *DangerMedia*

"*Under the Overtree* is as wonderfully twisted and dark as the deep roots of an ancient tree, steeped in secrets and dripping with evil. James Moore knows how to grab to reader's nerves and squeeze until the sweat pours down and their eyes bug out. This is 'horror' fiction—or 'dark fantasy'—at its dazzling best. Wonderfully human and touching and frightening, *Under the Overtree* is everything a good novel should be."
—Rick Hautala, author of *Bedbugs* and *Twilight Time*

"Fans of *The Shining* and *Phantoms* will welcome James A. Moore into the ranks of horror master. *Under the Overtree* is fresh, complex, and totally enthralling. Summitville is an intriguing town that should serve as the backdrop for future novels. Though the characters are fascinating, what makes Mr. Moore's novel so entertaining is the author's ability to make the supernatural seem so scientifically natural. Fans of urban fantasy and horror need to put this on their must read list."—Harriet Klausner, *Midwest Book Review* March 2000

"James A. Moore has a produced a fat treasure chest of a novel with his oddly titled *Under the Overtree.* The Overtree is a lake in the insular small town of Summitville, Colorado. What's under it causes major problems for new residents and townies alike."

"Moore takes a large group of well-developed characters through their paces in this involving tale. Whenever he flirts with predictability he finds a surprising twist to keep it lively. The result is a thriller loaded with suspense and mainstream sensibilities. *Under the Overtree* has potential to be a breakout book for Moore. He's already writing at a level equal to many of his more successful brethren."—Garrett Peck, *Cemetery Dance.*

"With the publication of *Under the Overtree*, Jim Moore takes his readers into the very realm where wishes become nightmares, and going home again isn't easy at all. With epic scope, this new novel firmly establishes Moore as a major force in the world of dark fantasy."—Matt Costello

"Meisha Merlin is a publisher to keep your eyes on. Every book that I've received from them has been of the highest quality.

Though once I'd started reading *Under The Overtree*, I wasn't positive that I would like it. It seemed to be a mediocre tale told often of a nerdy kid, new in town, and all the baloney that he endures. Upon further reading, it became ever so much more with complexity upon complexity.

Though listed as a tale of dark fantasy it could be a horror story to chill your bones when your home is dark and you are not quite sure just what is making that noise under the bed. James Moore is perhaps the most talented writer of this genre to date."—*Buzzy's Review News* #34

"The novel builds slowly, establishing Mark's character, his many moves and his inability to make friends, and the gradual development of real friends in this unfriendly little town. Once They get to work, things get gruesome fast: The dead walk, nightmares become real, and blood spatters. The otherworldy, end-of-the-world final confrontation is way out of scale with the early small-town realism, but it's satisfying in a comic-book-ish, over-the-top, **Buffy The Vampire Slayer** sort of way. Definitely worth checking out, though."—Carolyn Cushman *Locus*, May 2000

"High school as a surrogate Hell is used to good effect on the *Buffy the Vampire Slayer* television series. James Moore employs it to a slightly different effect in his new novel.

The novel starts as a realistic coming of age story, then turns toward a nightmarish, apocalyptic climax. That may be the reason I heard this book compared to 'a Stephen King novel.' Moore's novel takes well-drawn characters and thrusts them into fantastic situations. There's a definite similarity to King's work in that respect."—Don Kinney, *Talebones* #19, Spring 2000

"An ambitious novel with echoes of Bradbury and King and McCammon, *Under the Overtree* treats us to fully-fleshed characters, an engrossing storyline crammed with surprises, and a sensational finale. James A. Moore has arrived."
—F. Paul Wilson

Come check out our web site for details on these Meisha Merlin authors!

Kevin J. Anderson
Robert Asprin
Robin Wayne Bailey
Edo van Belkom
Janet Berliner
Storm Constantine
Diane Duane
Sylvia Engdahl
Jim Grimsley
George Guthridge
Keith Hartman
Beth Hilgartner
P. C. Hodgell
Tanya Huff
Janet Kagan
Caitlin R. Kiernan
Lee Killough
George R. R. Martin
Lee Martindale
Jack McDevitt
Sharon Lee & Steve Miller
James A. Moore
Adam Niswander
Andre Norton
Jody Lynn Nye
Selina Rosen
Kristine Kathryn Rusch
Pamela Sargent
Michael Scott
William Mark Simmons
S. P. Somtow
Allen Steele
Mark Tiedeman
Freda Warrington

http://www.MeishaMerlin.com